# ROCK 'n' ROLL BABES

## from outer space

# Linda Jaivin

BROADWAY BOOKS
New York

# ROCK 'n' ROLL BABES

## from outer space

ROCK 'N' ROLL BABES FROM OUTER SPACE. Copyright © 1998 by
Linda Jaivin. All rights reserved. Printed in the United States of America.
No part of this book may be reproduced or transmitted in any form or by
any means, electronic or mechanical, including photocopying, recording,
or by any information storage and retrieval system, without written
permission from the publisher. For information, address Broadway Books,
a division of Random House, Inc., 1540 Broadway, New York, NY 10036.

Broadway Books titles may be purchased for business or promotional use
or for special sales. For information, please write to: Special Markets
Department, Random House, Inc., 1540 Broadway, New York, NY 10036.

BROADWAY BOOKS and its logo, a letter B bisected on the diagonal, are
trademarks of Broadway Books, a division of Random House, Inc.

First trade paperback edition published 1999.

Designed by Bonni Leon-Berman

The Library of Congress has catalogued the hardcover edition as:
Jaivin, Linda.
Rock 'n' roll babes from outer space / Linda Jaivin. — 1st ed.
p. cm.
ISBN 0-7679-0165-7 (hc)
I. Title.
PR9619.3.J247R63   1998
823—dc21         97-34622
CIP

ISBN 0-7679-0200-9

*The author is grateful for permission to reproduce lines from the following:*
"Laid," Booth/Glennie/Gott, © Blue Mountain Music Ltd.; "La Di Doh,"
Ed Kuepper, © Beyond the Sea/PolyGram Music Publishing Australia Pty
Ltd.; "Smelly," Ben Green, © Ben Green; "Majik," Susie Schlesinger, ©
Susie Schlesinger; "Oopsy Daisy," Hinchcliffe/Simic, © Geoff Hinchcliffe
and Mikel Simic; "Slacker Song," Hinchcliffe/Simic, © Geoff Hinchcliffe
and Mikel Simic; "Swing," © J. Walker, permission granted by J. Walker;
"Your Eyes," Giarrusso/Bennie, © PolyGram Music Publishing Australia
Pty Ltd.; "Violet," Lover/Erlandson, © Mother May I Music; "All God's
Children," Michael Moriarty, performed by The Gadflys, © Phantom
Records/Leosong Music Pty Ltd. Every effort has been made to obtain
necessary permissions with reference to copyright material.

99  00  01  02  03  10  9  8  7  6  5  4  3  2  1

FOR MY PARENTS

# Acknowledgments

Big thanks to Geoffy Weffy Hinchcliffe and Mikel "Mickey Boy" Simic of Prik Harness for agreeing to appear in the novel and for permission to reprint the lyrics of "The Slacker Song." Kisses also to David, Gabrielle, Paul, and Pete the Hat, to my angelic flatmates, and, of course, my rockin' editor Michael Heyward and everyone else in the mothership of Text Publishing, my Australian publisher, as well as the Galactic Enterprise that is Broadway Books.

*T*onight's *my* *first* night on Earth. It's been a big one so far. I've been out on the town, I've been to a gig, I've even abducted my first Earthling. That's you, of course. Yeah, it's the whole alien catastrophe and you're part of it. Ready to rock 'n' roll?

Me? I'm Baby.

Baby Baby. Sound familiar? I got it from the lyrics of my favorite rock song. You know the one. My real name, well, I don't think I'll even bother telling you. You wouldn't be able to pronounce it anyway. You need at least two extra tongues and another set of denticles. Teeth. Whatever. Yeah, Baby Baby, that's me—extraterrestrial extraordinaire, alien sex fiend, wannabe rock star, designated driver on the highway to hell. Leader of the pack. Don't always look before I lead, but there you go.

It's not a big pack I lead. There's just Lati and Doll and me. Lati's a turbo-chick, full-on, fun, always looking for a good time. Her energy levels are near-on nuclear. You never know what Lati's gonna do next. Lati is the butterfly wing fluttering through all your chaos theories. Doll's another kettle of badfish altogether. Bit of a punk too, our Doll, and when she's mad, she's bad. Keeps Lati and me in line. Underneath all that attitude, she's actually quite sweet. But don't tell her I said so. She'd kill me.

We blew in this afternoon on Galgal, our flying saucer. Finding a park for a saucer is no easy feat in Sydney. It took us as long to find this parking space as it did to get to Earth from the dark side of the moon. That's where we ditched Mum. The mothership.

Doll handled the landing. She's the only one who managed to pass the perpendicular parking test back home. I never got a license. While doing my test I managed to trash three landing pods and take out a control tower. Nearly wiped the examiner too. Oh, it wasn't *that* bad. He was just a borg. You know, a cyborg. They were able to fix him up with a brand-new face and limbs. But they banned me from driving for life. Nufonians have a *very* limited sense of humor.

Nufon? That's the planet we're from. Don't get me started on Nufon and Nufonians. I know I shouldn't bag them all the time, but then I do a lot of things I shouldn't.

Anyway, we were stoked to land on Earth. First off, we turned our four-fingered little alien hands to shape-shifting. We wanted to take on Earth-girl form. To get some credit in the straight world. You know, Earthling world. Straight means something different here, does it? Oh, right. You see, space is so bent that even though Earth is round it's still sorta straight by comparison. Know what I mean? Never mind.

It took us a while to get the hang of shape-shifting. On the first try, we all came out looking like Keith Richards. That was *scary*. Yeah. We eventually got it right. Well, as right as we could under the circs. For one thing, we can't seem to make the damn antennae go away. Still, they've got their uses. For another—well, you'll see.

Of course, we didn't have a *thing* to wear. So we scored a few jars of Enigma Cream from Galgal's Special FX room and hit the consumption centers. Enigma Cream? It's concealer. A drop or two will cover up the odd zit or love bite. But if you're having a *really* bad hair day you slather it all over and disappear completely. Disguise-o-rama. We acquired some top gear. Like this orange PVC mini. You think it's filthy, do you? Really? I didn't notice any stains. What? Oh, I *see*. Fucken Transling-a-tron. Translation chip technology never keeps up with the lingo. Filthy, eh? Cool. Anyway, Lati went straight for your classic Bond T's and jeans, and Doll hit up some shop on Oxford Street for leather trousers and boots. We also managed to flog a whopping great stack of CDs. How? Easy. We just used your standard off-the-shelf Abduct-o-matic, you know, the minimodel you can buy in any supermarket. I see. Any supermarket on Nufon anyway. With the Abduct-o-matic, you just zap what you want, and what you want is yours. Ching ching! Instant gratification. Just what the doctor ordered—retail atrophy. What? Therapy. Whatever.

You understand. We'd been cooped up in a spaceship for what seemed like eons without even a shopping channel. I can tell you, we were pretty keen to cut loose. Mum isn't bad as motherships go. But let's face it, it's still basically a tin fucken can with boosters. Lati, Doll, and I are the best of mates and we've known each other since we were only knee-high to a mushroom spore. Still, put us in a flying antennae-spray container for that long and we can really get on each other's tits.

It doesn't help that by nature we're not much inclined to dormition. When you're awake most of the time like we are, you want to be entertained. The recreational facilities on board were *pathetic*. Fully tragic actually, considering how many trips to Earth the craft had made before we came along and borrowed it. Stole it. Whatever. On the other hand, our fellow Nufonians being what they are, and being that what they are is terminally fucken boring, I suppose it shouldn't have been *that* much of a surprise. Anyway, there was one Scrabble set, a selection of nonviolent computer games, a collection of CDs that consisted entirely of recordings by Bing Crosby, one copy of *Men Are from Mars, Women Are from Venus*, and, dig this, *heaps* of stamp albums.

Of all the things in the yoon that you could collect, Nufonians *would* concentrate on postage stamps. You can see why we had to get away from that planet. Absolute dweebsville. Bogans of the yooniverz. You want to know what Nufonians are like? All you need to know is this—they wear trek-suits in public.

Sorry. I won't go on.

There just aren't that many places you can stop off at on the way here, either. On the advice of the *Hitchhiker's Guide to the Galaxy* we tried the Restaurant at the End of the Yooniverz. That guidebook was published years ago and the restaurant must've changed hands or something, cuz it had been turned into a Sizzler. Family fucken restaurants. They're *everywhere*. Plague-o-rama.

We managed somehow. Doll amused herself by putting Mum on manual, taking over the controls and playing chicken with asteroids. Scared the living nightlights out of us a few times. There was this one asteroid, don't know his name, but he was a *big* mother. Doll took us close enough to see the dust on his nose. You should have seen the look on his face when we zipped by! Anyway, we had fun with him. We all blew kisses and Lati mooned him. Lati will moon anything. Even moons, though that joke wore pretty thin after a while. As for me, I just played a lot of air guitar.

I *love* rock music. We all do.

Thankfully, we'd managed to smuggle an Intergalactic Yaddayadda Receiver on board, so at least we could tune in to some decent music and keep up with the *Simpsons* and *X-Files*. We ayles love *The X-Files*, by the way. It's much more popular in the outer than *The Twilight Zone* or *My Favorite Martian* ever was. There's a huge *X-Files* fan club based on a planet near Alpha Centauri. The Sirians threw a fabulous party there shortly before we left. All the ayles got dressed up as Fox Mulder and Dana Scully. You gotta meet the Sirians some day. They're full-on space trash. We love 'em. Anyway, we thought of having an *X-Files* party during the trip. But it wouldn't have been much of an event with just the three of us. Well, four, if you count Revor.

Revor is our pet. See him? He sees you now. Isn't he cute? Haha. Stop that, Revor. Heh. Stop it. Ha! C'mon, Revor, lay off. You're making the Earthling nervous. Oops. Don't worry. You should be able to wash that out. When he cums that fast it's usually pretty watery. At least on Earth it doesn't float around like it did when we were up in the zero. What d'ya mean, what is it? It's only an oioi. Don't you have them on Earth? Funny little creatures. They're hybrids actually. Half Madagascan aye-aye, half space elefent. You know space elefents? They're teeny-weeny little pink things not much bigger than a quark with long noses and excellent mammaries. Oh, look. I said *"only* an oioi" and now he's acting all hurt. Oh, Revvy-wevvy. Don't be like that.

Come here, Revor. Come here. That's right. Oooh. What *are* you doing? Get outta there! Oooh. Whoawhoawhoa. No! Don't do that! Well, oooh, maybe do that. Yes, do that. Oh, yes. Oooh, *Rev.* Oooh. What have you found there? Mmmmm. Oh, Revor, *baby.* Yeahhhhhhh. Bit to the left. That's it. Ohhhhh. Don't stop. Good boy. Goooood boy.

Mmmmmmmmm.

What's wrong, Earth boy? You're looking a trifle on the pale side. Isn't sex what life on Earth is all about? I've seen Earth movies. I read *Cosmo.* I listen to rock songs. You know, this bed is on fire, I wanna rock you all night long, the birds and the goats. Oh, man. What d'ya mean, it's slightly more complicated than that? How complicated could it be?

By the way, is that a rocket in your pocket or are you just

happy to see me? I'm pretty happy to see you, actually. Very happy. There's definitely something about you, Earth boy. Something I want. Something I just might take.

Oh, look at Revor, chasing his stupid tail again. He did that a lot up in the outer. That's a sight in the zero, I can tell you. Yeah, Revor was definitely an oioi on the verge. When he wasn't chasing his tail, he was howling at comets or sucking the knobs off the control panel. Can't blame him, really. We were all bouncing off the walls. I remember how excited we were just to see some dumb NASA space probe. Lati mooned it.

I shouldn't complain. Space travel is a breeze compared to what it used to be in the bad old days of arkships. I couldn't deal with an arkship myself. You know, get on board as a yunggin, grow up, progenerate, watch your own yunggins grow up, and expire knowing that their yunggins will probably still be alive when the ship finally gets where it's going. Boring, boring, boring! I'm an instant grat girl myself. The old deep-freeze concept was pretty poxy too. People were always waking up in the Hiber-pod with their ears or eyebrows on the pillow next to them. Spewsville.

The discovery of wormholes has done a lot to make the yoon a smaller place, if something infinite can ever really be made smaller, that is. Wormholes are the autobahns of the cosmos. You know black holes, right? Picture one shaped like a cigarette. That's a wormhole. Imagine going in a strand of dried tobacco at one end and coming out the other as smoke. Which is the only problem with wormholes. They tend to rearrange your molecules. You wouldn't want to have seen the casualty wards up on Nufon when they first began testing wormholes for intergalactic travel. There was this one guy who came out with his nose where his—oh, you really don't want to know the details. Trust me. I'm an alien.

Anyway, we managed to arrive with all our molecules

more or less in place. And, following an afternoon of top shopping, there we were, ready to *party* when we clapped oculi on a poster advertising that Agent Mulder gig. Sweet! We'd caught some of the band's vids on the Yaddayadda on the way over. Besides liking the name, of course, we're fully into that sort of indie music. Well, *great*, we thought— serendipity city!

We knew then for sure that we'd come to the right place. Sydney! The Big Toke. Smoke. Whatever. We checked out quite a few different cities on the way. We went to New York first, it being the self-advertised center of the yoon and all. Just as we were coasting in on the saucer for a closer look, this crazy little bean suddenly pulled an Uzi out of his jacket, aimed it at us, and began firing. You've never seen a warp drive reverse so fast. We left skid marks on the *air*. We weren't sure where to go next. We'd seen the Eurovision Song Contest on the Yaddayadda, so continental Europe was out. Out out out. That's scary stuff. We like African and South American music, but it's not rock, and we *detest* Canto-pop, so Asia was out as well. The skies over Seattle and London, meanwhile, were gray as a Nufonian's tit and wet as a Sirian's sense of humor. And, well, you do hear so much in the outer about the Opera House and Bondi Beach and that cute little band, whatchamacallit, tinstool. What? Oh, right. Anyway, to make a long story short, here we are.

Yeah, I know, I know, silverchair's not really from Sydney. But look at it this way—when you're a billion trillion light years away from Earth to begin with, a few hundred kilometers here or there is spitting distance.

Go ahead, have a good look around. Groovy little pad, ain't it? Bit of a mess-o-rama, sure, but life's about more than just keeping your room clean, hey? We call this funky piece of furniture the Voodoo Lounge Suite. Abducted it this afternoon too. Galgal came with the most poxy furnishings. We trashed 'em all on the way over. Had to. They were all covered in beige Ultrasuede. That about sums up Nufonian taste. Just cuz it was once featured in *Saucer Beautiful*, they all have to have it. Jeez. You getting a sense of what we're running away from? Anyway, the saucer itself's not too shabby. Don't know if you know much about spacecraft, but Galgal is your typical bi-convex domed disk model. She's got some history, does the old Galgal. You know Ezekiel? No, not the heavy metal band. The prophet. Anyway, the Cherubim—they're another species of alien—did a big fly-by on Ezekiel in Galgal. Made quite an impression, it did. He raved about "wheels of fire" this, "wheels of fire" that for ages.

Galgal inspired the first mirror ball in the 1920s when she performed a spinning loop-the-loop in full sunlight with all her laser beams firing. Isn't that cool? Oh, and she pulled some spectacular wheelies over Tahiti some years ago. People assumed it was the aftereffects of French nuclear testing in the Pacific. Sparked renewed protests and all. We were pretty chuffed about that.

Environmental issues tend to be fairly high on the extraterrestrial agenda. But you probably know that from *Millennium Watch* and *UFO Quarterly*. You've never heard of those magazines? Oh, you're not missing much. They're just full of long articles on how ayles supervised the construction of the pyramids and shit like that. That's news? Give me *Rolling Stone* or a good fanzine any day.

It's funny, you know. It's like, we think we know heaps about Earth and Earthlings but here I am, face-to-face with you, a bona fide human bean, and I'm practically speechless. Well, maybe not speechless. Sorry. I must still be a bit hyper from all that space travel. But you know what I mean. It's like, you're so familiar and so strange, all at once.

You're our first abductee, you know.

That's not to say you're the first Earthling to get an

inside view of Galgal. Just the first since we've taken it over. Yeah, this little beauty has been responsible for the abduction of heaps of Americans alone. What happened to them? They all appeared on talk shows, of course. You'd have seen some on *Oprah*, surely. Australians? Let's see. There were three taken from back o' Bourke a few years ago. They asked to be dropped off at the pub; I'm not sure what happened after that. And then there were a handful of Kurds from Iraq. Apparently they were just happy to get away for a while.

Galgal is the subject of investigation by an entire secret division of the U.S. military. Full-on, eh?

We learned all that from the log book. Show it to you later, if you like. Typical of Nufonians to keep such detailed records. They're as regular as a test pattern, and half as interesting. Zzzzzt. New day, same picture. Zzzzzt. New day, same picture. Zzzzzt. Know what I mean? I really should stop dissing Nufonians. I'm kinda Nufonian myself. What do I mean, kinda? I'm a hybrid. Yeah, that's right. We all are, all three of us.

Let's talk about sex.

You've seen those tabloid headlines—"I WAS ABDUCTED BY A UFO!" "I WAS SEXUALLY EXPERIMENTED ON BY CREATURES FROM OUTER SPACE!" "I WAS IMPREGNATED BY ALIENS!" "EXTRATERRESTRIALS TOOK MY FETUS!"? Well, it's true. Shit happens. Believe it. The three of us, we're Earth's little alien love children. Yeah. Alien plus Earthling equals the sum of us. As a matter of fact, we were conceived right here, on Galgal.

Lati's mum was an American from the Midwest. The principal of a school that only teaches kids what's in the Bible and won't let them listen to rock 'n' roll—the *devil's* music. Ha. Anyway, the dumb-arse Nufonians thought she'd be a safe bet, and scooped her up one night after a PTA meeting. She hasn't been the same since. She has these blackouts and wakes up to find herself at Metallica concerts—*in the mosh*.

Doll had an Earth father and a Nufonian mother. He was another predictable Nufonian choice—an English accountant with three identical gray suits, a pantry full of Savoy biscuits, and a pathological fear of nose rings. He doesn't remember very much about the experience. But he gets erections whenever he sees a rerun of the original *Star Trek*.

*My* mother, funnily enough, is Australian. She's married to one of your leaders. Can't remember which one. Earthling names all sound alike to me. Anyway, she's middle-class-o-rama, all nylon pantyhose, family values, and received opinions on marijuana use. Boy, would she get a mega-shock if she ever met me. She's never mentioned anything to her husband about the experience. Didn't want to hurt his feelings. It was the best fuck she'd ever had.

Don't get the wrong idea. Nufonians aren't just sex maniacs who spend their free time cruising the yoon for talent. If they were, we might never have left. Nah, the Nufonian libido leaves a lot to be desired. Plus, the somatic form we usually get around in is what I think Earthling UFOlogists call "small gray." You don't know what that means? Never mind. I'll show you in a minute. I was actually in small gray mode when we first got back to Galgal, but you looked a bit out of it, so I'm not surprised you can't remember. But the crucial thing—as far as sex is concerned anyway—is that small grays have *no fucken genitals*. That's right. Even *we* can't tell if we're Arthur or Martha. Can you believe that?

How do we what? Reproduce? Like Earthlings, Nufonians only come in two genders. Boring, eh? Anyway, when it's that time in his cycle, the male Nufonian starts hacking away like someone who's just snorted a line of Mars dust. *Very* attractive, I can assure you. Keck-o-rama. Eventually, he hawks up a batch of phlegmy sperm into his cakehole.

He then finds a receptive female, and spits out all this gnarly cum into her ear. If it hits the bull's-eye, the fertilized egg then tumbles down a tube to a cavity in her throat. A few months down the track, she starts coughing as well, and eventually, just as you think she's going to gag to death, out pops a yunggin. The very thought makes me want to spew. When I'm on Nufon I keep my ears to myself.

Not that I have anything against aural sex. I've got nothing against sex of any kind. If you ask me, true love waits for no man or woman, ayle or bean. Lust doesn't linger for long and good times tend to slip away if you don't grab 'em by the short & curlies when they're passing through town.

Good times come in all sorts of shapes and sizes in the outer. Some aliens have funny, limited ideas about who they'll get involved with. Pleiadians tend to avoid Sirians, and Andromedans won't even look at an Alpha Centaurian. Me, I like all physical types. Senocular, simous, scombroid. Whatever. Don't care if you've got scales or fur or eyes in the middle of your head, or polka dots or stripes or twelve fat fingers on each of your twenty-two hands. It all boils down to chemistry, really. Know what I mean? I think you do, Earth boy. I think you do.

Chemistry, hey?

What was I saying? Oh yeah, sex. Age doesn't matter to me, either. The wrizzled voice of experience has always been the sweetest music to my ears, particularly since, as a Nufonian, my ears are all I've ever had to play with. I'm attracted to nearly all of the seventeen known genders in the yooniverz, though I must admit I've always preferred vuggier types. When it comes to sex, holes are a good thing. Holes are useful. Holes are fun. That's what's wrong with us Nufonians, you know. Not enough holes. Literally closed to new experiences.

Speaking of new experiences, I'm an Earthling virgin. Never done it in Earth-girl form or with one of your types before. Despite being part Earthling, we could never really manage the Earth girl shtick outside of this atmosphere—just as you think you've got a fix on it, *skikk*, it all kinda slips away and you're back in small gray mode. Unbelievable. You see, our Earthling genes have given us heaps and heaps of sexual drive but our Nufonian circs meant that we've never been able to get it out of first gear.

Sex-wise, you folks are a legend. I don't want to make you feel bad or anything, and this may be a bit of a generalization, but we up in the outer have never exactly been interested in you for your minds. In yoonal terms, you barely qualify as an intelligent life form. Your crufty little computers are a joke, most of you can't remove the caps from childproof bottles and you prefer dumb Hollywood remakes to the original French films. And look what you're doing to your planet. Not to mention each other. We occasionally tune into *NYPD Blue* and *A Current Affair* and I'll tell you, we're fucken *shocked* by what we see. I mean, Ricki Lake is one thing, but murder and mayhem and advertisements for slimming salons—they're not exactly signs of higher intelligence. Don't take it personally. It's not like you don't have potential. And anyway, it's clear you've got *something* going for you, or no one could be stuffed making the trip here in the first place. As I was saying earlier, space travel is no beatnik. Sorry? Picnic? Damn chip.

Where was I? That's right. And you did invent rock 'n' roll. I *love* rock music. Did I say that already?

Live wild on the edge or die bored in the middle, that's what I say. The surf's never up in the great mainstream. They try and tell you otherwise on Nufon. They're so clueless they wouldn't know if a shuttle was up them till the astronaut emerged for a spacewalk. They're as captive to innate Nufonian blandness as they are trapped for life in those wretched bodies. We're lucky. We're AC/DC. No, not like the band. Like this. I'm really getting the hang of shape-shifting here. See? Now I'm an alien. Now I'm an Earth girl. Now I'm an alien. Now I'm an Earth girl. We call shape-shifting into Earth-girl form "slipping into something more comfortable." Fun, isn't it? What's the matter? Something wrong? Why are you on the floor?

Speaking of shape-shifters, here are the others. This grrrl here is Doll. Doll Parts. And that's Lati. Lati Dodidohdoh. Where *were* you two?

Sorry. Looks like we're scaring you. Why don't you just sit down over there, next to Doll. It's okay. She won't bite. Not till she gets to know you better, anyway. Ha ha. Just kidding. Sort of. Hope you're all right. You're looking a bit pale, you know. Never mind. Sit next to me, then.

What's your name, Earth boy? Jake? You're very cute, you know. Very sexy. I bet you know it too. What's that on your head? It looks like the wrong end of a sheep. So *that's* what you call dreadlocks? Hmmm. Very sweet. No, I do like them. Really, I do.

Jake. Nice name.

All that stuff about the abductions, the sexual experimentation on Earthlings that produced us and so on is supposed to be fully hush-hush. Oh, I know you're not going to tell anyone. As if I really cared. Thing is, the experiments weren't exactly considered a raging success. From the Nufonian standpoint, we're too Earthish. As we see it, we're not Earthish enough. Anyway, officially, we don't even exist. When we're on Nufon we're expected to act like everyone else, and we're not supposed to attempt to shape-shift into Earth-girl form or talk about our origins or anything. They get really fucked off with us when we disobey, which is, like, every chance we get. The authorities up there would be shitting bricks if they knew we were sitting here yakking on about all this to you down here. Actually they'd be shitting bricks if they knew we were here full stop. No, I stand corrected. They wouldn't be shitting bricks because

THEY DON'T EVEN HAVE ARSEHOLES. Fucken anal retentives, the lot of them.

But no, you don't want to hear my theories on Nufonians.

Maybe you'd like to tell us a bit about yourself.

No? Oioi got your tongue? Ha. Maybe later. But if you're not gonna talk, then we'll go about our business. First, however, I'd like to say, on behalf of all of us, how delighted we are to have you here with us on Galgal. We went to the gig not really knowing what to expect. It was the first time we'd ever heard rock 'n' roll live. Oh, man. I love saying that here—"oh, man." It just doesn't have the same ring when you're talking to an ayle. Know what I mean? Never mind. Anyway, it was so totally grouse. That steaming mash of Earthling bodies, smelling of animal passion and sex. The pounding of the music. The screaming. The excellent T-shirts. The mad energy billowing off the stage and through the mosh. And that's when I saw you. Climbing up on stage and diving off it into the crowd, and doing it again and again. I looked at you and knew in an instant that you were everything I've always wanted. Sex, drugs, and rock 'n' roll. In one convenient package. I hope you understand. I just had to have you. And so I took you. With the Abduct-o-matic, of course. Such a handy tool. Never leave the home planet without it.

There wasn't much more to it than that, really.

You're a quiet boy, Jake. Didn't really expect an Earth boy like you to be so quiet.

You look a bit scared. Don't be. Try to stay calm. Whatever you do, don't struggle. There's no point. That's it, just relax. And welcome to the sexual experimentation chamber.

**S**pun out. Uh-huh. Whacked. Yeah. Confused. Sure. Freaked. Maybe. At this particular moment in the history of the yoon, Jake was feeling lots of things. Cool was not one.

This was not a minor point. Jake was a boy who liked to think he was so cool that he came with the instructions: defrost before use. So cool that cucumbers used *him* as a standard. So cool that, when he walked into Newtown's Sandringham Pub, all the little grungelettes and punkoids and baby deros and other critters of the rock 'n' roll night drew a collective, beery breath and exhaled, *kyoool*. Kyoool, of course, being even kyoooler than cool.

Kyoool/Cool. You have to keep up with these things. And Jake kept up. Not in any obvious way. In Jake's world, it was important not to be seen making an effort. Unless it was toward some truly heroic goal like getting so trashed on Saturday night that you managed to wipe out all of Sunday and most of Monday in the one go.

Getting laid on a regular basis was another laudable ambition, but the effort rule applied with double force here. The idea was to work it so that the girl thought *she* was chasing *you*. This not only made it hard for her to lay a guilt trip on you when you decided to bolt, but it had the advantage of her being keen to pay for your meals while she was still courting you. And the girls did court Jake. He was the lead singer in a minor but reputable band called Bosnia. He was seductively lazy, amusing, and not very together, a combination that many women found irresistible. He had the big brown eyes of an innocent and the slow white smile of a seducer. Women tended to lose themselves somewhere in the middle—in the vicinity of his modest little nose—captivated by his tall, grungy, dread-headed, rock 'n' roll boy charms.

Dreadlocks—now that was another perfect illustration of the effort rule. Dreads were the ultimate slacker hairstyle. No cut, no comb, no worries, right? Wrong. Good dreads demanded hard work, TLC, and regular rolling between the palms with wax.

There were also crucial aesthetic decisions to be made. How big was big enough? To wrap or not to wrap? Crazy Colour or natural? Then there was the problem of what to do when a loop of hair escaped halfway down a dread, sticking out like a teacup handle and looking *quite* ridiculous. You also needed to decide whether to wash the hair at all and, if so, whether to use shampoo—opinion was divided on the shampoo issue, but universally against conditioner. Jake shampooed once a fortnight. He rolled daily. He was not a natural blond.

People didn't understand how difficult it was being a slacker. That's why even younger kids were abandoning the pose altogether. Didn't have the stamina.

How Jake had developed his extraordinary kyoool, his raw sexuality, his sophisticated approach to hairstyling, even his rock 'n' roll talent was a bit of a mystery, for he had grown up in the weirdly sanitized environment of Canberra, the nation's capital. Canberra was as thrilling as a Nufonian honeymoon. It was a planned city where seasons actually began on the day they were supposed to, where inspired criminal activity was pretty well confined to Parliament House, where sex was a regulated industry, and where, not long before Jake was born, the bakers sold rye bread under the counter to immigrants on prearranged days so as not to frighten the Anglos with the sight of a nonwhite loaf.

Nor had Jake traveled much outside Canberra in his twenty-three years on the planet. He'd only ever made a few short trips to Sydney before moving there two years earlier with his best mates, the twins Torquil and Tristram. He'd gone to Melbourne once, to try to get a band together with some friends. He'd been here and there on the coast for some surfing, though Jake's surfboard was always more accessory than lifestyle.

Whenever Jake had traveled, it had always been by car, train, or bus. He'd never flown. Like the song went, music was his aeroplane. He sang, he strummed, he went as far as it—and a variety of chemical cocktails—could take him. But rock had never rolled him so madly, dope never lifted him so high, speed never sped him so fast, nor acid taken him to stranger places than Galgal, where he now inexplicably found himself, spun out, degravitated, giddy.

His vision was blurred and shaky and his chest felt as tight as Gene Simmons' pants. Taking a few deep breaths, Jake attempted to make out his surroundings.

The room he was in was shaped like a wedge of pie. It appeared to be windowless, though he could make out the outline of portholes and a door on each of the side walls. It glowed with a weird, lime green ambient light that would have made focusing a challenge even if his eyeballs hadn't been doing the lambada.

With a start, Jake detected a small silvery figure gliding toward him on delicate hooves. Its slim shoulders supported a disproportionately large head dominated by wraparound, almond-shaped eyes. They were all pupil, a daunting, fathomless black, and oddly reminiscent of the sort of sunglasses that boys like Jake all sported. They gave nothing away. Similarly, the creature's mouth was an expressionless slit. The ears were recessed and all he could see of the nose was a slight indentation where the nostrils might have been. In contrast to the inert blankness of its face, the figure's spindly, multiply jointed hands were almost insanely kinetic. Four long knobby fingers twitched on the end of each hand. Each tic and flutter produced a mysterious, bell-like vibration. His heart sounding a drumroll of fear within his chest, Jake tried hard to focus on the creature, but its skin was bright with a metallic sheen that repelled his gaze.

Maybe he was dead. He'd gone to heaven, and this was what angels looked like. Dead. That was it. He'd made his final stage dive into that great mosh pit in the sky. Happened to people all the time, if you believed the papers. Jesus. After that incident with the cracked collarbone, Jake had promised his mother he'd never stage-dive again. If she found out he'd done it anyway and now he was dead, she'd kill him.

Hold on. He didn't *feel* dead.

Nup. Whatever he was feeling, it was definitely not deadness. Jake tingled in his fingers. He tingled in his toes. Each fluttering contact of his Kyuss T-shirt on the winter-pale skin of his chest caused a tremor to run down his spine. Closing his eyes, he listened to his breath rushing his nostrils and the blood pulsing through his veins. Jake had never been a particularly attentive student, but he did remember this from biology: breath and a pulse were a pretty fair indication that you weren't dead.

*Tonight's my first night on Earth. . . .*

His eyes flew open again. It would have been tempting to liken Jake's expression to that of a stunned mullet. No fish, however, could register in its simple piscine orbs quite the degree or combination of shock, confusion, and sudden desire that were roiling Jake's big browns at this very moment.

For, right before those now almost distressingly clear-sighted eyes, the strange silvery creature was metamorphosing into the kind of girl that represented all that girldom could to boys like Jake. She was a rock 'n' roll dream. Her hair was a mass of braids in every color under the sun—and under every other star in the yoon as well. Under violet bangs, large uptilted green eyes sparkled out from thick lashes with a mischievous intelligence. Parenthesized by killer cheekbones, her longish nose arrowed down to the bow of her full lips. A *filthy* plastic minidress the color of burning rocket fuel, meanwhile, encased a body that could only be described as awesome: antigravity tits, a waist tiny enough to orbit with a pair of hands, two full moons for an arse, and strong legs as long as jet streams.

So, her skin was a touch on the green side. Green was cool. If Jake ever got around to registering to vote, he was sure he'd vote Green. Especially now.

But antennae?

Hold on a tic, he thought. This is tipping the weirdometer. Of course. Doh! It was the acid. Had to be. Jake had popped a microdot before heading out to the Agent Mulder gig. Still, this was one full-on, wacky trip. Acid had never kicked in for him like this before, not even the time the Vegemite jar grew legs and tap-danced around the room to Regurgitator. Maybe he shouldn't have had those four bourbon-and-cokes as well. Bourbon wasn't the worry. *No* one knew what was in Coca-Cola.

C'mon, Jake, work it out.

The very last thing he could recall was scrambling past the bouncers at Selinas and up onto the stage for a record sixth time. One moment he was airborne, palms away, sailing over heads and hands. Then there was a brilliant flash of light, an eerie silence, and a sweet, melting feeling. The next thing he knew he was swaying on his tingletoes, this alien girl's mellifluous voice lapping at his ears, her stream-ing words wilding his brain. Yaddayaddayaddayadda.

*Alien girl?*

Baby, she said her name was. Baby Baby. Where had he heard that before? As she chattered on, she answered each of the questions that popped into his head. The bizarre thing was, it occurred to him with a jolt, he hadn't actually asked them. He hadn't so much as opened his mouth, ex-cept to gape. She was reading his mind. How'd she do that? This was seriously spinning him out.

Her gaze was so intense it hurt.

Baby may have had the rock-chick look down pat, but she didn't have a clue how to behave in an acceptable rock 'n' roll manner. As any bean could tell you, contemporary rock 'n' roll manners are very much tied up with slacker eti-quette. And slacker etiquette requires, among other things, that no one look anyone else in the eye for too long or too attentively, particularly a person you are speaking to. To a slacker, excessive direct eye-contact goes beyond rude to approach the physically painful. Instinctively dodging the javelin of her regard, Jake glanced nervously around him.

Things were slowly coming into focus now. She had sat down upon a ripe-strawberry-red sofa, the rolling surface of which suggested a giant tongue. Voodoo Lounge? Did she say something about Voodoo Lounge? The linguiform sofa appeared to be licking her bottom. Trying not to stare, he shifted his gaze slightly and noticed that facing the lounge at a slight angle was another sofa, this one covered in blue-berry suede and shaped like a giant shoe. A wall-mounted control panel of some kind pulsed luminously in the corner. It was all very SciFi.

Yet for all the high-style high-tech, the place was a brothel, a total, absolute, shambolic, slobbiferous mess. Clothes and zines and CDs were strewn everywhere. A bit like his own room back in Newtown really. Except the clothes were all new, and this place lacked that ambient *je ne sais quoi* that comes from spicing up the dry goods with a few near-empty beer bottles and half-eaten brownies and a grease-soaked pizza box or two. He noticed that there were a few plaques that looked like stolen street signs but which bore names like Red Giant and White Dwarf. Star signs? She stole star signs? Posters also decorated the walls. Jake made out the familiar face of Kurt Cobain on one of them. He found the sight comforting until it occurred to him that Kurt was dead too.

Not dead *too*. He's dead. I'm not. I'm not dead. I'm not dead. Jake thought if he repeated this enough he might even convince himself.

*Alien girl?*

Visions of body-snatchers, brain-suckers, fire-starters, cocoon artists, cosmic apes, liquid skies, parallel universes, purple people-eaters, David Bowie, Sigourney Weaver, Men in Black, and the second-to-the-last Dr. Who tumbled helter-skelter through his mind. He searched for the right response, but the right response was quaking in some dark corner of his brain with the rest of his rational faculties as the visions shot through.

Yorp! Yorp! Yorp! It was at this moment that a small reddish creature with hideous fur like an old shag-pile rug, a long narrow snout, floppy ears, and prehensile toes bounded into the room, making a peculiar sound that was halfway between the yap of a small dog and the pop of a cork from a champagne bottle. Instead of pupils, its bulging round eyes pinwheeled yellow and black. Although it utilized both its front and back paws, it relied more on the back ones, hunching over with a peculiar gait that Jake had only ever previously observed in roadies. Yorp! Yorp! Yorp! Before he had time to consider the implications of this fresh apparition, it hurtled itself across the room and onto his left leg.

Its tiny body wrapped tightly around Jake's left knee, the creature began humping furiously. The alien girl hooted with laughter at this. That was a bit mean. No time to reflect on that now, however. Until he removed this furry tumor from his leg, he was in no position to reflect on anything. Revor was way beyond disgusting. What's worse, his snaky pink tongue, poking out of his puckered and off-center little mouth, had threaded itself through a rip in Jake's jeans and, with a series of moist ministrations, embarked on an upward exploration of his thigh. Jake vainly attempted to shake it off, push it off, pry it off, peel it off, and slap it off, all the while trying to maintain some semblance of cool. As Baby, wiping tears of mirth from her eyes, finally suctioned the little creature off him, Jake felt something wet dribble down his knee. He looked down to discover a stream of bright pink fluid. His stomach slam-danced against his ribcage; nausea diluted his original cocktail of wonder and fear. "What *is* that thing?" he gasped.

"It's only an oioi," shrugged Baby, tickling its ear. "Don't you have them on Earth?"

It was Revor's turn to look shocked. *Only* an oioi?

Hearing her matter-of-fact tone, Jake cringed at his own display of panic. Wherever this girl came from, alien nation or hallucination, he desperately wanted to impress her. At the same time, he suspected he was already failing miserably. This was a new experience for Jake. Jake usually found it much harder work extricating himself from a woman's arms than insinuating himself between her legs in the first place. Tears sprang to his eyes.

Tears had sprung to Revor's eyes as well. Ignoring Jake for a moment, Baby ootchikootchikooed her by now thoroughly pathetic pet. Sniffling, it wriggled around on her lap.

Jake found what happened next simply unbelievable.

He'd always fancied himself quite the sophisticate. To his friends, Jake was a walking encyclopedia of sexual knowledge: he could extemporize for hours on such arcana as the relative merits of the cat position and the doggie style, the joys of butterfly kisses (done with the eyelashes), the advantages of mint-flavored condoms ("freshens her breath at the same time"), and how to handle piercing emergencies—for instance if your eyebrow ring catches on her labial jewelry ("make no sudden moves"). Jake was also an avid reader of his flatmates Skye and Saturna's subscription copies of *Australian Women's Forum*.

But nothing he'd ever seen or done or heard or read could have prepared him for what happened now. It had to be the light. . . . Fucking hell. That was her thigh, for Christ's sake. Her body was writhing with unabashed pleasure. He could see Revor's long pink tongue darting in and out of the—what was it? Jesus Christ!

Revor suddenly jerked his head back, sucked in some O and buried his entire echinoid snout up to the eyeballs. Where his tongue was at this point, Jake didn't even dare imagine. Gnumgnumgnum came the muffled sounds from way inside.

Jake was so embarrassed he didn't know *where* to put his eyes. He wanted to disappear. He wanted to die. He wanted to throw up. Most of all, he wanted to be Revor. The sensation that, whatever it was he'd gotten himself into, he was already *way* over his head, grew nearly as fast as his erection.

After what seemed like an eternity, Baby tired of Revor's attentions. "Mmmmmm," she sighed. She extracted him from the tiny orifice on her thigh—his snout popped out with the sound of someone plucking a string on a double bass—and gave him a hug. Revor panted happily, then, squirming out of her grasp, dropped with a kathunk to the floor and began chasing his tail, whirling-purling, until his form began to shimmy and blur like the blades of a propeller. Revor always found there was nothing like a good twirl to clear his mind, refresh the soul, and renew the tastebuds.

*Space travel rarara . . . Agent Mulder rarara . . . flying saucers rarara . . . Earthling virgin rarara . . .*

Though Jake's mind was racing, it still lagged whole laps behind Baby's spiel. When she began to shape-shift, *Earth girl . . . alien . . . Earth girl . . . alien . . .* he sensed he'd lost control of the wheel altogether. Now he crashed into the barricade.

Knees a-wobble, Jake floored with a thud. As he reeled dizzily into a faint, it occurred to him that this had to be the single most disastrous, humiliating experience he'd ever had with the opposite sex.

When he opened his eyes again, his chin was resting on the reinforced toe of an exquisitely small army boot.

"Oi," spoke the voice that belonged to the foot which occupied the boot that was supporting his face. "Don't scuff the leather, Earth boy."

His eyes tracked upward. From the laced-up boot-tops rose a thin leg encased in black leather. Above that, a ripped black T-shirt. Wiry arms were folded over a narrow, boyish chest. *This grrrl here is Doll.* The face that peered back down at him with a fusion of mild contempt and high amusement was long, angular, pale. A silver bone pierced her elegantly hooked nose and a snarl surfed dangerous lips. Her dark eyes had the intensity of black holes. Through her eyebrows were looped half a dozen silver rings. Her head was shaved, leaving only a short bristly bridge across the front connecting two curved and stiffened devil's horns of hair that poked out from above her temples. An intricate spider tattoo peeked over the top of her right ear; its delicate web stretched down her neck. She had a dozen shimmering rings on her hands. Apart from the fact that she was green and antennaed, she vaguely reminded Jake of Trent Reznor from Nine Inch Nails. And Trent Reznor, so far as Jake was concerned, was a god. He was kissing the feet of a god. Goddess. It was still terribly awkward and wasn't helping his self-image. With a grimace, he levered himself up to a sitting position. His brain felt like it was wrapped in cotton wool. *Doll Parts.* Doll Parts? That name was really familiar too. Where'd he heard it before?

"In your dreams," said Doll wryly. Noting his look of surprise, she added, "These antennae ain't just decorative, sweetmeat." Doll had her doubts about Baby's choice of Earthling. He was, after all, their very first abduction and, while there'd surely be more to come, the first carried a kind of symbolic significance, not to mention a certain sentimental value. For one thing, she didn't see why it couldn't have been a girl. "Where's Lati?" growled Doll, ignoring Jake. "I'm sure she's taken my new, whatshernames? Moc Dartens."

"Doc Martens," said Jake helpfully.

With an open palm, Doll whacked the side of her head so hard that Jake jumped. "Damn Transling-a-tron," she growled. "Think there's a bug in it."

Jake was now smacked in the gob by a third apparition. *And that's Lati.* This one he took in from the top down. *Lati Dodidohdoh.* An untamed mop of hair as red as the dust of Mars. Widely spaced gray eyes smudged top and bottom with kohl. The kind of girl referred to in Jake's circles, with deference and awe, as a grunge queen. Her body was as curvaceous as space itself: soft full breasts straining against a short white T-shirt, sexy rounded belly humping out of low-slung jeans, big, luscious arse. Standard green skin and antennae. Encircling the waist of her jeans was a belt that appeared to be woven of the very fabric of the night sky, along which planetary fragments vibrated, collided, and smashed.

Jake's reality systems were crashing fast.

25

Why's the Earthling sitting on the floor, Lati wondered. Baby shrugged, reached down, grabbed Jake by the hand and hauled him to his feet.

Jesus! The girl was strong as a mallee bull. What's more, the touch of her hand was literally electrifying. Jake felt the hairs on his arms and legs stand on end. She patted the seat next to her.

*What's your name, Earth boy?*

"J-Jake," he stuttered. God, this was getting worse and worse. He'd never stuttered before in his life. He wanted to press rewind and start again. What was this movie anyway?

"He speaks," noted Doll, not overly impressed.

Latidodidohdoh, Latidodidohdoh. The syllables rocked and rolled in the vertiginous funride of his mind. Of course! The Ed Kuepper song! "Just sing Ladidodidohdoh." And Doll Parts—the Courtney Love hit, of course. As for Baby Baby . . . Doh! Did he feel dumb.

"Well, well, I suppose I should give him *some* credit," said Doll. "He's not exactly quick. But he got there in the end. I was beginning to worry."

Her eyes fell upon Lati's waist. "Lati, you bitch! That's my asteroid belt. I've been looking for it since we got to this galaxy and you know it."

"You said I could borrow it," Lati defended. "Besides, you've got all my rings of Saturn."

"You could've asked," Doll sulked. "I want it back. And"—she pointed to the boots on Lati's feet— "my Moc, Doc, *thingos* as well."

"Take 'em back then." Putting her hands on her waist, Lati raised her eyebrows and threw Doll a look so cheeky it could've been Mama Cass's arse. Doll stomped over to where Lati stood. She looked her straight in the eye. Keeping her gaze steady, Doll reached down, undid the belt, snaked it out through the loops, and tossed it to the floor.

The corners of Lati's mouth curled up ever so slightly. Doll knelt down on one knee with firm, deliberate movements, untied the laces of Lati's Docs and loosened the tops. With an upward wave of her palm, she indicated for Lati to lift one foot, then the other. Jerking the boots off, she tossed them aside as well. Doll now hooked a finger in Lati's waistband and pulled till her stomach was flush against her lips. Lati's mouth twitched. Doll licked and sucked Lati's stomach, which, Jake suddenly noticed, *had no navel*. Queasy-o-rama.

That was nothing compared to what Jake saw next. He felt like he'd entered some mutant jigsaw world where all the pieces had been put together in the wrong place. His hand flew to his mouth. "I think I'm gonna hurl," he moaned weakly. "Wherezaloo?"

Doll looked up and the three aliens exchanged mystified glances. "Hurl" was coming up "to rush, to dash, to throw, to fling; undecipherable in this context" through their Transling-a-trons. "Wherezaloo" wasn't coming up at all.

The moment passed. Jake swallowed, closed his eyes, took a deep breath, and opened them again. Four pairs of curious alien eyes—three humanoid, one animaloid—were fixed upon him. Revor, an incurable romantic with an instinctive empathy for any sort of emotional turmoil, scampered over and, intending to comfort, stuck his tongue in Jake's ear.

That was the final straw. Jake jumped up, knocking Revor to the ground. Revor landed neatly on his feet, unhurt except in his little furry heart. He'd only meant to help.

Baby pulled Jake down next to her on the Voodoo Lounge, and leaned toward him. The sweet plum of her mouth was just inches from his. . . . *you were everything I've always wanted.* Inhaling her honeyed breath along with her words, Jake's stomach settled. His loins began once again, almost imperceptibly this time, to stir. Imperceptibly, perhaps, to your average Earth girl. Aliens, however, are known for nothing if not the sharpness of their senses. They all stared with frank interest at the subtle sinuations of Jake's trouser snake under the fabric of his jeans.

Bruise-arsed, dumbstruck, and, despite everything, hopelessly on-turned, Jake flushed and covered his crotch with his hands.

*You're a quiet boy.*

Reaching behind her, Baby pressed a button on the faintly glowing control panel. One of the doors slid open, revealing another pie-slice shaped room. This one was more brightly lit. A laboratory table occupied the center of the room, behind which stood a bench and cabinets. Hanging from the wall were all manner of sterile-looking tools like medical instruments. *Now* what?

*Try to stay calm* . . . Baby rose and, standing in the doorway, gestured to him. *And welcome to the sexual experimentation chamber.*

Struggling to hang on to some last thread of cool, Jake steadied his voice and said, as casually as possible, "So, what brings you to Earth?"

Baby smiled. Her smile was so dazzling that he had to narrow his eyes and, finally, turn his head. Light poured in sweet, seductive waves from her minty skin, lime-lolly eyes and coconut-ice teeth. It washed over him, embracing him in warm, fragrant tendrils and making him feel suddenly, irresistibly sleepy. A sweet musk with a touch of nutmeg and orange peel filled his nostrils, and his eyelids succumbed to the pull of a strange, hot gravity. "You want to know what brings us to Earth?" she was saying. Jake perceived Baby's answer but dimly as he slumped down, slid off the lounge and passed over the threshold to Out. "Three things, Earth boy," she was saying. "Just three. Sex, drugs, and rock 'n' roll."

## Sex, drugs, and rock 'n' roll indeed.

For all their cosmic nous, yoonal kyoool, and Moc Dartened sophistication, the girls didn't understand certain crucial things about life on Earth. They didn't realize, for instance, that Eros was potentially a *big* problem for Earthlings. The truth was that Eros was practically out of control. In fact, it was believed in some circles that Eros might just destroy the world.

Eros. Greek god of love and sexual desire. Son of Aphrodite. Winged nudist. Hormonal hoon. *Australian Women's Forum* man of the month, every month. The French tickler of the soul. The imp in every impulse.

Eros. Biggest motherfucker of an asteroid ever to orbit the 'hood. Remember that meteor that got T Rex and all the other Dinosaurs Jr. and Sr.? Next to Eros, that was a mere pebble-ette, a flyweight of a flyby, a gentle lentil.

Now Eros, 433 Eros, member of the Amor group to you astronomers, was falling in lust. Love. Whatever. The point is, Eros was falling. Or trying to. And it was all the Babes' fault. You don't moon or blow kisses at an asteroid and expect life to go on exactly as before, do you? It's just common sense, really.

You want Tales of a Scorched Earth, Miss Mellon Collie? Just wait for Eros to come crashing into your life.

## Back in the saucer . . .

Baby looked down at Jake's prone form. She prodded him

with her foot. Though sound asleep, his mouth pursed slightly, as though anticipating a kiss. Underneath heavy lids and a thick fringe of curly brown lashes, his eyes darted, chasing a dream. The bold arcs of his eyebrows lay motionless on his high, clear forehead. The silver ring that pierced the left brow glinted in the clinical light streaming out of the sexual experimentation chamber. Baby bent down and touched his cheeks, then brushed her lips lightly over his neck. A potent Earth boy smell, part bourbon-and-Coke, part sweat, wafted up into her nostrils and set off delicious vibrations in her antennae. She closed her eyes and breathed in deeply.

"When you're finished . . ." Lati yawned.

"Oh, sit on my faculae," Baby retorted, snapping out of her reverie. "And don't just stand there. Give us a hand." Together they picked Jake up and carried him into the chamber, where they dumped him unceremoniously on the gleaming laboratory table.

Doll watched with studied indifference as Baby and Lati pulled off Jake's boots and socks and tossed them onto the floor. Next, they hoisted him up to a sitting position and yanked his Kyuss T-shirt up over his head. His long arms slid out of the sleeves and slapped heavily down on his sides. There was a sharp intake of breath but he didn't wake up. Around his neck hung a leather thong upon which were threaded a couple pieces of flattened metal. Pulling this off, Lati experimentally bit into what was in fact Jake's house key. "Yum," she approved, tossing the second key to Doll, who was perched on the side bench, swinging her legs back and forth. Doll caught it easily and popped it into her mouth.

Baby traced with her finger the tattoo of a scorpion that decorated Jake's right shoulder blade. "Looks a bit like one of those guys from Zeta Reticuli," she observed. "I hope this doesn't mean he's had contact before," she added, a trace of apprehension in her voice. "I was hoping we'd get an alien virgin."

"Oh, I reckon he's pretty pure," said Lati. "He could barely cope with us, and we're nothing compared to some of the ayles out there. I think it's probably just a coincidence."

Baby nodded, untying the flannelette shirt from around his waist. As they laid him back down, Baby's eyes roamed over the breadth of his shoulders, the gentle curves of his long freckled arms, the soft, light down carpeting his forearms and chest, the lean lines of his torso, and the neat pink mounds of his nipples, one of which strained erect over a small silver barbell. A wee tuft of brown hair poked up out of the top of his trousers and curled around the strange little hole in his stomach. Now where would that line of fur lead to?

Baby tugged impatiently at his jeans, but couldn't pull them down past his slender hips. "Damn," she cursed.

Lati, who was wearing 501s herself, shouldered Baby aside and unbuttoned the fly. Together, they shucked the jeans off Jake's long legs and threw them on the floor as well. Some coins fell out of the pocket, making a chinking sound which caught Lati's attention. She bent down, scooped up a handful and held them up to the others. Doll was still munching thoughtfully on the key and shook her head. Baby didn't even notice her offer.

Baby was rapt. Jake's smell clung to her nostrils, the touch of his skin set hers aflame, and the very sight of his handsome face was causing a liquid longing to mist her ears. (Nufonians had *very* sensitive ears.) This Earth boy, she was thinking, was truly a thing divine. Lati, if asked, would have said she was having fun. Then again, she always had fun. As far as she was concerned, Jake wasn't a bad biological sample, but that was about it. Doll, for her part, was utterly unmoved. She was thinking about drum kits—Pearl or Brady? One of each?

It all boils down to chemistry, really.

While Lati amused herself by tossing the coins in the air and catching them, one by one, in her mouth, Baby slipped trembling fingers into the waistband of Jake's red jocks and eased them off. She gasped. What was this? The other parts of the Earth boy's body had not contained so much surprise, for they were but variations on the forms the girls themselves had taken. But this fat pink plaything resting on its plump pillow and crowned with a coarse burst of hair, this was something else. She put a tentative finger upon its head. It twitched under her curious touch.

Lati began to spool out Bind-a-Bean tape. According to the manual that came with the Abduct-o-matic, Bind-a-Bean was the best method for securing a live abductee. Bind-a-Bean felt like silk and held like steel. Baby reluctantly stepped aside so that Lati could tape Jake's hands and feet to the table.

"Well, girls, this is it!" Baby exclaimed breathlessly when he lay spread-eagled and naked before them. She rubbed her hands together. "The moment we've been waiting for."

"*One* of the moments we've been waiting for," Doll corrected. Earth girls were *her* weakness. Still sitting on the bench, she picked up a speculum and began tapping out a beat on a row of carefully labeled beakers and jars. "Personally, I'm hanging out for the day we become rock stars. I wanna be the biggest fucken rock star in the yoon. Bigger than Been Her."

"What's Been Her?" Lati asked.

Doll shrugged noncommittally. "Dunno. Could be an all-girl band. It's something I heard one of the Earthlings say at the Agent Mulder gig. He turned to his friend and said, "Marilyn Manson, dude, they're bigger 'n Been Her."

Baby had picked up a magnifying glass and was examining Jake's skin. "This is so exciting," she marveled. "It's full of tiny holes. Have a look."

Lati sauntered over. "Weird-o-rama," she said. "Wonder why he doesn't leak?"

"They've got holes everywhere," Baby observed wistfully. "Wish we did. You know, on a permanent basis."

"We do all right," said Doll.

"Yeah, yeah, yeah," said Baby, leaning over and sniffing at Jake's armpit. "Sweet," she remarked.

Lati poked her nose into the other one. "Smells like teen spirit," she joked.

"Teen Spirit's a brand of deodorant," Doll commented. "Betcha didn't know that."

"No way," exclaimed Lati.

"Way," insisted Doll.

"So," Lati asked after a pause, "what's deodorant?"

"Who the fuck knows," shrugged Doll, hammering out the beat of "Israel's Son" while managing a startling imitation of the song's subterranean bass with the lower registers of her voice. "I just read it somewhere. Doesn't this song just make you feel like going out and killing someone?"

"You're a sick puppy," remarked Lati appreciatively, walking around to the other end of the table. Scrutinizing Jake's crusty toes, she recoiled at the smell. "Eeyuurgh!" She waved a hand in front of her face. "What d'ya reckon we should do now?"

"According to the manual," Doll replied, "You wake him up. Then you get some long hollow steel needles, point them at his head, and scare the shit out of him."

"It doesn't really say that, does it?" Baby protested, shocked and a little excited, too.

"Nah, it doesn't," Doll admitted. "I got that from the film *Communion*. Remember that scene?"

"Sure do," said Lati. "I say we throw Earth boy here into

33

a bathtub with lots of dry ice for effect, bring him to, and see what he does."

"Har har har." Baby shook her head. She picked up a probe and examined his navel with it. "Funny little crater," she remarked.

"Looks all wrong to me," Lati asserted. "Could have been an accident."

Doll was kicking her ankles together. Doc on Doc. A good sound. Solid. "Did you know that *Communion* was based on a true story?"

"No way!" cried Lati. "You don't believe in *aliens*, do you?"

They all fell about laughing hysterically. Jake slept on oblivious.

"You know," said Baby, wiping a blue tear of mirth from her eyes, "this is making it really hard to get into the mood. Oh no! Now look at *this.*" One hand resting possessively on Jake's thigh, she pointed under the table with the other.

Um um um! Socky wocky wocky! Um um um! Chp chp chp. Ooooooh. Smelly welly welly! Um um. Shlrp shlrp. Um um um um! Nnf nnf. Shlrp. Nnf nnf. Socky wocky! Oooky woooky! Grrrrrrrrrrrrrrrrrrr. Rrrrrrrrrrrrr.

"*Someone's* in the mood," she chuckled. Even Doll had to smile. Revor had insinuated his snout deep into one of Jake's woolly black socks and, clutching it to his face with eager claws, was rolling and tumbling and wriggling ecstatically around the floor, burbling and sniggling and cooing. The sock may have been old, unwashed, threadbare at the toe and down at heel, the kind of footwear that was an embarrassment to mothers, a disgrace to sheep, an aesthetic and olfactory repellent to normal affection. To Revor, it was sex incarnate. Um um! Um!

"Now *that's* a sick puppy," commented Doll dryly. "Music anyone?" Without waiting for an answer, she jumped down from the bench and disappeared into the rumpus room. Soon, a wave of energetic rock swept through the saucer. Doll returned, headbanging as she came. Her antennae and horns of hair were bobbing madly, and she sang along to the music. The lyrics had something to do with fingernails.

"Who's this, Doll?"

"Foo Fighters."

"Foo Fighters? That's a band?" Baby's jaw dropped. "That's hilarious," she hooted. "What a cack. How do Earthlings know about Foo Fighters? That's pretty specialized knowledge even on Nufon. I mean, we didn't know what they were until Lati pressed that button on the spaceship and one just kinda popped out." She shook her head. "Earthlings are *so* cool," she sighed, snapping on a pair of rubber gloves. "Damn," she cursed, looking down. "These only have four fingers."

Doll laughed, still thinking about Foo Fighters. "We sure scared that pilot," she chortled, recalling how Mum had ejillulated a thick white stream of electricity that congealed into a tight sphere and cannonballed off toward Earth. Whooping encouragement, they had watched the Foo Fighter's progress on the Foo Monitor, a previously blank screen on the control panel. The Foo Fighter had homed in on a U.S. Air Force plane on a mission of intimidation over some Middle Eastern nation. The fiery ball had loomed suddenly in the pilot's sights, filling his vision with light, and causing a celestial music to ring in his ears. The trembling pilot had a vision of God as a small silvery creature with hooves. Upon returning to base, he quit the military, let his hair grow long, and joined a troop of feral firestick twirlers with a sideline in environmental activism.

The Foo Fighter incident had definitely been a highlight of the babes' trip to Earth. Almost as good as when they shot through a small cloud of ash that turned out to be the remains of Dr. Timothy Leary, and Mum herself had a hallucination that she was the alien who abducted Elvis.

Lati was getting antsy. "Pass the strigil." She indicated a small instrument near where Doll had resettled herself on the bench. "Something has to be done about these toes."

Baby, meanwhile, turned her attention to Jake's testicles. "These look like fun." She stroked and pulled the dark, cool scrotal skin curiously. "Ohhhh," groaned Jake, now semiconscious. She cupped the balls in one palm. She bounced them up and down. She rocked them back and forth and pinched them between latex fingertips. She pulled off her gloves and did it all again. "I wonder if maybe this sexual experimentation thing isn't a bit overrated," she posited, a trace of disappointment in her voice.

Something occurred to her. "Maybe," Baby wondered, her antennae trembling at the thought, "it would be more fun if he were awake?" Performing sexual experiments on an Earthling who was actually conscious—it was too *transgressive* for words. She leaned over and, not too hard but not too gently either, bit Jake's balls. Jake's eyes flew open.

"It's awake now," Doll noted dryly.

"Oi," yelled Jake, trying to raise his head. What the hell was happening to him now? Who the fuck *were* these girls and what were they doing to his *balls?* "Oi!" he repeated. "Oi!"

Revor looked up from his sock with spermy eyes. Did someone call me?

"Mind telling me what's going on?" Jake asked in as normal a tone as he could muster.

Baby shrugged. "Sex," she replied, gripping his balls in her hand. He was *very* cute, she thought.

"Sex," Jake echoed flatly, attempting to pull an ankle free of its Bind-a-Bean. No go. Now Jake was not into bondage. Sure, he'd tied up a few girls with scarves when they'd asked for it, and had even used handcuffs on one kinky older woman. But he had never let anyone tie him up. Ever. He did not like feeling vulnerable and powerless. Not one bit. And finding yourself utterly starkers, bound hand and foot to an examining table under mysterious circs at the mercy of three very attractive but sexually predatory aliens did tend to inspire feelings of vulnerability and powerlessness. Not to mention intellectual confusion and spiritual crisis. Christ. It was almost as bad as being in a relationship. He tried to jerk a hand free. "Ow," he miserabled.

"What's a relationship?" asked Baby curiously, reading his mind. She wasn't making fun of him. Relationships were, if you'll pardon the expression, an alien concept in the outer. Alien civilizations had evolved way, *way* beyond relationships. Earthling society, which in yoonal terms was still dragging its knuckles on the ground, was only just beginning to shed the concept that a moment's fuckability did not automatically lead to a lifetime's compatibility. Aliens had long ago figured out that it was usually best just to give the night's mateling breakfast and a kiss and send it on its way.

Jake's jaw dropped. He stared at Baby. He stopped struggling. His eyes widened and his whole body visibly relaxed. A bright white light filled his vision and formed a shining halo around her head. It suddenly occurred to him that here standing before him—looming over him, whatever—was a beautiful, clever, full-on chick who *didn't know the meaning of the word relationship.* This was the girl of his dreams. Granted, his dreams had never accounted for antennae or green skin, and he'd have to have a serious word to her about this bondage-and-discipline scenario, but . . . *kyooool.*

"Oh, you know," he explained, gazing at her with eyes gone soft with longing, "relationships are when you hang out a lot, you know, for more time than it takes just to get each other into bed, and pretend to like the same films and music and each other's friends, and have really dumb arguments over things like, you know"—the pressure of her hand on his balls was starting seriously to distract him—"you stealing the covers at night and stuff, which really is dumb because, if you're bigger, you need more covers, right? Or like her getting jealous cuz you once said you thought Kylie Purr was a hottie?"

Baby was nodding her head in agreement, but what she was thinking was: why would anyone steal the covers at night? Weren't they just old songs sung by new people? How did you steal a cover anyway? And who was Kylie Purr? Was she that little blonde thing who sang "Locomotion"? She was also studying his long legs with their soft matting, his lean torso with its coat-hanger shoulders, and the geometric manner in which the fur grew over his chin. Goatees hadn't yet caught on in the outer, mainly because when aliens grew fur, it tended to be in places like behind the knees, or just under the eyes, or in other bodily sectors where it was either too difficult or painful to shave.

"The worst thing about relationships," he continued in a voice choked with confusion and lust, "is that they inevitably lead to a situation where one person starts talking *love*, when the other person was still just thinking *like*, and that turns the *like* into *fear*, and things start fucking up." Jake paused. Jesus. He sounded like a cynical bastard. If the truth be told, Jake had been in one or two relationships where he'd been the one who started talking *love*. Not that he was prepared to admit that. Not even to himself. "Yeah," he concluded, breathing heavily, "relationships are the pits."

God, her hand felt good. He had to call on all his willpower to resist the temptation to thrust his pelvis into those warm green hands of hers.

"Relationships sound *awful*," Baby commiserated, absentmindedly tugging and tickling and squeezing Jake's cock. She wondered what it would be like to fall in love. It could be fun. On the other hand, she had the impression that love was, oh, she didn't know, suspiciously *pop* or something. She wasn't totally ruling it out or anything, but she needed to know more about it first. Now sex, on the other hand, *that* was definitely rock 'n' roll.

Holy Hyades! Now what was happening? This Earthling was *full* of surprises.

"Check this out," she called to the others excitedly. Before their eyes and under Baby's fingers, Jake's penis was dramatically lengthening, the flesh hardening, the skin stretching taut and smooth. Jake was breathing fast now, his head twisting from side to side, his hands and feet struggling against their bonds.

"This bit . . ." Lati grabbed the *Whole Earthling Catalogue* off the shelf and turned the pages frantically until she located the reference. "The, uh, inseminator," she read, " 'the inseminator is not of static proportions.' " She yanked open a drawer marked "Measuring Implements" and began rifling impatiently through its contents. "Where the hell . . ." Calipers, rulers, scales, oscilloscopes, photometers, thermometers, hydrometers, hygrometers, potentiometers, sphygmomanometers, odometers, drosometers, eudiometers, audiometers, sonometers, tachometers, nephelometers, and—what joker put that in there?—even a parking meter clattered to the floor at her feet. "This'll have to do," she said, holding up something that an Earthling scientist might have recognized as a micrometer screw gauge but to Jake looked frighteningly like a miniature vise. Fresh fear churned the rapids of weird emotion that were surging through him but, instead of counteracting his desire, it only served to harden it.

Baby reluctantly relinquished her hold on Jake's penis so

that Lati could insert it between the micrometer's anvil and spindle. Lati took a reading. "It's already thirteen illion nufokips. And it's still growing," Lati said, impressed.

Doll had turned her back on them and continued to leaf through the catalogue till she found the section on females.

"Twenty-four illion," Lati announced.

"You can make a clitoris grow too, you know," Doll said. "If anyone's interested."

Baby nodded vaguely. She was interested, sure, but *later*. She didn't know whether it was the novel sight of an expanding Earthling inseminator or the appealingly demented lust in Jake's eyes or just her own general excitement at having finally abducted an Earthling after dreaming about it for abso-fucken-lutely *ages*, but she was feeling *very* turned on.

"Thirty-five illion."

Maybe it also had something to do with the little pill Baby had found in Jake's pocket. Whatever it was, her skin was tingling like a solar sail under a bombardment of photons. Dreamily, she put a hand on her neck and slowly ran it down over her body and back up again. Each movement drew ribbons of sensation over her skin, and she played them like the strings of a guitar, strumming herself and listening to the music. A tiny oscule appeared on her neck, and smacked its juicy lips. Baby drew her fingers slowly across the glistening little orifice, which nibbled back hungrily. Jake's eyes hadn't been deceiving him when he thought he'd seen a cunt on Baby's thigh and another on Lati's stomach. The babes were more blessed than most Nufonians in the genitalia department. It's just that the damn things appeared in the oddest places and weren't too *stable*. Baby pushed her finger in, slowly pulled it out and tasted it.

"Fifty-one illion!" Lati whooped. "But, hey, look at

this," she cried, doing a double-take. "There appears to be a spot of seepage."

Indeed. A small pearly drop had oozed up through the glans of Jake's cock. "Hello!" it cried. "It's me, Pre-cum! All systems are go! The balls are in position, the shuttle's all set for launch. We're starting countdown, *now*. Ten. Nine . . ."

"It *talks!*" exclaimed Lati. "*Cool.*"

Baby stopped fingering her neck. Jake raised his head and eyeballed his talking cock with alarm. *Fully* trippy.

"Eight."

On a whim, Lati opened her mouth and bent over.

"Don't touch it!" cried Doll, waving the *Whole Earthling Catalogue*. "It says here that it's necessary to build up a tolerance to Earthling bodily fluids over a period of time. It says here—"

Baby dived at Lati to shove her aside before she could touch her lips to Jake's cock. If anyone was going to do that sort of thing to Earth boy here, *she* was. He was *her* Earth boy, she fumed. Who was the leader here anyway?

Too late. They were both too late.

*CHICK-A-BOOM!*

It wasn't entirely clear what happened, but next thing they knew, Lati lay panting and disheveled on the floor. Her T-shirt was twisted around her torso as though she'd dressed in a tornado. A lemon yellow aura pulsed over the surface of her skin, heat poured off it in visible waves, and her form oscillated for a few seconds between Nufonian gray and Earth girl. A smell like that of jonquils filled the room. Her antennae vibrated and hummed. "Wowie zowie," she murmured. "Atomic electric."

Baby was paralytic with jealousy. Typical fucken Lati, jumping in like that. God! That girl really pissed her off sometimes.

*Of course she does, Baby. That's because she's actually as wild and free as you just like to think you are.*

Huh? Who's there? Is that you, God?

*No, it's Will Smith. What d'ya reckon? Of course it's Me, God. The One and Only.*

So, God. You don't think I'm wild and free?

*Don't go putting words into My mouth. I merely said you're not as wild and free as Lati. But you'd like to be. Of course, the problem here is also that you've become rather bizarrely attached to this Earth boy. Get over it. Abduction isn't the real thing, Baby.*

But—

*Look, I'd love to stay and chat but I've got to see an oracle about a prophecy. Hooroo for now.*

Hoo-what?

*It's an Australianism, Baby. If you're going to stay in Sydney, get with the lingo.*

Hooroo to you too, then.

"Countdown temporarily suspended," announced what was left of wee Pre-cum with a sigh. Jake wasn't feeling quite so robust as a moment ago. In fact, he was feeling rather disoriented. "Mum," he whispered. "Mum. I wanna go home."

ZzzxxxssssssZZZZT! The PA system crackled into operation. The response came in tinny cyber-syllables: "Come. in. Gal. gal. Mum. here. Please. con. firm. re. quest. to. go. home."

I will never take drugs again, Jake promised himself, palpitating, sweating, clutching the sides of the table. I can't take this shit.

Baby grasped Jake's flagging cock possessively while addressing the PA. She'd deal with Lati later. "Negative, Mum. Operational error. Go back to sleep. Over."

"Night. Night." Zzzzzzzzt.

The Foo Fighters sang on.

Under Baby's warm green fingers Jake's shuttle was soon ready for launch once more.

Lati was still lying motionless on the floor. Doll crouched by her side. She shook her shoulders and stroked her cheeks. "I bet this wouldn't have happened if we'd started with an Earth girl," Doll grumbled. "Baby, leave it alone for a second and come over here, will you? I'm not sure that Lati's all right."

Baby reluctantly turned her attention to her misdemeaning mate. "You okay, Lati?" she asked, secretly hoping she was suffering for her sins. She was *out of fucken order*, that girl.

They were both attending to Lati when a bevy of anxious squeals and groans drew their attention back to Jake.

"Ow! Oh! Aaargh!" hollered Jake.

"For love of Saturn . . ." Doll exploded with laughter.

"Aaaaaaargh!"

Revor, unnoticed by any of them, had abandoned the sock, shimmied up the legs of the table, and was now sitting between Jake's spread legs. He sucked Jake's erect cock up his tubular snout. It was a snug fit. As Jake struggled in vain to shake him off, Revor drew on Jake's cock with a manic intensity that made his little pop-eyes protrude even further. His shag-pile fur stood on end and small arcs of electricity rainbowed the spaces between his tensely splayed toes and fingers. His little tail was wagging so fast that it was a cherry-colored blur.

Jake was practically weeping by now. With a final shriek, he came in Revor's mouth. A huge crackling sound traveled the length of Revor's little body. Revor flew backward into the air with jet propulsion, a small furry meteor that cratered the wall and then slid down it to fall, a tangle of damp fur and wild eyes, to the floor.

Lati picked up her dizzy head. "Rev," she cried weakly, her shoulders sinking back to the floor again.

Revor threw her an unfocused glance. Then the lids snapped shut over his eyes.

Baby picked him up and held her hand up to his snout. "Still oxygenating," she noted. How was it that Revor and Lati had managed to have *all* the fun?

"So that was sex, eh?" remarked Doll, not quite as unimpressed as she liked to make out. She snuck another glance, this one lingering, at Lati's prone and peaceful figure.

"I think there must be more to it than that," Baby said wistfully. "Still. Yeah, I reckon that was sex."

"But was it rock 'n' roll?" asked Doll.

Jake, feeling like he'd just returned from a very long journey, picked his head up and looked at them, blinking. Rock 'n' roll? Did someone say rock 'n' roll?

Baby gave him the carotic smile treatment and, with a surge of affection, watched him fade back into unconsciousness.

"So," said Doll, indicating Jake's sleeping form with her chin, "what'll we do with Earth boy now?"

Baby didn't answer. She felt a little like someone had just opened a window on a spaceship. Emotional decompression. So, that was it. Their first abduction. Awopbopalooopbalopbamboom. Oh, she knew there'd be other abductions, other Earth boys. But Jake was her first, and, well, it was just all over so quickly. She couldn't figure out why she was feeling so flat. Was it always like this after sex? She needed a cigarette. Badly. Which was strange, for she'd never smoked before in her life.

Doll broke into her ruminations. "Touch of Memocide perhaps? It's recommended. Otherwise, the poor beans tend to get a bit traumatized."

Memocide. Comes in a convenient nonaerosol spray or powder.

"Sure," Baby nodded, indifferent.

"And here's something else that could be useful," Doll

continued, wondering what was wrong with Baby. She hadn't actually fallen for this Earth boy, had she? That would be ridiculous. Baby wasn't going to go around falling in love with every bean they abducted, was she? Doll shook her head. Too pathetic.

"I am *not* falling in love, Doll. Don't be fucken ridiculous."

Doll laughed. "Good. Now look at this."

Baby studied the page that Doll was holding open to her in the manual. "Sure. Let's do it." She turned and studied the labels on the drawers behind her until she found the one marked "homing devices." "Anal or oral?" she asked.

"Anal," replied Doll decisively.

"Mmmm," moaned Lati in her sleep, her rosebud mouth curled into a smile.

They untied Jake and flipped him over. Doll, studying the diagrams on the page, pulled on the rubber gloves, smeared them with Forbidden Planet lube, took the miniature device and inserted it up Jake's arse. "There," she announced. "All done. This little lemonhead can get back to where he once belonged."

"And we can find him whenever?" A note of hope sounded in Baby's voice. She wanted another go with Jake. On her *own*.

"Whenever. And let's give him another little memorative of the visit." Baby saw what Doll was proposing and nodded her assent.

When Doll finished, the two of them raised him from the table and dressed his still zonked-out form. Baby souvenired a pubic hair and they retained one sock for Revor, but got the rest of his gear back on him more or less as it had come off. He was heavy to move, but it didn't worry them. Their energy levels were nuclear. They ate uranium for breakfast. Heavy metal chicks.

45

Baby spotted a small piece of paper on the floor. It had slipped out of Jake's back pocket. It was a business card on which was printed an impression of black lace over a skull. "PHANTASMA. The one-stop Goth shop. For all your spectral needs." The address was on King Street, Newtown. "I reckon that's as good a place to drop him off as any," she reasoned.

Doll picked up the Abduct-o-matic, coded in Phantasma's address, and pressed REVERSE. Jake dissolved into a cloud of glittering particles, hovered for a moment, and vamoosed.

"Miss you already," sighed Baby.

**M**iss *you more* thought Jake. Now why'd he think that? Jake was unsure how the words had popped into his mind. Then again, he was unsure about a lot of things. Like how he came to be standing on King Street in his Sydney suburb of Newtown at the ungodly hour of eight o'clock on a Sunday morning, staring at the "CLOSED" sign on the door to his flatmates' shop, and tingling from head to toe. His head hurt. He was missing one sock.

Newtown, with its dominant population of crusties, punks, rockers, ravers, piercing artists, tattoo artists, installation artists, wannabe artists, bullshit artists, and piss artists, wasn't exactly a morning kind of place. It never felt particularly perky at this hour. In fact, just like Jake at this precise moment, Newtown felt like it had Kitty Litter for a brain. Newtown wanted to crawl onto its old stained mattress on the floor and pull its unwashed covers over its face. Newtown craved a Berocca and a darker pair of sunglasses. Newtown needed to spend less time in pubs, less money on drugs, and to pay more attention to the pamphlets given out in its health food stores, vegetarian restaurants, and natural healing centers. Newtown needed to get a haircut and get a real job. Newtown swore it was going to get its shit together next week. The week after that at the *absolute latest*. Definitely. If not, the week after that. For sure. Looking up at the same brilliant blue spring sky that prompted the denizens of beachside suburbs like Bondi to grab their surfboards and the residents of Darlinghurst to swarm the cafés, Newtown covered its eyes with the back of its hand and said *get fucked*.

Jake rubbed his dry and aching eyes with his fists. Little orange men in green leprechaun suits were jumping up and down on his optic nerves and rafting the throbbing veins in his temples. Other strange smurfs claw-toed his guts while sucking on the lining of his stomach with tiny, toothy mouths. His arse itched too, from way inside. What *had* he been doing all night? A vision of Revor suddenly floated up into his consciousness and he felt a sudden urge to dial a pavement pizza. The moment passed. Thank God. Jake had barked at a few lawns in his time—yorp yorp!—but it wasn't really what he thought of as a Good Look. Not in the middle of King Street anyway. When it was time to make those long-distance calls on the big white telephone, he preferred to do it in the privacy of his own home. Home. He wanted to be there five minutes ago. Yorp yorp? What the fuck was that supposed to be, hey?

The Last Nuclear Family in Newtown walked past, making a polite circle around where Jake stood dazed and confused, a generational cliché. Dad and son veered to the right, mum and daughter to the left. Reuniting ahead, they continued toward the church. Maybe it hadn't been a polite circle, Jake reflected, abashed. Maybe it was just a cautious one.

Maybe, Jake considered, what he needed was religion. He contemplated following this little vision of normality into the church.

Nup. Couldn't do it. He didn't think he believed in God. That was all right, for God didn't particularly believe in Jake, either.

Jake did, however, require some sort of immediate salvation. He pressed the inside of his wrists to his temples. DOOF. DOOF. DOOF. DOOF. It sounded like a fucken rave party in there. When a rock 'n' roll lad starts hearing techno in his veins he *knows* it's time to call it a night. Home, James, and the other one too, he instructed his feet.

He lowered his hands, and a mark on the inside of his right wrist caught his eye. Blue, and about two and a half centimeters wide, it depicted a flying saucer streaking through space. Jake's heart skipped a beat. Where'd that come from? What *had* he done last night? Agent Mulder. Of course. He'd been to the gig. The mark. It was just the stamp they applied to your wrist at the door. An image of a gorgeous green chick with antennae momentarily flitted into his head and then, just as abruptly, flitted out again. He must have been really off his face. Maybe he'd met a girl and she'd taken him home. Where else could he have been all this time?

Where had he been all his life?

Licking the tips of his fingers, Jake was attempting to rub off the ink when he noticed a mark on the inside of his other wrist as well. Unlike the clean, elegantly described image of the flying saucer, this one was just a string of blurry letters. Jake rubbed at the saucer. It didn't come off. It didn't even streak. He rubbed harder. The skin chafed, the image remained. Sharp and clear. Licking the fingers of his right hand now, he wiped experimentally at the mark on his left wrist. The ink stained his fingers. That was definitely the stamp from the door. He looked from one wrist to the other. He hadn't been so out of it that he'd gone and gotten a tattoo as well, had he? But wait, tattoos took some time to get to this stage. The scorpion on his right shoulder blade had been crusted over for a week before it finally came good.

Jake was in no state, mental or physical, to make sense of any of this. He had to get home. Turning a bit too quickly, he nearly tripped over the gray furry legs of a bedraggled Planet Rescue bear slumped against the window of the shop.

"Sorry," mumbled Jake, stepping away.

"Give us a dollar?" pleaded the bear. He'd obviously been on the street all night.

Jake sighed. He fished in his pockets and came up with a two-dollar coin. That's odd. He was sure he'd had more money than that. He looked at the coin. Considering what was needed to save the planet, it wasn't much. Considering what else he had in his pocket, it was everything. Then again, he had just had what some people would call a life-transforming experience and he was feeling a little giddy. He farewelled the coin with his eyes, and extended his hand toward the donations tin. Before he could drop it through the slot, a paw swung over and scooped it up.

"Thanks, mate," nodded the bear. "It's actually for me. I need a beer bad."

Jake opened his mouth to say something and thought better of it. A girl with a blue crew cut, a dozen face piercings, and jeans that were more rip than fabric, padded by on bare feet, arm in tattooed arm with a thin boy in green dreads and a long tie-dyed skirt. "Do you believe in angels?" the girl was asking. The boy shook his head. "Do you believe in fairies?" He shook his head again. Jake shoved his hands back into his now empty pockets and loped around the corner.

"Aliens?" she persisted. "Do you believe in aliens?"

Aliens. This rang a bell in Jake's mind, but it was too cluttered and smoky in there for him to actually reach the door and let it in.

"G'day." The tobacco-stained voice of George, his neighbor, cut into Jake's thoughts. George's dark little eyes shined brightly from under circumflex brows that lent his wide, leathery face an air of perpetual amazement. His thin lips twitched—George often appeared to be chewing something. In fact, he was chewing *over* something. What he was chewing over—and had been for years, in fact, ever since the death of his wife Gloria—were the twin issues of the end of the world and the arrival of aliens on Earth. George was a man obsessed. He was convinced—no, he was absolutely *sure*, he *knew*, he was *dead certain*—that human civilization was preparing to take its final bow. This was something predicted by the ancient Mayans and confirmed by the daily newspapers.

He also knew that, when it came time for that final tick of the earthly clock, benevolent aliens would save those who believed in them. He knew that when this happened there was a good possibility that he would be reunited with Gloria in another dimension. He knew this because he subscribed to magazines like *Millennium Watch* and *UFO Quarterly*. He corresponded with women in the Dandenongs and policemen in Gladstone and other people who'd actually seen flying saucers, including one mysterious dweller of caravan parks in South Australia who was in regular contact with extraterrestrials disguising themselves as dolphins. It all pointed to one thing, really. The need to Be Ready for Anything. Specifically, Be Ready for Uplift.

George was ready. His entire yard was a meter deep in dead and dying electrical appliances. Where some urbanites in their rural nostalgia might have planted frangipanis or ferns, farmer George sowed rows of Cuisinarts, electric pencil sharpeners, cyclostyles, transistor radios, daisy wheel printers, and fondue pots. A snowy river of old washing machines and fridges snaked along the side of the house; the roof was thatched with stacked television aerials. Why exactly this was the way to prepare for the apocalypse, George couldn't have said—it all came down to intuition, really.

His intuition told him that all was not quiet on the alien front. For one thing, the papers were full of signs that the end of the world was nigh. The government had recently announced it would service the national debt by selling off most of the country's environmental and cultural resources—including all World Heritage areas, the Opera House, Uluru, half a dozen dance companies, and a stand-up comic or two. It was directing shipments of nuclear by-products through urban electorates in which there were too many artists and homosexuals and women who used words like "chairperson." It had canceled reconciliation with Aboriginal Australia because reconciliation was considered a "politically correct" thing to do, and the government didn't want to be caught doing anything that could be misinterpreted as correct. It was also turning the ABC, the national broadcaster, into a commercial enterprise cum hamburger franchise. Elsewhere, American teenagers were swearing to remain virgins until marriage while their parents pledged to kill gays for Jesus. The one ethnic group left in the world that was not trying to wipe out another ethnic group had perished in a bus accident. Barges of toxic wastes were drifting aimlessly on the oceans, occasionally tipping over into the mouths of whales. And that was just last week.

Tick. Tick. Tick. The good news was that there had been a flap of UFO sightings around the world with at least a dozen reports from all over New South Wales the day before. General Jackal somebody-or-other in the Pentagon had issued a formal statement blaming errant weather balloons, lubbock lights, and other IFOs. He'd failed to comment on an international bumper harvest of new crop circles in the shape of CDs, vinyl records, and cassette tapes.

Then there was the matter of that strange dream last night. In it, George was strolling through the bush when he came upon a large flat stone. He bent down and turned it over. A beautiful sylph lay there, smiling and fluttering her wings. *I'm the girl from Mars*, she'd said. *If you don't believe me, just ask Jake.*

*I believe you*, George had replied.

*Well then*, she'd challenged, *gonna go my way?* George had woken up bolt upright in bed.

*Just ask Jake.* George waved Jake over.

Jake wasn't in the mood for a conversation. All things considered, however, having one required less effort than avoiding one. He ambled over to where George was unloading pulleylike gadgets from his pickup truck. "Whatcha got there, George?" he asked.

"Tummy toners," replied George.

"Fair dinkum," nodded Jake. He thought that would probably do it for neighborliness. He yawned. "Sorry," he apologized, covering his mouth. "Had a bit of a big one last night."

When Jake raised his hand, George's sharp eyes zoomed straight in on his wrist. "New tattoo?" He tried to control the tremor in his voice.

"Uh, sort of," Jake mumbled.

"Is there a story behind it?"

"Not really," Jake replied. "Well, maybe. I dunno. Can't really talk about it now. I'm *shagged*. Catch ya later."

George shrugged, hiding his disappointment.

Jake dragged himself over to the ramshackle terrace house next door where he lived. He pushed open the squeaky gate, stepped over the overflowing carton of bottles and tinnies that, one day, they were going to put out for recycling. Heading for the door, he just avoided putting his foot down into a fresh cigar of dog poo. Jake felt for the leather thong that held his keys. It wasn't there. Shit! This was too weird. He did a quick stocktake. Lost: a sock, his keys, a night. Gained: a tattoo and one whopper of a hangover. Surely, a night to remember. Now if *only* he could remember it.

He banged on the door. No answer. His flatmates would all be asleep. He could hear Iggy Zardust, his bull terrier, come running to the door, claws clicking on the unpolished floorboards in the hall. Iggy was doing his Unbelievably Happy to Have Master Home routine, scratching at the door, wriggling and wagging his tail, and whining with an enthusiasm that wasn't entirely feigned, but which did not go a long way toward letting Jake into the house. Jake sighed and shuffled round the block to the back, clambered over the fence, and excavated the spare key from its hiding place underneath a deformed garden gnome.

Inside at last, he scratched Iggy behind his pink floppy ears, and breathed in the familiar smell of the sharehouse—a comforting musk of stale beer, unwashed dog, over-flowing ashtrays, sleeping bodies, dirty dishes, and the legendary Missing Banana. Aromatherapy. It felt good to be home.

Jake crept up to his room. It looked like an explosion in a laundromat. Soiled and clean clothes coupled promiscu-ously in piles on the floor, or lazed on the precarious, three-legged chair he'd salvaged from the Tempe Tip. The only thing in the room that wasn't covered with undies, T-shirts, old suit jackets, retro shirts, socks, and jeans was the clothes rack by the wall from which half a dozen hangers dangled in a state of long-term unemployment. Jake shoveled a path to the mattress with his feet. He fell heavily on his bed, dis-tressing whole colonies of dust mites, frightening a pair of mating cockroaches, annoying a flea who'd been in a bad mood since misplacing Iggy two days earlier, and generally disturbing the room's delicate ecological balance. Jake com-pleted the outrage by kicking off his boots. The ensuing odor sent all the life forms racing out the door.

Jake's head was spinning like vinyl on a turntable. A 45 on 78. Alvin and the Chipmunks on speed.

Ever since finding himself on King Street all he'd wanted was to sleep. The second his head hit the pillow he'd be out like a light. But the light wasn't turning off. Hallucinatory fragments replayed themselves in his brain. Yet, as sobriety slowly percolated through his system, something told Jake that what he was recalling was not just a hallucination. All right, he conceded, it was real. It happened. I'll deal with it in the morning. Afternoon. Now can I get some sleep?

Why yes, replied the frankly relieved Sleep Fairy who'd been hovering impatiently over his bed. All you ever had to do was ask. Looking at her watch and shaking her head, she sprinkled sleep dust in his eyes and flew out the window to her next appointment, for which she was already late. Beans. Why did they make this such a complicated business? And then, she thought huffily, you get people like that guy on the street earlier. Doesn't believe in fairies. Hmph. Just see if *he* ever gets to sleep again.

In Jake's dreams, he reclined in a verdant field under an emerald sky. Baby's soft mouth hovered in the air like a daytime moon and her sexy drawl floated in a dewy mist around his head. As much as he strained to understand what she was saying, he couldn't make out the words. He reached out and caught one of her feet in his hand. It was exquisitely small, plump, pink, and seven-toed. Jake stiffened, moaned, and came in his sheets.

About two-thirty that afternoon, Jake, his head feeling like one of Iggy's well-masticated tennis balls and his gut like it had found the Missing Banana, wrapped a towel around himself and hirpled down the hallway and into the toilet. He sat down on the seat and reached automatically for the copy of *War and Peace* that lived on the toiletries shelf. He put it down again as soon as he noticed an old issue of the zine *Skills of Defensive Driving* under the sink. He still hadn't made it past page two of *W&P*. Never mind. He'd read it when he was old.

For now, he was content to lose himself in the *SODD* editor's ruminations on why he was a dud root. Jake was beginning to feel slightly better now. Without removing his eyes from the page, he groped at the wall and pinched a cardboard tube between his fingers. "Guys!" he bellowed. "Cooee! Anyone home?" He paused and sighed. "Why're there never any shit tickets when it's *my* turn to have a crap?"

"Whinge, whinge, whinge," commented Tristram, who happened to be passing by the toilet door at that moment. "Keep yer pants off. I'll see if we've got any spare cobs in the closet." Tristram wandered off, walking straight into the wall and bouncing off it, walking into another wall and careening off it in turn, thus angling his way toward the closet. He was pretending to be inside a pinball machine.

This was not unusual behavior for Tristram. He and his identical twin Torquil were what you might call Self-Amusing Units. The progeny of a Scottish mother and Egyptian father, they were pharaonic of eye, proud of nose, and slight of build. Their skin had a latte hue and their hair was the color of the week. This week, Tristram's hair was purple and Torquil's was blue. He was wearing a salmon-colored frock with a lace collar that he'd found in a thrift shop. Tristram's personal hero was Kwong José Abdul Foo of the Brisbane band Chunderer. Kwong José was another multiculti rock 'n' roll lad who liked wearing frocks. Tristram thought Kwong José was cool as.

Eventually, Tristram returned with a roll of loo paper. Just as he was about to open the door, Tristram noticed that Iggy appeared to be standing guard. "What's up, Iggy?" said Tristram. Iggy acknowledged Tristram's presence with a wag of his tail and a throaty little sigh. His pink piggie eyes were fixed on a spot about halfway up the door. Tristram now saw that Iggy was eyeballing a large cockroach that was slowly scaling the door. He wondered how long

Jake had been in there. Tristram smiled and patted Iggy on the head. In his weird bullie way, Iggy smiled back, showing teeth.

Careful not to disturb the cockroach, Tristram opened the door a crack and tossed in the toilet paper.

"Torq! My man!" cried Jake gratefully from his porcelain perch.

"It's Trist. I'm the purple one this week. Remember? Hey, where'd you go last night, dude?" asked Tristram through the door. "We saw you do this hell stage dive and then, like, you disappeared. We looked for you after the gig but couldn't find you anywhere. We thought you might've scored with some chick."

"Actually," Jake said cautiously, as an evanescent vision of himself strapped to a table winged into his consciousness, "I think I was kidnapped by aliens and made to have sex with them in their flying saucer."

Tristram jerked open the door. The cockroach lost its grip, fluttered its mahogany wings and fell backward in a perfect arc, right into Iggy's open and waiting mouth. The dog's wide jaws clamped shut and his smile widened. Shaking his head, he trotted off to the kitchen to play with his snack. Tristram, meanwhile, fixed Jake with a sardonic stare. "Yeah right," he said, poker-faced. "And my mother's a Klingon." Tristram whipped around and stared at the spot where he'd just been standing. "Don't you say that about my mother!" he snapped.

"Do you mind?" huffed Jake, pulling the door shut. "Can't a man get some privacy around here?" He regretted saying anything.

"Well?" Tristram demanded through the door.

"Well what?"

"Were they cute?"

Jake considered the question. Try as he might, he couldn't bring to mind a single detail of their appearance.

"Yeah," he ad-libbed. "Cutest little aliens in the whole yoon."

"Yoon?"

Jake frowned. "Dunno where that came from. I meant to say 'universe.' "

"You know what I think?"

"What?"

"We ought to go out more on Wednesday nights."

"Wednesday nights?"

"I think you're watching too much *X-Files*."

"Wait, wait." Jake struggled to recall something that was being chased around his brain by an eager little particle of Memocide. "They, uh, they watch the *X-Files* too," he said tentatively. His arse suddenly itched very badly.

"Let me get this straight," said Tristram. "You were abducted and sexually experimented upon by a bunch of aliens who also happened to be *X-Files* fans."

"Yeah. I think so." Jake shook his head. He wasn't so sure anymore, now that he thought about it. He *had* been tripping.

"What's their phone number? Zero-zero-five-five-Space Cadet?"

"Actually," Jake said, "I think they said they'd be in touch." He regretted saying anything at all. It had probably just been a hallucination. Now Tristram—and no doubt Torquil as well—would be paying out on him on the subject of aliens for days to come. Maybe he should just have a few Panadols and a big glass of water and go back to bed. He emerged from the loo, knotting the towel around his waist. "Oh, that's right," he added, scratching his head, "*and* I was scabbed by a Planet Rescue Bear."

"No way." Tristram really looked shocked now.

"Way. He got my last two dollars. Said he needed a beer." Jake frowned. He shook his head again. His hand was stuck. "Oh, fuck," he cursed.

"What's wrong?"

"Ring's caught," said Jake, waggling his wrist. His dreadlocks occasionally took prisoners: rings, small particles of food, the stray beetle. "Give us a hand, will ya?"

Tristram rolled up the sleeves of his frock, grimaced theatrically, and dove in heroically. After he liberated Jake's hand, they meandered downstairs and into the kitchen. The reasonably spacious kitchen, with its mixed antipasto of found plates and scavenged cutlery, its bread-crumbed floor, sautéed walls, butter-basted table, flambéed stove, and sugar-dusted benchtops, was the warm and nourishing center of sharehouse life.

Their housemates Saturna and Skye, who were sitting at the table, didn't even look up at the boys' entrance. Saturna and Skye were drinking coffee out of black bowls and talking about the end of the world, which, along with George, they believed was imminent. Whereas it worried George, it rather excited them. Doom and gloom were their favorite topics. They were Goths. They were also lesbian lovers and business partners. They ran Phantasma, the one-stop Goth shop and hairdressers where they sold everything from white face powder to futons tailored specially for caskets. They also specialized in purple, scarlet, and black hair dyeing. The petite Skye wore layers of scarlet and black lace; the voluptuous Saturna was a purpurate creature with a particular fondness for velvet, even in summer. They covered their skin with slabs of ghoulishly white foundation makeup, shaved off their original eyebrows so that they could paint on more dramatic ones, and tinted their lips the color of eggplant. They lived in the basement of the house, in a room that was way too dark for anyone else even before they'd painted the walls matte black.

"You girls were home? Didn't you hear me calling for dunny documents?" Jake affected outrage. Real outrage took too much effort and commitment. Without waiting for their answer, he yawned again, opened the fridge, and stuck his head inside.

"*We* always replace the toilet roll when we've used it up," Saturna remarked to his back, exchanging a conspiratorial glance with Skye. "Thought you boys could learn a lesson."

"*Boys?*" Tristram objected, offended. "What did *I* do? Unfair as."

Jake performed a quick inventory of the inside of the fridge: a small bowl of week-old lentil soup, some dubious tomatoes, a six-pack of VB, half a jar of Thai curry paste, and a saucepan with some rice crusts stuck to the sides. Well, that accounted for the boys' half, anyway. Saturna and Skye's side featured a few pieces of reasonably fresh fruit and some vegetables, a bowl of chili, a thick slab of tofu in a bowl of water, a loaf of bread, a jar of coffee beans, and half a carton of free-range eggs. Jake extricated a beer. "Protein breakfast," he remarked, patting his unreasonably flat stomach. "Where's Torq?" he asked. "We're supposed to have a jam this afternoon."

"He took a walk down King Street," replied Tristram. "He had some idea about feather boas he wanted to follow up. Said he wouldn't be long."

Iggy, having finally swallowed the cockroach, slurped loudly and contentedly at the water in his bowl. Saturna and Skye exchanged glances. Iggy was such a *boy*. Despite his unaesthetic pink skin and his atrocious and seemingly unalterable smell, the girls were actually quite fond of Iggy. They weren't about to let Jake know this, however. They only played with him when Jake was out. Iggy was quite cool about this. He seemed to understand the game rules, and normally kept clear of the girls until Jake and the twins had left the house, at which point he would dash into their room, roll onto his back and let them tickle his tummy as he wriggled and groaned and stretched his neck and batted the air with his legs. He licked their ears, instinctively careful not to wreck their elaborate makeup.

The phone rang. Tristram picked it up. "Sam and Tony's Pickled Pizzas," he said, earning a bored sneer from the girls. "Jake? Uh, who's calling? Larissa?" Tristram looked questioningly at Jake. Jake was shaking his head emphatically. "Uh, Larissa, he's not here right now. How about I get him to call you? Yeah. Yeah. I will. Yeah. No, I won't forget." Tristram rolled his eyes at the others. "No worries. See ya. Bye." Tristram hung up and tossed Jake a look of exasperation. "I hate that shit, man," he griped. "From now on, you root 'em, you take their phone calls."

Jake shrugged. "You seen George's new tummy toners?" he said, changing the subject.

Skye sipped at her coffee. "Have you ever heard him talk about why he collects all that shit?"

"Nup," said Jake. "What's the story?"

"He thinks that just before the final apocalypse, flying saucers are going to appear in the sky and aliens will whisk off those of us who, as he puts it, are 'prepared.' "

"Prepared? You mean, like, with stacks of broken keyboards and cappuccino machines?"

"Obviously."

"Far out. You know," Tristram remarked, watching Jake drain the last drops of beer from the can, "Jake told me he was abducted by aliens last night and sexually experimented on in their flying saucer."

"Great," approved Saturna vaguely. If he'd said Jake had been abducted by vampires or zombies she'd have been more interested. She noticed something on the kitchen table, and wrinkled her nose in disgust. Gingerly pinching the offending object between thumb and forefinger, she held it up for all to view. "Whose pubic hair is this?" she demanded accusingly. "*Jake?*"

Jake shrugged and held out his hand. "Dunno," he replied, deadpan. "But I'll take it. I'm one short."

He was, too.

Meanwhile, elsewhere in the cosmos . . .

"We have a situation here." Captain Qwerk cleared his throat, producing a tinkling noise like the song of bellbirds. Nufonian skin may look cold, but it can produce awfully pleasant and often unpredictable sounds. There is no other sonic vibration in the universe, for instance, that has quite the clear crystalline ring and symphonic range of a Nufonian fart.

An emergency meeting had been called of the Interplanetary CRAFTE (Council of Responsible Aliens For Terrestrial Exploration). In the room were gathered representatives from several planets. The Nufonians, who were hosting the council, were in the majority. Among the others were several Cherubim from the planet Cherubi. Of all the aliens, the Cherubim were the most humanoid in appearance. Even those who were well over a hundred Earth years old had flawless pink skin, yellow curls, and limbs cute with baby fat. Beautiful snowy white wings sprouted from their plump backs and they shared a mischievous sense of humor that their innocent appearance belied. They were also hopeless exhibitionists with a fetish for posing nude for artists. Some time after the Renaissance they grew bored with this. They began to skip their live modeling appointments or masturbate during them. This resulted in the decline of religious art and prompted the rise of the secular state in Europe. In recent years they had become obsessed with the idea of abducting Wim Wenders.

There were also a number of delegates from Sirius. Sirians, who had six eyes, were highly intelligent but so terminally silly that their prime cause of expiration was laughing to death (the second was fatal disorganization). There was also an Alpha Centaurian and one representative from ET's home planet, though she didn't say much—her people were still living down the embarrassment of ET's awkward but well-publicized little adventure.

The aliens didn't often have a chance for interplanetary get-togethers. So, despite the alleged seriousness of the crisis at hand, when Qwerk called the meeting to order, most were still chatting excitedly, catching up on news, and showing each other some of the knickknacks they'd abducted on recent trips to Earth. A Cherub had scored a dolphin-shaped dildo, which a Sirian was now sticking up one of his three nostrils, to general amusement. A small cluster of grays surrounded another little angel playing with a Gameboy, all of them jingling and jangling in their excitement. Reluctantly, they made their way to their seats and quieted down. The Alpha Centaurian was still munching on a quartz crystal snack when stillness descended on the room. He tried his best to muffle the sound of his chewing, but each cautious crunch caused one of the less mature extraterrestrials at the table to shake uncontrollably with laughter.

Qwerk cleared his throat again. Ding ding ding tinkle tinkle ding ding.

Several of the non-Nufonians exchanged surreptitious glances. Just because Nufonians were the only intelligent life forms around that were organized enough to launch the Earth-bound expeditions of which they all loved to be a part, they thought they were the masters of the universe or something. Nufonians were oh-just-so rational and reasonable. Their dwellings were without exception neat and tidy, they never had arguments over who should take out the garbage, they thought bureaucrats were Just Doing Their

Jobs and they found the idea of doing anything on a whim not so much suspicious as incomprehensible. Their auras were perpetually aglow with good health from self-healing and clean living, and they actually remembered to take out insurance each time they went astral traveling. No Nufonian ever had trouble programming the VCR or putting together any furniture that they'd abducted from Ikea. They were, in other words, the most annoying ayles in the entire yoon. A couple of Sirians had hoped to break the Nufonian monopoly on serious space travel but it was, like, the engine was in one place, the boosters in another, someone said she could get the fuel from a contact but then lost the number, and anyway, no one knew quite where the launching pad had gone.

Nufonians, for their part, would have vastly preferred to carry out their terrestrial expeditions without involving the rest of these cosmic clowns. The sad truth, however, was that the special rocket fuel required for such long-distance travel was made up of a number of minerals and chemicals that were not native to Nufon. They had no choice but to court the others' cooperation. And the others were more than happy to cooperate, in their own way, in exchange for free rides to Earth.

Earth was an alien magnet. They loved the place. It was just such a funky, low-tech, high-chaos, wild and crazy sort of planet. They couldn't get enough of it. Some aliens, like the Cherubim and Sirians, simply enjoyed slumming it there. Others, like the hopelessly naughty Zeta Reticulans, played pranks on Earthlings, popping out of children's closets at night, creating mystery tracks on CDs, and running past-life seminars for very silly people who all believed they were Cleopatra.

As for the Nufonians, they claimed they just wanted to make the world a better place. "Now is that," they were in the habit of remarking, "such a bad thing?" They somehow neglected to mention that they had a Hidden Agenda. The Hidden Agenda was 1475 pages long, exactly one page longer than Vikram Seth's *A Suitable Boy*, making it the longest book in the entire yoon. There were exactly two copies.

Qwerk motioned to the interstellar policemen guarding the meeting to close the door and step outside. "What I am about to reveal," he announced, a tremor of importance cymbaling his voice, "is a bit sensitive."

A Cherub yawned loudly. Qwerk looked over with exasperation.

"Sorry," she giggled. "Late night."

"I'd appreciate it if this information does not leave the room. But what we have here is a suboptimal . . . uh, what has happened is that, well, quite frankly, what we are facing are the consequences of an experiment gone wrong."

"Cool," enthused the Alpha Centaurian.

If these are supposed to be the *responsible* aliens, Qwerk thought, not for the first time, the yooniverz was in big trouble. The Alpha noticed the look of dismay on Qwerk's face. "Sorry," he said. "Go on. *Ouch!*" He slapped away a Sirian who'd crawled under the table to nibble at his toes. Alpha Centaurians had particularly sexy toes, and there were twenty of them on each foot.

Qwerk put his shiny gray head in his hands. "Can we get serious, please? Just for one minute?"

"Yeah!" cried a Cherub. "Get Sirius!"

"Get Sirius!"

"Get Sirius!"

The Cherubim led the others to jump the Sirians, whom they held down and tickled to within an inch of their lives. Whoops of laughter, the flapping of fat white wings, the clink and squish of alien bodies wrestling and rolling around the floor and gasped pleas for mercy reverberated off the walls of the room. Involuntarily,

Qwerk's antennae vibrated and a big blue tear dribbled out of one big black eye.

One of the Cherubim signaled to the others. "Sssst. Ssssst." With much puffing and panting and a few surreptitious pokes and jabs, they settled down again.

"Briefly," Qwerk soldiered on, "we have been conducting experiments with hybridization, Earthling-Nufonian crosses to be specific. This is, er, a rather difficult and risky endeavor. We had hoped that an infusion of Nufonian genes into the human gene pool would have a calming effect on Earthlings. I really can't understand why you're rolling your eyes at that, by the way. We hope they can become saner, straighter, more balanced, less aggressive. We think they should stop grumbling when they have to stand in queues or fill out forms in triplicate. After all—"

"Bureaucrats are Just Doing Their Jobs," came the ironic chorus.

Like all Nufonians, Qwerk suffered from a severe irony deficiency. He did not realize they were making fun of him. He merely thought they were finally getting the message. About time too. He would have smiled but Nufonian faces are by their nature expressionless, so he continued blankly, "A small but growing number of Earthlings understand and support our efforts; we have made useful contacts in communities from Sedona in the American southwest to Mullumbimby on the Australian east coast."

"I once scored the *best* dope in Mullumbimby," a Cherub whispered to the Alpha. "Had a vision of Nirvana. It was wicked. Thirteen Dalai Lamas and Kurt Cobain all sitting on these giant lotus pads, having this *filthy* jam session."

"You're so lucky," the Alpha sighed. "All dope does for us is make us want to go around sticking our elbows into things."

"That could be interesting."

"Yeah, well, it's got me into BIG TROUBLE in the past."

"*Do* tell."

Qwerk rapped on the table. "Can I *please* have your attention?"

"Later, dude," promised the Alpha.

"As you might imagine, there has been much trial and error. We've had to conduct quite a number of, uh, sexual experiments on Earthling subjects, both male and female." *Now* Qwerk had their full attention. "Although we have tried quite a variety of, er, biodynamic positions and, ahem, mechanical apparatuses, we initially encountered enormous difficulty in getting Earthling, uh, sperm samples to impregnate Nufonian eggs. Similarly, Earthling eggs are not easily, er, penetrated by Nufonian sperm. Through, uh, perseverance and diligence we finally did manage to work out the kinks in the process." Qwerk, blushing pale blue, paused and looked around the room.

Except for the whispery flutter of angel wings—for all their modeling experience, Cherubim had a big problem holding themselves perfectly still when excited—the room was silent. Even the Sirians were rapt. So, the boring old Nufonians did get up to a bit of hanky-panky after all. The others couldn't wait for tea time so that they could have a great big gossip session.

"We did finally manage successfully to breed three hybrids, all females, for convenience of further interbreeding. As they grew up, however, we discovered that the Earthling genes were apparently dominant. They were constantly breaking out of their Socialization Center and hitching up with itinerant Klingons and other unsavory types." Qwerk's voice grew stern. "They failed to respond appropriately to directive improvement. Which is to say"—here, he paused and sighed—"they turned out incorrigibly wild, undisciplined, uncontrollable, and, while quite intelligent, incapable of being educated in Nufonian values."

"Whoowa!" hooted the Alpha Centaurian, impressed. "When can we meet them?"

"Well, that brings us to the purpose of this convocation," responded Qwerk, relieved that someone was taking a real interest in the issue. "You see, we hadn't yet worked out what to do about them when somehow they managed, we don't know how, to steal a spaceship as well as all the fuel reserves on the entire planet. We have every reason to believe," Qwerk concluded gravely, "that they have already reached Earth."

"Far out!" cried a Cherub, envious.

"Cool!"

Just when you think you're finally on the same wavelength with them, thought Qwerk, you realize that they could all be from Mars. He exhaled a delicate silver bell of a sigh, and continued. "In sum, we need to send an expedition to Earth to, uh, recapture them, in a caring, sharing sort of way of course, and bring them and the spaceship back. Do we have your support?"

"Yay!" A Sirian jumped onto the table, flipped over onto his hands, and clapped his four fat green feet in the air. "We're going to Earth! We're going to Earth! We're going to Earth!"

The room exploded in gleeful pandemonium.

"Far out!"

"Far away!"

"Count us in!"

"Us too!"

"When are we going?"

"What'll I wear?"

"Are we there yet?"

"What are we waiting for!"

"ET, phone home!"

"Please. You're not going to bring that up again, are you?"

"Just kidding."

"I need to go to the toilet!"

"Wardrobe stress! Wardrobe stress! I really don't have a *thing* to wear to Earth."

"Don't wear anything."

"Yeah!"

"Beam me up, Scotty!"

"Yippee!"

"Rock and roll!"

Elizabeth Bay, on the genteel side of King's Cross, was not, on the surface of things, a particularly rock 'n' roll suburb. It was no Newtown, that's for sure. When Elizabeth Bay wore blue in its hair, it tended to be a rinse. Even Elizabeth Bay's bohemians, the artists and filmmakers and musicians and actors who hung out in the tiny suburb's chic little cafés instead of doing their work, didn't hang out *too* long, for they tended to be old enough to realize that if you didn't do any work at all you wouldn't get to *stay* an artist or filmmaker or musician or actor, a thought that hadn't fully dawned on some of their younger peers in Newtown.

Yet there in Elizabeth Bay stood the rock 'n' rollingest little hotel in all of Sydney, the Sebel Townhouse. The Smashing Pumpkins, Björk, Green Day, Alanis Morrisette, Billy Idol, Queen, Rod Stewart, Joe Cocker, Cyndi Lauper, and even the extraterrestrialoid Michael Jackson had all roomed at the Sebel at one time or another.

On this fine Sunday, the Rock Star in Residence at the Sebel was none other than Ebola Van Axel, lead singer of the American death metal band Twisted Mofo, on the final leg of his F*** the World Tour. Normally, Big Eb wouldn't have been caught *dead* up at this hour, this hour being about three in the afternoon. But the combination of jet lag, weird drugs, and the ministrations of a bevy of energetic young groupies saw him this afternoon lounging on a deck chair beside the rooftop pool, a pale, hairy sausage in a casing of black leather and dark sunglasses. Eb, feeling delicate, was scoffing peanut butter and oyster sandwiches from the room-service trolley by his side and barely enduring the happy squeals of the evites cavorting in the water.

Ebola Van Axel was having a hair crisis. The members of Metallica, probably the most important metal band in the world, had cut their hair short. Did that mean, Eb fretted, that short hair now had more cred? How can you play heavy metal with short hair? What would you toss? Your ears? He'd feel ridiculous. He'd look worse than ridiculous. In fact, Ebola Van Axel, total guitar hero and idol to millions of troubled and confused teenage boys, was convinced that he'd look like a real estate salesman. That's because his brother, whom he resembled, had short hair and *was* a real estate salesman. Maybe shaving would be better. But what if he turned out to have a pointy skull?

Oh, *Jesus*. Would these girls ever shut their silly traps? He had a *serious* headache.

Ebola was in the midst of these tortured reflections when he noticed something funny in the air: a vibration, an effervescence, a shimmering, a hint of mystery, a touch of magic. It was the sort of spiritually incandescent moment that in bygone days might have signaled to mortals that they were about to be enchanted by a nymph, or bewitched by a fairy, spellbound by a sprite, close-encountered by an elf or leprechaun. It heralded a head-on collision of worlds in which neither side could ever have enough third-party insurance.

Whatever it was, it was making Ebola very horny. "Hey,"

he beckoned, "one of you chicks wanna come over here and blow me?" They ignored him. They were hanging off the side of the pool and staring transfixed up at the rooftop water tower. "Hey." Still no response. Ebola burped and hoisted a bottle of Dom Perignon—the second of the day— to his lips. He was about to take a swig when a flash, a gleam of sparkling light from the tower, caught his attention. He raised his shaded eyes to see what the girls were looking at and was rewarded with a most extraordinary vision. Eb quickly looked down again lest he be trampled by a herd of pink elephants. The affluence of inkahol could be a scary thing. He squeezed his eyes to within an angström of shut and snuck another look.

There it was. Clear as day—and the day was very clear. God's Frisbee on the spire of Our Lady of Contemporary Hedonism. The hi-hat in the Infinite Drum Kit. The funkiest disco ball in the entire yoon. A one-hundred percent-guaranteed-or-your-money-back, genuine flying saucer.

Atop the tower, Galgal pulsed and glowed and beamed in the sunlight. Whirrrr. Whirrrr. Sssssssssss. A crack appeared in the saucer's apparently seamless exterior and widened to become a door. Weird green light poured out of the opening. Baby was the first to step into the light. Silhouetted there, with her Amazonian stature and hourglass figure, she looked like something out of a Japanese comic strip. Doll and Lati emerged at her sides, variations on a theme of yoonal babedom. The antennae of all three were particularly striking in profile. With a loud hiss, a porthole beneath the door slid open and expelled a cloud of sparkling purple and blue gas. The gas formed itself into a grand staircase spiraling down to the pool deck.

Ebola dropped the bottle of champagne. Landing upright, it ejaculated a celebratory geyser of thick white foam into the air.

"Yorp! Yorp!" Revor shot out from between Baby's legs,

scampered down the steps, flew through the spurting foam, and executed a perfect triple backward somersault into the pool, plummeting down through the water and coming up between the legs of one of the groupies.

Revor had excellent lung capacity. It had always made him a popular guest at pool parties in the outer.

The babes, meanwhile, descended their steps of ether, which dissolved behind them. Baby had changed into a hot pink fake fur miniskirt, skintight black Lurex top, fishnets, and knee-high lace-up boots. Doll was still in black leather, though now she was wearing the asteroid belt and Doc Martens. Lati wore her white T-shirt, jeans, and Converse All-star sneakers. She'd tied colored ribbons in bows around her antennae.

"Oh, *baby!*" exclaimed Ebola, scrambling to his feet and grabbing his crotch.

"Yes?" replied Baby. How had he known her name? She grabbed her crotch in turn, thinking, when on Earth . . .

"*Phwoah!* You chicks sticking around for a while? Maybe, uh, we could, you know, *do* something?"

Now what would he have in mind? Doll decided to find out. Scanning his thoughts, her antennae stiffened with annoyance. "I don't think so, butt-face," she hissed. "Of course," she conceded, "I only speak for myself."

"Speaks for me too," Lati said cheerfully.

"Me too," Baby nodded.

Shit! Chicks hadn't reacted to him this badly since he'd become a rock star. It *had* to be the hair. He'd get it cut this afternoon. Maybe.

"The hair's the least of your worries so far as I'm concerned," Doll commented, smiling as the singer's corpse-like countenance turned an even whiter shade of pale.

"Look!" cried Lati, gesturing excitedly. She'd gone to the balcony to check out the harbor view. There she noticed a bas-relief on the wall depicting Cherubim at an orgy. "Guess who's been here before us?"

"*Cool,*" enthused Baby. "We've obviously come to the right place. Now where'd Revor go?"

A stream of bubbles broke the surface of the pool, which was further agitated by the thrashing about of the groupies fighting for Revor's attention. They'd take Revor over some hotshot rock star anyday—rock stars never went down on *you.*

Not unless you were an alien babe from hell, of course. Baby felt something on her foot. It was Ebola's lips. She watched, bemused, as the pair of pink slugs slimed up her booted ankle to her knee, followed by a lot of hair and squeaking leather. Gently, she kicked him off. Ebola, on his hands and knees, gazed up at her, a pitiful and questioning look crinkling his stubbly mug. She shook her head. Funny, she thought to herself, wiping his saliva off her boots with the back of her hand. This Earthling was no less sex, drugs, and rock 'n' roll than Jake. Yet she felt no urge whatsoever to perform sexual experiments on him; in fact, the idea rather repulsed her. "Keck," she said.

"Use me," begged Ebola, senseless with lust. "Abuse me."

Lati approached Ebola from behind and, applying a boot to his upraised arse, sent him sprawling on the deck.

"More," sighed Ebola.

Lati placed an obliging foot on the small of his back and shrugged at the others. Earthlings. Strange-o-rama.

Baby signaled to the others and whistled for Revor. Revor wriggled out of the groupies' collective grasp. Energetically shaking himself and spraying water all over the still stunned and supplicant Ebola, he bounded across to where the babes stood waiting for the lift. The doors slid open and the party entered.

Emerging into the lobby, the babes sparked a near riot of erotic confusion. Normally staid matrons squashed ample, pearl-covered bosoms against the thin, eager chests of green-uniformed porters. Businessmen in Armani suits crazily humped the columns on which hung plaques from Phil Collins and Cliff Richard. A pack of Twisted Mofo fans knocked the enormous floral arrangement off the lobby's center table in order to ravish and be ravished there by a pair of well-heeled honeymooners from Taiwan.

The babes noticed all this frenetic activity. Having no other experience of Earthling behavior, however, they just took it as normal.

On the Sebel roof, meanwhile, Galgal, which had automatically shut down its Glow-matic lighting system after the babes departed, went largely undetected by passersby. Those who looked up and noticed the saucer didn't think twice about it. If people gave it any thought, they assumed it was just another one of those trendy shampoo advertisements that had nothing to do with the product. What could an advertisement tell you about washing your hair that you didn't already know anyway? Stepping out of the chaos of the hotel into the sun-soaked street, Baby fished in her bag for the homing device's Locate-a-tron. She held it up, and dialed in Jake's code—SPUNKNIK 1.

Over in Newtown, Jake and Tristram were trying to convince Saturna and Skye that the bowl of chili straddling the halfway line down the fridge was actually part theirs by virtue of location when the homing device in Jake's arse suddenly emitted a soft, flat beep.

"Gross," commented Skye.

"Mister Natural," Jake sang back, unfazed, scratching his arse.

"That's it," declared Saturna. "No chili for you boys. It'll only make you worse."

"Why *me?*" Tristram complained. "*I* didn't fart. Unfair as."

Registering the signal, a light flashed on the Locate-a-Tron. Baby took a reading. From the Sebel Townhouse in Sydney's eastern suburbs, Newtown, in the inner west, represented a major hike-o-rama in Earthling terms. To a pack of intergalactic jet-setting alien babes, it was a mere rockin' stroll. "Unless you girls have something else you'd like to do," she said, as casually as possible, "I'd actually like to go find Earth Boy again. I feel like we haven't really finished with him yet."

"Whatever," said Lati agreeably, licking her lips at a small gray cat. The cat turned into a tiger, growled sexily, and then, cat again, rubbed itself against her legs.

Doll shrugged. Earth boy shmearth boy. But you could never tell who else they might meet along the way.

Revor vaulted into Baby's shoulder bag and the babes strolled up Elizabeth Bay Road, soaking up the rays of the sun. Amazing star, the Aussie sun. Its daily schedule of arrivals and departures prompted the sky to riot and party. While it hung around, colors sang and danced upon the sparkling beaches, the mirrored towers of the central business district winked at the sandstone edifices glowing softly beside them, and a peculiarly Australian combination of physical vigor and sensual languor coursed through Earthling veins. Its impact on ayles was even more dramatic. All three were visibly pulsing now with an erotic energy: the sunlight suffused their skin, made sultry their gaze, and left a glossy dew upon their lips. It also left them looking less vividly green, which was probably not a bad thing in context.

Crossing through a small park, they found themselves in the heart of the Cross, a magnet for sleazebags and booners of every description. A carful of hoons revved by in a purple Valiant. "Oi!" one shouted out the window. "What planet are *youse* from?"

The girls looked at each other, bemused. Was it that obvious?

"Nufon," answered Lati.

"I wanna lick your anus," shouted another, as the car sped off, the sound of raucous laughter thinning into the air behind them.

"Did you hear that?" said Doll. "Uranus? I mean, who'd want to lick Uranus? It's a *disgusting* planet."

As they passed by the strip joints and adult bookstores and doorways overhung with signs promising GIRLS GIRLS GIRLS, hawkers whistled, sex workers cheered, bikies revved their engines, and all along the street men dropped to their knees. In Alien Planet, the video game arcade, baseball caps spun around on adolescent heads, virtual villains crawled out of their screens and surrendered, and plastic machine guns turned into plastic ploughshares before the dazzled eyes of the players.

Gone, perhaps, were the days when any old alien crew landing on Earth could count on being received as gods or having monumental temples or cave paintings dedicated to them. But rock 'n' roll babes from outer space could still make a fairly big impression.

The babes crossed the Williams Street intersection. There was utter chaos as both drivers and pedestrians forgot where they were going and tried to follow them. They were now approaching the King's Cross fire station. A discreet doorway led upstairs to a needle exchange and STD testing center. A woman with vacant eyes was putting a dollar coin into a vending machine in the doorway. The babes crowded round her, thoroughly engrossed. What sort of game was this?

"Oh, *baby*," Baby greeted the woman, grabbing her crotch.

Sadly, it must be reported that there *was* the occasional Earthling who proved immune to alien charms. "Fuck off, ya slags," snapped the woman, pressing a button labeled "fit." As the girls watched, oblivious to her annoyance, a thin black plastic container popped out and the machine chirped tinnily, "Thank you for your custom." The woman, after giving them the finger, slouched off with her prize to the tiny park around the corner. A fireman, who'd been enjoying a smoke in the driveway of the fire station observed the babes with interest.

"Cool," said Lati, pressing her finger to the same button. Aliens had a way with machines. Something to do with the amount of electrical current running through their synapses. That's why, as is frequently reported by "experiencers," when aliens or their craft are in the 'hood, cars tend to stall and television screens dissolve in static. With that sort of power over the mechanical world—no money, no worries. Out popped a similar package. Lati fished it out of the tray and unwrapped it. After they'd all examined the hypodermic syringe it contained, cooed and clucked over it, she popped the needle into her mouth and ate it.

This sight prompted the fireman to drop his cigarette, which ignited a scrap of litter. This, in turn, blew up the street to the cafe next door and landed on a pile of weekend papers, setting them alight.

By the time a waiter had put out the flames with an eccoccino, the girls were well up the street. They didn't really understand what the fuss was all about. Earthlings eat animal and vegetable, ayles fang down on mineral. It would be quite ridiculous, not to mention rude, don't you think, if every time an alien spotted an Earthling troughing out on a bowl of pasta its response was to set the place on fire?

Tristram wandered up King Street in search of his twin. He found Torquil standing with folded arms and gazing into the window of their favorite thrift shop, The Fifth Scarf. Torquil was wearing the sort of baggy, low-crotched cotton trousers colloquially known as poo-catchers, and a Mambo theology T-shirt depicting the descent to Earth of a three-eyed alien rock god. His olive-complexioned brow was furrowed and his large black eyes half-closed in contemplation of an aqua blue feather boa which happened to match, almost exactly, the color of his hair.

"Yo, bro," Tristram greeted him. "Am I my brother's beeper, or what? Time for our jam."

"What d'ya reckon?" Torquil replied. "Do I absolutely need this feather boa or what?"

"What."

"What?"

"You said 'or what' and I'm answering. What. Like, you don't need this feather boa."

"Right. That settles it." Torquil spun on his heel and entered the shop, emerging less than a minute later with the boa coiled around his neck. "Well?" he said. "What are you hanging around here for? We've got to get home and re-hearse."

Tristram agreeably turned in the direction of home.

"Whoa! Whoa," Torquil called out. "No need to rush. Besides, dunno 'bout you, but I need a nosebag. Got any moolah? I spent all mine on this." He flapped the end of the boa at Tristram. A feather escaped, and they watched it float away. It landed on the street, where it was promptly run over by a truck. Torquil laughed. "Cool," he said. "I thought it came with too many feathers. Well?"

"Well what?"

"Got any dosh?"

Tristram shook his head. "Zilch. I just checked. And my next dole check doesn't come till tomorrow."

"Spewin'," Torquil was outraged. "How does the government expect us to budget our money when they give us so little to begin with, hey? Tell me that."

"I tell you nothing," said Tristram, fishing a bag of Maltesers from the pocket of his leather jacket and handing them to his brother. They were walking in the direction of home now. They copped a fair amount of staring. Identical twins usually did, even those who didn't go to the additional trouble of dyeing their hair bright purple and blue and tying it up in rows of tiny rosebudlike knots, à la Björk *circa* "Violently Happy." Then there was the matter of Tristram's frock and Torquil's feather boa, of course.

A boy stepped out in front of them and pointed. "Are you guys twins?"

They each looked around them in confusion. "Sorry?" said Tristram. "Do you see someone else here?"

Torquil, meanwhile, began contorting his face and slapping it while tapping his feet on the pavement. Without taking his eyes off the kid, Tristram joined in, snapping his fingers, knuckling his head, and making popping noises with his mouth. The twins were nothing if not percussive. They were Bosnia's rhythm section. Tristram played bass and Torquil played drums. Sometimes Torquil played bass and Tristram played drums. In fact, they could play anything. Their bodies, plate glass windows, the lids of garbage bins, lampposts, the tops of twelve-year-old heads. And they did.

By the time they finished, passersby, including the boy's mother, had thrown $6.35 in change at their feet. "Easy as," remarked Tristram as they advanced on their favorite Leb-roll shop with a bouncing gait, counting the coins as they went.

Soon, Torquil was wiping chili sauce from his mouth with the back of his hand and Tristram was munching down the last of a falafel roll. "What's the time?" asked Torquil.

Tristram glanced at his watch. It was twenty past three. "Late as," he accused.

"Well get a move on then, you slacker bastard." Torquil flicked the boa at Tristram. "So what did Jake have to say for himself, disappearing like that last night? What happened to him? Or should I say, *who* happened to him?"

"It was aliens, apparently." Tristram raised an eyebrow.

"You mean aliens as in foreigners?" Torquil was confused.

"No. Aliens as in *doodoodoodoo doodoodoodoo*." Tristram sang the Twilight Zone theme.

"Aliens as in *doodoodoodoo doodoodoodoo?*"

"Aliens as in *doodoodoodoo doodoodoodoo*. He says they performed sexual experiments on him." Tristram drew a circle around his ear with a finger, the yoonal sign for loopy as.

"Yeah, right," Torquil laughed. "That's one thing I don't get about aliens," he said. "Why would they come all the way to Earth for that? Don't they get enough sex in outer space? Oh, g'day George." They came to a halt in front of where George stood belly-bent over his treasure trove. "Watcha got there?"

"Tummy toners. Which one are you?"

"Torq. Torquil."

"Right." George pointed a fat finger at each in turn. "Torquil. Blue. Tristram. Purple. When you're not color-coded anybody tell you apart?"

"Nup. Not even us," conceded Torquil cheerfully.

"Every time I begin to develop a bit of individual personality," complained Tristram, "he just turns to me, inhales hard and *whoop* there it goes. Sucked right up through his nostrils and into the bloodstream. Then it's, like, his too. Spooky."

"Bullshit," argued Torquil, punching his brother lightly on the arm. "That's you. The human hoover."

Slowly polishing a machine part with a greasy rag, George studied the twins. Tristram was wearing a frock again. Interesting. They'd once told him their father was Egyptian. Later, in one of his books, George read that Egyptians traditionally believed that twins were connected somehow to the star Sirius.

"Do you two ever think about aliens?" George ventured.

Torquil glanced at Tristram. What was this? International Alien Week? "All the time, George," he said, straight-faced. "As a matter of fact, we're right into aliens at the moment. Jake was apparently kidnapped by some last night."

If George had had any hair left on his head, it would have stood on end.

"What?"

"Torq! Trist! Get your fucken arses over here!" Jake's voice thundered across the yard from next door. "Chop chop."

That tattoo. George was about to say something when Tristram cut him short.

"Gotta go," Tristram shrugged. "Catch ya next time, George."

"Yeah," said Torquil. "Dad's calling." He took his brother's hand. They turned and skipped off home.

George sat down on the ground with a thump. It was all happening. He was sure of it.

*The babes were now approaching* the eternally popular Café Da Vida, its latte-laden tables spilling out onto the pavement, its customers jargling and laughing, plotting and scheming. At this particular café, nearly everyone was an aspiring, has-been, or even occasionally practicing filmmaker, writer, or actor. This contributed to the theatrical levels of the conversation—a relationship drama here, a career tragedy there, a raucous farce in the middle.

"I've got this idea for a movie." An earnest young man with a ponytail and black rectangular glasses leaned across the small table toward his friend. Like everyone else at the café, they were dressed entirely in black.

"Yeah?" said his friend, turning to exhale smoke and catching sight of the babes. "Whoa. Marty, hold on for a sec. Chick alert."

Marty frowned. "You listening, Bret, or what?"

"Yeah I'm listening," he sighed. "Can't I listen and look at the same time?"

"Can you?"

Bret sighed and angled his head so he could at least keep the babes in his peripheral vision. "Lay it on me." Were they *green* or was it just the light?

"It's about this guy in his mid-twenties, inner-city type, who strives to overcome his alienation and ennui through drugs, alcohol, and sex."

Bret winced. "It's been done before. Besides, that's not art. That's life."

"Aw *thanks*," said Marty, a little hurt. "But before you dismiss it out of hand, there's a subplot." He paused for effect.

"Well?"

"It's about how, like, blond guys, I mean, natural blonds, not bottle blonds, can have a really hard time cultivating proper goatees, particularly those little caterpillar or triangular numbers underneath the bottom lip. Even if they've got enough facial hair to pull it off, the results hardly show and they can suffer *unbelievable* trend-angst as a result."

Bret considered this a moment. "Now you're talking," he nodded. He snuck a look over his shoulder. "Oh, man," he said. "You gotta check 'em out."

Marty did. "I think they're *green*, Bret."

"Hey," Bret shrugged. "This is a multicultural society."

"Hi there," he saluted them.

"Oi!" Lati declared, cheerfully grabbing the crotch of her jeans and tonguing a bit of needle from between her teeth. Her wide gray eyes sparkled from beneath her tousled hair. "And what planet are *youse* from?"

"Mars," gulped Bret. "And you?" Did she just grab her *crotch*?

"Mars?" Baby shook her colorful head and wagged a finger at him. "Fuck off, ya slags," she laughed. "You're nothing like a Martian. Martians are just dumb microbes. Prehistoricville. Cold and rocky." She reached out and stroked the skin of his arm. He felt like he'd just been dunked naked in a bath of warm milk and licked all over by a cat. "You're not cold and rocky. No, you're no Martian." She touched a finger playfully to Marty's nose. "And neither are you," she said. Marty had the distinct impression that she'd taken his entire face in her mouth and sucked on it. He shivered. "You're just an Earthling," Baby continued, coquettishly smoothing the teeny circle of pink fur down over the tops of her extraordinary thighs. "Not that I have anything against Earthlings. We love Earthlings, don't we girls?"

Lati panted like a dog who'd been offered a T-bone.

Doll scuffled the pavement. "I'm bored," she announced. For emphasis, she whipped round and applied what is known in kickboxing as a spinning back fist to the brick wall behind Marty and Bret's table. With a small crunch, the wall reshaped itself. Two men at the next table felt close to fainting. Another found himself with an instant erection. Doll inspected her hand, blowing off its dusting of plaster and brick fragments. She threw her head back and laughed. Her devil's horns of hair waggled in tune with her hilarity. Cappuccinos frothed and bubbled in their cups, anchovies swam through Caesar salads, and Turkish bread sandwiches stood up to belly dance.

Marty and Bret were speechless. Everyone at the café had grown quiet. Their collective vision was saturated with silvery light and their ears rang as though with a symphony of triangles. They all felt like, somehow, they had fallen in love. They were gripped with a kind of yearning that was so physical it made them ache, and they looked at each other with fresh looks of confusion and desire. They were all a little hard, a little wet.

Lati picked up the spoon from Marty's saucer, inspected it in the light and popped it into her mouth. She burped, a small, metallic sound that rang softly and distantly, like bells under water.

"Shall we?" she proposed.

"About time," Doll replied.

Badabadabadabadabadabadabum. Ra-dabadabadabadabadabadabum. Badadabum. Badadabum. Tatatatata. Boomtaba. Boomtaba.

Wunnekadankadank.

Wawawawawa.

Tristram looked up from his bass, a dubious expression on his face. "Think we should go easy on the wawa?"

"Nah," Jake shook his head. "You can never have too much wawa."

"It's your song."

"Take it from the top?"

"Can't take it from the bottom." Torquil lifted his drumsticks high over his head.

"Yeah yeah yeah. Everyone's a comedian."

Bosnia had a gig at the Sandringham in three weeks' time and Jake had written a new song, "Big Toe Beanie," that they needed to run through. Some might say it sounded a lot like every other song Jake had ever written, though Some, in Jake's opinion, would then certainly reveal himself or herself to be a philistine of rock, a guitar illiterate, the sort of person who didn't know their Blind Melons from their Smashing Pumpkins, their Celibate Rifles from their Single Gun Theory. Anyway, it wouldn't really matter, because Some never went to gigs at the Sando anyway.

Badabadabadabadabadabum went the drums. Tsssssss went the cymbals. Whookookookookikookikoo dldldlanwawa went the guitar. Downstairs to the basement went Iggy, in search of some peace and quiet and the company of girls. Iggy liked rock 'n' roll, but he had his limits and, terrible as it is to say in context for what it implies about the pet-master relationship, he had standards and taste.

He also had, it must be noted, a peculiar way of going down stairs. At the top step, he flattened his thick bullie body on the floor, splayed his legs flat out to either side, and raised high his chin. Then, pedaling with his back paws, he propelled himself over the top and went stiffly bumping down the narrow stairs like a canine skateboard, moaning gruffly as he went. Whereas this apparently awkward and potentially painful habit mystified Saturna and Skye, the boys of the household understood immediately and intuitively. It was an extremely efficient if slightly dangerous method for scratching one's balls. Enviable, really, though not particularly advisable for humans.

Badabadbadbadabadabadabadabum.

Unheard over the bang and twang of the Bosnia experience, a breathless shriek emanated from the basement. "Iggy! Stop it! Stop it!"

More squealing and giggles.

"Saturna! You're just encouraging him . . . oh . . . ohhhhh . . . nnnnnnn!"

Onward the babes strolled. They reached an intersection. Lati elbowed Baby and stuck out her chin in the direction of a car parked just around the corner. In a big old Buick cozied against the curb sat two fat men with bad suits and worse language. One was handing a thick wad of bills to the other, a man with a good position in the Kings Cross police force and a bad cocaine habit.

Later, officers of the Independent Commission Against Corruption would sweat and swear and shake their heads as they replayed the tape of the transaction, filmed by a secret camera in the glove box. Intended to be the clinching piece of evidence in a major sting, the tape contained the following mysterious sequence: Fat Man One pulls piles of cash out of a beat-up black briefcase. The cash, all old fifty-dollar bills, is bundled into packets of ten. Fat Man Two smirks with satisfaction, and holds out his hand. Fat Man One is about to put the grease on the palm when the money—and you could only see this in super-slow motion with lots of freeze-framing—breaks apart into pixels, each of which further disintegrates into tiny fractals of gold and green and white, which then dissolve into sparkles of colored light, cascading outward and dispersing into nothingness.

Both men paled under their ill-shaven jowls. By the time Fat Man Two composed himself enough to demand,

"Where the fuck did that go?" all he really wanted to do—inexplicably, because he was no woolly woofter, no siree, he was a *real* man—was dive into One's daks and worship thoroughly what he found there. So he did exactly that. "Anyway," he muttered about half an hour later, picking a pubic hair out of his teeth, "all property is theft, eh?"

"Don't stop," murmured One in reply.

Alien contact can be a beautiful thing.

The babes, meanwhile, put away the Abduct-o-matic and studied with great interest a picture printed on the rectangles of paper they now clutched in their hands. It was this picture which had drawn their attention to the bills in the first place. "Not bad," Baby conceded. "It's kinda cute actually."

"Pretty groovy," concurred Lati, "in a retro sort of way."

On the note they were looking at was a drawing of the CSIRO telescope at Parkes, in outback New South Wales. It was, as they spoke, systematically channel-surfing the yoon for radio signals from extraterrestrial civilizations. What the scientists at Parkes didn't realize, of course, was that extraterrestrial civilizations had long ago abandoned radio for TV.

Silly scientists.

Even if they did detect such signals, it was likely they'd be at least 150 years old, which is much older than even, say, *Gilligan's Island* or *Leave It to Beaver* or *Countdown* or leisure suits or Gary Glitter and would therefore be potentially very embarrassing for the extraterrestrial civilization that had put them out in the first place. It's conceivable that there are whole civilizations out there who are sitting on their planets with their head-equivalents in their hand-equivalents, blushing whatever color represents mortification to them, dreading the day some other intelligent life form happens upon whatever it was that they ill-advisedly broadcast all those light years ago.

The babes stuffed the decorated notes into their pockets and bags and continued on their way.

Their way took them up past a small park, a large hospital, and onto Oxford Street, where Earth boys stood in the doorways of pubs pashing off other Earth boys, and Earth girls knit their fingers together in lust. This was nothing unusual for this particular street. What was slightly out of the ordinary was that the Earth boys in question hadn't even noticed each other until our aliens passed and the girls had previously considered themselves straight.

Every other doorway displayed a sign showing a pink triangle and the words "safe area." "Do you think that means the same thing as it does on Nufon?" Baby asked nervously.

"What else could it mean?" Lati frowned. "Maybe 'safe area' means they've set up some kind of protective force field. But I never imagined that the Cyborgs of 49 Serpentis had made it to Earth."

"Is no place in the yoon safe anymore?" Baby shook her head. "I don't want to sound like a paranoid android, *but.*"

"Fucken hell," said Doll. The notorious three-sided Cyborgs of the double star 49 Serpentis could make even Doll quake. "Hate borgs."

"They're not as bad as bots," Baby replied, her teeth chattering. "At least they've got a heart."

"Yeah," Doll retorted, "a black one. I'll never forget what they did to Michelle."

As if any of them could. Qwerk hadn't been telling the truth, the whole truth, and nothing but the truth when he told CRAFTE that they'd bred only three hybrids. There was also Michelle Mabelle, the first hybrid, and the wildest of them all. When Captain Qwerk and the other leaders of the Qohort had had enough of her riot grrrrl antics and decided to "cap" her they'd called in the borgs. Baby, Lati, and Doll had been forced to watch. It had been horrible. By the time they'd finished with her, Michelle was a quivering wreck, a shadow of her former self who would now wear only navy blue and beige twin sets, didn't see why it was necessary to swear, washed the dishes after every meal, and went to bed at what was stupidly known as a "reasonable hour." The girls knew that if they were ever caught, the same—or worse—would happen to them. After all, Michelle had never stolen a spaceship.

They hadn't much time to ponder the matter of the pink triangles when they were distracted by an insistent ringing sound. It was coming from a clunky silver and orange device decorated with numbers and perforated with holes and slots. It hung off the wall of a rectangular glass box. Lati was the first to recognize it. "It's Dr. Who's time machine!" she exclaimed.

A well-groomed older woman stopped and stared at the device as well. "Waiting for a call?" she asked. The aliens shook their heads. The woman picked up the receiver. "Hello?" Seconds later her smile evaporated, and she slammed the receiver back down again. "Fucken arsehole," she muttered angrily in what was now clearly a man's voice. "Ahem," she cleared her throat. Her voice rose a few octaves. "I mean, darling, that's *no* way to treat a lady." Turning to Baby, she cooed, "By the way, I *love* the outfit. You didn't get it at Drag Bag by any chance? I've been looking for a little something just like it. No? Oh well. Cute dog too. Ciao for now." Blowing a kiss, she high-heeled off in the direction of the Albury Hotel.

Rrrrring. Rrrrring. They looked at each other. Doll picked up the receiver, holding it to her head as she'd seen the other woman do. "Hello?" she mimicked.

"Wanna suck my cock?" came the voice at the other end before it collapsed into an aria of exhalations. "Ohh, ohhh. Huhhuhhuhhuh. Ngngngg. Sssssss."

"Maybe," Doll replied into the sibilance. "How would I do that?"

"Sssss. Huhhuh . . . How?"

"Yeah. How? How should I suck your cock?"

There was a brief silence at the other end.

"I mean, I'm open to suggestion. For instance, I could suck it real hard and then bite it off if you like."

The nasal whine of a dial tone sounded in Doll's ear. She shrugged and hung up.

"What was that?" asked Lati.

"Some kind of Earthling sex, I think," Doll replied. "This guy asked me to suck his cock."

"Cool," said Lati. "What's a cock?"

"Fucked if I know."

A young Queenslander just off the bus from Brisbane approached the phone booth. "You finished with the phone?" he asked politely.

"Wanna suck my cock?" replied Doll experimentally.

He flushed bright red. The first thing that had popped into his mind was: yes, I do.

Onward and westward they went. At the corner of Hyde Park, they bumped into a pair of conservatively attired, short-haired Mormon missionaries. "How are you today, ma'am?" one said.

"Wanna suck my cock?" asked Doll, obviously pleased with her new expression.

"P-p-pardon?" he stammered, paling, his own cock stirring sinfully within his official, masturbation-proof garment. The girls waved a pleasant good-bye, turned left, then left again, then right, then left, then left again. They'd be in Newtown before you could say "Babes in Toyland."

The asteroid Eros had been to one good party his whole life. It was an absolute blast. It was, in fact, the planetary explosion that had given birth to him in the first place. But that was a long time ago, and not much of interest had happened to Eros since. In the great dodge 'em car arcade of the asteroid belt, Eros hadn't even managed a near miss with another celestial body. And now he was trapped in this dead-end orbit around fucken Mars, of all planets. *Spewin'.*

Eros was big, bored, and very restless.

"Oi! Little star! Star light, star bright—yeah, you!—first star I see tonight. 'Course it's true. You were the first. The very first. Swear to God. Just let me finish, okay? I wish I may, I wish I might, I wish—what do you mean only Earthlings get to say that? That's fucken *off*. What's so special about Earthlings anyway? Tell me that, huh? Huh? Fucken Earthlings, they get to do *everything*. What d'ya mean, like what? They get to live on Earth. Isn't that enough? It's *so* unfair. Why aren't I an Earthling? Did I ask to be born an asteroid? Hey, little star! Little star! Won't you just stay for a while? You know, have a chat, get to know each other? Oh, piss off then. I didn't want to talk to you anyway.

"No one *ever* pays any attention to me. What am I? A creep? A weirdo?

"Those babes in that rocketship, they were pretty nice, though, hey? That was so cool. Total deep space quiet and then, suddenly, that *boomboomboomboom* bass beat and I look up and there's this mothership bearing down on me, stereo blasting, and those *babes* inside. I'm sure one of them mouthed, 'See you on Earth!' I'd see her on earth. I'd see her anywhere. Name the galaxy. Damn! Why didn't I get their phone number? Damn. Damn. Damn.

"Earth, hey? Oh, God. Maybe I should just try and follow them there."

*Don't even think it, big boy.*

"God? That you?"

*No, it's Sun Ra. Who'd you think it was? You, my aspirational little asteroid, are going to orbit Mars until I say you're free to do otherwise. It could be 150 thousand Earth years, it could be 1.4 million. Depends on my mood. So don't go getting any ideas. No unannounced slamming into Earthie-poo. I'm in charge of this yooniverz and don't you forget it.*

"Yes, God," sighed Eros. "Anything you say, God. God? God? You there?"

Once he was pretty sure that God had taken off, Eros defiantly wriggled and wiggled and waggled and wobbled. God shmod. He'd achieve escape velocity if it was the last thing he did.

**Knock knock.**

"Is that the door?" Torquil nudged Tristram. The twins were nestled in the large brown beanbag chair on the beige-carpeted floor of the lounge room. The original owners of the house must have been proud of the carpet, for they extended it about a foot up the walls, from which point cheap wood paneling took over. Jake was lying on another genuine seventies artifact, a blobby mud-colored sofa so shapeless and malleable that at the end of the evening it was not un-common for people to discover that they had somehow slid, together with most of the seat cushions, all the way onto the floor. The decoration and furnishings of the lounge, a trib-ute to the excruciatingly bad taste of a previous generation, had always been a key attraction of the place to them all. Tristram exhaled a long stream of smoke. He leaned for-ward, replacing the makeshift bong, a small plastic juice bot-tle filled with a murky brown water, back onto the coffee table. The movement caused beans to shift and rustle under-neath him. That's a nice sound, he thought.

Door? Door. Doooor. The word floated through the air like an autumn leaf and drifted, ever so languidly, into Tristram's air space. Doooor. Dooooor. His radar was picking something up. Blip blip blip. Control tower, how-ever, was in a bit of confusion. It ordered the word to go into a holding pattern till someone could deal with it. Doooor. Doooor.

Rehearsal over, the three boys had stacked their instru-ments against the wall and were using the room for its intended purpose: lounging. The telly was on. The sound was off. They watched Fred Astaire sing and dance silently across the screen. For sound, they were listening to the latest CD by Three, a band with exactly two members. They were pulling cones. Jake was also leafing through the latest copy of *On the Drum*, and Tristram and Torquil were practicing strange pulling faces, using each other as a mirror. There'd been no sign of the girls or Iggy for hours.

It seemed like hours anyway. You kinda lose track some-times. You know. When you're stoned. It's not a bad. Feel-ing. But you do. Lose the plot. Uh, the track. Track. Yeah. Sometimes.

Knock knock.

DOOR. The traffic controller inside Tristram's head finally put down his coffee and joint and looked at the screen. The door! Of course. Tristram looked over at Jake. "Is that the door?" he asked. No response from the supine figure on the brown sofa. "Jake?"

"Dunno," drawled Jake, moving only his lips. "Depends what you mean by *the* door. There are many doors. There's door-to-door. There's doors in. There's doors out. There's indoors and outdoors. Then there's the Doors."

"I reckon there are more windows than doors," declaimed Torquil, pointing for some reason at the ceiling. "There are windows of opportunity. There are windows to the soul. There are windows on the world. There's Microsoft Windows."

"Yeah," objected Tristram. "But they copied all that from, you know . . ."

"Who?" asked Torquil.

Tristram looked at his brother blankly. Who what? What was he talking about?

Knock knock.

Jake took a deep breath. "*IGGY!*" he yelled. He paused a moment to gather more energy. "*THE DOOR!*"

"That's fucken ridiculous," objected Tristram, after thinking about it for a minute. "Iggy's downstairs. He'll never hear you."

"It's worth a try," Jake shrugged. "He needs the exercise. *IGGY! IGGY!*"

"Jeez you guys are hopeless," grumbled Tristram, clambering off the beanbag and drumbling out to the hallway. "Fucken stasibasiphobics."

"I know what that means," Jake called out after him. "Them's fightin' words. And if I ever get over my aversion to standing up and walking I'll deck ya for it."

Tristram gestured grandly at the door. "Open Sesame," he cried.

It was George.

"Yo, George. What's happening, man?"

"They've landed," George replied, face alight. "Just like I said they would."

Tristram stared at George's gut. He could picture it tumbling off those stick legs and bouncing merrily down the street. "Who've landed?" he asked it.

"The aliens."

Tristram's gaze crawled back up to his neighbor's face. "Well, that's great, George," nodded Tristram, deadpan, as the word "aliens" danced in his head, whirling Ginger Rogers around in its arms as it went. Aliens! Wheeeee! Aliens! Wheeeeeee! Wheeeeeee! "So, uh, where are they?"

"My place."

"I see. What exactly do these aliens look like, George?"

"Three sheilas and a dog."

"Uh huh." Tristram pondered this information. "But, George, uh, not to be a major skeptic or anything, but, like, how do you know they're aliens? How do you know they're not just, like, three sheilas and a dog?"

"Their antennae," replied George, smugly, tapping his head.

"Their antennae," repeated Tristram, solemnly, tapping his own head in reply. He wondered if George hadn't a kangaroo loose in the top paddock. Kangaroos. Kangaroos. Boing. Boing. Skippy. Ts ts ts ts. Boing boing.

"Who's there, Trist?" Jake demanded from the next room. "And if there's a party, why wasn't I invited?"

Fifteen Sirians, twenty Cherubim, twelve Zeta Reticulans. Captain Qwerk put his shiny gray head in his four-fingered hands and shook it. Ting-a-ling. Ting-a-ling. He was doing his passenger-to-fuel supply ratios, which is to say, he was figuring out how many of his fellow extraterrestrials he would have to shlep to Earth in exchange for the ingredients they were supplying for the rocket fuel. Seven Alpha Centaurians.

Did there have to be *fifteen* Sirians?

It was going to be a long trip, even if they did manage to install the new antimatter drive in time.

What else was there?

Oh, God, the registration.

It was nearly expired. God.

God was the single, immortal inhabitant of the planet Genesis, which having produced one of Him, saw Him and saw that He was good, or good enough, and thus neglected to provide any instructions on the further reproduction of the species. Which was probably sensible, considering that one of God's main characteristics was His omnipresence. It was difficult to see how there could be room in the yooniverz for another one of His kind. God, who was occasionally mistaken for Phil Collins, was a bit of a creative spirit; He went around letting there be light here, letting there be a firmament in the midst of the waters there. That was cool with the other aliens. More worlds to explore and all that sort of thing. What occasionally got up their spotty blue noses, however, was the fact that He had such big tickets on Himself. Not to put too fine a point on it, He was the biggest bossy-boots in the cosmos. He went so far as handing down commandments and visiting plagues upon those who told Him to get stuffed or simply refused to return His calls. Another one of His dominant personality traits—one He'd surely list in a personal ad were He looking for a partner—was omnipotence. He liked to help His mates. Yet, the sad truth of the matter was, He didn't always do what He could. God didn't overly exert himself when it came to stopping senseless warfare or looking after His chosen peoples or even showing mercy to poor suckers who could use a break. On such matters He was the original slacker. On the other hand, He could be diligent as hell when it came to busting space cowboys for expired rocket registrations and other intergalactic traffic violations. It wasn't like you could sneak anything past Him. He was, after all, omniscient.

Qwerk sighed and added "reregister the spaceship" to his do list.

"That's one thing I never ex-pected, you know, that the food on Earth would be so good," Baby enthused. "All those cafés we passed seemed to be serving only the tiniest portions and no variety either. Knives, forks, spoons, spoons, forks, and knives. For fuck's sake."

"I know exactly what you mean," said Lati, ripping apart a toaster oven. She sniffed the dial, licked it, and drew it sensuously across her cheek before finally opening her lips and stuffing it inside. Doll was troughing down on the grill tray.

Baby sucked contentedly on a plug. "I'd love to get the recipe for this thing," she said. She swallowed a prong and smacked her lips. "It's a hell alloy."

"The Earthling George seems a good sort," Lati commented. "We rock up unannounced and he acts as though he's been expecting us his whole life."

Eeeeek. Revor, who'd been licking out an abandoned vacuum cleaner, had got his snout stuck in the hose. He waggled his head with increasing desperation. Eeeeek. Eeeeeek. Help me. Eeeeek. Eeeeek.

"Silly pet," laughed Baby.

Lati picked up an electric carving knife, retrieved a whipper snipper from across the yard and the starter motor for a Kombi van, and began to juggle.

"Stop playing with your food, Lati," Baby ordered, mock-serious.

"Yes, Captain Qwerk. Whatever you say, Captain Qwerk." Without warning, Lati tossed the whipper snipper at Baby. Baby's arm flashed out, caught it and in one smooth motion threw it back. Lati snaffled it midflight and kept it airborne. "It is fucken *great* to be out of reach of Qwerk and those other deadheads," she whooped.

"I'd say it's a fair bet they're not missing us much either," said Baby.

Missing wasn't exactly the word Qwerk would have used. But if Baby thought he didn't care if he never saw them again, she had another thing coming. In fact, they all had another thing coming, and that thing was Qwerk himself. He just needed to work out a few final details.

Eeeeeeeeeek. Eeeeeek. Eeeeeeeeeeeek. Eeeeeeeeeek. Eeeeeeeeeeeeeeeeeeek.

Whoops. Forgot about the pet. Baby reached over, grabbed Revor by the rear legs and pulled. His head popped out with a great *phook*. He rolled onto his back, closed his eyes, and lay panting gratefully.

"We could sit here all day," said Doll, "or we could make a move. I don't wanna appear too impatient or anything, but I smell sex, drugs, and rock 'n' roll, and well, I dunno about the rest of *youse* but I'm ready." This got a laugh from the others. They knew about the difference between you and youse. Aliens might be innocent of many aspects of life on Earth, and their words might not spill out correctly all the time, but they weren't stupid. Or illiterate.

"Actually, now that you mention it," said Lati, letting her toys drop to the ground, "I smell sex, drugs, and rock 'n' roll too. And I think it's coming from next door."

Baby glanced at the Locate-a-tron. "Definitely next door," she affirmed. "But, Lati?" She'd put on her stern, I-am-the-leader-here voice.

"Yeah?" Lati hated it when Baby pulled that leader shit. It was so bloody Nufonian.

"Jake's mine this time."

Lati shrugged. "As if I gave a fuck. I didn't think he was so great the first time." Lati wasn't being particularly malicious. She just enjoyed stirring Baby.

Doll observed their exchange warily.

Just as Baby was about to retort that Jake had probably thought even less of her, George reappeared. "Thanks for the grub," she said to George. "We're off."

"You'll be back, won't you?" he asked anxiously.

Reading his mind, she assured him, "Wouldn't lift off without you."

*Tristram ambled back into the* lounge. He flopped back down on the beanbag next to his twin.

Jake and Torquil looked at him blankly. Where had he been all this time, they wondered. It felt like he'd been gone for *years.* Torquil, overcome with emotion, threw his arms around his brother. "Bro," he cried. "Where *were* you?"

"Where d'ya reckon?" Tristram wriggled out of Torquil's grasp. "At the door."

"*Really?*" Torquil replied in a voice full of wonder. "That's *so* cool." He thought about it a moment. "Was anyone else there?"

"George."

"And what does old George have to say for himself, hey?" Jake interjected.

"He says the, uh, aliens have landed," Tristram answered, getting up again and wandering off to the kitchen to fetch a glass of . . . a glass of . . . Never mind. He'd probably remember when he got there.

*"Doodoodoodoo,"* giggled Torquil. *"Doodoodoodoo."*

Jake suddenly felt very warm. He glanced at his new tattoo. It appeared to be heating up. Bizarre. Fred and Ginger were getting on his nerves. He picked up the remote control and switched channels. Click. A flying saucer was attempting to uplift a new model four-wheel drive, but failing. Click. Someone was impersonating a Mintie by tying up his ears with elastic bands. Click. On the news, the government announced new laws making it illegal to laugh at the foreign minister or any other members of Cabinet, no matter how risible they became. Click. A little extraterrestrial danced around a giant bar of chocolate. Click. Back to Fred and Ging.

"Torq," he said.

Torq, eyes closed, had gone into screen saver mode. Flying toasters winged their way across his eyelids, followed by toast.

"Torq."

Torq slowly came back on line. "Mm?"

"I have this funny feeling that I'm about to meet the love of my life."

Torq rolled his eyes. "Yeah. Well. You say that every Saturday night."

"It's Sunday." Jake held up the paper and tapped an ad. "And speaking of Sunday. Smokey Stover's playing the Sando tonight. Smokey Stover. *The* Smokey Stover. Tonight."

Torq reached for the bong, pulled another cone, and contemplated Jake's professed excitement. "But, Jake," he said.

"Wha?"

"I forget. What were we talking about?"

"Dunno. Nothing?"

"No. There was something. What'd you say just then?"

"I said," Jake said, yawning again, and scratching his arse, which suddenly itched something fierce and had just released another small *blaaaat*. "Smokey Stover's playing the Sando tonight."

"Oh, that's right. But, Jake. Stokey Smover. Skokey Mover. Smovey Stokey always plays the Sando on Sunday nights."

Jake sighed and shook his head. "You know, Torq, all I ask is—what?—a little enthusiasm. A little zeal. A little passion." He drew smoke into his lungs thoughtfully. That's exactly what he needed, it occurred to him with a blinding flash of self-awareness: a little enthusiasm, a little zeal, a little passion. Torq didn't need these things *half* as much as he did. What was he saying? Oh right. "Besides, someday, I know it's hard to imagine, but someday Smokey Stover might not play the Sando on Sundays. And then, you know what? Life would be different."

"Life's full of surprises," Torq submitted.

"It is," agreed Tristram, who'd reappeared with a tea towel in his hand. He wasn't sure why he had picked up the towel, it just seemed to be the right thing at the time. He sat down again and hung the towel over his brother's head. Then he bent over and examined the hem of his frock. The stitching was fucken *amazing*.

Knock knock.

"Trist," Jake said. "The door."

"I got it last time," Tristram protested.

"Which," Jake explained with exemplary logic, "is exactly why you should get it this time too. You're in practice."

Tristram frowned. He felt intuitively that there was something wrong with that argument but he couldn't put a finger on it. He hauled himself out of the beanbag once more. There was definitely a flaw in Jake's line of reasoning. Line of reasoning. Why was it a *line* of reasoning? Why couldn't reasoning be a dot, or a plane, or a solid even? Maybe logic was a rhomboid, sorta circular but with *angles*. Tristram snudged out of the room to answer the door.

Torq extended a mental claw and scratched in the dirt of his memory. "Uh, Jake," he said, sloughing off the towel. "Wanna hear a joke?"

"Dunno. Is it a good joke?"

"Dunno. Who's to judge?"

Jake pulled the cushion into a more comfortable position under his neck and repositioned his long legs. "Well?" he said. "Lay it on me."

"Have you heard the one about the dyslexic agnostic insomniac?"

"Nup."

"He lay awake all night trying to figure out if there really was a dog."

"Arf arf . . . what the fuck?" The hair on Jake's arms and legs suddenly stood straight up. Full-body horripilation. Even his dreads were doing their best to scramble to their feet. Being fat and heavy and unaccustomed to exercise, however, they only managed to heave themselves halfway up before tripping over again exhausted. Three faded to zero as the CD wound down. A trancelike silence enveloped the room. Fred Astaire transmuted into a swarm of butterflies and fluttered off screen. Jake's eyeballs were bathed in a dazzle of icy, diamantine light and he had a distinct sensation of centipedes in steel-capped boots marching up and down his spine. Hesitantly, he turned his gaze to Torquil. Judging by the other's bug-eyed expression, he knew that, whatever it was, Torquil was experiencing it too.

You have to give it to them—alien chicks really know how to make an entrance.

There, in the door of the lounge, stood a very pale-looking Tristram and three positively glowing rock 'n' roll babes from outer space.

"Oi," greeted Baby. "Remember us?"

Jake sat up straight and blinked. Déjà vu déjà vu déjà vu vu vu. But. How. When. Where?

Doh! she thought. Forgot about the Memocide. "Never mind," she said, unreasonably disappointed. "We just had *sex*. But it's not your fault you don't remember."

Jake was goggle-eyed.

"Really. It's not."

Lati studied the twins, who were looking equally flabbergasted. They were *heaps* cuter than Jake. Baby could have him. She'd have *them*. "How are you today, ma'am?" she inquired coquettishly. "Wanna suck my cock?"

Doll sighed and grabbed her crotch. Boy-o-rama. Where were some *girls*, hey?

"Well," gestured Torquil, when he found his voice again, "do come in. And, oh, Jake?"

"Uh, yeah?" answered Jake, not taking his eyes off Baby.

"You're a legend. Fucken *leg of lamb*."

*I wonder if we could get away* with fewer Sirians?

Let's see. Given that $Zn^{2+} + 2e == Zn$, and the solubility product of $MgNH_4PO_4$ at $25°$ C is $2.5 \times 10^{-13}$, if we installed a few extra solenoids here and a synchrocyclotron there we might not need quite as much vanadium or molybdenum, and that way—Qwerk brightened—we just might be able to knock down the Sirian component a bit.

Qwerk rose from his desk and walked to the door. He looked down the corridor. No one was around. He shut the door and returned to his desk. Opening his mouth wide, he inserted a long silver finger. With just a twinge of guilt, he thought of the things that excited him most—tidy suburban shopping centers, pocket calculators, and Michelle Mabelle—and devoted the next twenty minutes to pleasuring his uvula. Dongdong dingding dongdong dingding dongding dongding dongding dingdong dingdong DING-DINGDINGDINGDING.

Before rock 'n' roll, before rhythm & blues, before jazz, before Mozart and Bach, before Gregorian chants and German lieder, before sitar and marimba and gamelan and dulcimer and pipa, before *Cats* and *Phantom* and revivals of *Hair*, before reggae and house and ska and dub, before Hanson, before Elvis, before Orpheus, before Throbbing Gristle and Nine Inch Nails, all living creatures grooved to one beat: that of the heart.

Baboom. Baboom. Baboom. A stethoscopic survey of the living creatures gathered in the lounge room of a particular Newtown sharehouse late on a Sunday afternoon early in the spring but late in the twentieth century would have revealed some highly generalized cardiac confusion. Was it rampant, uncontrollable lust? The first wild intimations of true love? The unpredictable physiological effects of alien contact upon the Earthling constitution and vice versa? A cosmic vibration caused by an adjustment in the orbit of the asteroid Eros, which at that precise moment had shifted minutely closer to Earth? Just springtime? All of the above?

Woof?

Woof?

Iggy came trotting into the room on clickety claws, insinuated himself between Lati's legs and licked his lips. He was followed by Saturna and Skye, tugging bits of lace and velvet and strands of hair back into place. Revor was the first to act upon his impulse. Trotting up to Iggy, he stood up on his back legs, curled his front paws up like a kangaroo, cocked his head to one side and howled.

Iggy looked down at Revor with startled eyes. He opened wide his powerful jaws and, with an economical swing of his neck, scooped him up and shook him high in the air.

Wowowowowo. Put me down. Wowowowowowo. Wowo. Oooo. Is that your tongue? Ooooooo. Oooooooo. Ooooooo. Don't stop. Ooooooo. Nfnfnfnfnfnfnf. Mmmmm. Rrrrrrrrrrrrrrrrrrrr. Ahhhhhh. Ahhhhhhh. Nf. Nf.

All the assembled bipeds, ayle and bean, stared in consternation and amusement, unsure what, if anything, they ought to do. Before any of them had time to react, Iggy expelled Revor with a cough, turned and, head held high, padded off to the kitchen. Revor, fur damp and curly, eyes moist, landed on his feet and shook himself vigorously. Sniffing the air for Iggy's unmistakable scent, he cantered off in hot pursuit.

"Let's turn the electricals back on," Lati suggested. Doll aimed her antennae at the CD player. It started up again instantly.

*I can smell your sweet sweet sweet fuzzy armpits, woman, I can smell you,* sang one of two of Three.

Thus followed a pause thoroughly up the duff with erotic possibilities.

Jake squirmed. He felt oddly responsible for the situation. This was not a totally comfortable feeling, for Jake felt almost as squeamish about responsibility as he did about commitment. He much preferred to think things just happened, and he was either there, or he was not there.

Another bun browned in the oven of time.

"Well, cool," ventured Torquil. "Aliens, eh?"

Baby nodded. She didn't think she'd be particularly keen on responsibility or commitment either. Whatever they were. They sounded a bit like that, what was it, that's right, that *relationship* thing. They didn't sound very rock 'n' roll in any case. Too many syllables, for one thing. She indicated the CD player. "I like the music," she commented amiably.

"Yeah?" said Jake, inexplicably proud, as though he'd had something to do with it.

"Fully. That's why we're here."

"Here? In this house? Because of Three?" Jake was at a nonplus. Not to imply any negativity.

"On this planet. Because of rock 'n' roll."

"Cool!" said Tristram. Was the redhead licking her lips at him? Outrageous. Tristram *loved* outrageousness in girls. He didn't know *where* to look.

Doll was checking out Saturna and Skye. Now *they* were what she'd call Abduction Objects. Yum-o.

"So," Jake proposed, "we all going to the Sando then?"

"The Sando?" queried Lati. "Is that the local locus for sex, drugs, and rock 'n' roll?"

"Uh, depends how you define sex, drugs, and rock 'n' roll, I guess," replied Jake, amused. "But, yeah, I suppose it is."

"I like this girl," whispered Torquil to Tristram. "Wacky *as*."

"I liked her first," Tristram whispered back. "And I," he added, "*saw* her first, which has got to count for something."

Lati smirked with satisfaction. She'd have both of them on toast. Whatever the fuck toast was. "Let's jet," she said.

Jetting wasn't quite the word for what happened next.

First, Saturna and Skye disappeared downstairs to repaint their eyebrows. Then Jake and the twins embarked on a vague, epic, overlapping search for socks that involved peering under cushions, shifting the TV, grabbling around on top of the fridge, and ferreting in the cupboards where the cereal and peanut butter lived. It entailed the inconveniencing of entire communities of insect life, forcing spiders and cockroaches and several species of ants to flee their traditional homelands. It took the boys out to the shallows of the small courtyard and into the depths of the junk closet, and finally, when they'd exhausted all other possibilities, upstairs to their rooms.

Left to their own devices, the babes curiously examined their surrounds. Brown-o-rama, Baby noted to herself. She hadn't quite expected Jake's pod—pad, whatever—to look like this. She'd expected something a little more colorful, a bit more kinetic, with shifting perspectives perhaps, for she'd got all her ideas of how rock 'n' roll boys lived from the interior scenes in music videos. She was more disoriented than disappointed, but it occurred to her that, despite everything that had happened the night before, she hardly knew Jake at all. Had she talked too much? Maybe she should've asked him more questions about himself.

"Wouldn't have been a bad idea," Lati mumbled, having read her mind. "Especially since you're so keen on him and all."

"Fuck off, ya slag," Baby replied.

"What's with you two?" Doll asked, not really wanting to know. "Hey, dig this chick." She pointed to a poster of Kylie Minogue blu-tacked to the wood paneling. "Looks familiar. Wonder who she is?"

"Remember 'Wild Roses'?" Baby prompted. "She was the corpse."

Baby picked up the bong and sipped the murky fluid inside. How odd, she thought. Even their drugs are brown. She had a sudden vision of beige Ultrasuede dolphins in a tan sea by a chocolate beach.

Doll picked up a drumstick and hit Torquil's drums. "Enough oioishitting around. I wanna make that spunky music, green girls. Let's not lose sight of the main story here. And rock 'n' roll, as far as I'm concerned, is the main story." Doll was as focused as the Hubble Space Telescope. Doll may have been the least obviously flamboyant of the three. But she was also the one who made sure things got done. Sure, Baby and Lati came up with the idea of running away to Earth, but who worked out how to steal the spaceship, hey? Who managed to flog the fuel, tell us that? Lati was great fun, and Doll rather fancied her, but she was all over the place. Baby, for her part, had big enthusiasms, but they didn't last. Doll gave the Jake thing about, oh, two more days, a week tops. Doll knew, moreover, that Baby and Lati could go on about wanting to be rock stars till the cows came home—whatever the fuck that meant—but if she left it up to them, they'd never even pick up an instrument. This was actually a trait they shared in common with most Earthlings who wanted to be rock stars, but Doll couldn't have known that.

Thinking of something she'd seen on a video clip, Doll put down the drumsticks and picked up Tristram's bass. Lifting it over her head, she was preparing to smash it across the arm of the sofa when Tristram wandered back in.

"Whoa whoa whoa!" he exclaimed. "Easy on the equipment, alien girl." He relieved her of the bass. "Dunno about your planet, but around here these things cost a lot of bikkies."

Doll rolled her eyes with exasperation. Baby and Lati were giving her the shits and these Earthlings weren't turning out to be that much fun either. She plopped down into the beanbag as heavily as possible for someone so light. "BORED," she announced. "BORED, BORED, BORED."

This struck Lati as hilariously funny. Throwing back her head, she unfurled a wave of xylophonic laughter. The music of her merriment danced about the room, flung itself into the corners and bounced off the walls. Eventually, it grew languid and soft and slow and wove its fluttery way back to her. Sucking it back in through her nostrils, she released another peal. The action of laughing elongated her strong, beautiful neck and caused her lovely rounded stomach and full breasts to shake and strain at the cotton weave of her T-shirt. Her antennae quivered amongst the sensuous mass of her red hair.

Tristram, seeing her laughter, hearing the sinuations of her body, grew so enchanted he forgot entirely about Doll's threat to his bass. In his mind he was pressing his lips against the near-translucent skin of Lati's neck, nibbling on the delicate shells of her emerald ears, flicking her verdant nipples with his tongue, pressing his body against hers, kneading her arse, needing her arse . . .

Torquil, who'd ambled in just as Lati had started to laugh, was similarly struck. His mind's eye perved on a vision of himself burying his face in her sweet fuzzy armpits, of devouring the soft flesh of her side and tummy in a frenzy of little lovebites and then plunging his nose and mouth and tongue into the folds of her cunt, which would be wet *as* . . .

Baby stood rapt, enjoying Lati's performance, and the twins' reaction to it—they'd keep Lati safely occupied for a while, she was sure, when suddenly—

Lati farted.

Having recently consumed half a toaster oven, an entire fondue pot (including forks), a handful of ball bearings, most of a car axle and an electric can opener—not to mention the hypodermic needle and cappuccino spoon—Lati's flatulence was no mere triangular ting-ting. If her laughter had been a zesty xylophonic, her fart was a full-on fugue. A harmonic weave of trumpetoids, trombonoids, and tympanoids, blowing a shower of gold and bronze sparks into the air. The smell was rather astounding in its own right, a gingery funk with an underlay of oriental spices and a hint of musk.

Doll, who'd sat sullen and impenetrable until that path-breaking, ice-breaking, wind-breaking moment, now cackled with delight, hoo-ing and ha-ing and kicking her legs in the air.

Baby collapsed giggling onto the floor.

Pleased with herself, assured of the full attention of everyone in the room, Lati then scooped up the lighter from the coffee table, turned her back on them all, pulled down her jeans, let go with another doozy—and lit it.

FFFOOOOM. The violet flame shot forth with a flourish and then extinguished itself with a scorching little riff that seemed to Torquil how the heavy metal band Pantera might sound if they used bells instead of guitars. Lati wriggled her plump arse back into her jeans, spun back around, buttoned, and grinned.

"Biggest hoon in the yoon," cackled Baby.

Torquil and Tristram looked at one another. Torquil gulped. Tristram gasped. Torquil gasped. Tristram gulped.

Love moves in mysterious ways. In this case, it moved Torquil and Tristram to complete and utter surrender.

"What did the Russian say to the dominatrix?" asked Torquil.

Tristram blinked. In the next instant they fell to their knees, raised their arms and touched their heads to the floor. "I want to be your slav," they chorused.

"Hmph," Doll snorted, sprunting out from the clutchy folds of the beanbag and stomping from the room. At this rate they'd never even move on to *drugs*.

"She didn't like the joke?" Tristram picked up his head and shot a guilty look at Baby.

"Don't worry about her," Baby assured him. "That's just Doll. She'll be all right." Then, as casually as possible, she added, "I'm going to see what's become of Jake," and exited after her.

Lati surveyed the twin set at her feet. "If music be the food of love," she commanded, "play something already."

In his mind, Torq jumped to his feet, searched efficiently through the pile of CDs by the player and selected a superbly seductive album, Dave Graney's *Soft and Sexy Sounds* perhaps, or Beck's *Odelay*, or maybe *Henry's Dream*, or even whatshisface unplugged. Maybe the Perkins, Walker, and Owen thing. Yeah. Perkins, Walker, and Owen. He rolled over onto his back and gazed upon Lati with helpless infatuation. What a *woman*. Did she just ask him to do something? She did, didn't she? What could it have been? Damn. Oh well. If it was important, she'd probably ask again. Tristram, meanwhile, was thinking *Porno for Pyros*. What was he doing kneeling on the floor? He raised his plumbummy bones, plodded over to the CD player, and found the album. Holding it up, he looked questioningly at Lati.

"You'll make great pets," she approved.

In their own stoned stunned way, Torquil and Tristram were beside themselves with lust and fascination. They wanted nothing more than to possess and be possessed by, singly or doubly, this extraterrestrial minx. They had no doubts, no second thoughts, no prior commitments, no real problems with green skin, no reason to hesitate. On the other hand, they were total slackers. So what they did was this: nothing.

Here's a picture of seduction, slacker-style. Tristram is collapsed loose-limbed on the beanbag, eyes at half-mast. Torquil is passed out on the floor, eyes closed. Lati dances by herself. Many minutes pass. Tristram sits up and reaches for the bong.

"Hey, space girl," he says. "You smoke?"

It was awfully quiet up in Eros' corner of space. Eros didn't have a lot to do but think. One thing he thought about a lot was crashes and collisions. It was a typical asteroid fetish. Every time some other 'roid whizzed by, Eros pictured it hurtling into another one and both of them exploding into myriad fragments. In great detail, and over and over again, he imagined that spectacular moment of impact, the exact instant of simultaneous gratification and annihilation, the *grand mort* of the asteroidal orgasm. But Eros didn't really fancy the notion of thumping some other 'roid himself. Eros had bigger plans and more exotic fantasies. Eros wanted to crash into Earth, to thrust into her soft soil and drive through her crunchy rocks, to break through her crust and penetrate her mantle, to shake her to her very core.

That'd impress those babes, hey?

"Hey, don't bite it, girl!" cried Tristram. "Just suck on it!"

Torquil's eyes flew open in alarm. What had he been missing? He looked around anxiously. Lati was seated on the sofa now. Tristram was bending over her, examining the bong for damage.

"Haven't you ever pulled cones before? No? You're kidding. You *must* be from another planet." He handed it back. "Sorry. Anyway, you light that, yeah, that's right, and suck in the smoke from the top. Nice and deep. That's it. Now hold it in as long as you can before exhaling."

This turned out to be a very long time indeed. Just as the twins were getting worried, Lati blew the smoke out her ears. In a series of perfectly formed rings.

"Oh, man," sighed Torquil, shaking his head. "How *do* you do what you can do?"

"I told you. I'm an alien. You just won't believe me. And I

recognize that line, by the way. It's from Vesuvia. *Fear of a Flannel Planet* EP."

"C'mon, Lati," coaxed Tristram. "How do you know that?" The effects of the dope were wearing off, and he was beginning to feel much more clearheaded. *Fuck*, she was sexy.

Lati shook her head. "I told you. I've got a perfect memory for music and lyrics, especially with any sort of galactic reference. Just have to hear it once and it's here." She tapped her forehead. "And by the way, one of the advantages of being an ayle is that I can read your minds when I feel like it. So, to answer your unspoken questions, sure, Torq, I'm sure I could do that. I'd certainly be willing to give it a go. But you'd have to do the same with another feather boa. And Trist, what you're thinking also excites me a lot, but you're going to have to guide me . . . OH, GOD!"

*Yes, Lati?*

What the fuck is happening to me, God?

*Effects of the drug, Lati. You've just been smoking cannabis. Cannabis causes an intense biochemical reaction when it enters the Nufonian ichorstream. Prepare to shapeshift a few times and give off a lot of heat. I mean a lot. And, luvvy, don't forget you're half Earthling as well, so expect to be off your tits for at least an hour or so as well. If that's all, I've got a UFO doing eighty googolplex in a sixty-five zone. Gotta book the bastard before he gets away.*

Sure. Thanks. But, hey, hold on a minute. If it's an *Unidentified* Flying Object, how do you know it's a he?

*He she it. I still think "he" works as a universal pronoun.
Call Me unreconstructed. But the feminists sure were wrong
about Me, weren't they? I get so annoyed when I hear them
call Me "She." As if. I just feel like visiting My wrath upon
them, you know, smiting them or something.*

Lati sighed. You couldn't argue with God.
I thought you had something to do, she said.

*I do. I'm outta here.*

Lati blinked. She felt more than usually hot-headed; her
antennae felt as though they were burning up. She realized
the twins were now staring at her with a far more shocked
expression than was warranted merely by the revelation that
she had read their naughty minds.

Right before their eyes, Lati appeared to be self-com-
busting. Her red hair was aflame, and the air around
her bent liquid with heat. Her features had begun to
mutate: she had Bette Davis eyes, Chrissie Amphlett lips,
and Salt 'N' Pepa thighs; she was Prince in Purple Rain,
she was Kurt Cobain; she was You Am I and Faith No
More; she was Jim M the original Door; Annie Lennox
and Madonna, Courtney, PJ, and Summers, Donna; she
was Velvet as the Underground, a silver CD spinning
round . . .

Doh!

Torquil and Tristram found themselves staring at the CD
player, which was emitting a low hiss. They were alone in
the room. They were sweating profusely. The windows
were all steamed up and condensation dripped down the
screen of the TV.

Tristram pinched some mull between his fingers and examined it closely. "What *is* this shit?"

**Baby, meanwhile, discovered Jake** in Torquil's room, appropriating a sock.

"I've got this theory," he remarked as she came in and sat down on the bed beside him. He bent over and pulled on the sock. His big toe protruded through the hole at the top. He studied it as though he'd never seen a toe before. Truth is, Jake, the serial lady-killer of the laid-back set, playful playboy of the Newtown world, was utterly smitten. He was also confused as hell. He had *sex* with her? And *forgot?* "You know how, like, one sock always goes missing from the pair?" he remarked. "I'm sure that all of the single socks have been sucked into a black hole somewhere in space. The black hole then expels them onto a distant planet where the inhabitants have only one foot."

"It's true," she confirmed. "The planet's near Arcturus. I know someone who's been there. He said that they hold weekly sock hops. They operate the clutch in their space-ships with their noses, which are extremely long, and play Twister by special rules. They don't feel guilty about the sock gambit cuz they figure if they can get by with one foot, the rest of the yoon can manage with one sock."

Jake raised his head and studied her. She didn't seem to be kidding. She stared right back. Eye contact city. Jake felt like she was vacuuming his eyeballs. With an effort, Jake sucked back his vision and applied it to his boots, which he now laced with full concentration. Baby liked how the lean muscles worked under the freckled skin of his long arms and how the big matted pipes of his hair flipped and flopped about when he moved his head. For his part, hot desire was burning off the marijuana mist in his brain. She read both his desire and his awkwardness and smiled to herself.

"What's so funny, space girl?" Jake had sat up again. His

hand was now making an uncharacteristically nervous foray into the vicinity of hers. It hovered briefly but the landing gear didn't seem to be working. Come on, he thought, put down those wheels, you can do it. By now, they were both staring at his hand. As nonchalantly as possible, he reversed the engines and piloted it back to base, where it taxied straight into the hangar of his jeans pocket.

Shit! What now?

Jake was a great believer in diversion therapy.

"You know," he said, addressing her extraordinarily kissable lips, "I once took this incredible hash. At first, I thought I was God."

"You're nothing like Him," she interjected, wondering why he didn't seem able to speak his mind, particularly since she was so clearly on it. "Really. I know God. Believe me. You couldn't be more different." And thank God for that, so to speak, she thought. Couldn't really handle two of them.

She knew God? Jake considered the implications of this remark. She couldn't be a born-again, could she? Born-agains were such a worry. Could never get them into bed and, from his experience, they didn't even have great taste in restaurants. But he refused to believe that she was a born-again. For one thing, if she were, she'd have knickers on.

He'd come to the conclusion that she wasn't wearing any underwear while he was bending over his boots. He'd noticed she was sitting pretty casually for someone wearing such a short skirt and he'd, uh, *accidentally* glanced up and caught a flash of flesh. Actually, it was a bit weird, now that he thought about it. No hair and, in fact, it looked like there was nothing else there either. Barbie doll city. No, he shivered involuntarily. That was ridiculous. He hadn't dared to *stare* or anything. She was probably just one of those kinky chicks who shaved her pubes. Of course.

What's this born-again business, who's Barbie doll, and what the hell is underwear? Baby wondered to herself.

Jake dropped the religious problem into the too-hard basket and began again. "Anyway," he hazarded, "I realized I wasn't God, but I had the feeling that whoever was God was trying to speak to me. And then I saw that God was, God was, uh, an alien." He paused for effect. "A female alien."

Bullshit, thought Baby. Wonder what he was going to say before he decided he needed to impress me?

Wilma Flintstone is what he was going to say. He'd had a vision of God as Wilma Flintstone. This had impressed other girls, but he wasn't sure it would work on Baby. What kind of name was Baby, anyway? "Shall we go?" he proposed.

When they reached the lounge, they found the twins shuttlecocking a Big Mac carton back and forth between them. "Where are Lati and Doll?" asked Baby.

Tristram winced. Torquil screwed up his face. "Doll's downstairs with the girls," he mumbled. "Lati, uh, kinda, disappeared."

Baby shrugged. She knew Lati well enough not to worry. And she was not sorry to have Jake to herself, either.

"You two coming?"

"Don't think so," said Torq. "Think we'll just hang around and wait for Lati to come back. Oh, and Doll said she'd catch up with you guys later."

The phone rang. Before Jake had time to react, Baby picked it up. "Wanna suck my cock?" she said, deepening her voice. On the other end, a woman burst into tears. "Jake, you're a bastard," she sobbed, slamming down the receiver.

Baby turned to Jake. "Jake, you're a bastard," she informed him.

"So they say," said Jake, flinching. "So they say."

"They're all bastards," shrugged Saturna. "But there are different sorts of bastards. There are lovable bastards, there are tolerable bastards, there are irredeemable bastards. The boys in this house range from lovable to tolerable, with occasional bouts of irredeemability. *Love* the spider tattoo, by the way. Are you sure you're not a vampire? Sure you're just an alien?" Saturna, Skye, and Doll were sitting cross-legged on the Goth girls' king-size four-poster, which was canopied in extravagant loops of black muslin. "Don't you want to make double-sure?" Black candles placed around the room released a musky scent and glimmered through the muslin, creating an artificial gloaming full of mysterious shadows and unpredictable light. Saturna reached out and placed a soft hand on Skye's neck. She pulled Skye's hair back from her face and tugged her lace choker downward. Skye's bare neck glowed golden in the candlelight. "Don't you?" she repeated.

"I do," Doll said huskily. "I really do." She placed her lips on the proffered flesh. Her devil horns of hair tickled Skye's cheeks. Wrapping one arm around Skye's waist, she buried the other in her hair, where it found Saturna's hand and came to rest upon it. "Whaszavampardoagen?" she queried through skin.

"A vampire bites the neck and drinks the blood of his victim," instructed Saturna. The authority in her voice was undermined by a slight tremble. She shifted one black stocking-clad foot slightly so that the heel pressed against her stiffening clitoris. Reaching out, she stroked Skye's thigh through the layers of lace and crushed velvet. "We've fantasized about this for ages. It should be totally transporting." Her hand slid upward to tease Skye's cunt gently through the soft fabric. Skye let out an uneven breath and closed her eyes.

Doll felt fully happy for the first time since they'd landed on this planet. There'd been altogether too much Earth boy this, Earth boy that for her taste. Boyzone city. This was more like it. She bared her teeth and sunk them into Skye's neck. These were the teeth of a girl for whom taking a mineral supplement meant crunching on a rock. Breaking the skin easily, she sucked on the salty nectar trickling out from the shallow wound. The taste of the blood caused a shiver to run up her spine, and her whole body was suffused with a sudden intense warmth. Skye, panicking, tried at first to twist away. Saturna, however, held her firmly, and Doll kept an iron grip on her as well. Eventually, Skye stopped struggling. Trembling, she rested palely against Saturna's breast, as Saturna continued her intimate caresses.

Doll's antennae were now quivering and her breath was coming in shivers. A rainbow of colors cascaded over her skin like a fluttering Mardi Gras flag. "Mmmm. Mmmmm." The bodily fluids of Earthlings didn't require *that* much getting used to, really. Typical cautious Nufonian claptrap.

Doll lifted her head and licked the blood off her teeth. "Let me," said Saturna, twisting her neck round to tongue the blood from Doll's mouth without removing her hand from Skye's cunt.

"Maybe I am a whatchamacallit after all," Doll meditated, probing her eye teeth with a finger. What was this on the roof of her mouth? Oh, *yes*. "Have a look at this, girls," she said, opening wide.

"I enjoyed the Vampire Chronicles. But *Cry to Heaven* bored me to tears, and I thought *Exit to Eden* highly overrated."

"Have you read the witches series?"

"Not yet. How is it?"

"I didn't mind it. Skye and Saturna are reasonably big readers, so I spend a lot of time checking out their bookshelves. The boys, on the other hand, are *hopeless*. The only time Jake's ever had decent books around the house was when he was chatting up this librarian chick. Jake will happily walk into a pub and spend upwards of fifty dollars on booze in a night, and yet he won't fork out fifteen bucks for something decent to read. I don't get it. If I weren't so genetically programmed to afford unquestioning loyalty, I'd have bolted ages ago. How 'bout you, little fella?"

Iggy lay on his side. Revor was snuggled up against his pale chest, clamped between the bull terrier's front paws. He sighed. "The babes aren't what you'd call big readers either. Classic rock chicks. Not that I've got anything against rock. You into music at all?"

"Of course, though I'm a bit old-fashioned in my taste. I've always had a soft spot for the Animals and Three Dog Night, for obvious reasons, not to mention Beasts of Bourbon. I do like some of the new music, though. Portishead, for instance. Again, at the risk of total obviousness, the track 'Biscuit' is my personal favorite. What's your taste run to, Revie-pie?"

"We are *so* compatible it's ridiculous. Though I'd have to add the Beach Boys' *Pet Sounds* album."

"For sure. Oh shite! Here come Jake and Baby. Act animal." Iggy jumped to his feet, trotted over to the doorway and licked Jake's hand with thoroughly calculated subservience, indicating uncomplicated joy by wagging his tail at the same time. "Ruff!" he said. "Ruff! Ruff!"

"Yorp!" cried Revor. "Yorp! Yorp!" He rolled onto his

back and paddled his feet in the air as Baby arpeggioed his fluffy tummy with her fingers. "Nnf nf! Eheheheh! Ticklewicklewickle!"

Jake filled Iggy's water bowl, patted him good-bye, and left with Baby. "There goes the master race," commented Revor as the door shut behind them.

Iggy collapsed on the floor next to Revor and yawned his crocodile yawn. Gnaaaaaaa-*snap*. "Doesn't all this ootchi-kootchi-koo crap ever get on your nerves? Don't you wish sometimes that we could just can the pretense when they're around and act like the intelligent life forms we are?"

"Oh, I dunno," shrugged Revor, taking Iggy's paw in his own and licking the pads. "They'd probably want us to start feeding and walking *them*. Quite frankly, I couldn't be stuffed. Why let on you can drive when you've already got a first-class ticket on the gravy train?"

Iggy laughed. "You little bludger."

"Hi ho, hi ho, it's off to Earth we go." The Sirians, disembarking from the interplanetary shuttle to Nufon, were doing a conga line down the steps. Having four feet meant they could do this rather sensation-ally. They were also singing, an activity for which they had infinite enthusiasm and infinitesimal talent. Due to the space limitations and weight requirements of the interga-lactic craft on which they were to travel to Earth, they were allowed one backpack and one handbag each. Together, these were not to exceed 86.3 nufograms. Being Sirians, they had trouble complying with even these relatively sim-ple regulations.

In fact, one Sirian was at this very moment sitting on the tarmac bawling his six eyes out and sniffling out of all three nostrils because he'd forgotten his handbag, which held, among other things, his favorite hair clip, the cybernovel he was reading, an access-all-areas backstage pass to Kyuss, a packet of psychedelic snacks, and his gold Amex card. A somewhat impatient Nufonian official stood beside him, tapping his hoof, and trying to console him by saying that once they got to Earth he could abduct replacements for all those things. "No you can't," snuffled the Sirian. "Kyuss split up. They're not playing anymore."

The Nufonian, ever-logical, shrugged. "So what good's a backstage pass then?"

"You don't understand," blubbered the Sirian.

It was true. Nufonians were incapable of understanding such things. Nor could they comprehend how anyone could pack the way the Sirians did. You'd think that aliens preparing to go on an interstellar voyage would have an interest in traveling light, taking only what they needed, and placing everything in their luggage so that it could be readily retrieved in good condition. Nufonians themselves were naturally efficient and neat packers, but as for the rest of the aliens . . . From the knapsacks of the Sirians protruded or extruded any number of strange and outsized objects, including whole wardrobes of Elvis jumpsuits (Sirians led the yoon in Elvis impersonations), golf clubs (they adored golf because of the shoes), bowling balls (ditto for bowling), and easel-and-paint kits carried on the off-chance they might want to take up art along the way. One had even packed an ET mask. As if all that weren't enough to send your average Nufonian round the twist, one Sirian was simply shlepping a laundry basket full of rumpled outfits and smelly socks. Three to the pair. Natch.

Quietly, in the background, Nufonian underlings (who were never resentful of their status but worked diligently and with the understanding that Somebody Had To Do It) unloaded the bags of special chemicals and minerals that were the Sirians' ticket to Earth.

With a sudden whirr and mighty splash, a Cherub landing capsule belly flopped into the pond by the airstrip. A door slid open and an inflatable slide popped out. Within seconds, the slide was bouncing and squeaking under a tumbling squelch of fubsy bodies.

As they scrambled on shore the Cherubim shook their wings dry and exchanged greetings with the Sirians and Alphas, who were just leaping out of a shuttle on which someone had graffitied the words "Love you. Mean it. Swear," a greeting some Alpha had overheard on her last trip to L.A. Paddling down the steps of the shuttle with their ridiculous feet, the Alphas had just begun the process of slapping hands and licking the nostrils of the others in greeting when the black hovercraft of the Zeta Reticulans buzzed the field. No sooner had they swarmed onto the ground than the horrid Zetas were hoisting Cherubim in the air and swinging them around by their wings, playfully stomping on Alpha Centaurian twenty-toed feet, and telling jokes to the Sirians just to see how faint they could make them from laughing.

Captain Qwerk approached one of the underlings and, after glancing around shiftily to ensure no one else was watching, handed her a bulky parcel. He whispered instructions in her ear. She nodded. Entering the spacecraft, she found the Secret Hiding Place, which was clearly marked for identification, placed the Hidden Agenda inside, shut the latch, and removed the sign.

Jake and Baby walked down King Street towards the Sandringham, the rolling glide of his leggy gait perfectly complemented by her bouncing ebullient step. Jake noticed how everyone they met smiled at her. When she smiled back, some sank blissfully down onto the pavement, as though their bones had turned to water. This made him simultaneously happy—she was with *him*—and nervous. Clearly, she could be with *anyone* she wanted. On the board outside the pub were chalked the words "Smokey Stover"; underneath it said there'd be a two-dollar cover charge.

"A cover charge? What is this about covers?"

Jake looked at her blankly. "Pardon?"

"You know, that thing you were telling me about relationships and cover stealing?"

What the hell was she talking about?

"You know, at night?" She suddenly remembered that Jake wouldn't be able to recall any of their conversation. She was beginning to regret the Memocide gambit. "Never mind," she said.

She was a strange girl all right, thought Jake as he trawled his pockets and came up with four dollars. "I'll get this," he offered. He'd always thought that tactically it was best to pay for a girl on the first date, preferably something fairly cheap like a gig at the Sando, and then, once she'd come to understand his precarious financial situation, graciously to allow her to pay for everything after that. Not that he was in a particularly calculating mood on this night; it was more just a matter of habit.

"Hey, Jake." The girl doing the door, into whose short pink hair was carved a yin-yang symbol, and who wore a brief Chinese embroidered satin top over tight black trousers, greeted Jake with a flirtatious wiggle of slim shoulders.

"Hey, Kya," he said, trying not to look as worried as he felt. Ever since he'd had that little affair with Kya, she'd displayed an unnerving tendency to say the raunchiest and most embarrassing things to him in public, without any regard for circumstances. And tonight's circumstances, he felt, were in special need of regard. "Two, please," he said in his most businesslike voice.

"Oh, you've got a *date*. I *see*." She took a good look at Baby. She hadn't intended to let her gaze linger, but gazes had a way of getting trapped by alien babes.

"Kya, you taking the money or can I assume you're letting us in free?"

Kya shook off Baby's spell with difficulty. "Taking your money, Jake. It's not often a girl has that privilege and I think I'll make the most of it, if you don't mind."

Jake glanced over at Baby, but she appeared oblivious to the conversation. She was peering over his shoulder and into the pub with undisguised excitement.

Jake gave Kya his wrist. While stamping it, she tickled his palm. He snatched his hand away. "Do you *mind?*" he said. Baby's eyes met hers for the first time. Kya was so dazzled that she found a wide smile had come to her lips and tears had sprung to her eyes. Her heart was pounding in her chest and her hands were shaking.

Baby held out her hand. Kya stamped it. "Do you *mind?*" said Baby, snatching her hand away just as she'd seen Jake do.

Kya's jaw gaped. Baby let hers drop as well, smiled again, and followed Jake into the pub.

She looked around. The art deco tiling that covered the bottom two-thirds of the walls and the burnt orange paint with occasional black-stenciled drawings above it exuded a yoonal charm. The punters boasted hair and clothing in a range of colors that Baby hadn't seen since she last met an Alpha Centaurian with freckles. They wore more metal on their faces than your average cyborg. Her antennae picked up a scent of febrile sexuality and the gentle hum, inaudible to normal human ears, generated by a roomful of altered consciousnesses. The clink of glasses, the electronic gurgling of the video games, the drawn-out *thringgg* of the pinball levers and *plingpling* of the pinballs themselves reminded her of half-forgotten alien tongues. Smoke hung in the air like white clouds over Titan. In short, Baby felt right at home. And to make what was perfect even more so, here was another *rock 'n' roll band*, live and playing within a few meters of where they stood.

The band, Smokey Stover, was a regular institution at the Sandringham. Baby got right into them, and jumped around enthusiastically to the music. Jake swayed coolly next to her, wondering what it was about Baby that had such an electrifying effect on people. While she danced, Baby looked at everyone around her with a gaze so direct and curious that their eyes went to the ground with embarrassment. But the crowd, in its own low-key, tribal, unhyped, rock 'n' roll sort of way, was checking her out too. Big time. The Sando, haunt of the great semi-washed and demi-employed, Newtown's answer to whatever particular question was being raised at the time, the ultimate hang for the high-rock, low-techno crowd, commonly played host to any number of uncommon characters, but they'd be damned if, mirror mirror on the washroom wall, Baby wasn't the fucken uncommonest of them all.

Now that the effects of the dope had nearly worn off, Baby's aphrodisiacal effect on Jake was growing all the stronger. He didn't think he could handle it without the aid of some kind of chemical palliative. He glanced over at the bar. A drink would be good. "What do you want?" he asked Baby.

"To be a rock star. To take lots of drugs. To have heaps of sex. You know, with you again too. Everything. Anything. Just as long as I can get it *now*." Baby was nothing if not frank.

Jake couldn't believe she'd just said that. Particularly the bit about having sex with him again. No, he decided. She hadn't said that. She couldn't have said that. He was imagining things. He'd better try again. "Sorry?" he said. "What did you want? Like, to drink?" he clarified.

To drink? Why hadn't he specified that in the first place? It really was going to take some time to get the hang of Earthling communications. Baby had never had a drink of any sort—aside from that bong mud, of course. The liquid element of the Nufonian ichorstream consisted of mercury. She racked her brain for an appropriate answer. "One bourbon, uh, one scotch, uh, one Cooper's Ale? No that didn't sound right. "One bourbon, one scotch, one . . ." Now what was that song title? That's right. "One fizzy drink."

Approaching a corner of the huge, nearly square bar that dominated the center of the room like Mission Control, Jake signaled to one of the commandos within. "Hey Greg. One Coldie. And, uh, one bourbon, one scotch, one fizzy drink."

The bartender raised an eyebrow, which was no easy task given the number of silver rings that were weighing it down. "Joking, right?"

"I'm not. She might be."

Gregory leaned over the bar and looked to see who Jake was indicating. "Phwoah!" he exhaled, smiling ingratiatingly. "Who's the babe?"

Jake shrugged. Who was she indeed?

"Reckon she's the sickest bitch I've ever seen you with, hey," Greg complimented as he laid the drinks on the bar. "And you've brought in some scary betties in your time."

Jake, privately pleased, palmed the change. "Keep up the good work, Greg," he said, deadpan. He wrangled the four drinks over to where Baby was waiting. She relieved him of her three. "Cheers," he said, raising his to his lips.

Trying the bourbon first, Baby gagged at the taste. Before Jake could react, she held the three glasses out at arm's length and tipped them over, letting their contents cascade onto the floor. Then she ate the glasses. It's hard to say whether the slack-jawed astonishment of all those within splashing distance was due more to horror at the public menace of it all, terror at the sight of her crunching glass, or just simple amazement at the waste of perfectly good piss.

"Oh man." A crustie boy examined his bourbon-and-scotch soaked trousers and scratched his head, raising a small cloud of dust. A dazed smile crept over his features. "Whatever she's on," he sighed enviously, "I want some too."

Jake felt faint. Just when you think you're back on Reality Road, something like this happens and you realize you're so far off it you could be, well, on the moon. He started to put an arm around Baby's waist to lead her out of the circle of interested stares when his hand, having got *that* close, suddenly beat a hasty retreat. He indicated the back of the pub with his chin. "Shoot some pool?" he suggested.

"Sure," replied Baby gamely, picturing rifles and backyard swimming holes. "How do you shoot a pool?"

Jake studied her. If it was an act, it was a very good one. "Pool is a game?" he ventured, wondering if he was making a complete fool of himself. "You play it on a table?" He pointed to the back of the pub. "Like that one. You must have seen a pool table before? Surely."

"How do you swim on that?"

"You having me on?"

"On what?"

"Never mind."

Baby shrugged. "I told you. I'm from outer space. There's a lot I have to learn about Earth."

"We all have a lot to learn about Earth," nodded an earnest girl with a nose ring and a Celtic tattoo on her upper arm who'd been listening in on their conversation. "I really believe that. Otherwise we're going to destroy it."

Jake led Baby to the pool table and put a coin down on the side. A game was just beginning between a stick-thin bloke with a shaved head and another fellow, also in his late twenties, whose looks hung on the knife's edge between seedily handsome and just plain seedy. "We'll just have a go when they're done," Jake said. The players were tossing for the break. Baby didn't get it. What was this heads or tails business? Jake explained. He was just about to make some other comment to Baby when something in her eyes made him hold his tongue. The look on her face was a blend of studious observation and rapture.

Surveying the table, Mr. Stick leaned almost parallel over his cue and hit the cue ball sharply, scattering the balls and sending one of the stripes straight into a side pocket. The cue ball came to a halt in a perfect position to sink a second. He pocketed that and two more balls and set up a fourth within a centimeter of a corner pocket. Mr. Seedy stood unperturbed, leaning on his cue stick, his eyes half-lowered, one corner of his mouth pulled up with an expression that said, I eat players like you for breakfast.

Baby had never seen a game as sexy as pool. The intense, predatory circling of the table, the slow grinding of the chalk, the gentle sawing of the cue stick over the bridge of the hand, the sharp crack of the balls, and the subterranean, hungry gulps of the table. The soft green felt and smooth polished wood. The cigarettes dangling lazily out of the corner of the mouths of the players. Their jaunty, jut-arsed, cock-hipped stances.

Her eyes never left the game. Occasionally, she asked Jake questions that sounded so basic—mainly stuff about rules and scoring—that he grew convinced that she really didn't know anything about the game at all. The two players, overhearing their conversation, exchanged knowing glances. Their obvious air of superiority and condescension annoyed Jake just as their transparent envy—she was with *him*—secretly pleased him.

Jake wished they'd finish their game and leave. He was looking forward to playing with Baby. He wasn't nearly as good as these two were, but he was good enough. He was feeling quite unnerved by her. He needed to demonstrate competence, show off some style, redress the imbalance between them somehow. The sex thing. Maybe it was just her idea of a joke. No *way* he'd forget.

When Mr. Stick potted the black, winning the game, Jake politely asked the pair if they wanted to play doubles, privately hoping they'd just cede the table. When they grinningly accepted and suggested a small wager on the result, Jake could practically hear the theme from *Jaws* playing in the background.

"What's happening?" Baby was puzzled.

Jake shook his head disparagingly. "They want to play for money."

"Money?" Baby asked. She pulled a fistful of fifties out of her bag, the fruit of the afternoon's abduct-o-heist. Jake paled. Jake had a practical notion of money. He didn't just see a handful of bills. He saw rent. Electricity. Chocolate bars. Pizza deliveries. Café lunches. Dinners for two at the Thai Potong. Breakfasts of eggs Florentine and champagne. Fresh seafood. Top wines. Stuffed quails and grilled figs. Not to mention ounces and ounces of excellent gear. Heads. No loose stuff. "You mean these rectangular tokens?"

"You ain't wrong, sweet thing," said Mr. Stick, mouthing "jackpot" to Mr. Seedy, and then, "Rectangular tokens? Where's she from—outer space?"

"Yes, I am, actually."

"Baby," panicked Jake. "Can we have a little talk about this? I don't think this is a very good idea." Where'd she get all that moolah anyway? She was sexy, smart, *and* rich. Jake felt faint at the thought.

"She looks like the type to make up her own mind, mate," said Mr. Stick with a cold smile. Jake could have sworn there were a few large fishtails caught between his teeth.

Smokey Stover announced a break. The word that this bizarre, antennaed, bottle-eating chick was about to put more money on a game of pool than many of the Sando's regulars saw in a month of dole checks spread through the pub faster than herpes at an orgy. The space around the table was soon filled with a crush of bodies.

Baby ended the discussion by picking up a coin. "Heads or tails?"

"Tails," leered Mr. Seedy.

She flipped the coin into the air and, discreetly, took aim with her antennae. *Zaaap.*

It was heads.

"I'll break," Baby announced before Jake could say anything. She liked the sound of the word "break."

At this point it would have been highly impolitic for Jake to have expressed any doubt that this was a good idea. He forced a little smile. "You know what to do?" he whispered nervously.

"Sure. You just told me," she answered in a normal voice. "You slam the white ball into the others. They scatter and if you're lucky you sink a colored ball at the same time." Several observers sniggered into their beer. This was going to be rich.

Without the slightest trace of self-consciousness, Baby ran her fingers lightly over the several cue sticks leaning against the wall. Picking one, she held it up. She drew it through her closed palm and then slowly twirled it. Eyes closed, as though in a trance, she registered its weight and balance. She then lowered it parallel to the table and leaned right over it, the hot pink fake fur of her mini-skirt stretching taut across her full buttocks and hiking up to the tops of her muscular thighs. Two mohawked boys standing directly behind her passed out from sheer sexual excitement. One fell into the willing arms of a Goth girl standing behind him; the other crumpled to the floor and was given prolonged mouth-to-mouth resuscitation by Smokey Stover's drummer.

Baby, meanwhile, took aim and executed what could only be described as a perfect break, spreading the balls evenly across the table, even sinking two solids. A murmur of approval rose from the crowd. Jake gaped at her with barely concealed surprise and relief. Mr. Stick frowned at Mr. Seedy. Beginners' luck.

"My turn again, yeah?" asked Baby, her mind whirring with equations of force, mass, speed, and direction. Complex calculations of friction, action, and reaction. Newtonian physics were first-grade maths where she came from; Newtownian physics were play school. She stalked the table like a tigress. Practically purring, she chose her first victim. With a crisp crack of the cue on the cue ball, she sank the red. And the blue. Then the green. She stopped for a moment to survey the table, and picked up the chalk. Slowly, she crushed the soft stone against the tip of the cue. Three more people fainted at the sight, two girls this time, and one boy.

For the next shot, she perched on the edge of the table, one long leg reaching to the floor and the other curled underneath her. She lifted the cue over her head in an almost balletic movement, and executed the shot from behind her back. It was a perfect double. By now, a hush had fallen over the room. Like quite a few other males in the room, Jake could feel a hard-on stir in his trousers as, cool as Ice-T, she proceeded to gangsta her way through the rest of the solids. All that was left was to pot the eight ball. She did this, no wucken furries at all. It took a moment for the Earthlings to snap out of their trance. But, when they did, everyone in the room except Mr. Stick and Mr. Seedy burst into ardent applause. As for Stick and Seedy, looking like the cats who were swallowed by the canary, they shook hands unsteadily with Baby, then, as though by after-thought, with Jake.

"On ya!" shouted a group of young women who'd been watching with particularly keen interest. "One for the girls!"

Baby looked up at Jake with an innocent smile. "Now what happens? Don't the rest of you get to play?"

For the first time in his life, Jake was speechless. Guile-less. Legless with infatuation.

**Back at the house, Lati** reap-peared as suddenly and mysteriously as she had disap-peared, beaming and patting her stomach. "Boy, have I got the munchies," she announced, advancing on the stereo.

"NO!" screamed Torquil, jumping out of his seat as Tris-tram hid his eyes in his hands. "NOT THE BLACK GOODS!"

**M**onday morning—morning in the rock 'n' roll sense of the word, which translates to approximately two P.M. Other People's Time—saw Jake slither down the stairs, towel around his waist, clutching a Panadol, in desperate need of a glass of water. He'd briefly considered drinking from the tumbler that had been in his room since about the Year That Time Began, but the liquid within had begun to resemble a long-neglected swimming pool. Jake was certain there was a lot more than two Hs and an O in there. While he had nothing against chemicals in general, he didn't want to abuse any mystery molecules on a morning when his head already felt like a bodgy lab experiment.

It's reasonable to wonder—a Nufonian certainly would—why Jake had never bothered to take the glass of fetid water downstairs, dump it out, clean the glass, and take a fresh one to his room. The answer was simple really. The principle was the same one that resulted in his failure to throw away the infamous Rainbow Loaf. This was a loaf of bread that Jake had purchased, left on top of the fridge, and forgotten about. Its increasingly complex moldy veneer had progressed from green to blue, with spots of vivid orange and red. One day, Saturna confronted Jake, demanding to know why he hadn't thrown it out.

"I wanted to see where it was going," he shrugged. "It'd be such a pity to throw it away now. When it's doing so well."

"*Pity,*" said Saturna distastefully, as she pulled on her

black rubber dishwashing gloves, plucked the loaf from the top of the fridge, and tossed it in the bin, "is not the word I'd have chosen."

The Rainbow Loaf Incident was a lifetime ago, which, when you're twenty-three as Jake was, means it actually happened about two or three months earlier. But today, Jake was struggling just to make sense of his weekend. Entering the kitchen, he found the twins slumped over the table with their heads in bowls of cereal.

Torquil lifted his head at Jake's approach. His face was dripping with milk and cornflakes that adhered to his forehead and the tip of his absurdly regal nose. "Oopsy," he warbled, dropping his head back into his bowl.

That was Tristram's cue. He raised his lactescent features, scattering soggy flakes. Bellowing, "OOPSY DAISY," he plunged back into the primordial breakfast.

With friends like this, Jake thought, who needs aliens?

Aliens. Who'd have thought, hey? Oh, Baby Baby. Where was she now? What was she doing? She wasn't *with* anyone, was she? Those *antennae*. At the soft moist touch of a tongue on his feet, Jake jumped. He looked down sharply. Doh! It was only Iggy, coming in to snuffle his master's toes in greeting.

Iggy looked back. Yes, it was his master all right. But Jake's toes were somehow different since the last time he'd examined them. Softer, less crusty. Had Jake had a *pedicure?* Iggy was shocked.

The phone rang. No one budged. It rang again. "I'm sharing an important bonding experience with Iggy," Jake informed the twins. "Could one of you get it?"

"We're sharing an important bonding experience with the Kellogg company," Tristram gurgled through dairy. "Intense as."

"Yeah," Torquil pronounced through bubbles. "It's for you anyway."

Jake sighed. "C'mon Ig. We've got to answer the phone cuz no one else in this house is sane enough to be trusted."

It was Tim, the lead singer of Umbillica, another Newtown band. Umbillica was a heavy metal band that specialized in loud electric guitar sounds, macho stage posturing, and bad haircuts that tossed well. They'd heard the news about Metallica, but were waiting to see what other key metal bands did, hairwise, before making any big decisions.

"Timbo," said Jake. "How's it hanging, mate?"

"Not so well, actually. I'm in big trouble. I thought I'd surprise my girlfriend for her birthday, which is tomorrow, and take her to see Twisted Mofo at the Sydney Entertainment Center."

"I thought she hated heavy metal."

"Oh, mate, you're not wrong. But it being a special occasion and all, and Ebola Van Axel being, like, a total metal god, you know, I figured she'd at least be a little excited."

"I take it she was not a little excited."

"Yeah. No. I mean, she was pretty pissed off, actually. Spat the dummy. Said she'd told me ages ago what she wanted to do for her birthday."

"And what's that?"

"Fucked if I can remember. Or, more accurately, fucked if I can't. I've got twenty-four hours to try and come up with it or I'm up shit creek."

"Well, Timbo, that's quite a tale. Is there a moral you wanted to impart?"

"Jeez. Nearly forgot. Yeah, so I've got two tickets to Twisted Mofo. Going very cheap. Going free. Pity to waste them."

Jake scrunched up his nose. "Look, mate, don't want to be rude or anything, but Ebola Van Axel's not really my cuppa. The man's an embarrassment to us new-style, caring, sharing sorta rock stars. But the twins might be interested. I'll ask them. Hang on a tic."

Jake meandered back into the kitchen. The twins were actually eating their breakfast now. "You've got a cornflake on your ear, Torq. You two wouldn't be interested in tickets to Twisted Mofo tomorrow night, would you?"

Torquil jumped up, grabbed his crotch and, in perfect imitation of Ebola Van Axel, shrieked, "I'm gonna fuck you on the table, gonna fuck you on the chair, gonna fuck you over here, and gonna fuck you over there."

"Cuz I love you, baby, I do, and couldn't love you more. Yeah, I've got a big big dick, oh baby *yeah!*" Tristram had leaped to his feet as well, and was thrusting his hips and waving an imaginary guitar over his head. He burst out laughing. "Oh, man, that guy's a legend. Ridiculous as. What should we *wear?*"

"So, I tell Tim you want the tickets then?"

"Is the bear Catholic?" replied Torquil.

"Does anyone want to tell me what the fuck has been going on!" Mr. Spinner, the manager of Kissed for the Very First Time Records, was fuming. It was Monday afternoon. The young sales staff exchanged covert glances, shuffled their feet, and then stared at them. They were in fact entirely innocent. They felt guilty anyway. As you do.

Well, maybe not *entirely* innocent. They'd all knocked off the odd CD in the course of their career. But the sum of all the CDs they'd ever pinched from the stockroom, combined with all those flogged by every other teenager who'd ever worked there, didn't come close to the number that were missing. It certainly looked like an inside job. The secure crates in which the CDs were stored hadn't been forced open or otherwise tampered with.

An excruciating ten minutes passed without anyone saying a word.

"Mr. Spinner?"

"Yes, Zach?"

"Uh, maybe aliens done it."

"Zach."

"I mean, I read in this comic? Like how these aliens had this machine? An Abduct-o-matic? It was really cool an' it—"

"Zach." Mr. Spinner closed his eyes, lowered his head, and cupped his face in his hands as though praying to Allah for deliverance from teenagers, his job, everything. "Shut up."

Across the city, similar scenes were unfolding at shops with names like Drum Warehouse and Guitar City. The babes had had a very busy day.

The door of the sexual experimentation chamber opened. Doll swaggered out. She approached the Voodoo Lounge where Baby was reclining. Doll's wiry little body was glazed in black latex. She was wearing a rubber cat suit with a partial hood that she'd newly abducted from the House of Fetish. She'd cut four little holes in the hood—two for her horns of hair and two for her antennae.

Lati entered at the same time from another door, lazily yawning and stretching. She was wearing jeans and a T-shirt advertising the film *Aliens 3*. Lati managed to be both the most manic of all of them and the most voluptuously languid. She performed a leisurely double take at Doll's outfit. "Rrrrrrrrrrr," she growled sexily, "What's new, *pussycat?*"

Doll tried not to appear *too* pleased with herself. They both looked at Baby. She hadn't said a word since they'd come in.

A Fender Stratocaster lay across Baby's raised knees. She was practicing slide lines up and down its long, handsome neck. For some reason the guitar reminded her of Jake. Why hadn't Jake been at Ebola's concert last night? He wouldn't have been *with* anyone, would he? With their super-keen senses and sharply focused antennae the babes had easily spotted the twins among the large crowd. But while Baby must have scanned the entertainment center crowd a hundred times she just couldn't pick up any sign of Jake. And she'd left her Locate-a-tron at home. Wasn't that always the way?

Doll indicated the sexual experimentation chamber with her chin. "This one wants to stay, too," she announced smugly. "She's a real stunner. You girls happy with that?"

"Whatever," Baby replied without much interest, staring into the Betty Boop holograms that patterned her new frock, which was designed to look like a nurse's uniform. She'd gone for a stroll in it earlier. As she passed through the Darlinghurst café belt, the Earthlings had torn off their clothes, knocked their cups and glasses to the ground, and draped themselves over the tables singing, "Doctor, doctor."

Baby had been amused, but she couldn't help thinking, why isn't one of them Jake?

"Lati?" Doll asked. She was keen to return to her new abductee. "You happy?"

"Happy as Larry."

"That happy?" A smile forced its way through Baby's melancholy. The girls had never seen anyone quite as happy as Larry. Larry was as happy as a Sirian with a feather duster. Larry was as happy as a little indie band with a big record contract. Larry was as happy as happy could be. Yet, just two days before, Larry had been having a mid-midlife crisis crisis. His midlife crisis, contrary to all his expectations, was not bringing him much joy. In going from bank branch manager to carpenter he'd gained little more than splinters. Then there was the problem of his love handles—since he'd left his wife, no one was handling them at all. On Monday, he'd been sipping a black coffee at Café Da Vida and mournfully observing all the streetside Pretty Young Things who were pointedly not observing him back, when suddenly he felt a sensation like a thousand tongues licking the inside of his elbows.

Victoria Street faded from his vision. Stars danced before his eyes, which he opened only to find himself, naked, on his knees, with one of Lati's antennae up his arse, and Baby's legs locked around his neck. Doll, in a black velvet riding jacket and jodhpurs, was playing with Lati's breasts with one hand, and her own stomach with the other. The only jarring thing in this otherwise idyllic scene was the sight of Revor sliding back and forth across Baby's face, but after the initial shock Larry even found that exciting. His dreams had come true, down to the last detail. Larry, as the twins might say, was happy *as*.

"How's the spare room situation?" asked Baby.

"Reckon we can squeeze heaps more in."

"Why not, then? The more the messier."

"Merrier."

"Whatever."

The girls had had a very busy few days. In addition to their massive swoop on Kissed for the Very First Time Records and the musical instrument shops, they'd acquired whole wardrobes of clothing with labels like Mission Earth and Space Time. They'd been to see a band called Venutian Vixens at the Annandale Hotel, wondering if it was anyone they knew. Most excitingly, they began writing songs and playing their own music. Doll had worked out the formula. Three chords, twelve bars, four beats, and a tune—how hard could it be?

Baby wrote the first song. The lyrics went like this:

*Screamin' outta Hangar 99*
*Feelin' hot, feelin' fine*
*Leavin' Nufon far behind*
*We're the rock 'n' roll babes from outer space*
*And we're gonna disconnect your mind.*

When she finished, Baby put down her guitar and looked up expectantly at the others. "It's not Patti Smith," commented Lati candidly. "But it's a start."

"I wouldn't overdo the rhyme thing," opined Doll.

Baby slumped down on the Voodoo Lounge in a pout. "Everyone's a critic."

"I think we can work with it, though," mulled Doll, sitting down at her drum kit. Within minutes, they were bashing away at their instruments and "Hangar 99" began to fly. They all began writing songs after that. In their lyrics they sang of their frustrations with the patriarchal planet, of the joy of coaxing chaos out of order, of rocketships fueled by desire, and other yoonal themes.

Their abductions of Earthlings, meanwhile, continued apace. Their abductees included both male and female, old and young, able-bodied and infirm, beans of all sexual persuasions and bents. And, hoowah, were some *bent*. They were so bent that they had to sleep in circular stairwells. And that was *before* the babes got to them. In the great classroom of Earthling sexuality the girls were on a steep learning curve. They'd dispensed with the long introductory getting-to-know-you spiel and tended to wack the beans straight into the chamber. It didn't seem to make much of a difference to them. The babes didn't automatically tie them down anymore, either. In fact, some of the Earthlings tied *them* down. A number of them, like Larry, had begged to stay on. With a few exceptions, Memocide didn't seem all that necessary.

Lati yawned again and turned to go. "It's been real, groovers, but I've got to go. 'Happy as Larry' reminds me— I've got to take him over some panties I've been wearing for the last two days." It hadn't taken long for the girls to suss out why Earthlings wore underwear. It was so much fun to play with! Especially after a few days.

Doll took a step closer to Baby and smiled sweetly. Baby found this a disconcerting if not downright frightening sight. Doll? Smile? The girl had *fangs*. "By the way, Baby?" Doll said. "I just want to tell you how much I appreciate your leadership, and how much I love you and care for you. Your friendship means so much to me. I want to give you a big hug."

Enduring the hug, Baby squinted at Doll suspiciously. "What are you on now, Doll?"

"Oh, just a little pill the last girl gave me. I think she said it's called an ooky." Doll slapped the side of her head. "An ekky. Jeez, this language chip is driving me crazy. I think it must have a wire loose. There don't seem to be any cybernetic workshops listed in the Yellow Pages either. God, they're primitive here."

*Complaints, complaints. You're having a good enough time, though, aren't you, Doll?*

Yes, God.
Doll rolled her eyes at Baby.

*I saw that, Doll.*

Yeah, yeah, big boy. Sit on my face.

*I don't think that would be a very good idea, Doll. Not that I wouldn't enjoy it. But I'd hate to see your face afterward. It'd be spread from Perth to Pluto. Not a pretty sight I'm sure. So do we have anything more to say about my handiwork? My precious Project Earth?*

No, God. I love you, God, she added.

*Watch it with those pills, Doll. You're losing your edge.*

Yes, God.

*I'll be off then. There's a cute little nun calling to Me from some convent in Belgium. I think I might go present her with a vision. What do you reckon—a vision or voices? Or maybe a miracle?*

An instant later, He was gone. He didn't even wait for her answer.

Boy does He give me the shits sometimes, Doll thought. Makes a girl really want to get into, oh, I dunno, satanic metal or something.

Revor tapdanced into the room, plopped down on Baby's foot and nuzzled her ankle with his elephantine snout before sucking each of her toes in turn. "Iggywiggywiggy. Iggywiggywiggy. Nf nf."

"What's with him?" Doll looked alarmed.

"I think he's lovesick," Baby observed. Funny that. She sort of felt the same way herself. Despite all the sex and fun they'd had with other Earthlings since their abduction of Jake, which, though just a few days earlier, already seemed a very long time ago, she felt strangely disconsolate. In the classic Nufonian manner of expressing dejection she spent an inordinate amount of time nuddling soft cushions and licking the ceiling. A medley of love songs played in her brain.

Love? That was ridiculous. She was a hardcore rock chick, she reminded herself, not some sentimental country queen. What she felt was, oh, *curiosity*. Lust. Interspecial pheromones. Whatever. Certainly not love. Probably not love. "What do you think, Rev? Time to go back to Newtown?" Revor rolled onto his back and paddled the air slowly with his feet.

Jake lay on his back on his mattress, paddling the air with his feet, and staring out the window above the bed at nothing in particular. It was Thursday. Not that time had much meaning for him anymore. No, Jake was *over* time. Space, on the other hand, now *that* had heaps of potential.

Unobserved in the doorway, Torquil watched bemused, for several minutes. "Uh, Earth to Jake, Earth to Jake," he said finally. "Beaming you down, dude."

Jake rolled his head to the side. "Torq. My man. Or is that Trist? What'd you do to your hair?" Torq, who was wearing extremely wide jeans and a very narrow T-shirt with the word "Sportsgirl" across the chest, had unknotted his hair and redyed it. It stood up in frightened clumps, as though trying to escape his head in all directions at once.

"Torq. I reckon green's the color of the hour. What are you doing anyway?"

"Exercising," Jake replied. "It's like riding a pushbike, but better for you. No traffic. No stress." He turned his head from side to side, stroking the air with his hands. "*And* you still get to wave at all the cute girls. Except, unlike in real life, they always wave back."

"You're a very strange boy," commented Torquil appreciatively, as Jake's foot caught on the piece of Indian fabric that served as a makeshift curtain and the cloth came tumbling down over his face. Jake groaned, his limbs stiffened, and he tumbled rigidly onto his side.

"So dead," moaned Jake from underneath his shroud of maroon paisley. "Remember that line from *Tank Girl*? I'm *so* dead."

Torquil shook his head. "If I didn't know you better, dude, I'd think you were in love or something."

Jake wrestled off the cotton and propped himself up on an elbow. "Hey, Torq."

"Hey, Jake."

"Do you think they're really aliens?"

"Well, Lati's outta this world."

"Seriously."

"Seriously, I think we've got to stop taking so many drugs," said Torquil. "We didn't even remember to get their phone numbers before they disappeared on Sunday night."

Jake sighed, flopped onto his back, and returned his stare to the ceiling. "Nice day," he commented mournfully.

"Exactly," concurred Torquil. "Spring has sprung and Trist and I are going swimbos. You coming or what?"

"Dunno. I've just had my exercise."

Torquil scanned the clothes mountain. "Jake. You are lazy as." Hoicking up a pair of swimmers with a toe, he kicked them over to where Jake lay. They landed on his face. "Get yer gear on. Ready for blastoff in ten."

Jake peeled the bathers off his nose and rolled toward the wall. "You guys go without me. No, don't. Go with me. No, go without. With. Without. Oh, I don't care."

He hauled himself up on his elbows. "Which beach you going to?"

"Just Bondi."

"All right, all right. I'll go. Just this once. But don't say I never did nothin' for ya."

"Uranium."

"Check."

"Titanium."

"Check."

"Samarium."

"Check."

"Praseodymium."

"Check."

"Californium."

"Check."

"Valium."

"Check."

"Kryptonite."

"Check."

"Coke 'n' Sprite."

"Check."

"Iron supplements."

"Check."

Qwerk frowned and ran his eyes over the list one last time. That should do it for the food supply. "All the beings can take their own nuts, bolts, and other snack foods."

It was only a matter of days now.

*On Friday, George arrived home* to find the babes troughing down in the yard. "Watch the skies," he saluted.

The girls squinted up into the sun. "For what, George?" asked Lati.

"Just a joke," George apologized. "There was this movie, *The Thing*? It was about an alien carrot monster that fed on human blood. That was the last line of the film."

"Oh," exclaimed Doll. "They're revolting. We've never had much to do with them, really."

"Sorry? Didn't have much to do with what?"

"Alien carrot monsters."

George took this on board. "You wouldn't, though, would you?" he remarked, shaking his head.

"Mind if I do?" Baby had picked up a battered mold in the shape of a trout and raised it to her lips.

"Help yourself," nodded George, lugging over a portable computer and depositing it at her feet. He grinned. "Here. Why not make it fish and chips?"

Doll picked up a tool with a sharply angled arm and flying saucer–like top. She flicked the switch just under the bend in the handle. It whirred into action for a moment and then died. She hit it again, but whatever life it once had was gone now. Turning it over, she read the words Breville Multi-Reach embossed on the side. She took a small bite off the top. "Weenie beenie!" she cried. "Oh *yum!*"

The others looked at her. "What's that, Doll?" Baby asked.

"Dunno," Doll answered, turning the tool over in her hands. "But it's got the most fabulous garnish."

Lati looked up from where she sat nibbling on a clock radio. "What's wrong, George?" George was blushing so intensely that his scalp glowed from underneath his thinning hair and his ears had turned quite red.

"Nothing," he mumbled, bending over and ostriching among the gadgets. The vibrator had been his late wife's, God rest her soul. He wasn't sure how it had ended up in the yard.

Baby inserted a finger in her mouth and pulled out a keyboard space bar that had wedged between her back teeth. She was too wrought up to eat much. "You two ready?" she asked, trying to mask her excitement at the thought of seeing Jake again.

Lati could see how anxious Baby was. She felt like winding her up a bit. "What's the hurry?" she taunted. "I want to finish this first." She held up a mobile phone and began, very slowly and deliberately, to suck the keys into her mouth one by one. Then she extended the phone's antenna and pushed it back in again, extended it and pushed it back in again.

Baby was starting to grind her teeth. "Must you?"

"Just tenderizing," Lati retorted.

"Cut the crap, Lati." Doll was longing to see Saturna and Skye. She snatched the remains of the phone from Lati and popped it into her own mouth. "There," she crunched. "Let's go."

"Thanks for the feed, George," said Baby.

"Anytime," nodded George. He really wanted to talk to them sometime about the end of the world. What they knew about it. He was sure it was getting very close. In that morning's newspapers, the government had declared that it was removing all Aboriginals from the land pending a final solution of the Native Title problem. It was going to eliminate youth unemployment, meanwhile, through a comprehensive program of forced labor on public works, primarily the building of casinos.

Overseas, an entire nation that had once been part of the Soviet Union had managed to blow itself up with nuclear devices before anyone had even learned to spell its name.

And astronomers were plotting the course of the mega-asteroid 433 Eros, which was beginning to look unstable in its orbit. A spokesman from the London Observatory assured the public that Eros presented no immediate danger, but they were keeping an eye on it.

**Knock knock.**

"Wanna suck my cock?" Doll yelled through the door. No answer. "Why are our favorite Earthlings not in their nest?" she grumbled. Revor leaped out of Baby's carry bag and sniffed at the crack under the door.

Iggy, on the other side, wagged his tail deliriously. He cursed under his breath. Why didn't the humans ever leave him a key? They were all out. Saturna and Skye were at their shop, Tristram was at his part-time job in a King Street newsagent and Jake and Torq were at the CES, earnestly explaining to their case managers how difficult it had been, once again, to find any work. The door was deadlocked. Oh God, oh God, please, somehow, let me open that door.

*Oh, all right. Just this once. But don't make it a habit.*

A shiver crept down Iggy's spine. His fur, such as it was, stood on end and his ears pricked nervously. He sniffed at the air. Who the hell was talking to him?

*It's God, dog-face. Remember? You called me?*

God??!!

*Who'd you think it was, the Sisters of Perpetual Indulgence?*

Iggy's knees went weak and he sank to the ground.

I promise I'll go to church from now on, and . . .

*Cut the crap. I'm just doing this as a favor to the babes.*

The bolt sucked in and the door swung open. Revor bounded up to Iggy, jumped on his face, and humped his nose in greeting. Gnyah! Gnyah! Gnyah! As the girls watched in amusement, Iggy's big pink tongue extended out of his mouth and disappeared up Revor's arse.

Doll shook her head. "How beastly," she said appreciatively.

"Anyone home?" called out Baby, her heart racing.

Silence.

Oh, how foolish of her. She hadn't even checked the Locate-a-tron. Quickly she punched in the code.

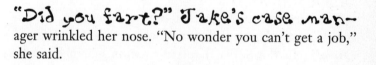

"Did you fart?" Jake's case manager wrinkled her nose. "No wonder you can't get a job," she said.

Masking her disappointment, Baby led the others into the lounge. "Did you do that, Lati?" she chuckled, fingering the bite marks on the stereo speaker. "What a naughty little ayle you are."

Lati burst out laughing. "You should've seen their faces," she chortled, wiping away tears of mirth. "Shock-o-rama." She picked up Torquil's bass.

"I wouldn't eat that if I were you," said Baby. "I don't think he'd be very happy."

"I wouldn't eat a *bass*," Lati resiled. "What do you take

251

me for?" She twangled the strings while Doll dragged Tristram's drum kit out from the corner and seated herself on the stool. Doll picked up a drumstick, twirled it in the air, and attacked the drums. Digitidigitidigiti. Baby discovered Jake's guitar behind the sofa. She threw on the strap and struck a pose. "One two three four!"

Revor and Iggy were in the midst of a little game called the Gerbil and the Movie Star (Iggy being the Movie Star and Revor the Gerbil) when the girls began to play. Iggy's ears pricked and a smile widened his bullie jaw. His tail began wagging furiously, the movement of his backside evoking muffled groans from Revor. Finally, Revor's little head appeared from its salmon-colored collar. He blinked a few times. Wriggling out, he landed on the floor, shook himself and galloped after Iggy into the lounge, where they positioned themselves in the front row and listened with total absorption, tapping their tails to the beat. "You said they were good," whispered Iggy excitedly, "but you didn't say they were *this* good."

The girls ran through their entire repertoire, including "Comet Karma," "Close Encounter You," "Warped Drive," "In the Sexual Experimentation Chamber (Anything Goes, Everything Cums)," and, of course, the seminal "Hangar 99." They were so absorbed in their jam that they didn't even see Torquil and Jake come in until they'd been standing there for some time.

"That was *filth*," Torquil exclaimed, awed.

"Fully," agreed Jake. He grasped the sides of the doorway to prevent himself from floating away.

On Saturday night, Jake had promised to do the door at the Sandringham for two Canberra bands, Prik Harness and The Angel Pygar. He'd gone to school with the drummer of Prik Harness. He thought Baby might enjoy hearing them and suggested she go too.

Doll was accompanying Skye and Saturna to a CD launch by Pitch Bitch, a new all-woman Goth band. No one was sure where Lati had gone. While dropping acid with the twins on Friday night, she turned into a giant chicken with sparkling blue feathers, flew straight into the television set, and was yet to reemerge. The twins felt they ought to wait for her to return.

About an hour before Baby was due to arrive, Jake tried on all his shirts. He settled finally on a purple paisley polyester number. Being a tad too tight, it looked excellent on his lean frame. He considered striped leggings but opted in the end for red jeans. He gathered his dreadlocks into a ponytail, and studied his reflection in the bathroom mirror. Nup. He shook out the ponytail and swept his dreads up on top of his head, where they fanned out in a magnificent geyser of yellow piping, but decided he wasn't feeling enough in touch with his feminine side at that moment to carry it off. He let them flop back down au naturel, and examined the result. He tweaked one or two till they stood out at interesting angles, and applied a dab of Fudge to ensure they stayed that way. He then rummaged through Saturna and Skye's considerable collection of makeup, smearing concealer on a zit, experimenting with a smidgen of eyeliner, and painting one nail black. He tweaked another dread. He unbuttoned the bottom button on the shirt, buttoned it up, and then unbuttoned it again.

It took just over an hour, but by the time he was finished, Jake managed to look like he'd just rolled out of bed and pulled on the first availables.

Knock knock.

Who's there?

Ali.

Ali who?

Alien.

Jake opened the door and was almost blown backward by the sight of Baby in a silver lamé shift worn over purple tights and basketball sneakers. She'd tied a velvet ribbon around her neck and stacked black and silver bangles on her long green arms. She'd wrapped her braids around her antennae so they stood up in a giant V from her head like a TV aerial. She was the most stunning thing Jake had ever seen in his life.

Upon recovering his breath and balance, Jake searched for the right words to tell her how beautiful she was, how magnificent, how totally fantastic, but also that it wasn't *just* that, it was her talent, her energy, her intelligence, her confidence, her style that made him want to lie down and die at her feet. He wanted to carve the pounding heart from out of his chest and present it to her on a platter. He rehearsed all these thoughts in his head before finally managing to speak. The words came out like this: "What d'ya reckon?" he said. "Should we just head straight to the Sando?"

Baby smiled. She'd read his thoughts. "Yeah, sure," she replied.

At the pub, Jake dragged a small table and two stools over to the doorway. Before he had a chance to fetch the small tray with the stamp and the one-hundred dollar float from the bar, Gregory, noting Baby's presence, sailed over with the tray in hand. "Hi, gorgeous," he greeted Baby, offhandedly passing the tray to Jake without even looking at him. "*Filthy* frock," he added, giving her the once-over.

"Thanks, Greg," Baby purred. "Nice shirt, by the way."

Gregory patted his genuine seventies nylon black-and-white op-art shirt and smiled with intent. "It *is* good, isn't it?"

"Nice to see you too, Greg," Jake interjected, trying not to sound as sour as he felt. She hadn't said anything about *his* shirt, he thought petulantly.

"I like your shirt too, Jake," Baby said, turning her dazzling smile upon him. "I like it a *lot*." It was suddenly as if there was no one else in the room. As if there had never been anyone else in the room.

"Cool. Well, I'll just get back to it, then," Greg said giddily, weaving his way back to the bar.

A tall boy with the hair of an electrocution victim and an Unsane T-shirt shuffled up to the door. "How much?" he said, doing a double take at the sight of Baby.

"Three dollars," Jake answered.

No reply. Unsane was in love. You can't talk when you're in love. Unconsciously, he moved ever so slightly toward her, drawn into her orbit at just the precise moment that, way up in the outer, the asteroid Eros shook himself a wee bit farther out of his. Unsane's mouth opened. His tongue rolled out. His eyes drooped at the outer corners and his cheeks flushed pink.

"Three dollars, mate," repeated Jake. He looked at Baby to see if she was in any way encouraging this moronic display. She appeared oblivious, happily tapping her feet to the music—they were playing *Songs in the Key of X* over the PA—and watching the bands set up.

Unsane tried to remember where he was and why. Curiously, he took in the orange walls of the pub, the stage, the mammoth bar, his own feet. *That's* right. He pulled in his tongue. Speaking slowly, as though coming out of a dream, he asked, "Any concession?"

"Sorry, mate."

Unsane pulled three coins out of his pocket, one at a time, farewelling each individually with tragic eyes. He held out a skinny wrist and Jake stamped it with a little picture of R2D2. He gave Baby one last look of pure devotion and disappeared up the back of the bar.

Next to front up was a sophisticated-looking girl with sparkles on her face and cartoons on her stockings. She was handing over her three dollars when the bouncer stepped in. "ID," he demanded.

"Tosser," pouted the fifteen-year-old, turning on her heels and walking off.

"Friend of the band," announced the next comer, a skinny fellow in a huge Prik Harness T-shirt that said "Choose Satan" on the front and had a cartoon of what Baby recognized as Andromedans on the back.

"Name?"

"Fizzer." He pointed to his name on the list.

"Cool." Jake crossed off the name and stamped his wrist.

"Sorry." Fizzer apologized as he squeezed past Baby and into the venue. His leg accidentally brushed against hers. He jumped as though shocked and, if Jake's eyes weren't deceiving him, the Andromedan on Fizzer's T-shirt suddenly grinned and winked its one eye. Fizzer gulped and hurried on inside.

The person behind Fizzer had been straining to read the list. "Friend of the band," he mumbled, eyes darting every which way.

"Name?" Jake demanded.

"Uh, Chomper."

"Three dollars, mate. Chomper and I are like this." He held up intertwined fingers. "Better luck next time."

The fellow scowled and walked away, muttering under his breath about how he'd complain to someone or other.

"Who's Chomper?" asked Baby, moving her stool a centimeter or two closer to Jake's.

"Fucked if I know," shrugged Jake, hoping she wasn't *just* making more room for the punters. "But the list says 'Stomper.' He read it wrong."

Next in the queue was a clump of crusties. They were standing so close to each other that it looked as though their dreads had all Velcroed together. In fact, that's exactly what had happened. A friend of theirs was supposed to have come over that afternoon to help separate them. But she'd had a few spliffs and forgotten all about it. So they were condemned to another day or two of deep communal living. Which was fine with them. They were into that anyway, even if it was slightly awkward when one of the girls had to go to the toilet. One of them handed over a five and a ten and the entire coagulation shuffled forward, holding out six wrists for stamping. Jake stamped five, and did some sums. "That's another three dollars, mateys."

They grimaced collectively. "That's all we got," a small voice piped up from the center of the cluster. "And we couldn't exactly leave one at home." Jake stamped the sixth wrist. Grunting gratefully, they amoeba-ed into the pub.

At least three others who fronted up claimed to work at the pub, six said they just wanted to use the toilets, and four were "looking for a friend." One explained she worked at the café next door: "We've got an agreement." Another said he just wanted to get a bottle from the bar. Like those who'd only come to use the toilets, he disappeared till the end of the evening.

One young fellow, obviously a student, emptied one pocket of his oversized trousers, which hung perilously around the crack of his arse, placing eighty cents in ten- and five-cent pieces on the small table in front of Jake. Then he emptied the other pocket. The total came to $2.20. He held it out to Jake with a mournful expression. Jake waved him in. He understood. He'd been there. He *was* there.

"This," he explained dryly to Baby, "is the glamorous and exciting world of rock 'n' roll."

Baby didn't pick up on Jake's sarcasm. She was entranced. Earthlings had such peculiar and fascinating rituals. Nufonians would have all just queued up, handed over their three dollars, and gone in without a fuss. If they didn't have three dollars, they'd have stayed at home. She was enjoying every minute.

Prik Harness mounted the stage wearing macramé bikinis. The bikinis would have looked bizarre enough on any woman, but the band was all male. "Why is everyone laughing?" Baby asked Jake. On Nufon, everyone wore macramé bikinis in the summer. Not only were they very practical, but they were aesthetically pleasing against silver skin shimmering under the stars.

A girl with a cheeky grin came to the door, leaned over the table, and whispered, "I have a very large pair of underpants for the band."

Jake waved her in.

"Is underwear an accepted currency in the rock 'n' roll world?" Baby was curious.

Jake considered the question. "Yeah," he replied. "It is, actually." He'd turned back to the door to collect money from a girl wearing a baby doll nightie over woolen stockings, and sucking on a large carrot. Baby smiled at her and she smiled back, her lips stretching around the carrot. Baby felt so at home at moments like this. Aliens and Earthlings weren't all *that* different when it came down to it.

"We wrote this next song for our mate Jake," the drummer announced. Baby looked at Jake, impressed. He was pretty impressed himself. He had no idea they'd written something for him. He tried to look nonchalant, though secretly he was thrilled to death. "It's called the 'Slacker Song,'" explained the drummer. A titter rippled through the crowd. Jake felt mildly alarmed.

"What's a slacker?" Baby asked curiously.

"Some bullshit term invented by the media," he replied. "I could never figure out what it means, myself."

Baby, reading his mind, understood that, whatever slacker meant, Jake privately feared he was a quintessential.

This wasn't something he objected to as a matter of principle, or found particularly offensive, but he did hate being a caricature. It offended his dignity. And even quintessential slackers have a certain amount of dignity.

*I need a cup of coffee*
*but there isn't any milk*
*so I have some cordial*
*and I'm feeling ill.*

*Why am I so tired?*
*Why am I so bored?*
*I couldn't get off my arse*
*to save my own life*

*I need a piece of toast*
*but there isn't any bread*
*so I search through the fridge*
*and eat a carrot instead*

*Why am I so tired?*
*Why am I so bored . . .*

How embarrassing. The crowd greeted the song with huge applause and howls of laughter. A number of people turned, midguffaw, and gave Jake the thumbs up. He did his best to ignore them.

"Are you often bored, Jake?" Baby asked.

"Nup," he replied. "I used to be bored."

"What happened?"

"I got tired of it."

Baby cocked her head. She wasn't quite sure what he meant, but she also suspected he was joking. It was hard to tell sometimes with Earthlings. Personally, Baby didn't see how it was possible to be bored on Earth.

"You should like this next song," he informed her. "It's called 'Space Food.'" He drained the last drops from his bottle of beer and handed the empty to her. He watched as she greedily munched and swallowed it down. He was no longer shocked by her feeding habits even if they still scared him. Baby was beyond a doubt the most astounding woman Jake had ever met. Alien. Hybrid. Whatever.

"Nup," he disabused two boys in grunge beanies. "No discount for Canberrans. Three dollars each, thanks."

He watched her now, listening to the band. He loved the way that, listening or playing, she threw herself into the music. It was so sexy.

At the end of the evening, after repaying the $100 float by the bar, Jake counted out $265.30. The bands paid him $20. "I'm a wealthy man," Jake informed Baby.

She shrugged. "Money can't buy you love," she replied, without meaning to impute anything in particular. Jake felt as though he'd been stabbed in the heart.

"**Look!**" cried a Cherub, bouncing up and down on podgy feet in front of the Space Monitor. "It's the Red Dwarf!"

"Cool!" Next to the *X-Files*, probably the most popular program in the outer was the BBC's *Red Dwarf*, about a mining craft lost in deep space. The craft was populated by one surviving human, a hologram of a dead crew member, and a character who had genetically mutated from a cat.

A Sirian, who'd been lying on the floor of the control room asking Captain Qwerk, "Are we there yet? Are we there yet?" leaped to his feet and gave the Red Dwarf salute, a particularly absurd gesture that involved extending one arm and making a limp-wristed circle with it before snapping it up to the side of the head, military style. Another Sirian, seeing this, laughed so hard he had to be given resuscitation. Meanwhile, more Sirians pogoed around Qwerk, begging him to alter course so Red Dwarf wouldn't see their spaceship. In the TV show, there were no aliens, no other spacecraft, nothing, just space. "You'll ruin it if they see us," they begged.

"We'll lose too much time if we take a detour," argued Qwerk.

"Please please please," they pleaded, swarming around him, stroking his pointy little chin, running tentacles over the thin slit of his silvery mouth, licking his funny little hooves, and pinching his knobbly knees.

"Get off me," exclaimed Qwerk desperately, swatting

them away. "Off me, you mutants!" This only encouraged them.

"We love it when you call us names!" chuckled a Sirian.

"If you don't let me go," Qwerk growled, "I won't be able to swerve away in time and they definitely will spot us." The Sirians were off him faster than you could say "Start Me Up."

**Baby, Doll, and Lati practiced ev—**ery afternoon at the house in Newtown. The saucer had become too much of a zoo for them to concentrate there. Then there was the Ebola plague. At the close of his concert at the Sydney Entertainment Center, Ebola Van Axel stunned his fans with the announcement that he'd be staying in Australia indefinitely. He took up what appeared to be permanent residence by the Sebel pool, leaving a daily tribute of red roses at the base of the water tower, writing "I luv U, Baby" in whipped cream on the deck, and crooning love ballads to the saucer.

Those weren't the only reasons the babes hung out in Newtown, of course. They felt thoroughly at home there. Lots of people had weird hair and green skin in Newtown, especially the morning after a big night out. But mostly, the babes liked being in Newtown because that's where Their Favorite Earthlings were. Doll had decided that she could easily have been a vampire in another life. Lati, meanwhile, had become the best of drug buddies with the twins who, while continuing to lust after her, were always somehow too slack or too stoned to do anything about it.

As for Baby and Jake, they continued to circle each other like birds who couldn't get beyond the mating dance. It had been, what, *three weeks* already. What was this, the 1950s? Baby, who coupled with complete strangers at the drop of an Abduct-o-matic, somehow couldn't bring herself even to give Jake a proper kiss.

She tried to talk to the others about it. Doll curtly replied that she was the last person to consult on a matter concerning Earth boys. Lati, for her part, offered to seduce Jake herself. After all, she wickedly enjoyed reminding Baby, Jake had provided her very first taste of the bodilies. Baby made it abundantly clear that if Lati so much as laid a finger on Jake, she'd find her antennae wrapped around her fucken neck.

To make things even more complicated, Jake and Baby were becoming the closest of friends. They hung out together all the time, played music, laughed, and talked about everything except their feelings for each other.

For his part, Jake was coming to grips with these feelings. He recognized that he was falling more in, uh, whatever, with her each day. He wanted her more than any girl he'd ever met. He even kind of wanted, he'd decided, sort of, a, uh, you know, thing-o. A, uh, relationwhatsee. And, if that happened, he might even give commitment some thought.

Yet he still couldn't bring himself to make a move.

At least there was progress in the musical department. With an alacrity that was almost alarming, the babes were developing a huge repertoire of original songs. Their playing was fast and furious at times, seductively slow at others. It was passion-fueled, spontaneous, rough enough around the edges to be called loose, which was considered a good thing in the rock world, and yet controlled and synchronized enough to be called tight, which was also considered a good thing. Baby's voice was a true chameleon. It could come growling out from under a stone one minute and turn the color of air the next.

But what was truly extraordinary was the way the music actually changed shape according to the desires of the lis-

263

tener. Everyone heard it differently. Saturna and Skye perceived a dark undercurrent, a touch of Marilyn Manson, Siouxsie and the Banshees or Sisters of Mercy. To Jake and the twins, the babes clearly came out of the girl punk tradition of L7 or Bikini Kill with satisfyingly grungy touches like fuzzy guitars and more than a hint of metal. George, whose grasp of the genre was a bit on the vague side, simply understood that they were better than ABBA, or the Rolling Stones, or whatever the group with that Elvis character called itself. Iggy and Revor understood it for the unique skate- and surf-influenced postindustrial grunge-punk-power-pop-acid-funk synthesis that it was.

"Kurt Cobain was right," sighed Torquil after hearing another new song. "The future of rock belongs to women."

It was Saturday and they were all hanging out in the lounge. The phone rang. "I'll get it," offered Tristram.

"Crazy Joe's Rock 'n' Roll Warehouse. No, yeah, that's right. Uh, who's calling?" They could all hear the conversation. "Julia? Let me see if he's here."

By the time Tristram came back into the room, Jake had a pillow over his face. "I take it you're not here?" Tristram asked. Saturna and Skye rolled their eyes.

"Extremely not here," replied Jake from under the pillow. "Like dead or diseased not here. Gone walkies never expected to return not here."

Tristram returned to the phone. "Uh, Julia? He just stepped out for a minute. Can I get him to call you? Yeah, no worries. No, I'm sure he has your number. No, I won't forget. Yeah, I'll tell him."

Back in the lounge, Tristram pulled the pillow off Jake's head and whacked him across the arse with it.

The phone rang. Everyone looked at Jake.

"Want me to get it?" Baby offered.

"Uh, no thanks," demurred Jake, remembering the last time she'd taken a call for him. "I'll get it." He levered himself off the sofa. "Lazy bastards," he addressed the others. The phone was on its seventh or eighth ring by now.

"Hullo?"

"Jake. My man."

"Timtam." It was Tim from Umbillica. Umbillica was to support Bosnia the following evening at the Sando. They were filling in for Smokey Stover, who were doing their annual stint in detox.

"I know it's a bit on the last minute side of things," apologized Tim. "But do you know anyone else who could do the support for you tomorrow?"

"What's happened?"

"Oh, it's sorta embarrassing. My girlfriend's really pissed off at me."

"So? What's new?"

"Yeah, well, she cut off all my hair in my sleep."

"That's a bit foul. It does rather resolve the Metallica problem though."

"And she cut up my clothes with scissors."

"Really? Ripped's a good look."

"And trashed all our instruments."

"Full on. What're ya gonna do?"

"Marry her."

Jake held the telephone receiver away from his ear and screwed up his face at it, incredulous. "Well, that's fine for the short term," he finally said, "but I mean, what about the band?"

"Well, when Styx heard about what she'd done to his drum kit, he decked me. Even if I had my hair, my clothes, and my guitar, I couldn't front up on stage with this doozy of a black eye. Two black eyes actually. I look like some bamboo-cruncher in a Chinese zoo."

"How'd the others take it?"

"Much more civilized. They're just refusing to talk to me."

Jake shook his head. "Bastards."

"I know. It's fucked. But anyway, I was wondering if you could line someone else up or if you wanted us to do it. We should probably call Trace at the Sando in any case and let her know. She's always got zillions of bands with their tongues poised at her arse, just waiting for their big break."

"Timbo, you just whack a few beefsteaks on those shiners and chill. I think I've got just the solution."

"You're a real mate, Jake."

Jake wasn't motivated just by mateship.

"How about Zaygon?" Tristram proposed. "The evil planet in *This Island Earth*?"

Lati stopped munching on a spoon long enough to stick her nose up and her thumb down.

"Scotty?" suggested Torquil, with a drum roll on a soy sauce bottle.

"Too boy," Baby vetoed.

Although it had been Torquil's suggestion, Jake felt himself blush at the rebuff.

"Abduction Theory?" Now Jake was making himself blush.

"Mmm." Baby considered. "Let's put that one on the list."

"Succubus," Skye submitted.

"I like that," Lati conceded. "What's it mean?"

"I'm not sure," admitted Skye, trundling downstairs to find a dictionary.

"How about Spinar Tap?" said Baby.

Torquil laughed. "You mean Spinal Tap. Been done."

"No, Spinar Tap. Don't you know spinars?" Blank looks all round. "They're black hole suns," Baby explained. Didn't Earthlings know anything?

"Black Hole Suns?" repeated Tristram, nonplussed. "Like the Soundgarden song?"

Skye reappeared in a flap of maroon and black velvet. "It's a female demon who fucks men in their sleep," she announced.

Jake choked on his beer.

"What's a female demon who fucks men in their sleep? What are you talking about?" said Tristram, now thoroughly confused.

Lati jumped up from her seat, clambered up onto the table and, clutching the pepper grinder like a microphone, boomed out, "Ladies and gentlemen, I give you the one and only, the magnificent, inimitable, fully fucken fabulous— Rock 'n' roll Babes from Outer Space!"

**Back at Galgal the following af-**ternoon, it was all systems a-go-go as the babes readied themselves for the gig. Doors whirred open and shut as they scurried from one section of the saucer to another, trailed by abductees, searching for outfits, lipsticks, and guitar picks. The saucer was by now a complete brothel— clothing strewn everywhere, graffiti on the walls, Sebel room-service plates and pizza delivery boxes on the floor, and sex toys wherever you looked.

Baby emerged from her room wearing a tartan mini, tight white T-shirt, and black opaques disappearing into ankle-high leather boots. She was doing a catwalk turn for the others' benefit when Revor skirred in, sprang up on her leg, and slid down, ripping her tights with his claws and riddling them with holes and runs. Before she had time to react, he did the same to her other leg.

"Revor's right," Doll nodded. "That's definitely the look." Doll was wearing what she always wore. Leather.

Black. In a concession to stage glam, however, she'd rubbed glitter all through her hair-horns and over her scalp.

They could hear someone calling from outside the saucer. Doll pressed a button and a porthole opened. She peered down. "It's that keck-bag again," she reported.

Baby rolled her eyes. "Better let him in. Otherwise, he'll just stand out there bellowing and drive us all nuts."

Doll sighed. She fiddled with a few more buttons, and the saucer exhaled its magical stairway. Ebola struggled up, unable to get a firm grip on the shifting and ethereal steps.

"Hi, Eb." Baby felt she ought at least to be nice to Ebola. She wasn't the least bit interested in him. She still could not imagine performing even a teeny-weeny sexual experiment upon Eb, what with his collection of ugly silver skull rings setting off the black hair on his pale knuckles, the awful corseting of his paunch in the tight black leather, and his coke-snorter's habit of constantly jerking his head back while sniffling and touching the tip of his nose with his forefinger. If this was love, and he insisted it was, she wanted no part of it. She did enjoy his tales of life as a big-time international rock star, however. She was also happy to satisfy him on one level, for Ebola desired to be as thoroughly abased by her as he had abased thousands of groupies in his time. It was all rather karmic, really.

By the time Eb launched himself into the rumpus room, he was huffing and puffing. "Polish my boots, Eb," she greeted him. Without even stopping to catch his breath, he fell gratefully to the floor, tongue out, and began with the heel.

"I could do a tattoo for you if you want," Doll offered to Baby, ignoring the homunculus at her feet. "We've got time." Doll loved doing tattoos. She practiced on all the Earthlings. By the time Doll packed up her kit, Baby had a shooting star zinging its way around her left bicep, and a rendering of the mothership on her right, adorned with hearts and ribbons and the word "Mum."

Ebola, having finished her boots, watched the tattooing with tears in his eyes. "I'm sharing your pain," he informed Baby. "I really am. I'm here for you, Baby."

"It's been real-o-rama, Eb," Baby replied indifferently. "But we've got to be in Newtown in about half an hour."

"You spend *all* your time in Newtown," Eb whined.

"Yeah, well, we've got a gig tonight."

Ebola jumped up and down, squealing with delight. "Can I come?" he begged. "Can I come?" Doll shook her head decisively. He burst into tears.

Baby telepathed Doll, "Now look what you've done. The guy's more sentimental than a Guns N' Roses ballad."

"There, there," Baby comforted. "We need you to guard the saucer, Eb. It means a lot to us. You just sit there by the pool, and don't let it out of your sight, okay?" She tickled him under his hairy chin. He made a brave effort to smile as a little stream of snot fought its way through the stubble to reach his upper lip. "Good boy, Eb," she praised. "We'll see you later. We've got to find out what Lati's doing." She signaled to Doll and they zapped Ebola back to pool-side.

Entering Lati's room was like walking into a blizzard of clothes. Lati was going through her wardrobe at the speed of light, trying things on, pulling them off, throwing them into the air, retrieving something from the bottom of the pile, and starting all over. A gabble of abductees perched on her Reinvigoration Platform offering spirited and mutually contradictory sartorial advice of which Lati cheerfully took no notice whatsoever. In the end, she donned her favorite Bond T-shirt, jeans, and Converse All-stars, looked into the mirror, and grinned. "That's it," she concluded. Most of the abductees, including Larry, who hadn't left Galgal since being kidnapped nearly three weeks earlier, were coming to the gig. They were almost more excited than the girls.

"Yorp!" Just as they were about to leave, Revor came running up to Baby and nipped at her ankles.

"Go away, Rev. You can't come. They don't allow pets in the Sandringham. Enough. Off." She kicked out her leg and sent him flying. Revor landed upside down with his back against the wall and his head sideways on the floor, looking like some demented yogi.

"You're a strange bean, Rev," said Lati. "Catch ya later."

*All I wanted was a lift to Newtown. Unfair as.*

Weary eyes peered out of a face that was an asymmetric wreck of blue wrinkly skin, bright green lips, and fat orange ears. The eyes stared at a control panel glowing nuclear green, upon which spiraled endless patterns. In the next seat hunched a smaller creature, with the face of a mutant dog and bobbing antennae a foot long, also fixated on a small screen. The third chair was filled by a lumpish beast with simian features topped by a propeller beanie.

Aubrey, a middle-aged Earthling of ordinary appearance, entered the room carrying a tray loaded with scones and tea. He put it down on the console, espied the mutant canine, and threw up his hands in horror. "I married a monster from outer space!" he exclaimed, bending over to nibble on its ear. The dog glanced at her watch, picked up a stick upon which was mounted a small flying saucer, and spun it round. The whirling disc shone blue and green and yellow. "Teatime," she announced, lifting her mask. The others followed suit, and soon they were all fanging appreciatively into the scones.

It was 31 October, and the scientists on duty at Project Beam Me Up, Beam Me Down were celebrating Halloween. Beam Me Up, Beam Me Down was the nickname Professor Luella Skye-Walker and her colleagues had given to a task that was, on a quotidian basis, almost excruciatingly dull, but which had the potential to lead to the most exciting scientific discovery ever. Well, Earthling scientific discovery anyway. They were at Parkes monitoring the very same large satellite dish pictured on those old fifty-dollar bills. The satellite dish that was methodically eavesdropping on several hundred stars in the galactic 'hood to see if anyone out there had anything to say.

"Obe-Wan Kenobi," the cosmic ape greeted Luella's husband, swallowing a scone. "This is a treat."

"Pleasure," replied Aubrey. "So, how many radio channels have you checked today?"

"Twenty-four million, give or take ten thousand."

"Any talkback yet?"

"Nup, but I can see it now," Jason said. "With our luck, we'd finally make contact and it would be with an extraterrestrial John Laws or whatsisface in America, Rush Limbaugh."

The blue-skinned alien, otherwise known as Aaron, was reaching for the strawberry jam when he happened to glance back at his screen. "Hey!" he shouted. "I think we've got something."

"Well I'll be . . ." Plates clattered to the floor, scattering scones and cream.

Ten minutes later, having run a check on "Elmer" (the Follow-Up Detection Device—FUDD), Luella looked up from her equipment, white as a ghost.

"What is it?" Aaron was almost beside himself.

Her face twisted into a funny little smile. "I think they just said, 'Hello, Mum.' "

**Jake's orange Kombi van chugged**
and clunked its way up King Street and lurched to a stop in
front of the Sando. "Good girl, Kate." He patted the dash
and praised her for making the distance.

The girls piled out noisily. Lati elbowed Doll who, upon
seeing what Lati saw, grabbed Baby by the wrist. They all
stared excitedly as Gregory the barman chalked in "Rock
'n' roll Babes from Outer Space" just under "Bosnia."

"Hey, hey," flirted Gregory, looking up, "it's my favorite
purple people-eater."

"How do you know I'm a people-eater?" teased Baby,
raising an alarm in Jake's chest.

"G'day, Gregory," Jake loomed. "Don't let us interrupt
you."

"Interrupt away," smarmed Gregory, checking out Doll
and Lati. "These girls can interrupt me anytime."

"That's us, you know," Lati said importantly, pointing to
the name of the band.

"Is it?" Gregory whistled. "Now I'm *really* looking forward to tonight. Funny I've never heard of you before.
Where d'ya usually play?"

"Their place," Baby replied, jerking a thumb at the boys.

"I bet," smirked Gregory.

Jake, annoyed, extended a possessive hand toward Baby's
back. A charge passed between them, strong enough to
knock Jake off the curb. He nearly crashed into two girls
with pink crew cuts who were so impressed with his acro-
batic display that they gave him the finger. Trying to act as
if nothing had happened, Jake brushed himself off and addressed Baby and the others in a voice he hoped was not
shaking. "Gregory works the bar. You have to be nice to

him, cuz he hands over our money at the end of the night. But not too nice."

Torquil, grunting with exertion, was hauling the drums out of the van and placing them on the pavement. "Careful, they're heavy," he warned Doll, who picked up the entire kit and carried it into the pub as though it were a handbag. Torquil was still trying to slide shut the generic Fucked Kombi Door when Doll reappeared and waved him aside. She stretched the metal frame with her bare hands, slipped the door back into its slot, slammed it shut, and readjusted the frame.

"You," palpitated Torquil, "are a *groover*."

Kate the Kombi was thinking the same thing.

Observed with idle curiosity by a handful of drinkers who'd been at the bar since early that arvo, the bands began setting up on the makeshift stage—strips of carpet laid over thin boards balanced on a great array of milk crates, all crammed up in one corner and shaped to accommodate the overwhelming central bar. Lati, Doll, and the twins finished first, and went to the back room to play some pinball. Jake and Baby were still kneeling at the front of the stage, plugging in the guitar pedals. "What's that one called?" she asked.

"Tube screamer."

Baby hooted with laughter. "Tube screamer? *Tube screamer?*"

"I better get some gaffer tape," mumbled Jake, feeling uncharacteristically embarrassed. "If you go wild it's better to have the cables taped to the stage." He fled.

Baby was still giggling to herself when an intense young man wearing jeans and a black Frenzal Rhomb T-shirt advanced upon her with squeaking sneakers and a vague air of menace. His long lank hair was gathered in a loose ponytail at the back. The great clutch of keys, Maglite torch, and mobile phone jangling from his studded belt made him seem like some sort of rock 'n' roll prison warden. He came to a halt about a meter from where she knelt. Staring emotionlessly into her eyes, he raised his hands and clapped sharply. And again. And once more.

Baby raised her hands and clapped back.

Mr. Frenzal shook his head dismissively. "You don't do that. *I* do that."

"Who are you and why do you do that?" Baby wasn't sure whether to grab her crotch in greeting or not. From the response she got on the street, she'd gathered it wasn't always appropriate. Earthlings were so complicated. On Nufon, whenever you met someone, you simply put your hands on your hips, bent over to the left and stamped your right hoof twice. The all-occasions greeting. Here it was "Wanna suck my cock?" one minute, "How are you today, ma'am?" the next, and now clapping. How was anyone supposed to negotiate this social maze?

"I'm testing the resonant frequency in the room," explained the hand-clapper self-importantly. "I'm Henry. The mixer."

"Mixer?" said Baby. Her translation chip was giving her: nonalcoholic component of a cocktail; kitchen gadget; a person adept at mingling. "Are you adept at mingling then? Or are you just a tonic?"

Henry raised an eyebrow. He knew it wasn't said aloud these days, but Henry believed the proper place of chicks in rock 'n' roll was in front of the stage, screaming at the band. Or chatting up the mixer. Sucking in his cheeks to deepen his expression of grave misgiving, he retreated to the mixing board, flicked a few switches, and adjusted the faders. Then he rubber-soled back over to the stage.

Glancing at the amp, Henry shook his head. "I can't believe you're using a Marshall," he said. "It's such a rock 'n' roll cliche. I mean, Little Richard, Jimi Hendrix, Red

Hot Chili Peppers, Pearl Jam—everything sounds the same with a Marshall."

"But what—"

"I know, I know, most amps only go to ten and Marshall goes to eleven. I've seen *Spinal Tap* too. Frankly, if you want my advice, I'd use one of the lesser-known brands if I were you. You're looking for a distinctive sound, aren't you? Take Sovtek for instance," Henry steamrolled on. "Made in Russia from old tank parts. Or so they say. I like to believe it."

"What's the diff—?"

"Well, for one thing, Sovtek's got a crunchier distortion, more bottom-end drive . . ." Henry crapped on, and on, and on.

Baby's head was hurting. Her translation chip was giving her static. She couldn't make heads or tails of what Henry was saying.

"Sound check," is what he was saying now. "Shall we do a sound check? Or do you want to just stand there and let me imagine what your levels will be like?"

"Uh, what should I do?"

Henry rolled his eyes. "Play me something," he said. He went back to the desk. She'd no sooner started when he came flying across the room, waving his hands. "Wind your tops down," he ordered her. "It's too sharp. You're cuttin' my ears off." Baby began again. He was back in a flash. "Turn your volume down a bit. You're *way* too loud," he complained. "It's only a small room. You don't have to be that loud." Each word pricked another one of the lovely translucent spheres that made up Baby's bubbly confidence.

Where the hell was Jake? She slipped the Locate-a-tron out of her bag and with nervous fingers, hammered in his code. At the head table of a state banquet in Canberra, the wife of a very important government leader suddenly let rip with what sounded like the mother of all farts. Whoops! Wrong number. By the time Baby had worked out what had happened, Jake had returned with the tape. Baby clutched at his arm. Jake could have sworn she was burning neat little holes in his skin where her fingertips were gripping. He could almost smell the scorched flesh. "Jake," she whispered, "I'm nervous. I don't know what I'm doing."

"It's only rock 'n' roll," he reassured her, yanking his arm away before it turned into kebab meat. Immediately, he panicked at the thought that she'd misunderstand and think he didn't like her touching him. He loved her touching him. In theory anyway. If she could only wind down her tops first, that'd be ideal. "You don't *have* to know what you're doing," he said. "You just play."

"Just play?" she repeated despairingly, thinking, why'd he pull his arm away like that? Didn't he like her touching him? She was so agitated she neglected to read his mind. "Just play. It's that easy, is it?"

"Baby. If anyone makes it look that easy, you make it look that easy," Jake declared honestly, if somewhat distractedly.

Of course it was easy. She knew it was easy. What a silly little panic attack she was having. God! Why was she going on like this?

*It's simple, really, Baby. Basic Earthling psychology. A case of the Pseudo Blues. You're just using stage fright—a concept that is really just about as alien to you as, oh, staying drug-free for whole days at a time would be to your fluffy-headed friend here—as an excuse. What you really want is to get close to Jake. Don't ask Me why. Personally, I don't see the attraction. Not My type. Then again, few Earthlings are. Anyway. This schmuck Henry was clearly trying to intimidate you for his own, pathetic, ego-related reasons, and you were letting him in order to generate a minor crisis. Your hope in doing so was to rouse Jake from his characteristic emotional torpor so that he could assume a heroic posture, to save you, as it were, thus generating a sense that you'd been through something crucial together. Which would give you a good excuse to jump him.*

I see. You're so wise and all-knowing. What do you think I should do now?

*How the fuck should I know? I may be omniscient, but I'm not an advice columnist in some woman's magazine, for My sake. Figure out what you really want to say, what you really want to do. Say it. Do it. Be happy, don't worry. And, if that's all, I've got a sound check for a supernova I'm organizing on the other side of the yoon. Should be spectacular. I've abducted the guy who usually does the lighting for the Nine Inch Nails to help out with effects.*

Cool. Hey, thanks a lot, God.

*Catch ya round like a rissole.*

Baby focused her big, watery green eyes on Jake. She lowered her head and a tangle of pink and orange braids tumbled endearingly in front of her face, mixing in with the violet bangs. She managed a pathetic but thoroughly charming smile. "I don't know shirt," she murmured.

"That's shit," Jake corrected. " 'I don't know shit.' "

"*You* know shit, Jake. Don't give me that." A flirtatious tone had returned to her voice.

Jake wasn't sure how to take this. The joint he'd smoked when he stepped out for the gaffer tape was just beginning to kick in. He looked at Baby curiously. Who *was* she? She seemed very large at this moment, not just physically but psychically. She was *huge*. Why was she accusing him of knowing shit? What did he know? And why was she *green*?

What did it all *mean?* Par. Ah. Noy. Ah. Par. Ah. Noy. Ah. No! No! Don't hit me! Aaaaaah.

"You should see the expression on your face," laughed Torquil.

Jake jumped. "Don't sneak up on me like that, man," he sulked.

Torquil shook his head and watched Doll and Lati clamber on stage for their sound checks. "Oh, man, you ever play pinball with Doll? She's *awesome.*"

Lati tuned her bass and struck a few chords. "Oi! Henry! I can hear a bit of high and ring. Fix it, will you?"

Henry nodded and gave her the thumbs up. To Doll, who was bashing away at her drums, he advised, "I could put a short gate on it with a bit of delay to fill it out if you want."

"Yeah," she responded authoritatively, "make it about 1.5 seconds with a 35 millisecond delay."

"Cool," said Henry. "Done."

Baby looked at Lati and Doll in wonderment. Where'd *they* learn to talk like that?

Read their minds, Doll telepathed. It's that simple. Piece o' cake, these Earthlings, piece o' cake.

What's that mean, piece o' cake?

Fucked if I know.

Baby felt another surge of anxiety. She tugged on the hem of Jake's T-shirt. "We have to talk."

"What about?" Oh, no. Oh no. Not a *relationship* talk! Oh yes. "Us."

Aaaaaaargh. Help! Help! The threat of serious interpersonal communication, particularly of the "about us" kind, always triggered Jake's fight or flight reaction, even when he wasn't ripped off his tits. The fact that he had decided, pretty much anyway, that Baby was the one girl he loved, or something like that, made no difference to his primal instincts. He struggled to keep his legs from pedaling. "Mm?" he responded, with a forced smile and a sound akin to that of a strangulating cat as the knot of paranoia rose from his stomach. "Maybe later would be—"

"Jake. Not later. Not indefinite future. Now. Now. Now. I am getting, as you say, *angsty*."

"Maybe we should find someplace a bit more private," he stalled, looking around for a bolt-hole. He pointed to the back room just beyond the pool table, where the pinball and video machines were. They found the room empty except for Ozone, a member of another rock band. Ozone sat hunched over Major Strike, a video game that was like a golf tournament, but better, because you didn't actually have to go out into the fresh air or lug anything heavy around to play it. Ozone's hair looked like it had just escaped the laboratory of the mad scientist who'd created it. He was wearing a green polyester shirt, a greasy brown suit jacket, jeans, and Blundstones. A cigarette hung out of the side of his mouth. His eyes were bloodshot and puffy and, although he was just past thirty, too many late nights and too many weird chemicals had etched hard lines into his face. "Oi. Jake," he mumbled in greeting, slugging at his beer and jiggling the game levers.

"Oze," Jake replied, grateful for the diversion. "My man." Jake studied the screen over Ozone's shoulder. "Shit. Water hazard."

"*Jake*," Baby fumed.

"Just a tick. Crucial shot coming up here."

Baby's impatience was causing her ichor to boil. This, in turn, set off a chain reaction of riotous electrical impulses. Jake hardly had time to wonder at the current running up his spine when there was suddenly a loud explosion and smoke billowed out of the top of the golf game.

"Jesus Christ!" exclaimed Ozone, falling off the stool. Jake had flown backward and landed on the seat of a motorcycle race simulator. If he was getting paranoid earlier, he could definitely be said to have got it now. All three watched in silence as flames licked out the top of the game. The screen cracked and the small animated figure wielding a club began to melt down. His happy little face transmogrified into a mask of terror.

"Now do I have your attention?" Baby ground the words out from between gritted teeth.

"Barbecue!" cried Doll and Lati, attracted by the smell of melting hardware. Grabbing a handful of hot metal each, they went back to the pub's main room.

Ozone lay in fetal position on the floor, shaking like a leaf. "I nevva shudda left ennay," he slurred.

Baby's Transling-a-tron was shorting out. She looked at Jake, who had righted himself and was trying desperately to appear as though he'd only ever been leaning suavely against the motorcycle seat. "Who's Ennay?" she asked. "His girlfriend?"

"NA," he grimaced. "Narcotics Anonymous." Jake recoiled from this particularly uncomfortable vision of the rock 'n' roll future.

"I feel terrible," she said, abashed. "I was the causatrix of all this. Guilt-o-rama. But what's an anonymous narcotic? And do you think we should effect him to be vertically postured again?"

Jake bent down and slipped his hands into Ozone's armpits, perceptibly damp even through the jacket, and hauled. And hauled. "Oof," he groaned. "I don't think I can lift him."

"Move aside, Earth boy," said Baby. She looked Jake in the eyes, and did a quick mind scan. Holy Hyperion, what a mess it was in there! It was the psychic equivalent of his room. Lurking in the corners were men with evil faces, trench coats, and switchblades, hissing, "Jay-ake! Jay-ake! We're coming to get you!" Something had to be done. Baby shook her head, focused her antennae, aimed, and fired.

BOOM! Jake instantly felt as though someone had dunked him in a great big bathtub of warm milk upon which floated fragrant rose petals.

Oh, how he loved it when she called him "Earth boy!" He watched with a soft and gooey expression as she hooked a finger under Ozone's collar and gently brought him up to standing position.

Oh, man, she was cool. She was more than cool. She was . . . she was . . . she was whatever it was when you were *more* than cool. *More* than kyool. She *was*.

She was letting go of Oze's collar. Staring at her with uncomprehending, pinned eyes, Ozone crumpled back down on the floor.

"He'll be right," Jake said, smiling stupidly. "He spends a lot of time on floors." He looked at Baby with unadulterated tenderness shining out from his big browns.

"Ready to talk?" she said sweetly.

Jake nodded.

"I'm not quite sure how to say this, Jake, but I think there's something that's standing between us."

Jake looked at the space between them.

"It's sex."

He looked harder. Then he looked up. "Sex?"

"You know how I mentioned that we'd already had sex?"

"Uh, yeah," Jake squirmed. "I seem to recall you saying something like that, now that you mention it, yes."

"I wanted to clean the air."

"Clear."

"Sorry?"

"That's 'clear the air.' "

"Whatever. Anyway. You see, we sort of abducted you and—"

"Hey, green girl." Groovy Gregory popped his head in the room. "You're on in five." He lounged against the door frame and registered the awkward silence that ensued.

"Hope I didn't interrupt anything," he said, hoping exactly the opposite.

"—we, uh, performed a number of sexual experiments on you." She glanced up at Greg. She certainly had the attention of both of them now.

"Piss off, Greg," suggested Jake, adding, "and you know I mean that in the nicest possible way."

Gregory shrugged and off-pissed, flashing five fingers at them as he went. He didn't like heavy scenes anyway.

Jake returned his attention to Baby. What had she just said? *Jesus*. "Like, what sort of experiments?" And did that somehow, he thought with a shudder, explain his ridiculously itchy behind?

"Uh, yes, it does. We, uh, inserted a homing device up there," she answered, looking at the floor. Jake blushed bright scarlet, a sight that even his own mother would have paid good money to see. "Want me to take it out?" she offered. "I mean, we know how to find you now, and all."

Jake's hands instinctively flew to cover his arse. "Later," he mumbled. "But, tell me. What exactly did these experiments involve? Are there any photos?"

"Videoed the whole thing. Uh, but we use Betamax in the outer, so, like, you'd have to come to our place if you wanted to view it."

"Right. I see." He was trying to take all this in. "Was it all three of you?" This was not an unpleasant thought.

"Yeah. No. Four, actually. Revor was in it too."

The blood drained out of Jake's face. "What—" On second thought, he didn't think he really wanted to know. That thing had sex with *Iggy*, for Christ's sake. Eeeyurgh. Be cool, he told himself. Be cool. "So," he asked as jauntily as possible under the circs, "did I enjoy it?"

Gregory reappeared. "You're on," he said to Baby.

"Yes," she informed Jake, turning to follow Gregory into the bar area. "I believe you did."

It suddenly occurred to Jake that maybe that's why he found it so hard to make a move with Baby. He'd already *had* sex with her. He'd always found it difficult committing to a second time.

Baby stepped up to the mike and looked around at the dozen or so punters. The abductees, a motley crew if ever there was one, were flashing besotted grins. Two girls with leopard-print hair had parked their skinny arses on the ledge by the window and were skimming indifferently through the fanzines piled up there. One or two of the crusties from two weeks before, having been liberated from their hairlock, stared expressionlessly at the stage from under floppy dreads.

"We're the Rock 'n' roll Babes from Outer Space," Baby announced to desultory applause, most of which came from the abductees, the Bosnia boys, Saturna, Skye, and Gregory. "First up we'd like to do a kind of love song." Inadvertently she found herself looking at Jake when she said the word "love." Jake looked away. What else could he do? How could he possibly look at her at a moment like that? With her sharp eyesight, Baby caught one of the girls in the corner rolling her eyes at the words "love song."

"Close Encounter You!" she roared. Doll, who'd taken off her leather jacket and was wearing a black T-shirt with the sleeves ripped off, attacked the drums furiously. The muscles in her lithe arms flexed and rippled. Lati swooped in on the bass, dipping her shoulders and shaking her head from side to side with the beat. Baby came in on her guitar. The song was fast, furious, and yet instantly memorable.

> *I had a dream*
> *about a hill*
> *about a boy*
> *about a girl*
> *you weren't there*

*in the light*
*you weren't there*
*on the hill*
*I want you in my vision*
*I want you in my night*
*I wanna*
*Close encounter you*

By the second verse, the cat girls had put down their zines, jumped into the space in front of the stage, and were throwing themselves bodily into the music. The crusties had wrestled their dreads out of their eyes and the serious drinkers at the bar focused their bloodshot orbs on the babes. By the time they launched into their second song, "Space Dogs," the pool players had abandoned their game. Even Ozone managed to haul himself up off the floor and was leaning on the wall by the bar, an expression of total awe on his face.

On stage, the three girls exchanged animated glances. It was working! Then, bizarrely, just as they started their third song, the pub began to empty out, leaving only Jake and the twins, Saturna and Skye, and the faithful abductees. Jake felt himself break into a cold sweat, as though it were his own band dying on stage. Torquil and Tristram fidgeted in unison. They couldn't understand it. The Babes were fucken brilliant. The energy pulsed off the stage in great waves, they played like they'd been at it for years, they were sex in motion, and the songs had hard rocking cred and excellent hooks. Why was everyone running away?

The answer came by the start of the fourth song. Every single person who had run off now reappeared, dragging in tow entourages of friends, flatmates, colleagues, case workers, even complete strangers they'd run into on the street. On King Street, cafés were emptying, and other pubs and clubs deserted as the intense gravitational pull of the babes' alien charisma sucked half the population of Newtown into the Sando. Soon, the pub was so packed out that the walls were beginning to bend under the pressure.

Wham! Bam! "And how are *you* today, ma'am?" Baby yelled out to the newcomers as she introduced the next song, "AstroTurf." If the babes were *cooking*—hot as—the punters were broiling and baking and steaming. Those lucky enough to get a view didn't care if they were turning into dim sum. If they ended their lives the following morning on a wheeled trolley somewhere in Chinatown, it would have been worth it. One person, then another, then another, clambered onto the bar to dance until there was no space to rest a beer. Others hung from the rafters, shimmied up the columns, perched on the pokies and pinball machines.

There was Doll, arms a blur, head banging, choppin' out on the toms, sending the beat straight into people's feet. Lati swayed and dipped infectiously over her bass, teasing amazingly complex rhythms out of those four simple strings. Baby, for her part, and her part was major, was one-thousand-watt electric ladyland. The punters up the front could have sworn they saw sparks streaming out from her antennae. Her guitar was a magic wand. She was a cater-wauling Janis Joplin one minute, a soulful PJ Harvey the next, a riot grrrrl and a pop queen, with the hell-raising outrageousness of a premakeover Courtney Love thrown in for good measure. She was a red hot chili pepper, a smashing pumpkin, a delicious bowl of pearl jam, an entire, blooming one-woman soundgarden.

> *I wanna fold you in my bionic arms*
> *Wanna smother you with space-girl charms*
> *Wanna switch on all of your alarms*
> *Comet karma, Earthling of my dreams.*

Those who couldn't squeeze inside pushed their faces against the windowpanes. It became so wild out there that the police were called to clear King Street for traffic. The coppers ended up leading an impromptu dance party on the pavement that leached down several side streets.

"Who *are* these girls?" was the question on every pair of lips.

Jake's elation at their success was tinged with foreboding. He'd be in for some pretty stiff competition on the Baby front before long.

The last song of their set, "In the Sexual Experimentation Chamber (Anything Goes, Everything Cums)" went down like *cunnilingus*. YUM! screamed the punters. YUM! "We're the Rock 'n' roll Babes from Outer Space," said an elated Baby, soaking up the cheers and applause like a solar cell taking in rays. "Thank you very much. Bosnia will be on after a short break."

"More!" screamed the punters. "More!" The pub shook with the stomping of boots and clapping of hands. "More! More!"

Baby looked over at Jake questioningly. He shrugged assent. On the one hand, it was fantastic. He couldn't remember the last time he'd seen a support band besieged for an encore. On the other hand, it was a hard act to follow, and he had to follow it. The Babes finished up with a cover of the Stones' "2000 Light Years from Home."

Bosnia opened with their crowd-pleaser, "Away with the Paxies," a song voicing sympathy for a family of welfare recipients that the government and media had picked on for refusing to take mind-deadening jobs requiring ugly haircuts and the wearing of spewsome uniforms. The family had become national heroes for a significant portion of the population. All of Newtown, for instance. The crowd was so thoroughly warmed up by the Babes that it gave Bosnia the best reception the band had ever received. Baby, Doll, and Lati, besieged by fans, tried to do the right thing and at least look like they were listening to Bosnia. It wasn't easy.

After it was all over, Henry came over and solemnly shook the hand of each of the babes. "It was an honor," he mumbled, turning and exiting with dignity.

When Greg finally turned on the lights and shooed the last drinkers out of the pub, the two bands, dazed by the success of the evening, packed up and lugged out in near silence. Jake and Baby dismantled the stage—a ritual for bands playing the Sando—and were hanging round the bar waiting to get paid.

"Well," said Jake. "Well, well." It had been quite a night.

Torq and Trist, who'd been packing up the van with Doll, wandered back inside. "Where's Lati?" asked Baby. "Isn't she with you?"

"She's moved on," said Torq mournfully.

"To bigger and better things," added Tristram pathetically.

"To triplets," Doll clarified, "with a fast car."

"No way," Jake stifled a laugh.

"Way," said Torquil.

"Definitely way," confirmed Tristram. "She even persuaded them to let her drive. Laid down a strip of rubber several meters long. Unbelievable."

"That's how we know it was a fast car."

Doll sniggered. Baby looked worried. Like Baby, Lati had been banned from driving for life on Nufon.

"What a gal," sighed Doll.

Greg handed over the two hundred dollars the bands had been promised and then an extra one-hundred-fifty-dollar bonus. "That's for packing it out, guys," he said, looking at the girls.

"Kyoool," Jake exhaled, starting to divide up the money. He stopped. He put one hundred dollars in one pile on the bar, and two hundred fifty dollars in another, which he pushed toward Doll and Baby. "You earned the bonus."

Doll looked at Baby. "We wouldn't have been here if it weren't for you." She pushed it back.

Torquil and Tristram held their breath. "Let's go halves then," Jake said reasonably. "And our shout for drinks at Sleepers. We'll do cocktails. You'll love the margarita glasses."

**On a deserted road outside of Wol-**longong, a police siren whoopwhooped out of nowhere. Blue and red flashed in the rearview. "Shit!" chorused the triplets. "Stop the car, Lati," said Bob or Rod or Rob.

Lati shrugged and applied the brakes. The car went into a dramatic spin. Jerking hard on the wheel of the police car, Sgt. Alvin Pepa just managed to avoid crashing into them. When all bodies in motion finally came to a rest, the triplets had turned green as an Alpha Centaurian's toenails. Lati let loose a scale or two of wild xylophonic laughter and Sgt. Pepa stormtrooped over with one hand on his gun.

"Wanna suck my cock?" Lati greeted him.

"Better get a lawyer, son," he exploded at her.

"I know that song," Lati chirped, still exhilarated by her little joyride. "Cruel Sea, yeah?"

"License and registration."

"Who do you think you are—God?" Sassy *as.*

Sgt. Pepa was losing patience fast. "Out of the car." He waved his gun at her by way of emphasis. "Put your hands in the air."

"I know that one too—silverchair." Lati blew him a kiss. "Just kidding. Doan go off yer crumpet." Of all the babes, Lati was quickest with the local lingo. Ignoring the desperate, triplicated signals of caution emanating from her fellow travelers, she grinned at Sgt. Pepa, a big, juicy, magic, knock-them-Earthlings-dead alien grin.

Sgt. Pepa blinked. His anger drained out of him quicker than you could say "Lonely Hearts Club Band." In its place he felt himself filling with love and peace. Lati was the most beautiful woman he'd ever seen in his life, more beautiful even than Lily the dental hygienist who'd give him his first sexual experience, in the chair, when he was fourteen, more beautiful than his wife's sister in her red suspender belt and stockings, more beautiful even than Guy Pearce in *Priscilla*. He struggled to keep his mind on the job. He looked at the registration. "Uh, you're only registered to, oh, that's this year," he said. Pepa struggled to remember what he was supposed to be doing. "Guess that's all in order then." He sank to his knees.

"How'd you do that?" whispered Rod or Rob or Bob admiringly, stepping out of the car for a better look.

Lati ignored the question. "Eat me," she commanded, addressing Sgt. Pepa and spreading herself out for delectation on the hood of the car. The car glowed, imperceptibly at first, but with a brighter and brighter light. Small welts erupted in the paint where it came in contact with Lati's skin. Lati was *hot*. The sight of Sgt. Pepa in his cute little Earthling uniform, on his adorable big Earthling knees, had already been enough to excite the formation between her legs—more or less—of something for him to eat. To the triplets, she remonstrated, "Don't go away. You're next. And pass me an E, will you?"

"Allow me," said Sgt. Pepa gallantly, retrieving one from his shirt pocket as he shuffled forward on his knees across the bitumen. "We, uh, carried out a bit of a raid earlier this evening. Good stuff, I believe. Very pure."

"How many pairs of handcuffs do you have, sir?" asked Bob or Rob or Rod. Sgt. Pepa looked over as though seeing them for the first time. Three identical young men with lean muscular builds, randomly chopped hair dyed platinum blond, big blue eyes, red bow lips like those of angels—or, Lati thought with a smile, Cherubim—stretched over clean white teeth.

"Enough to go around," replied the policeman suggestively.

"Around what?" chorused Rob and Bob and Rod with a mischievous twinkle in their eyes, taking the suggestion.

Lati didn't make it back to the saucer for three days.

*Your faithful reviewer had a bit of truble waking up on Sunday morning, evening, whatever, and got to the Sando just as the chicks from Rock 'n' roll Babes from Other Space (dig the antennas, girls!) were halfway through their set. Someone at the bar told me they came from the Planet Newfon, but maybe he just said Planet Newtown. Newtown's sort of a planet unto itself, yeah? But getting back to the Babes, where have they been all my lyfe? Their sound is muscular and all-woman and taught and connected right to people's heads with killer hooks. My predicktion: these babes are going to go astrological.*

*I have to add, they're acid for the eyes. Oh, Baby Baby if you'll pardon the pun. Ladee's a Hole nuther thing entirely, yeah, that girl's definitely the Oz answer to the Courtney question. And Doll—love that snarl! Not that looks should be a factor in girls Becoming rock stars or anything. But I've never seen such sexual energy mulching off a single stage, male or female, and I've seen Paige and Plant (only kidding). Seriously, the Babes connect in a big way.*

*Bosnia's amp blewe in the middle of their fourth song, but they were riding on the excellent vibes which the Babes had filled the room and no one seemed to mind much. The rhythm twins were in fine fourm, and lead man Jake was fully intent, which*

*was good to see him into the music like that because sometimes
it's like he seems almost too likeadaisacle or something. Oh
shit, Bosnia's the lead band and I shoulda given them much
more space but sorry, guys, I'm outta room. Catch ya next
time.*

*Des Blight,* On the Drum

Iggy lay on his back. Revor was stretched out on top of him and, by gently wriggling, they were slowly rubbing all their nipples together. Considering Iggy had six and Revor seven, three of which were now pierced, this was a particularly sensual exercise. "Mmmm. That feels sooooo good, little fellow. Wutda wuld nee dsnow . . ."

Like all lovers, Iggy and Revor were developing a language of their own.

"Reen gmay bhel," Revor replied, "Shug ga pye hunn yeeboon ch. Mind scratching behind my left ear for me? Ahh. That's it. Ta." His eyes were spiraling like pinwheels in a cyclone.

Iggy laughed. "Oh, Rev," he sighed, looking into those mad little orbs. "Ever heard the Underground Lovers' song 'Your Eyes'? They wrote it for you." Iggy bounced Revor off, rolled over, gently swatted him to the ground, took one of his three lemony nipples in his teeth and nibbled. "Yaw eiff, yaw eiff . . ." he hummed, his lips vibrating against Revor's tummy, causing him to gasp and giggle.

"Eiwan na seeyoos wing!" cried Revor breathlessly.

"Eiwan na seeyoos ing," replied Iggy contentedly from between closed jaws.

"There they are," Saturna motioned to Skye. Skye stood

on tippy toes and peered over Saturna's shoulder at the two pets, curled up together in the junk closet. She stifled a giggle at the sight.

Back downstairs in their room, Saturna lit a musk candle and bent to kiss Skye on the side of her neck, where Doll's latest bite mark was still healing. "Let me put some aloe vera on that, Dark One," she said.

"Pets and girls," Skye mused, as Saturna massaged the ointment into her skin. "At least there's two categories of life form in this house that don't have problems with the concept of relationships."

"We're only on this Earth for a short time," Saturna replied, wiping her hands and turning down the bed's black satin sheets. "It's foolish not to make the most of it."

"You know, the funny thing is, I do believe that Jake thinks that in his own way, he *is* making the most of it."

"Maybe he is," Saturna conceded, unzipping Skye and watching layers of velvet and lace slither sensuously to the floor around her naked ankles. "Maybe he is."

Jake had a full day planned for Monday. First, he needed to pop into the bank and check that his dole money had come through. Then . . . well, that was about it, really. He set the alarm so he could get an early start. The telephone woke him first. Trring. Trring. Jake groaned and pulled the pillow over his head. Trring. Trring. He dragged the pillow off again and listened grog-gily for the pitter-patter of other feet going to answer the phone. Silence on the pitter-patter front. Trring. Trring. Maybe whoever was calling would give up. Hold on! Maybe whoever was calling was Baby! Wrapping a towel around his waist, Jake made a mad dash for the phone. Before picking up the receiver, he let his breathing settle. "Uh, hel-lo?" he murmured, playing the sexy sleepy voice thing for all it was worth. In his experience, it was virtual big bucks.

"That Jake?"

He knew the voice. It was Tracy, the woman who booked bands for the Sandringham. Blunt as the needle on an old gramophone, Tracy didn't have much time for niceties. Like "Hello," for instance. He pictured her sitting in her little office above the bar, a cigarette dangling out of the corner of her black lipsticked mouth, one hand threading through her unruly shag—an *ironic* haircut—the other white-knuckling the receiver as though it might run away if she loosened her grip.

"That's Jake," he confirmed with a sigh, sexy dropping out and leaving sleepy to handle the call.

"D'I wake you? It's Trace."

"Mm. Wozza time?" His tone was reproachful.

"Eleven-thirty," she snapped. Tracy was not easily intim-idated. Her job involved saying *no means no* to any number of rock wannabes who made up with persistence what they lacked in talent and originality. "Not exactly the crack of dawn, Jake," she observed dryly, taking a drag on her ciga-rette. "I think you need a *real* job."

Jake let that one go. He knew it was her standard way of stirring musicians. No one got up before well into the after-noon if they didn't have to. She should know that. "Waz-zup?" he yawned.

"Heard the gig on Sunday went *off*," she whistled. "Best response we've ever had to anything since I've been here anyway, and that certainly feels like a lifetime and a half." Tracy was twenty-five. She'd been booking the Sando for four months. "So I'm not gonna hassle you for not letting me know about the change in lineup. You know the drill. Anyway, we want both bands back as soon as possible. Week Saturday's the earliest I can book you in. Howzat suit?"

"Yeah, great," said Jake, cheered. Saturday night. That was a real break. Bosnia had been doing occasional Sundays and weekdays for ages.

"Wanna give me a contact for Rock 'n' roll Babes from Outer Space?"

"I can pass on the message. I'll be seeing them. They don't actually have a phone."

"Joking! Not even a mobile?"

"Nup."

"Unbelievable. Uh, Jake. Mate."

Jake pursed his lips philosophically, waiting for the blow. When some people called you "mate" it didn't mean "friend." It could mean sucker, wallie, dickhead, fuckwit. It could also mean the speaker, the mater, as it were, needed a favor from the matee and, what's more, knew it wasn't exactly going to make the matee's day.

"I'd, uh, like to have the Babes headline. You'll be the support, mate."

" . . ."

"Is that okay with you?" Her tone implied it didn't really matter if it wasn't.

"Yeah, whatever," he replied. One part of him, the not-that-I'm-looking-for-it-or-anything-but-if-success-came-knocking-on-my-door-I'd-say-come-in-dude-where-you-been-my-whole-life part, was outraged. "What?" it frothed. "We've been at this for years and these girls blow in and we encourage them and help them and get them their first gig and then we just stand back and watch while they shoot on past?" Then there was the Unreconstructed Male that lurked in the dark corners of even the most enlightened psyche and came up with sentiments as embarrassing as they were unspeakable. Like, but *they're GIRLS for fuck's sake! And we're BOYS! It's not fair! It's not fair!* But another part and, happily, the biggest part of Jake, was clapping its flippers and spinning a ball on its nose out of pure glee. The Babes were awesome and Baby was *so* cool. She was a fucken star and he'd be happy just tuning her guitar. And besides, maybe when he told her, she'd give him a big kiss, and one thing would lead to another and one thang would lead to another and . . .

"Week Saturday then."

"Week Saturday."

Slipping back into bed, Jake found it hard to fall asleep. He sat up, rolled his dreads for a while, and surveyed his clothing kingdom. He leaned over the side of the bed, searched for the least filthy pair of underpants, examined them briefly, turned them inside out and pulled them on. One of these months, he really needed to do his laundry.

Maybe not. The Newtown Festival was not far off. Two years ago, at the height of their sewing phase, Torquil and Tristram had made up a huge swag of clothes to sell there, and stuffed them into one of those big green garbage bags the night before. But on the morning, being not much better at mornings than Jake, they accidentally grabbed the wrong bag, the one with all their laundry. As it turned out, they sold every last piece, even items of underwear so crispy they crackled, and socks that not only were capable of walking down the street on their own, but had developed full-blown personality disorders. As it turned out, the twins were able to keep for themselves the clothes they'd sewn, and still made enough profit to buy new daks, a case of beer, and a dozen CDs. They never looked back. In fact, they looked forward to a Golden Age when all the people of Newtown—for only in Newtown was such a thing conceivable—simply passed on to each other their old clothes, and thus regularly acquired new wardrobes without ever needing to wash them. The following year Jake had chipped in his soiled clothes as well as his sheets. Shit. He still hadn't replaced the sheets. He'd have to get some new ones if Baby was to . . . if they were to . . .

Jake considered this possibility in detail. He pushed and pulled and rubbed and stroked it. Mmmmm. Those *anten-nae*. Oh, man. Mmmm. Where were the tissues when he needed them? He noticed the clock. Twenty past twelve. He really ought to get up. Yawning, he pulled the covers back over his head. Just ten more minutes and he'd be outta there.

Running feet thundered on the bridge overhead. A door slammed. An eerie quiet pervaded the Earth-bound craft. Suddenly, screams rent the air. Qwerk jumped. He could feel his ichor run cold. More screams.

"Not the liquid oxygen!" someone squealed. "Don't stir the liquid oxygen!"

What in Quagaar was going on? Preparing for the worst, Qwerk signaled to two of the borgs. They took the stairs three at a time, hooves clattering on the metal rungs, council truck meets Pablo Percusso. The screaming stopped as suddenly as it began. He threw open the closed door only to be greeted by a roomful of guilty, grinning faces. The aliens were watching a video of *Apollo 13* that some Alpha had abducted from Video Ezy on his last trip to Earth a year ago. Aliens, as a rule, found Tom Hanks devastatingly attractive. Most of them had already seen the film at least fifty times and could recite the dialogue off by heart. It was second in popularity only to *Independence Day*. They'd put the vid on pause at Qwerk's approach, and now all sat contrite, waiting for his upbraiding to finish so that they could return to their film. "Okay Houston," whispered a Zeta Reticulan, solemnly, "we've got a problem here." Someone giggled, and then someone else did, and soon the whole room was pffpffpffing with suppressed laughter.

Qwerk sighed, a shimmering little vibrato of a sound,

exited the room, and closed the door behind him. The video resumed and, shortly afterward, so did the screaming. Qwerk returned to the control room, and put his head down on the console.

God, this was trying. Wasn't there any way to get the other aliens to behave themselves?

God, this was trying. Wasn't there any way to get the other aliens to behave themselves?

*God, this was . . .*

Qwerk sighed again. God clearly was not going to come to his aid on this one. Sometimes he thought God didn't like him very much. It was a depressing thought. His eyes darted to the speedometer. Phew. Just under the limit.

"Jake, mate, that gig went off so much it went *on* again." The second gig at the Sando had proved even more of a triumph than the first.

"Cheers." Jake clicked his glass against Tim's. After the Sando closed, they'd all moved up the street to Sleepers, a pub for those who weren't, not at night anyway. From his position leaning on the bar, Jake was able to keep an eye on the swell of admirers around Baby, Doll, and Lati. There sure were a lot of them. Why couldn't Baby be with *him* and him *alone?*

"Sorry?" Jake realized that Tim had been speaking to him.

"Mate," Tim was saying, "you angsting out over something?"

"Angsting out? Me? Nah," said Jake, thinking, is it that obvious?

"Look, I know what you're going through."

"You do?" Jake seriously doubted it.

"They're just pop, man. It's *good* pop—don't get me

wrong—it's cool, it's sexy, it's indie, it's got some cred. But, like, ten, twenty years down the track, who are people gonna remember?" Tim answered his own rhetorical. "Bosnia, man. Bosnia."

Jake forced a smile. "Thanks, Timbo." Right. His male ego had been suffering so much that his rock star ego had forgotten that it was being mortally wounded as well. For fuck's sake. Thanks a *lot*, Timbo.

Jake turned so he wouldn't have to look at Baby, and found himself staring straight at a leggy girl with short hair, a shorter skirt, and a twinkle in her eye. Jake snapped automatically into flirt mode. "What are you drinking?" he asked suavely, nodding at her nearly empty glass.

She grinned. Jake took encouragement and grinned back.

"Sorry, mate," a deep voice rumbled from just behind him. The fellow who owned the voice edged between Jake and the girl, who threw her arms around his neck in greeting. Jake realized with embarrassment that she hadn't been smiling at him after all.

Jake had always maintained that if you couldn't chat up someone at Sleepers, it was time to hand in your membership in the Newtown tribe and move to . . . move to . . . Where else was there? Like most people who lived there, Jake almost never left Newtown and therefore had only a hazy notion of what else was out there, Sydney-wise. Now it looked like he was going to have to hand in his membership after all. Never mind, he consoled himself. No one had been watching.

Wrong. Tim had seen the whole thing. "I think you're losing it," he teased.

"At least," Jake replied dryly, "I once had it." He wasn't, like, totally *devastated* or anything. The girl was cute, and he wouldn't have Kicked Her Out Of but his heart wasn't in it. What his heart was in was standing about two meters and a million miles away sponging up the vile attentions of all manner of untrustworthy and insincere flatterers who had less than honorable intentions and whom she should be warned about, if not protected from. Well, that's how Jake saw it anyway. Christ, he knew all of them, and they were *just like him!*

There was a whole slew of new faces at breakfast on Galgal the following afternoon. Two gigs down the track and the girls had discovered groupies. Groupies, they found, were almost as much fun as abductees. Sometimes more so. And wasn't it fabulous how they all got along? Earthlings were *so* easy.

Well, most Earthlings anyway. Baby was sitting on the lap of a rather distinguished-looking older man abductee who had managed to coax five tiny cunts out of her side, one for each finger. She was also nibbling at a handful of nails offered up by a gorgeous young groupie with pert breasts and waist-length purple hair who was kneeling at her feet. Ebola was sitting a respectful meter or two away, on his hands and knees, ready to do whatever his mistress commanded. But was Baby happy? No. Baby was thinking about Jake, wasn't she? She knew he desired her. But something was stopping him from doing anything about it. And that, in turn, was stopping *her* from doing anything about it. Was it because she was an alien? She couldn't help that, could she? And why would she want to? Mmmm, those fingers felt good. Mmmm. Jake. Why hadn't he come over to her last night at Sleepers and taken her away from those other people?

No, she wasn't obsessed. That was ridiculous. She was just, oh, curious. Intrigued. Attracted. Perplexed. Infatuated.

Obsessed.

**"Jake! Why didn't you stick**
around last night?" The twins, closely followed by Saturna
and Skye, burst noisily into the house. "We all ended up
back at their place. Oh, man," exhaled Torquil, "you should
see where they *live.*" He plonked himself down next to Jake,
who was seated on the brown sofa tracking the tennis on
telly with morose eyes. "It was, like, this flying saucer? On
top of the Sebel?"

Jake raised one eyebrow. He kept his eyes on the tube.

"Yeah," enthused Tristram. "Can't believe we'd never
been over there before. It's cool as. You, like, look out the
windows and there's Bondi in one direction, the city in the
other. Fully viewsome. And what a night. You'd never believe who was there. You know how Ebola Van Axel announced that he was staying on in Australia? Well, guess
where he's hangin' out?"

Jake's head whipped round. *"No,"* he denied, horrified.

"Yes," Trist affirmed. "Oh, yes."

Jake suddenly noticed that Torquil was wearing one of
Baby's frocks, the lime green one with the diamond-shaped
cut-outs in the sleeves. Couldn't his world fall apart a little
at a time, like everyone else's? Did it have to happen all at
once? "Nice frock, Torq," he said, hoping those weren't
really tears that he felt in his eyes. For fuck's sake.

"Yeah," Torq smoothed the stretchy fabric over his legs
smugly. "Lati just *shredded* what I was wearing and I had to
have *something* to come home in."

Jake was feeling thoroughly alarmed by now. "Did you
guys, did you—"

"Did we what?" Tristram asked, looking suspiciously innocent.

Jake decided he didn't really want to know any more

about last night. He hadn't been there. Whatever happened, it hadn't happened to him. On a need to know basis, he didn't need to know. He blinked rapidly a few times. "I think we're ready," he declared, changing the subject, "for Bosnia moved up in the world. I've decided to call the Annandale to see if we can get a gig there. With the Babes, of course."

"Cool," said Torquil, staring hard at Jake. Was that a *tear* in his eye?

The Annandale Hotel was a notch higher than the Sando in the feeding chain of Sydney pub rock, if only because it had a stage that wasn't constructed from milk crates, its bar was in a logical place, and it could hold more people.

Old-timers compared the Bosnia/Babes night at the Annandale to the famous gig played by Midnight Oil at the Stagedoor Tavern in 1980 at which nearly 2000 people crammed into a space licensed to hold 129 while 500 more rioted outside. No one could estimate how many people managed to get into the Annandale that night—the bouncers, like everyone else, had fallen under the Babes' chaotic-erotic influence and were go-go dancing naked on the pool tables.

"I reckon it's time to hit the road," Jake observed to the twins afterward. They were leaning against the Kombi, waiting for the Babes to extricate themselves from the boisterous cluster of fans who'd besieged them the second they emerged from the backstage door and were still surrounding them now, an hour or so later. All they could see of the Babes were their bobbing antennae.

Torquil looked at Jake in disbelief. "You don't want to wait for the girls?"

"You're not, like, *jealous* or anything." Tristram was shocked as well.

Jake treated them both to a look of disdain. "I'm disappointed in you both," he sighed. "Deeply disappointed. As *if*. What I meant—obviously—was that it's time we took this show on the road. *Tour* time. I am looking into the future and I see Melbourne, Canberra, Brisbane, Byron Bay. Any prior commitments? Speak now, or hold your peace."

The twins' faces lit up like a pair of spotlights. "Let's do it," enthused Torquil. "I think I'm overdue for long service leave from the dole anyway."

"And I," announced Tristram, "will check my diary but I don't think I have anything planned for, oh, the next twenty years or so. So, like, whenever's good for me." He jumped up, punched the air, and whooped, "Rock 'n' fucken *roll!*"

Kate the Kombi grew alarmed. They weren't planning to drive to all those places in *her*, were they? At her age, just trundling off to the shops could be traumatic. She broke out into a cold radiator sweat. The more she thought about the toll such a trip would take on her aching joints and old starter motor, the more she became convinced she was on the verge of a breakdown.

Two cute girls with bindis on their foreheads, feathers in their hair, and lust in their eyes fronted up to Jake. Now this was more like it. Jake let rip his killer smile and snaked his posture into a sensuous, relaxed curve. He raised his cigarette to his lips, cocked an eyebrow, and looked from one to the other. "Hi there," he drawled.

"Uh, hi," said the one with the green glitter on her cheeks. "We're, like, really big fans?"

Jake puffed with pleasure.

"Of the Babes?" the girl continued. "And we were wondering if you could get them to autograph . . ."

It was deep into the wee hours by the time Baby, Doll,

and Lati finally bubbled up to the Kombi, high on performance and adulation, and full of apologies for the delay.

And then they still had to jump-start poor Kate. Baby did it with the tip of her little finger.

"Erotic," sang Eros tunelessly, "erotic."

"Neurotic," taunted a fellow 'roid, zipping past and refusing to indulge in even a minor prang. "Quixotic."

"Despotic," hooted a second. "Idiotic." He slammed straight into the first, just to annoy Eros. Asteroidal fragments flew off in all directions and their screams of pleasure echoed through space.

If they weren't going to play with him, why couldn't they just leave him alone!

Wretchedly, Eros huffed and he puffed and he still couldn't blow himself down. But he was having something of an effect. The Philippines experienced a series of minor volcanic eruptions, there was an intense gurgling in the boiling mud pools of New Zealand, and Peking shifted slightly on its geological plate. Feel the Earth move under your feet?

Inside the secret bowels of the Pentagon, close to where the small intestine of Offensive Strategy met the large intestine of Military Intelligence, stood a recessed and relatively inconspicuous door through which few people ever passed and behind which things transpired that Fox Mulder would have given his right arm—and Dana Scully's as well—to find out about. Upon the door was drawn a logo which to the uninitiated eye might suggest a ban on Frisbees. Below the logo, stenciled letters spelled out CONSPIRASEE.

It was the headquarters of the highly hush-hush, much feared Central Organization for the Non-civilian Secret Project Involving the Restraint of Aliens, Starpeople, and other Extraterrestrial Exotics. The offices behind the inconspicuous door were far from humble. They featured an extensive library, a bank of computers, and a well-equipped laboratory with a setup not dissimilar to the sexual experimentation chamber on Galgal. One of the things You Wouldn't Want to Know was what lay in the smallish coffinlike containers stacked in the refrigerator cabinet that dominated an entire wall of the room. The only decorations were Wanted posters with pictures and descriptions of ET, assorted Klingons, and Captain Qwerk.

When the phone rang the man in charge of CONSPIRASEE, General "Jackal" Mikeson, was studying a television advertisement that appeared to feature actual alien actors. Putting the vid on pause, he hit the button on his speakerphone. He settled his big armyman's frame into his leather swivel chair and jutted his enormous Roger Ramjet chin at the speaker. "Mikeson," he barked.

"Bo Davidey. Public Relations."

Mikeson was not particularly committed to a relationship with the public. He picked up a dart from an ashtray and threw it at the poster of Qwerk. It landed right in the middle of Qwerk's bulbous forehead. "Yes, Davidey," he said. "What is it this time?" He picked up another dart. "I haven't got all day."

"Ever hear of a group called, uh, let me just check my notes, right, 'Persons Aware of the Reality of Alien Networks for Organized Interplanetary Destruction'?"

Mikeson rolled his eyes. "PARANOID. Nutcases, the lot of them."

"That's a bit harsh."

Mikeson shrugged his broad armyman's shoulders. "You can spell, Davidey." He picked his nose and examined the findings for alien spore.

"I've got a journalist from *Time* who wants some comment on the group's allegations that the military is suppressing information on alien contacts."

"Deny it. Completely." Mikeson couldn't believe these guys in PR sometimes. That place was a real lights-are-on-but-no-one's-at-home scenario. Duh, he mouthed at the receiver.

"No other comment?"

"No. That all?"

"Well, there's one other thing, actually. I don't know if you really want to bother with this one. But there are some scattered reports from our spies in Sydney that a rash of green-skinned female aliens have landed and, uh, formed a rock band."

"Green-skinned female aliens. A rock band." Mikeson rolled his eyes again. "And you want a comment?"

"If you—"

"I don't."

"All right. No problem. Thanks, General."

"Pleasure." A *rock band* for Christ's sake. Where the fuck was Sydney anyway? And what kind of name was that for a place? "I come from *Sydney?*"

Gimme a break.

"Hot as," complained Tristram, wiping his brow on the sleeve of his Karen Carpenter T-shirt. Summer was a sauna in Newtown. Goths suffered most in their unrelenting black. But it was not the done thing for anyone in Newtown to wear white, even in summer. Oh, sure, the yuppies who were energetically attempting to gentrify the place—they wore white. But they weren't *really* Newtown. They didn't count.

"It would help if you didn't have the oven on, you know," remarked Saturna, who'd just popped back home from the shop to fetch her knitting needles and wool—a regular customer at Phantasma was having a baby and wanted a black bonnet and booties for her.

"You can't bake hash brownies without turning the oven on," Torq argued reasonably. "No pain, no gain." They watched the wall above the stove blacken with cockroaches. Turning on the oven always got the roaches going.

"Arthropodic as," remarked Lati, impressed.

Tristram and Torquil gazed besottedly at Lati. Sometimes she made *no* sense whatsoever.

Saturna shook her head in dismay and exited, fanning herself with a black lace fan. She and Skye adored Doll, of course, but they really couldn't understand why the other aliens, who were girls too after all, encouraged the boys in their worst habits and strange humor.

"You know, it'd really make a difference if we had demos to send around," Jake said. She wouldn't really, you know, be doing the *thing* with Ebola Van Axel, would she? Getting the two bands on the road as soon as possible, it had occurred to him, was an excellent way of taking her away from that troll.

"So? Let's make demos then." Baby was agreeable. Was it her imagination or was Jake avoiding her eyes?

"Not that easy," Jake said. He glanced at the twins. They'd agreed to present their plan to the babes together. But when Jake looked at him, Tristram contemplated the ceiling and paradiddled the table with his hands. Rightleftrightrightleftrightleftleft. Torquil scrutinized the table and paradiddlediddled his chair. Rightleftrightrightleftrightleft. Percussive types could always find something to do when things got awkward.

"Why not?" Baby asked. "Is there some sort of insurmountable popsicle or something?"

"That's 'obstacle.' Sort of."

The girls had already read the boys' minds. They knew they were about to be hit up for dough. They didn't care. They were perfectly happy to shell out. Abducting money was easy. They were just enjoying watching the boys squirm.

They creased their pretty brows and tilted their heads in a perfect imitation of Earthling befuddlement. "Well?" questioned Lati. "What is it?"

"Money," Jake blurted out with uncharacteristic nervousness. "You know," he blundered on, "for the studio and stuff." Jake paused. He felt like *such* a con artist. Yet it was a perfectly legitimate proposition. He was doing this for them, too, after all.

"Yes, we know," chuckled Baby. "And we appreciate it."

"Sorry?"

"Never mind." Doll emptied her pockets and dumped several fat wads onto the table. "How much do we need?"

"That's a good start," whewed Torquil. "That's a very good start."

Jake mailed the two CDs to venues along the east coast and then followed up with phone calls. When he wasn't on the blower, he was under Kate hammering her into shape for the tour. Ow! Ow! *Easy* on the exhaust pipe.

The girls had a word with the abductees. They'd look

after the saucer with the groupies. There'd been an emotional scene with Ebola, who'd pleaded to be allowed to come along as a roadie. A mixer. Anything. They'd already asked Henry to come with them. Anyway, there was no way that Jake was going to put up with Ebola on tour.

The twins, on the other hand, thought that it would be hysterical. "Now what do you know about being a roadie, Ebola?" they teased him.

"Everything," he answered earnestly. "I know the roadie's credo off by heart."

"What's that, Eb?"

Ebola puffed himself up and recited, "If it's wet, drink it, if it's dry, smoke it, if it moves, fuck it, if it doesn't, throw it in the truck."

The twins looked at each other. The guy was serious.

In the end, Baby managed to appease Eb with one of her magic smiles and the promise that, upon return, she'd let him kiss her feet for a whole ten minutes—without boots.

The bookers for the various venues, upon receiving the demos, put the Babes' CD on continual replay, and made love with whoever or whatever was available—boyfriends, girlfriends, neighbors, pets, television sets—for hours on end. It took days for them to remember to get back to work. Then the first thing they did was call and say they were megamega-keen to have the Babes. And they didn't really mind *who* supported them. Bosnia, whatever.

*"We'll have heaps of time to chat* when we get back, George. Promise." Baby waved good-bye to George. He'd wanted to have a talk with the babes about the end of the world before they left, but they kept putting him off. Young people. Always in a hurry. Young aliens, it seemed, were no different. What could you do? George waddled back over to his place.

Baby folded her large frame into the front seat of the Kombi next to Jake, who was at the wheel, revving up. The others were all in the back with the gear. "Let's vehiculate!" she whooped, pulling the door shut after her. The door promptly fell off its hinges. *Ouch*, whimpered Kate. That *hurt*.

"*Shit*," said Jake, stepping out to have a look. "I was expecting a bit of strife, but I was fairly confident she'd at least make it out of the drive." He kicked the bumper in frustration.

Now was that any way to treat a lady? Kate had been stressing out badly ever since the trip had been mooted that night at the Annandale.

Doll rummaged in her bag and came up with a roll of Bind-a-Bean. She hopped out and taped up the door. That seemed to work.

"Yeeha!" yelled Torquil as they finally pulled out of the drive.

"Hayee!" yodeled Tristram.

"Yabadabadoo!" hollered Baby.

"⚐⚒⚙⚖☉⚘⚓⚔⚕" whooped Lati.

"⚐⚒⚙⚔⚕-*what?*" exclaimed Torquil and Tristram in unison. The girl was fucken awesome.

"Sorry," giggled Lati. "Just a bit of Nufonian that slipped out."

About an hour down the coast road, Kate, who'd been feeling increasingly and ever more dramatically sorry for herself, gagged, coughed, spluttered, hawked, expectorated, sneezed, sniffled, went all stiff in the joints, and developed a high fever. Curling up on the side of the road, she refused to budge, only issuing the occasional pathetic moan or groan when Jake prodded her ignition.

Tristram was the first to speak. "Uh-oh, spaghetti-os," was what he said. Not much help, really, under the circs.

"Let me have a look," offered Henry, following Jake round to the back of the van. Doll hopped out, shouldered Henry aside, and waved Jake away as well. She opened the little hatch at the back and stroked the engine gently while speaking in low tones.

About five minutes later, Doll told everyone to get back in and announced that she would drive. She and Kate had come to a mutually satisfactory agreement. Kate would hold herself together and try to develop a more positive attitude. In return, Doll would juice her up with some of her extraordinary alien energy. Sliding the key into the ignition, Doll smiled smugly as Kate purred. To general cheering, she brought her up to the speed limit and then well beyond. This was a girl used to steering a flying saucer. She was a hell driver, taking to the meridian strips one minute, the shoulder the next, and just lifting off and flying over the rest of the traffic when that seemed like the more amusing thing to do. Kate was happy as Larry, who was still extremely happy. All the girls had their antennae tuned for radar, and Doll managed to get Kate under the limit and in the right lane, more or less, each time they approached a speed trap.

Jaded old rock musicians are always complaining about how boring it is to be on the road. Don't know which road they were on, but the babes and the boys must have been on a much better one, because they were having a *blast*.

Not long after they set out, Tristram and Torquil pulled out a range of pharmaceuticals and offered them around. The details of the trip get a little hazy after that. Sometimes, however, they get a lot sharper. Other times they become a trifle stretched around the edges, or plump and squishy, with great big swirls of color and eyeballs stuck on everything. Occasionally, they become sort of vibratory and bewitching, or inexpressibly sad, or manic and pepperminty. Then there are the details that just sort of slip away and get lost, never to be found again.

Here are some of the recoverable details: they played board games in parallel yoons. They conducted a scientific cross-cultural Earthling/Nufonian survey of what is considered unspeakably gross on each planet, with the goal of creating a cosmic Sliding Scale of Spewsomeness. They painted pictures and messages on Kate's doors, with her permission. They sang along with the radio, loudly and badly, while performing drum solos on the sides of the van and each other's craniums. And that was only the first six hours. They hadn't even reached Melbourne yet.

Acid. Speed. Booze. Speed. Dope. Speed. Hash. Speed. Ecstasy. Agony. Out there. In there. Here and there. Wheeeeee. Aliens. Wheeeeeeee.

Zzzzzzzzzzzzzzzzip! Melbourne! Zzzzzzzzzzzzzzip! Canberra! Zzzzzzzzzzip! Is this a flying blue wombat zone or was that just me? Zzzzzzzzap! Where the hell are we? Kalbarri? Where the fuck is Kalbarri? Who's got the map? Oh, *shit!* Zzzzzzzzzzzzzzzzzip! Zzzzzzzzzzzzzip! Brisbane! Phew. You *have* to let us in, we're the *band*.

Back in Newtown, George watched the five o'clock news with Iggy and Revor. He was seated in his favorite armchair, a worried expression on his face, a tinny of VB in his hand. The two pets were lying side by side on the floor, heads on front paws, eyes raised to the tube. The government was announcing a major deforestation program focusing on national parks. It was imposing a luxury tax on organic fruit and veg and setting up a hotline for people to dob in naturopaths and yoga teachers. It was targeting marijuana smoking as the biggest threat to national security and family values. George noticed they were playing music behind the news on the ABC now. Polkas for a Gloomy World.

George shook his head and took a swig of beer. Mad pig disease rampant among politicians. Aporkalypse now.

Also in the news: a Chinese satellite, the Red Star, had blown up on impact with a tiny piece of space debris. The debris was believed to be one of the missing pieces of Cosmos 1275, a Soviet satellite that fifteen years earlier had collided with other space junk. More and more pieces of debris were launched into unpredictable orbits by such accidents, the reporter was saying. There was the possibility they could trigger an uncontrollable chain reaction of explosions that might leave the planet blanketed in an impenetrable layer of flotsam and jetsam.

The news ended. George watched morosely as a tall dark moron in breeches pursued a rosy-cheeked young woman in a baby's bonnet across a meadow. Jane bloody Austen. The world's coming to an end and we're all watching Jane bloody Austen, thought George.

"You know, Rev," Iggy mused, "it's interesting that the Chinese satellite was blown up by a fragment from a Soviet one. I think it sheds some light on the problem my master and your mistress have in getting together."

"How so?"

"Simple," Iggy explicated. "Our past relationships come back to haunt us. No, it's worse than haunting. The fragments of exploded intimacies can come back and *blow us up*. Jake's been hurt a few times. He pretends he hasn't, that everything's cool. Yet there are some deadly scraps of psychic debris floating around his headspace, I'm sure of it."

"You're so wise," Revor cooed. "You blow *me* away."

"Maybe something will happen between them on tour," Iggy said. "It's got to, don't you think? All that lethal proximity? I think that's what Jake was hoping for anyway."

"Baby too," nodded Revor. "But somehow I don't think it's going to happen. The master race is very complicated about this stuff." He lifted his head and licked Iggy's tongue, which was hanging out in the heat. Slurp. "When there's no need for complication." Slurp slurp. "I mean, *we're* not complicated about this, are we? I mean, I can actually just look at you and say, I *lurv* you, Iggie-wiggie-poo."

Iggy's ears pricked, a smile widened his face and, with a sudden intake of breath, he sucked Revor straight down his throat. Revor's back paws and tail stuck out from between Iggy's teeth. His tail was wagging. "Letti troll bayb ee," he purred from somewhere inside Iggy's stomach.

By the time the babes and the boys rocked into Byron Bay for the last show of the tour, they were feeling totally triumphant, hideously burned out, fully into touring, thoroughly over touring, absolutely delirious, dangerously manic, unbelievably depressive, one hundred percent drugfucked and in desperate need of both less and more of whatever it was they'd sworn off the night before. They'd come to the right place.

Byron Bay, south of Brisbane, north of Sydney, east of everywhere else except L.A. was a small town that nestled between magnificent surf beaches and awesome rain forest. It enjoyed a reputation for being a *healing* kind of place.

Byron Bay will read your Tarot, teach you to belly dance, cure you with crystals, lead you in yoga, workshop your "stuff," float you in tanks, monitor your aura, deep massage your tissues, touch you for health, show you whales, introduce you to dolphins, play you music in its pubs, invite you to raves, and allow you to lie naked on its beaches. Byron Bay will provide you with naturopathic dentists and holistic chiropractors. Byron Bay will put dandelions in your latte, guarana in your smoothie, and any drug you can name in your hands. All you have to do is ask.

"Any mushies?" is what Jake was asking.

It was about ten A.M. The gang had left the Gold Coast after their gig at the Playroom and had arrived in Byron in the middle of the night. Balmy as. They headed straight for the beach, jumped in the ocean, and then slept on the sand. Come the morning, they wandered down the main street and had breakfast at Ringo's café.

Jake and Baby were strolling back up the main street toward the beach when Jake decided it was time to put some money into the local economy.

Jake and Baby fit right into Byron Bay. Byron was not unlike Newtown in some ways, except even fewer people wore shoes in Byron and there were more surfies. Every other person in Byron had dreadlocks and colored hair and some even had tinted skin. Byron was a perennial cosmic convention, a feral paradise. There was a greater volume of matted hair in Byron than in a warehouseful of Victorian sofas, more nose rings than you'd see on a dozen cattle farms. While few ferals would stoop so low as to take gainful employment, some were running completely mobile and not unprofitable business concerns. Jake was negotiating with one such dealer now, a young man with tangled blond hair and a narcotic smile.

While they talked weights and measures, Baby looked around her and met the bright and shiny eyes of a small teenage feral girl with enormous pink dreadlocks, green sparkles on her cheeks, and an ensemble that seemed to consist mainly of one tiny piece of purple cloth and a lot of ribbons and bells. She carried a small basket over one arm that held a failing bunch of grapes, a dole form, a small bottle, and an enormous collection of sequins and beads.

"What d'ya *use*, mate?" gushed the little feral, jingling in her enthusiasm. With all her bells, she sounded almost Nufonian.

"Use?" Baby didn't have a clue as to what she was talking about.

"On your *skin*, mate. On your skin. To get it that green."

"It's natural," Baby laughed, putting a hand up to her cheek.

"We're all natural," replied the little feral, happy with the answer. She was always happy. "We're all nature's children. I love your antennae too. Coming to the full moon party tonight at the Epicenter?" The Epicenter was an old beach-side abbatoir that was now the karmically disturbed but otherwise apparently happy home of yogis, artists, ferals, hippie couturiers, earth goddesses, and other dwellers of the fringe. It had a cafe, a gallery, and some of the best dance parties in town.

"Full moon party?"

"Yeah. Come be part of the universal family. And here, have some floral essence to prepare for the occasion. Stick out your tongue."

Baby stuck out her tongue. It was turquoise.

"Oh, man. You are so cool." Feralette pulled out the small bottle from her basket and administered a few drops of liquid. Immediately, Baby saw a pattern of brightly colored poppies unfold across the sky. When the poppies faded, the feral had gone and Jake was staring at her with amusement.

They continued up toward the beach. A van with ocean

waves painted on its doors and a stack of surfboards on the roof rack chugged by, stereo blasting. "There goes Lati," said Baby, noticing two pert antennae amongst the dreads and mohawks. The twins and Henry had driven out to Nimbin to score whatever was on tap in that ripped little mountain community cum drugs bazaar. For her part Doll had abducted a board and had taken it down to the Pass, where the surf cooperatively swelled into perfect tubes for her to ride.

Byron did funny things to people. At this moment, it was doing something so funny to Jake that he actually reached out and took Baby's hand. For one perfect second, they rose together and floated, hand in hand, high above the street. They gazed out over the ocean, where pods of dolphins frolicked in celebration. Then, ever so gently, they glided back to earth. Jake resolved to tell Baby he loved her. He would drop to his knees right there, in front of Earth & Sea Pizza, and do it. I love you, Baby.

He looked at her and opened his mouth. Come on. You can do it, Jake. He cleared his throat. "Baby."

"Yes, Earth boy?"

Damn! It just wouldn't come out. "Try one of these," he said instead. "Space cookies." He'd tried. He really had.

"Do you think you can ever take too many drugs, Jake?"

"Nah. Yeah. Depends on the timing, really."

They'd reached the Main Beach and were climbing down the rocks to the sand. "What do you mean by timing?" she asked. "Is it, like, take this, wait an hour, take that?"

"I meant the timing of when you think about it, really. The morning after, when your head is full of lumberjacks cutting down trees with chainsaws, and there are little men with hammers trying to nail things into the back of your eyes, and your stomach feels like you've just swallowed someone else's farts, then, yes, I think, I've just taken a few too many drugs. But that same amount of drugs, the night before, when they're doing the cancan in your brain, and you're starting to see the colors of music and you feel like a combination of Jesus Christ, Stephen Hawking, and Jim Morrison, that's just the right amount. That's what I mean by timing."

"I see," said Baby, taking another bite of cookie. "Ergh. Don't know how you palate this stuff. Spewin'. Do you have anything to take the edge off?" Jake pulled out a pack of cigarettes and offered her the foil. "Thanks," she said gratefully. Her antennae suddenly lit up like sparklers, spraying sparks.

"Nice place, Byron Bay," said Baby, looking dreamily at the sky, where the clouds were metamorphosing into white lilies and freesia. "What were we talking about?"

"Can't remember," said Jake, watching daisies sprout from between his toes. He was suddenly possessed by the urgent need to figure out how the alphabet was spelled. "A" wasn't too hard—A-I-Y would do—and "B"—B-E-E—was easy, but what about "C"? S-E-E? It didn't actually have the letter "c" in it. Was that okay? *Really* okay?

Jake was still occupied by this problem as they hiked up the dunes to where the trees met the sand and stretched their limbs across the fine white powder. Jake considered doing a line of sand. He concluded that this was probably not a good idea, rolled a joint, and passed it to Baby along with the bag of mushrooms.

As they sat there quietly enjoying the rush of heightened sensation, an insect debranched from one of the trees and fell with a little plop onto the sand beside them. Its head was bulbous and gold, with delicate antennae and a single, large black eye dead center. Its six spindly legs worked hard at hauling its wormy green body along behind it. Lest any other creature be tempted to laugh at its cycloptic head or labored gait, it brandished a menacing spike on its arse. The contractions and expansions of its ridged exoskeleton made it look like it was pulsing with electricity. With each pulse, it grew in size, until its body had expanded to the size of Jake's leg. Baby's heart skipped a beat. She looked at Jake, but he hadn't seemed to notice anything out of the ordinary. Sunbathers strolled by, glancing up at them but registering no particular surprise. Baby was thinking this drugs thing could get a little freaky when the creature tapped her with its antennae. "Pssst," it said. "It's me. Your cousin Zyggo."

Baby did a double take. "Zyg! I didn't recognize you. Then, how could I? What are you doing here? Why are you dressed like that? How did you get here?"

She glanced nervously at Jake. He was smiling placidly at the sky, his eyes hidden by his sunglasses. "H," he was thinking, how do you spell "H"?

"Whoa whoa whoa," laughed Zyggo. "One thing at a time. Doesn't that stuff mellow you out at all? First of all, I'm not actually here. Not in the physical sense, like you are. It's a parallel yooniverz shtick. As far as the rellies are concerned I'm still at Uncle Oyszty's birthday barbie chowing down on a uranium-burger and paying out on a couple of Vogons who'd invited themselves over."

"Oh, *yum.*" Baby's mouth watered. "I've had such a craving for uranium since we got here, I can't tell you. There's supposed to be heaps of it up north. Maybe we can go there together. How long you here for?"

Zyggo tried to sit up. His new body was not built for vertical mobility. He only succeeded in falling over, and lay on his back flailing the air with all six of his legs until Baby reached over and flipped him onto his stomach. "Ta," he said. "Not long. I've got to get back before anyone notices that I'm just a hologram of my former self. But I'm not here on a joyride, as joyous as it is to see you, my dear. Did you get any of my messages?"

"Messages? Where did you leave them?"

"Where else?" Zyggo rolled his one eye, not a pretty sight. "On the ether. Don't you ever check your e-mail?"

Baby answered in an abashed tone, "Nup. Never even occurred to me. I'm having too much fun, Zyg. Who wants to spend all their time in front of a compu-tron anyway? I'm over compu-trons. Good-bye, geek girl. Reject the virtual, embrace the real. Besides, I never actually learned how to log on. What? What are you doing now?"

Zyggo was clawing the air with his front feet. "Trying to put my head in my hands to emphasize my shock and dismay. Communications is the first thing they teach you in interstellar piloting."

"Zyg. They didn't exactly give us training and hand over the manual. We stole the spaceship."

"So you did. Which brings me to the point. Why I'm here. It's not for my health you know." With his one protuberant eye, Zyggo looked himself up and down with distaste. "This particular hallucination is giving me the shits. Why couldn't you have just dreamed up some giant flower or something? I just needed one good image hook to facilitate somatization. You know how it works. A nice little goblin would have done me fine, or a blue kangaroo, or even a bagel."

"I didn't know you were coming."

"Never mind. Anyway, it seems the whole incident has caused quite a stir in the Leading Qohort. A mate of mine, Exl, works as a metallurgist in the Qohort kitchens. He was hanging out after hours hoping to flog a few aluminum ingots and these two bigsters came in, Qwerk and this other guy. Exl did a quick shape-shift and pretended he was a smelting pot till they left, praying that no one would light a fire under him. As a pot his hearing wasn't brilliant, so he couldn't quite make out everything they were saying, but it had to do with 'neutralizing' you and your two pals. They said you had defective genes."

"Defective jeans? My Levis? I just abducted them a few days ago."

"Genes, Einsteinette. As in chromosomes? The point is, you're in what I believe Earthlings call 'the ship.'"

Jake slowly rotated his head around, removed his sunglasses, fixed his dilated pupils on Zyggo and drawled, "the shit, man, the shit." Then, with a dignified and deliberate gesture, he put his sunglasses back on and passed out on the sand.

Zyggo looked at Baby in puzzlement. "Who's the waste-oid?"

"Don't worry about him," said Baby. "He'll be right."

"The point is, will *you?* They're after you, Baby. If I were you I'd pack up and kiss your sweet Earth good-bye. Oh, don't look so sad. I can't bear it. There's plenty of other planets in the yoon. New ones are coming into existence every day."

"Yeah, but." Baby's eyes misted over.

"But what? You saw what they did to Michelle Mabelle. And she never even stole a spaceship. Or ran away to Earth. Or, bloody Betelgeuse, formed a *rock* band. Really, Baby! Don't you know rock 'n' roll is dead? Ambient, trance, jungle, even dream pop or lounge I could understand—but *rock?* It's so, so, I don't know, passé or something. Darling, if you weren't my cousin, I'd consider prosecuting you for fashion crimes. Oh c'mon, I'm only joking. Look at me, Baby."

"Rock 'n' roll will never die," Baby replied, her bottom lip quivering. "And I'm staying." She laid a hand on Jake's leg.

Zyggo looked at Jake as though seeing him for the first time. "Don't tell me you're—"

"No."

"In *love.*"

"Love? What's *that* got to do with it," she snapped.

"Sorry, Zyg," she apologized, abashed, "it's all a bit emotional." She looked up into the sky, where a lenticular cloud hovered, honking its horn. "Is that your ride?"

Zyggo tried to wave at it. "Coming!" he shouted.

*Beep beep.* The cloud, a saucer in disguise, was double parked. And everyone knew God's attitude toward double parking. *Beep beep.*

"Zyg, I thought you were parallel yooning. What's with the saucer?"

"Some blokes I met from Planet X. They're just gonna take me to a higher ground. I'll zip off from there. Great guys, by the way. They didn't even bat an eye at my present, uh, configuration. You should meet them, Baby. Get your mind off."

"I'm not interested in other ayles," she sniffed.

Zyg was about to say something when the saucer honked again. He decided to let it rest. "Well, cousin, it's been real. Chip chip."

"Chip chip. Oh, and thanks, Zyggo. Thanks a lot."

Zyggo flew into the sky like a Chinese dragon kite. A door opened in the cloud, and he disappeared into it. The cloud hung a u-ee, zoomed east, shot out over Cape Byron, and was gone.

*There once was a captain called Qwerk*
*The yoon's most silliest jerk*
*There's no hair on a gray*
*But he'd brush every day*
*Fifty strokes, up and down, the big berk.*

Qwerk compressed his expressionless little slit of a mouth into an even tighter slit as he scrubbed the latest graffito off the fathership's bathroom wall. Why did they torment him like this? Was it necessary? He honestly didn't understand why anyone did anything that did not have a safe and predictable, not to mention a sensible and constructive outcome. Besides, what was so funny about brushing? So what if he didn't have hair? What was so good about hair?

Squeezing out the sponge, he checked his chronometer. ETA was, let's see, about two Earth-months away. He mentally reviewed his plan for the hundredth time. First, offload the other ayles. Aliens. God, now he was even talking like them. Second, locate and capture the feral hybrids Ms. Baby, Ms. Parts, and Ms. Dodidohdoh before they could further insanitize the planet. A *rock* band. *Really*. He'd found out about it when one of the many bots, er, robots that Nufonians planted around the world to keep an eye on Earthling affairs beamed up an excited report on their Annandale gig. Overexcited, if you asked Qwerk. Were not even robots safe from the babes' pernicious influence? Clearly not.

Never mind. Once the babes were out of the way and they could begin to implement the Hidden Agenda, everything would straighten itself out.

**Back in Parkes, Professor Luella** Skye-Walker rubbed her bleary eyes and checked her screen for the hundredth time. "Getting anything, Aaron?"

"Not a thing. How 'bout you, Jason?"

"Nothing. No thing. No Thing," Jason said. He got up to put some music on. "*The Cult of Ray* okay with everyone?"

"Oh, why not?" Aaron said. They'd been listening fairly nonstop to Pee Shy's *Who Let All the Monkeys Out?* They liked singing along to the track, "Jason, I Thought I saw a UFO."

"Damn, damn, damn," cursed Luella. "We were *this* close just two months ago. I'm sure of it. They said 'Hello, Mum' and then they went silent. Are they out there, or not?"

"What if *we* sent out a message?" Aaron proposed. "I know it's not in the brief."

"It's definitely not in the brief," Luella affirmed.

"Oh well," sighed Aaron.

Luella shook her head. "Don't give up that easily. What were you thinking? Message-wise."

"Oh, I don't know," he replied thoughtfully. "Something like 'Hello Pop'?"

Jason laughed. " 'Hello, Pop.' I like it."

"Can't hurt," shrugged Luella. "Let's do it, rocket man."

Baby checked Jake's watch. She tapped him on the shoulder. He opened his eyes, sat up and shook the sand out of his dreads. "Wozza time?" he asked.

"Four."

Where'd the day gone? It was already time to meet the gang at the pub for their sound check.

Jake and Baby pulled up just as a bouncer was evicting a pair of quarreling drunks. The bouncer, Big Brian, was built like a brick shithouse, which is Australian for "he had no neck." He held the sobriety-challenged duo by the scruffs of their necks and tossed them onto the street as though they were chooks. Wiping his hands on his jeans, he sneered righteously and disappeared back inside.

Baby looked at Jake. "Rough-o-rama!" she exclaimed.

The two drunks had already forgotten what they'd been fighting about and were now sitting on the pavement lighting each other's cigarettes. When they clapped eyes on Baby, they fell over and kissed the pathway.

"Hey, Baby! Jake!" The surfie van had pulled up just behind Kate, and Lati jumped out. "See you dudes later tonight, hey?" She waved them off, straightening her clothing. Doll was padding down the street from the beach, still in her wetsuit. When she caught up with the others, they sauntered into the pub together.

"HOOHOOHOOHOOHOO!" yelled out a representative of Byron's least celebrated subculture, one in which the men sported non-Celtic tattoos, mustaches, and nonironic bad haircuts, and the women answered to names like Janelle and Shareen—specifically, what they answered was, "Oi? Youse talkin' to ME?"

"PHWOAH! OVER HERE *BABY!*" Several of the men around the bar grabbed their crotch in greeting.

"Now, how do you fellas know my name?" Baby asked, as sincerely mystified by this as when she first met Ebola, and, of course, grabbing her crotch back. For some reason, this only seemed to set them off even more. "WHYT-WHYOO," wolf whistled one, and then another, and then another.

To the catcalls and whistles and general testosteronal yodeling, Lati predictably replied, "Wanna suck my cock?"

Well, predictably for her, anyway. The rough-heads clearly were stunned by this. Several opened their mouths and curled their upper lips, which was an Earthling way of saying, "Are youse cruisin' fer a bruisin'?"

"Uh, girls," Jake interjected nervously. "I don't think—"

"Shut ya poofter trap," a wiry man with beady little eyes, dangerously pointy boots, and a missing front tooth instructed Jake curtly. Then he returned the full glory of his attention to the girls. "Youse dykes?" he challenged. Both his general demeanor and the tone of his voice suggested he was not a wholehearted supporter of the Gay and Lesbian Mardi Gras. "Oi reckon," he declared, without waiting for clarification regarding their sexual orientation, "all youse dykes needs is a good man." He scratched his balls and stood up. He was chewing gum slowly and ostentatiously. "That's what oi reckon."

"Oh, yeah?" Doll replied, walking straight up to him, a tiny little creature in body rubber, her horns flattened from the surf and pointing forward like those of a bull. Deliberately, she reached for his bottle of beer from the bar. Standing on tiptoe, she poured the contents of the bottle over his head, making sure quite a lot of it flowed over his face. Then, without taking her eyes off his, she took a large bite out of the bottle. "Is that what you reckon?" she said, crunching glass. "A 'good man,' eh? Then tell me. What good's a man?" She spat out a small shard onto the floor. "Don't make me take out your other tooth, Ratface," she cautioned. "It could have tragic consequences for your life-style. For one thing, you wouldn't be able to gnaw through the electrical wiring anymore."

"YOU—" Ratface pulled back his right fist and shook it at Doll.

"*Rumble!*" hollered Lati, vaulting up onto the bar and voguing like Michael Jackson in the video for "Beat It."

"Oh shit," said Jake under his breath. Jake loved Tarantino and all, *but*. He looked at Baby in alarm. To his horror, she seemed a million miles away.

Baby might not have been a million miles away, but she definitely wasn't quite all there. She was in fact in another dimension entirely, Dimension 865A, to be precise. Cavorting with a pack of singing daisies. They were so *sweet*. They were so *cute*. They were twirling and skipping and steering yellow polka-dot flying saucers around and around her head.

Lati bent over, pinched Ratface's ears in her fingers and pulled up. He had been staring at her and Doll as though in shock, but he was now clearly coming to his senses, and his senses were beer-soaked and furious. His mates were rising from their stools as well and doing the sort of thing that Earthlings did when they wanted to indicate that they were preparing to rearrange someone else's facial features— breaking glasses on the bar, cussing under their breath, snarling, and spitting.

Baby *loved* her daisies. They represented everything that was beautiful in the yooniverz. And the yooniverz was *such* a beautiful place. The daisies were smiling at her now. She smiled and smiled and smiled back.

ZING! The room was bathed in light more dazzling than that of the sun and softer than that of the moon. A scent like that of sun-warmed skin and sticky rice with mango infused the air. The ears of everyone in the room were filled with the sound of celestial harps and violins, overlaid, of course, with jangly guitar hooks and hell vocals. It was that old alien magic at work.

"YOU, YOU—BEWDY!" Ratface brayed. He stepped forward to give Doll a big hug as the others applauded enthusiastically, boozy eyes alight with good cheer and goodwill.

"Oh, retch," scowled Doll, pushing him off her with a look of extreme distaste. "I wish you wouldn't do that, Baby. I was just starting to have fun."

Baby blinked. "Pardon? Do what?"

Just then, Torquil and Tristram flopped and stumbled into the pub, moaning and groaning dramatically. They were wearing sunglasses and holding onto their stomachs. Sharp, oddly shaped lumps protruded from under their matching "I ♥ Tina Arena" T-shirts.

"Yo," squeaked Torquil.

"More poofs," noted Ratface approvingly. "That's really nice to see around here. It sorta takes the macho edge off things, doncha think? Welcome, boys," he gushed. "We here at this pub *respect* difference."

"Uh, thanks," replied Torquil uncertainly. He looked at

Jake for some help in deciphering this new and unexpected signifier in the great postmodernist landscape of life. Jake was too busy admiring you-know-who to notice. Lati hopped off the bar with an air of disappointment.

"What's going on?" croaked Tristram.

Lati had slacker communications down to a T. She shrugged in reply, an ironic twist to her mouth.

"Fair enough," said Tristram.

Doll was fed up with the lot of them. "We sound checking or what, then?" she snapped. She went out to the van to start lugging in.

"What's under your shirts?" Jake had finally managed to tear his eyes away from Baby as they shifted their gear into the venue.

"Crystals." Torquil frowned.

"*Crystals?*"

"We got some *wicked* shit in Nimbin. Not sure how we got back to Byron, but we just kinda came to on the beach an hour ago, feeling like furballs vomited up by a very large cat. Scuzzy *as*. We were toxing out when Tristram remembered seeing a sign advertising crystal healing. So we got some crystals and gaffer-taped them all over our bodies." He lifted his T-shirt and showed Jake.

"Is it working?"

"Not really," said Tristram.

"Maybe they take a while to kick in."

"That's what we're hoping."

"Where's Henry?" The twins grimaced in unison.

"Here." What was that? The others looked to see where the very small voice was coming from. "Over here." Henry was on his hands and knees in the doorway, looking like something a dog wouldn't even consider for dinner.

"Oh, dear," said Jake.

"I'll be right," said Henry. "I just need a Panadol."

After the sound check, the twins left to score some over-the-counters for themselves and Henry, whom they left chilling out on the side of the stage with his sunglasses on and the carrying case for a drum over his head. Lati and Doll headed up Jonson Street to look for an automotive repair shop—the little drama in the pub had only sharpened their appetites.

"What do you want to do?" Jake deferred to Baby. They still had some time before the gig was scheduled to start.

"Not sure," she said. "It's been quite an afternoon. I wouldn't mind staying here and shooting some pool, actually." She dropped a coin into the slot, and began to set up. Baby had become addicted to pool. On Jake's advice, she'd taken to flubbing a few shots now and then so that she wouldn't scare the other beans too much.

He strolled over to the doorway, squinted into the sunshine, put his sunglasses back on, and joined her in the side room. "Yeah, I reckon it's best to stay inside," he said. "I think it's possible to overdo this outdoors thing. Sunshine's a bit overrated. Don't you think?"

"Absolutely," she agreed, replacing the triangle on the green lamp above the table and chalking her cue. "I prefer the light from white dwarfs myself. It's a hell of a lot softer, more romantic."

God, he liked this girl.

*So why don't you do something about it, Jake? I'm getting bored already. I mean, foreplay and buildup are one thing, but it's been, what, nearly 230 pages already—in my diary, anyway—and you still haven't made a move.*

Who's that? Jake looked around him nervously.

*God. You called. Remember?*

Huh? *Fuck*, those space cookies were full-on. That's it. No more drugs. Ever.

*It's not the space cookies, my handsome little dread-headed one. I thought you were a thinking-girl's crumpet, Jake. I'm a bit disappointed in you. I don't detect much thinking going on at all. If you don't mind my being frank, I'd suggest you lay off the chemicals just a wee bit and concentrate on the chemistry.*

Sorry?

*Kiss her, you fool.*

Kiss her? Now? Just like that? Hello? God? Mate? Where'd He go?
(He hadn't gone anywhere; He was watching.)
Jake swallowed. "Uh, Baby."
"You wanna break? What is it?" Baby looked at Jake. He had a tulip sitting on his left ear. She went to pluck it, but it wasn't there after all, and her hand stroked the bouncy matted pipes of hair that were there. To say that Jake shuddered would be less accurate than to say he *vibrated*. From head to toe and back to head again. Jake's heart was beating. Digitidigitidigiti. He stared at her full red lips, the corners of which were curled upward, and noted how close the top of her lips were to the tip of her nose. Jake always loved that in a girl. Jake imagined himself shrinking and climbing into the bow of her lips as if it were a deck chair, dangling his legs down one side, tickling her teeth with his fingers, and blowing soft breaths up her nostrils at the same time. He imagined bouncing on the soft hammock of her thick blue lashes, swinging from her adorable earlobes, and rolling around on the springy mattress of her magnificent cheeks.

Baby pulled his head close to her own and sweetened her lips against his. The turquoise velvet of her tongue insinuated itself into his mouth and found a willing playmate in the fat pink organ that lived within. Her antennae were humming "What a Wonderful World" (the Nick Cave and Shane MacGowan version). Breathing unevenly but very deeply, she let go of her cue, which clattered to the floor.

Neither of them noticed Brian the Bouncer come into the room. After that business with the drunks, Brian had satisfied himself that nothing much was happening in the bar. He was in the bog laying a cable, checking the growth on his mullet, and thinking about Shareen's pasty thighs when that scene with Ratface and Doll had erupted. Now he emerged to find the place weirdly sedate. No fights. No arguments. Nothing. Just a hippy dippy happy atmosphere of love and peace. It made him damn uncomfortable. Something was afoot. He checked the backroom. He rechecked the bar. He looked up and down the street. He leaned against the wall and waited. When he heard the clamor of the cue striking the floor, he strode into the pool room.

Aw, Christ. Didn't these birds ever wash? She was *green*. And that bloke she was canoodling. Skinny fucken *wimp*. Brian watched till he could stand it no longer. He strode over and slapped Jake on the shoulder. "Oi," he said. "Feral face."

Quick time out for the tonsil hockey team.

Jake and Baby blinked uncomprehendingly at Brian's leering mug.

"Oi've bin watchin' youse," he scowled. "And youse makin' me sick, mate. You wanna do that shit, you do it outsoide. And woipe that smoile off yer doile," he further advised Jake. "Unless ya want me to do it for ya. Pubs," he informed them in a voice that brooked no dissent, "er fer sinkin' piss."

230

The main compu-tron on Pop crackled into life. "Mes. sage. re. ceived. 'Hel. lo. Pop.' Over."

Qwerk quickly checked the coordinates. Parkes? Where in Quagaar was that?

Standing in the doorway of the pool room, Lati could hardly believe her oculi. She'd come back for the Abduct-o-matic, which was with the rest of their gear next to the stage, just in time to witness the big kiss. Lati couldn't understand why Baby and Jake allowed that big oafy bloke to interrupt what had obviously been, for them—and everyone else in the pool room including Lati herself, who'd grown a little cunt between her eyes just from watching—a rather sensational moment.

Those two were fucken hopeless. Baby should have turned the bouncer into a barstool or zapped him off to charm school in Perth. Instead, she just stood there awkwardly, not even daring to lift her eyes and look at Jake. Brian smirked. He turned and, examining his fingernails, headed back toward the bar. Finally, Baby picked up her cue and began to shoot pool as though nothing had happened, except she was hitting all the wrong balls. Jake was affecting an equally absurd nonchalance. He'd picked up someone's empty schooner from the table next to him and was pretending to drink from it.

Well, if Baby wasn't going to follow through with Jake, then Lati figured she could pretty much do as she liked. And she liked to cause a bit of trouble.

The gig went down smashingly with the Byron crowd. Even Brian jumped up on a table to dance with Shareen. Poor things had to be carried off when it collapsed underneath them, but that's rock 'n' roll.

After the gang had lugged out, they all whizzed over to the Epicenter for the full moon party. Scrambling down the dunes to the beach, they discovered maybe a hundred people in feral finery dancing under the silvery light of the moon, skinny-dipping, twirling firesticks, and passing pipes and tabs. Torquil and Tristram joined the large drumming circle. Henry, mumbling something incomprehensible about "graphic EQs," passed out on the sand. Doll got involved in tattooing some woman's breasts, and the little goddess of the floral essences from that afternoon whisked Baby off to meet her cosmic family.

Jake sat on the cool sand, hypnotized by the waves and the drumming and thinking about Baby's lips. He'd scored some Mullumbimby heads and had a pipe. Or two. It definitely wasn't three. Maybe three. Yeah, please, do, kiss me again. Mmmm. That's *wonderful*. That's the most *wonderful* thing in the world. Mmmmm. I'm in heaven. Let me open my eyes and look at you, my gorgeous alien girl.

*Shit!* Jake jumped about a meter backward in the sand and covered his mouth with his hands.

Baby didn't see Jake recoil. All she saw was him kissing Lati. That was enough. She turned and walked straight into the surf. Swimming furiously through the water, she dived to the bottom and punched the sand as hard as she could. The ocean floor shifted under the impact and a new sand bank formed that, surfers would later swear, created the *filthiest* swells they'd ever seen on the north coast.

By the time she emerged from the waves again, Jake was frantic. He stumbled over to the water's edge and shouted, "Baby, it's not what you—" but before he finished his sentence she dived in again. He turned to stare straight into Lati's unrepentant eyes.

"Christ, Lati," he moaned, raising his hands to the sides of his head. His tattoo ached.

"Jake," she shrugged. "You know that Dave Graney song? 'You Wanna Be There But You Don't Wanna Travel'? Think about it."

With that enigmatic comment, Lati turned on her heel and tripped off to join in the dancing. Jake waited for Baby to come out of the water, but she didn't reemerge till dawn when it was time to hit the road again.

For the drive back to Sydney, Doll took the wheel. Baby sat in the front with her, staring out the window and not speaking for the entire trip, except to tell Lati in an annoyed voice to shut up when she sang the Foo Fighters' "For All the Cows" for the hundredth time after passing yet another fucken paddock. Lati didn't care. She snuggled up to Henry, who was still feeling very delicate. Jake, mortified, horrified, crucified, and drug-fried, huddled behind the passenger seat, torturing himself with the sight of the back of Baby's head. The twins, unaware of any psychodrama, lay side by side, trying to recall exactly where they'd misplaced their brains. "Somewhere between Kalbarri and Brisbane," Torquil was saying. "Definitely somewhere between Kalbarri and Brisbane."

"Couldn't you be more specific?" groaned Tristram. "Otherwise we'll never find them again."

"It's for you, Jake," Saturna called out. She hadn't actually answered the phone. As educated guesses go, however, it was a Ph.D. The phone had been ringing nonstop for days—more even than the time last year when the dozen or so girlfriends that Jake had accumulated suddenly found out about each other and felt compelled to share with him in detail their feelings on the subject of his general desirability as a member of the human race. As before, every call was for Jake. This time, however, they were the sort of which every musician dreams—venue and festival bookers, scouts for record companies, producers offering their services, journalists begging for interviews. Kwong José Abdul Foo wanting to do a gig together and Nick Cave hoping for a duet. Countless fans volunteered their sexual services or just pleaded for scraps of clothing or locks of hair. None of the callers was the least bit interested in Bosnia.

The career of the Rock 'n' roll Babes from Outer Space had taken off at warp speed. The word was spreading faster than warm butter on a hot toaster (the girls' current breakfast of choice). Radio Triple J, which was running on a shoestring now that the government had cut ninety-five percent of its funding, had snapped up the Babes' single "In the Sexual Experimentation Chamber (Anything Goes, Everything Cums)." They put it on high rotation despite government threats to razor the final five percent if the station didn't start playing *healthy* music. When the Babes launched their LP *Come to Mothership*, the Js defiantly made it their featured album of the week, as did Triple C, which billed itself as the alternative to the alternative. The commercial stations put several tracks from it on their top ten, and even the Christian community stations played "Hangar 99." (God had had a word in their ear.)

They continued to play live, to sellout crowds all around the country. The lingering tension between Baby and Lati over what had happened in Byron only added to their heat on stage.

One day Jake, who'd by now become the Babes' de facto manager, headed over to Elizabeth Bay to discuss the upcoming No Way Out festival, where the Babes were to be sharing the stage with top international acts. Arriving at the Sebel with Iggy, he took the lift up to the pool area, just in time to see Ebola laying his daily offering of roses at the foot of the water tower. "Hi there, Jake," Ebola gurgled ingratiatingly.

A shiver of disgust ran up Jake's spine. "Uh, g'day," he replied with evasive eyes. The man was an aesthetic offence. Jake couldn't even bring himself to greet Ebola by name. For his part, Iggy looked at Eb and growled at him, as he always did. Iggy *hated* death metal.

"Gonna see our Baby?" Eb asked.

*Our* Baby? The man was a fucken outrage. Iggy's growl deepened. Jake ignored him and called up to the saucer. "Baby?"

She looked out the window, waved, and let down the steps. Jake and Iggy couldn't believe it when Ebola, uninvited, followed them up.

As Iggy scampered off to find Revor, Jake pulled Baby aside. "How can you let this guy hang around like this?" he whinged. The mobile phone that the babes had abducted for him rang. As Jake took the call, a flash of annoyance lit Baby's features. Jake had some nerve telling her who she should or should not be seeing.

She hadn't gotten over the Lati incident. Doll, who saw the whole thing, told Baby what had happened as soon as they returned to Sydney. Baby had confronted Lati, and there had been a bit of antennae-pulling and name-calling, but at least they'd faced up to it. What still irritated Baby was how Jake had avoided all attempts on her part to raise the subject. Was he guiltier than Doll made out, she wondered. If not, what was his *problem?* Earthlings, obsessed as they were with primitive toys like mobiles and e-mail, still couldn't *communicate* to save their lives.

On a sudden impulse, she grabbed Ebola, who was lying prostrate at her feet, a rose between his lips. Hauling him up by his collar, she plucked the bloom and planted a smacking wet kiss on his mouth, right before the astonished Jake. This caused Eb's hair (which he'd recently cut back to his shoulders, as a sort of compromise with the Metallica thing) to stand on end and his ears to glow orange. Then she patted him on the arse and told him to go back to the pool and leave them alone. Stepping out of the saucer, the love-befuddled rock star fell straight down to the pool deck, for no one had activated the steps. He cried out as his ankle twisted beneath him. Sitting on the deck, he cradled the hurt foot in his hands, weeping tears of pain and gratitude.

Jake swallowed bile. He concluded the call and switched off the phone. "About the concert," he opened, a little harshly. They discussed details, neither looking the other in the eye, and Jake took his leave. "Iggy?" he called. "IGGY!"

Iggy was hiding behind the door to the sexual experimentation chamber, his tiny eyes wide with vicarious mortification. He'd seen and heard everything. He couldn't come out now. He felt terrible for Jake, but wouldn't know what to say to him—"ruff ruff" somehow seemed so inadequate under the circs—and desperately wanted to find Revor so he could talk it over with him first.

"IGGY!"

In a flat voice, Baby assured Jake that Iggy would be fine. He was probably having a good time with Revor. She'd return him to Jake's the following day when they were due to go to Newtown for a meeting with some record company executives.

Feeling like he'd lost everything that had ever mattered—his girl, his dog—Jake fumbled his way back down through the Sebel and over to where he'd parked Kate. Kate was grumpy. They'd had to take a stressful detour to avoid a demonstration by workers protesting the government's tough new industrial relations laws and demanding that lunch breaks be made legal again. She'd further suffered the humiliation of being ticketed by a snotty Elizabeth Bay parking inspector who'd actually been so cruel as to mock the state of her paint job. She had every intention of giving Jake trouble on the road back to Newtown but, when she saw his expression of absolute dejection, she decided that probably wasn't a great idea.

Jake couldn't have known that this was the one and only time poor Ebola was to get his hot slimy lips on Baby's, or that that was as far as it went, or that as soon as he left, she rushed to the saucer's bathroom, threw Revor out of the spa where he'd been luxuriating, and took a bath in Dettol. Repeating "keck keck keck" to herself, she pinched her antennae hard in punishment and regret.

"Iggles? Iggles?" Revor, his fur smelling like lavender bath oil, found Iggy in the chamber licking his crotch with an air of dejection. "What's wrong?" Revor poked his little snout into Iggy's genitals, but Iggy swung his body away, and attended to an imaginary nit on his haunch. "Sheel ivvson luvs treat?" Revor tested. No response. Revor scampered off to fetch a pair of sunglasses and a spangled jumpsuit that a Sirian had once given to him. He stood on his hinds, stuck out his furry little gut and crooned, "Ahyay ntn uthin buttahow nd ogg," at which point the melancholy Iggy finally raised his teary little beadies. On seeing the outfit, he smiled, then barked and woofed with laughter. He rolled on his back, shook his paws in the air, and finally collapsed onto his side, gasping for breath. That was more like it. Revor breathed a sigh of relief.

"What's wrong, Iggy Poop? Was it something I said?" By now Revor had snuggled up close against Iggy's chest. Iggy flicked the sequins on Revor's outfit with his claws. "It's Jake." As Iggy explained, Revor took his snout between his front paws in horror. "I realize it's probably hard for you to understand," sighed Iggy in conclusion, "but this whole overnight success thing . . . I mean, everyone in our house is delighted of course, we're overjoyed for the babes. But you have to understand. It's not that easy either. I mean, how do you think Jake feels? If it was hard for him to make a move before, he's completely paralyzed now. Let's face it. He's pretty cute by Newtown standards, but he's basically just a clever young thing who lives in a dump, smokes too much dope, and plays music that's not bad but will never be brilliant. She's shot way out of his league."

"Ebola doesn't deserve to polish Jake's boots," Revor sniffed.

Baby was thinking the same thing.

*Good-bye cock rock, hello frock rock . . .*

*Juice*

Where can you go once you've redefined the genre?

*Take Britpop brats Oasis, up the sex, drugs, and rock 'n' roll factors by about a googolplex, paint them green, make them girls, and give them antennae and you begin to get an idea of what Rock 'n' roll Babes from Outer Space are like. . . .*

*Rolling Stone*

Become a caricature of yourself?

*Babes on the Net! For information, gossip, lyrics, and on-line chats with Baby, Doll, and Lati contact the news group alt.fan.greenteens. . . .*

*The J Mag*

Interfaced with every wired gasbag from here to Hercules?

*Welcome to the Sexual Experimentation Chamber. We are about to find out all about alien sex, straight from the mouth of—who else—Rock 'n' roll Babes from Outer Space. . . .*
*Australian Women's Forum*

Spoken intimately to the public about matters you haven't totally sorted out with your intimates?

*Who wasn't there at the out-of-this-world launch party for X-Terrestrials, the new Oxford Street clothing shop selling space-inspired fashion for men, women, and, as the sign on the window says, starseeds of any gender. The label is the brain-child of the Rock 'n' roll Babes from Outer Space. . . .*
*Pulse (Sydney's "New Testament of Trend")*

Become a fucken commercial enterprise?

*Inspired by Rock 'n' roll Babes from Outer Space, Tulip King has announced a new line in green lipsticks with founda-tion and blusher to match in a range of verdant shades. . . .*
*Vogue*

An icon?

*Rock 'n' roll Babes from Outer Space frontwoman Baby Baby is all Woman Woman. The stunning green-skinned beauty claims she's got no special diet or beauty secrets—"I just eat whatever I want, anything including the kitchen sink," she jokes. She refused to confirm rumors linking her with male supermodel Troy Polloi, nor would she comment on stories that her lovers have included Bad Seed Nick Cave, Oasis's Liam Gallagher, Henry Rollins, Cruel Sea oarsman Tex Perkins, or the American country superstar k.d. lang. People did obtain the following exclusive photographs, however, which show Babe's basswoman Lati Dodidohdoh out clubbing with Brad*

*Pitt—the hunky American actor is said to have been a fan of the Babes ever since he got a copy of their CD* Come to Mothership *from Tom Cruise.* . . .

*People*

Everything you ever wanted to be? Extraterrestrial extrafucken ordinaire. A Rock Star.

**I**t's me again. Yeah, Baby Baby. And I'm talking to you, Earth boy. Earth girl. Bean. Whoever.

We've had a *filthy* time on Earth. Sex, drugs, and rock 'n' roll, hey? Full-on-o-rama. All things INXS. Forget One Hot Minute—we've had, what's it been now, One Hot Six Months?

It's all worked out a bit too easily for us. Take rock 'n' roll for example. We'd barely picked up our instruments when we became rock stars. Did you notice that? Nothing too difficult about sex or drugs either. We fucked everything in sight, used no condoms, caught no diseases, and, while we did stay away from the Big Heavy Stuff, we had an excellent time on drugs, and didn't lose too many brain cells in the process. Cheerin'.

Is this a purple kangaroos crossing zone or is it just me?

Just joking. But it's been one hell of a party. And now we're headed for the biggest bash of them all—*Come to Mothership*, our big gig at the Sydney Cricket Ground. We've got heaps of special FX planned. Hope you've got a ticket—they sold out megafast. If you don't, let me know. We've still got a few backstage passes left. We'll get you in one way or another.

But, I dunno. All this stardom stuff really shifts me. Shits me. Whatever. It's like, I can't even walk into the Sando to listen to a band these days without beans all over me like a rash. I mean, I've always enjoyed a bit of attention . . . all right, I've always enjoyed being the *center* of attention, *but*. It's funny, I almost feel a sense of relief thinking about what

Zyggo said, you know, that Qwerk is coming after us. It's like, yeah, Earth, it's been real, but time to move on. Other worlds to conquer and all that.

I know you're waiting for me to say something about Jake. What can I say? I've gone from No Doubt to Faith No More and back. You know the score. I know the score. But that doesn't seem to make it any easier, does it? Melodrama-o-rama.

No, that's *not* a tear in my eye.

"Well," observed Jake. "Tomorrow's the big day."

"Are you upset that the promoters knocked Bosnia off the program?" Baby tried to shift slightly closer to Jake on the lounge room sofa but the blobby pillows slipped and slid beneath her, and she actually ended up farther away.

"Nah," Jake lied. "I know you tried. It's probably for the best anyway. We never really intended to go mainstream. We'd lose our cred. I couldn't imagine Bosnia doing stadium rock. Wouldn't want to end up like silverchair."

Baby considered how silverchair had ended up. "You mean," she giggled, "rich and famous?"

Jake flinched. "Fame and wealth don't appeal to me," he said. He glanced at her, suddenly aware of the implications of what he was saying. "Not that I'm criticizing you or anything. I know you're not in it for the money. I think that it's been great, what's happened with the Babes. It's just that I'm not really into that kind of thing. Myself."

"You know I'm not into that, either. I just love playing music. But Jake, tell me. What *are* you into? You know, I've known you all this time and I still haven't figured it out."

"Oh, whatever." He studied the ceiling. A mysterious brown stain had spread over one corner from which a small plantation of mushroomlike growths hung like stalactites in the gloom. He briefly wondered if they were edible. "True love, maybe?"

Baby's antennae stood straight up. She tried to read him but Jake was too quick for her. He was batmobiling. His deflector screens had shot up—he was an emotional escape vehicle, complete with tinted windows. Bullet-proof, bomb-proof, utterly impenetrable. Her antennae were trembling with the effort by the time she gave up.

"Jake?"

"Yeah?"

"I might not be hanging out here much longer."

Jake's heart jumped into his throat and then dropped into his stomach, slid down his leg, and fell straight out of the hole in his sock. "What d'you mean?" he said, swallowing. "You going to the States or something? Australia too much of a small pond and all that sort of thing?"

"No." Baby gave a weak laugh. "That's not it at all. Of course not. I meant this planet."

"But—" Jake kept forgetting she was an alien. It seemed she'd been in his life forever. He couldn't imagine her leaving Sydney, much less Earth. Wasn't it just space and stars and shit out there?

"It's sort of hard to explain. But I've got this cousin, Zyggo, and there's this group of leaders, the Qohort, and this guy Captain Qwerk, apparently he's coming to get us, and—" she could tell Jake didn't have a clue as to what she was talking about—"do you love me?"

*Do you love me?*

Jesus Christ! What the hell was Jake to do now? If she'd said, "I love you," Jake would have been startled but he could have coped. When a girl says "I love you," you have a number of options, and they're equally applicable whether you love her back or not. You can change the subject, you can mumble incomprehensibly, you can say "I know" or

243

"thank you" or something equally heartbreaking, or you can say "I love you too." Or you can just slip the tongue in.

Jake's eyes rabbitted around the room, searching for a safe burrow. Hunching over the coffee table, and with great concentration, he licked the tip of a finger, pressed it to some mull on the table, and raised it to his nose. He sniffed it and put it back on the table. He reached for the remote that controlled the CD player. "Have you heard the new Dambuilders EP?" he asked, aiming it at the stereo and pressing buttons.

"Jake. I asked you a question." Baby's voice was small and tremulous. Wind chimes tinkling at the end of the verandah.

Jake fiddled more insistently with the remote. He frowned. "It's stuffed," he remarked.

"I know," Baby said, a touch of impatience in her voice. "Remember? I can fuck up the electricals when I feel like it."

*Do you love me?*

Silence. Jake was trying to think of what to say. Why the hell couldn't he just say "yes"?

"Oh, forget it," said Baby sadly. "It's just, you know, a bit of a shame-o-rama that we've never, uh, you know, constipated our relationship. Cuz you know I've been thinking a lot about it, and I reckon we actually do have a relationship. Already. You know. That's what I've learned in my time on Earth. A relationship is just a connection between two people. That's all."

"Consummated," he said in a voice suddenly gone hoarse and husky.

"Consummated," she echoed.

*Do you love me?*

There was a silence. Into it, Jake mumbled, "Yeah, probably." His voice sounded like it had been hooked up to a distortion pedal. "You know." She looked at him with questioning green eyes. He studied the floor. "Love you."

244

The CD player whirred softly into action. So did Baby. Now-or-never-ville. She picked up Jake's left hand with her right and pressed it to her lips. Electrical impulses danced up his arm and traveled in tingling pathways through his body. Baby, in turn, tasting the light salt of Jake's hand, felt her whole self tremble at the piquancy of it. His fingers sought her cheeks, stroking the smooth skin of her face. They kissed for a very long time.

Pushing her head gently down, he sucked one of her antennae into his mouth. The finely proportioned antennae, with their beautiful rounded tips, delicate aqua coloring, and fine, sleek membranous sheaths were made for sucking.

She, in turn, gasped as she felt Jake's mouth slip round the knob and nibble gently on the stalk. If the eyes are the windows of the Earthling soul, the antennae are the alien soul's eyes, ears, nose, and more. Through their antennae, aliens can see beyond that which is merely apparent to that which is veiled, they can hear the most secret sounds and perceive sensations that are beyond taste and smell and touch. The organs of the hypersenses, the antennae were hypersensitive organs. It wasn't by accident that evolution had left them on top of the head, where their random contact with breezes and floating pollens and sonic vibrations and the occasional fly was already enough to drive your average alien to sensuous distraction. And Baby was hardly your average alien.

Now, with Jake's tongue flicking up and down the skin made slippery with his saliva, with his wide lips closed tight round the shaft as he sucked it down his throat, Baby's whole self was flooding with sensations of every sort. She could hear the pounding of Jake's heart. She could hear the blood cells in his lungs slurping in the oxygen and bounding back with crimson sighs of contentment into the slipstream of his arteries. She tasted the salt crystallizing on his skin, whose dampening she could also sense as though it were her own. The thickening musk of his desire was enough to take her to the very edge of a faint. The heat of his body warmed her and, as he entwined his fingers into her thick braids, caressing her scalp with his fingertips, she could sense the tingling currents racing down the pathways of her own brain.

As for Jake, the psychic secretions of the antenna were such that he had the illusion of total weightlessness. Though in reality he was still sitting on the old brown sofa, the sensation that he was floating was so vivid that for a few seconds he was gripped with a terrible vertigo. When that settled out, he opened his eyes, or thought he did, and saw that he was flying through space. He beheld a cosmic panorama, he heard the beating of pulsars, the whoosh of comets and, beyond that, the astounding silence of deep space.

Baby's braids engorged with color and glowed with supersaturated greens and pinks and blues and purples.

They slippery-dipped to the floor on a cascade of cushions.

Rainbow arcs of electricity coursed through her body now, and her skin vibrated like that of a drum. Slowly, she rolled her head away from Jake, her antenna slipping out of his slackening mouth. Parting a path through his dreadlocks, she applied her own lips to the pale shell of his ear. He trembled as her tongue expanded soft and moist into the neat cavern, tickling the soft down of its sides. She chewed on his soft lobe, pulling playfully on it with her teeth and then slipping in her fattened tongue once more.

He bent to her neck now, and plumped his lips against her jade skin. Moistening, a small, rosy mouth opened to his lips and welcomed his tongue inside it. He stroked her leg and there, too, the skin grew warm and wet and parted to embrace his fingers. He marveled at this, and at how she was trembling from the tips of her antennae to her toes now. She rolled over on top of him, curling down to kiss the crook of his elbow. She stroked and licked the skin there in a kind of daze, as though half expecting that it, too, would open to her, when she felt his hand move underneath her skirt.

He caressed the smooth skin he found between her legs, making circles upon it with his fingers, tickling and then stroking harder. The magic happened again, and slowly, like the petals of a rose unfolding, moistness gave way to cleavage, and soon he felt the insistent pressure of lips no less soft or beautiful than those that were now crushed against his. Eventually, his whole hand disappeared into that most mysterious of orifices. Baby was groaning with pleasure now, and she rode his hand gently.

She leaned away and tugged on his T-shirt, pulling it over his head and tossing it onto the floor. She bent her head to his armpits, and remembered that first, naive encounter in the sexual experimentation chamber all those months ago. She breathed in his heady, boyish scent. Smells like teen spirit. Who'd said that? Who cares. Flicking the barbell that pierced his nipple with her tongue, she ran her fingers lightly over his chest and down to his stomach.

Jake had withdrawn his dripping hand and, with his face now pressed against her breast, he felt around the back of her skintight frock for a zipper. How the hell had she got the thing . . . shit. His eyebrow ring had caught on the fabric of the dress in the front. Sssssssst. He'd only meant to shake it loose, but instead the ring had pulled a thread that pulled another and suddenly her frock had fallen away, neatly torn in two. She laughed, unconcerned, and tugged at his belt. Soon most of their clothing lay scattered around the sofa, and what remained on their bodies was of no hindrance. As their tongues entwined, Baby rubbed herself against him, enjoying his fuzzy warmth and the hardness of his cock against her stomach, where yet another new mouth was parting its hungry lips. These lips suddenly sucked him inside and Jake gasped as the flexible inner tongue which gave pleasure in both directions began sliding itself around the swollen head and sensitive rim of his cock. Baby was in such a state of arousal now that her skin was shimmering with kaleidoscope-like images, loops and spirals and psychedelic patterns. Jake's tongue and fingers were burrowing into yet more *petites bouches* that had opened up in her breasts and on the plump cheeks of her arse. The tiny tongues inside each cunt swelled until, like overripe fruit, they felt as though they'd burst at one more touch. Juices flowed from these mouths bearing flavors of cinnamon and spice and cockles and lemon.

Jake reached again for her antennae. This time, the mere touch of his lips to the sensitive shaft caused her to explode in *simultaneous* multiple orgasms, the capacity for which is a rather big advantage of being an alien.

As she spasmed and sparked with extreme pleasure, her many cunts grew and widened and merged so that where they had sucked in a finger, it was now an entire hand that they ingested, and then an arm, until finally, her entire body gaped open and swallowed Jake whole. He filled her up, from head to toe—even her limbs were replete with him. Jake, meanwhile, found himself squeezed inside the most delicious, warm, wet space, at once profoundly comforting and deeply exciting. Come to Mothership indeed. He swam through her, surfing her waves. He felt an orgasm ripple through his body from his head to his feet and then back up again, through each vertebra, down every nerve path, even along his very marrow. Jake had never experienced an orgasm that was so powerful or that lasted so long. He felt utterly annihilated. Shaken and stirred to the core of his bean. Just as he was beginning to notice that it was a trifle difficult to breathe, Baby moaned and stiffened and came again, screaming with pleasure. *Odelay-yee-oo!*

Lati and the twins were just stepping into the house when they heard Baby holler. They rushed into the lounge just in time to see a gasping and totally slimed Jake come tumbling out of the largest, most extraordinary cunt any of them had ever seen, on a tidal wave of juices. He was a bit blue in the face, which made him and Baby an even more perfect pair.

Iggy and Revor had dashed in as well, and were squealing and howling and performing somersaults of sheer delight.

Baby looked up at their audience. "Sorry," she apologized breathlessly and with a naughty giggle, "I forgot. In space, you know, no one can hear you cream. Now, fuck off ya slags."

Lati grabbed the twins each by an arm and led them upstairs to make further inroads, so to speak, into the question of how much fun one alien girl with an infinite number of cunts could have with two Earth boys.

By the time Jake recovered, Baby's petals were folding back in on themselves, except for one spot on her neck that she was stroking absentmindedly, her eyes closed. He bent over her, scooped her up in his arms and, trying not to huff or puff too much (she was, after all, something of an Amazon and Jake wasn't exactly Mr. Jock), carried her up the stairs and into the shower. There, they made love all over again. Ending up in Jake's room, they fell asleep in each other's arms, or rather, Jake fell asleep in Baby's arms. Baby didn't sleep much anyway, and her mind was whirring.

Something told her this would be her final night on Earth.

Wheeeee, yodeled the Sirians and the Alphas and the Cherubim and the rest as Pop zipped through the Last Wormhole Before Planet Earth like a toboggan on a water slide. *Yeeha!* There was further hilarity, and not a little panic, when they discovered that they'd exceeded the recommended speed limit for wormholes and were starting to get some of their molecules confused—a Sirian and a Zeta Reticulan inadvertently swapped noses, for instance, and Qwerk must have traded a few brain cells with an Alpha, because he actually began *laughing at the others' jokes.*

Eros, meanwhile, had just caught wind of the fact that the biggest, baddest, bestest rock concert ever was going to happen the following night in Sydney, Australia, Earth. *Those babes.* Promises-shmomises, Eros was going to be *in the mosh.* What had God ever done for him, hey?

But twinkle twinkle Mazzy Star, how the hell do you get that far? *The Kirkwood gaps!* Eros jumped up and down in his joy! That's it! The ejection seats of the asteroid belt! If I can just maneuver into one of the gaps, Jupiter's gravitational pull will just whip me up and away!

Here we go! Yaaaaaaaaay!

After what seemed to Baby a very long time veering on forever, Jake finally woke up. "Morning, starshine," she greeted him, rather too brightly for that time of day.

"Mmmm," he moaned, stretching and yawning and rolling on top of her. He was still sticky with her juices and his own. "I feel seedy," he informed her.

"Why don't you take a shower then?"

"What—and spoil the moment?" he replied, yawning again, rolling off, and scratching his balls. Baby looked at

Jake with a new and disturbing clarity. Her antennae felt unusually sharp. They were picking up all sorts of things. Jake's air of postcoital complacency, for one. The Missing Banana for another. (It was hiding under a copy of Homer's *Odyssey*, another book Jake was planning to read when he got old.) She suddenly recalled the feeling of let-down she'd had that first night in the sexual experimentation chamber, when she'd wondered if that was all there was to sex. Now of course, she knew better. Last night—now that was Sex with a capital S. It was more than that, too, it was, you know, the pop thing as well as the rock thing. But now what?

Jake threw an arm over her. It felt heavy and confining. She needed *space*, she thought. Which, coming from an alien, could mean any number of things.

"Breakfast?"

"Sure," said Baby, thinking, go on, just leave me alone for a minute.

Jake trundled off downstairs. She could hear the toilet flush. Yuk-o-rama. She was still unused to Earthling evacuation habits. Alien systems were so much more efficient. They just turned food into energy. Full stop. Oh, there was the occasional fart, of course. But as we have seen, alien farts are in a category by themselves. Practically art. Arty farty.

Soon Jake returned with two plates. On one was a three-day-old almond croissant, some scrambled eggs, and some cheese he'd stolen from Saturna and Skye's half of the fridge, on the other was an electric pencil sharpener and some other bits and pieces he'd scavenged from George's place for her. They ate in silence. Well, not exactly silence. The whirring of the pencil sharpener and the sound of Baby scoffing metal lent the romantic little scene the soundtrack of an auto wrecking yard. Jake didn't care. *He was in love.*

After breakfast, they began to feel amorous all over again.

Jake knelt on the mattress and pulled open a drawer in the wardrobe by the bed. "So *that's* where all my socks are," he exclaimed in wonderment as he chucked the dirty plates in. Closing the drawer he turned back to Baby and, putting on his best Iggy imitation, proceeded to nuzzle and growl at her astounding breasts.

The little act with the dirty dishes and the sock drawer did it for Baby. *Rock 'n' roll.* She was definitely in love again.

For the moment, anyway.

## What do you want and what can you get?

"When I get what I want, I never want it again."

—*Courtney Love*

## Doll was the first to return to

the flying saucer on the day of the big concert. Skye and Saturna had risen early to open the shop. Lati was off with the chemical brothers, as usual, on some sort of pharmaceutical quest. Baby was still with Jake. Doll fumed. Boys. Drugs. Those two were so unreliable. They were due at the stadium in just a few hours for the sound check. Pacing, she found herself at the door to Galgal's control room. None of them had been in there in ages. She pushed open the door, glanced around, and was about to leave when something on one of the monitors caught her eye. "Jump-fuck-ing Jupiter!" she exclaimed, a chill running up her antennae.

There was no time to waste.

Mum had received a message. It was a simple message. "Hello, Mum." Only a Nufonian could have sent that message. Qwerk. It had to be him. He was coming to get them. She checked the date and spatial locus. Doing a few quick calculations, she worked out that he was probably through the Last Wormhole Before Planet Earth and nearly at the tollgate to the lunar orbit.

God operated the tollgate, of course. Fancying Himself something of a metaphysician, He'd set the toll at "something of yoonal value." The girls had gotten through by tossing the Bing Crosby record collection into the basket. It was originally Lati's idea of a joke, a brief diversion while they worked out a more plausible offering. They could hardly believe it when the light turned green and the turnstile went up. Doll had activated the boosters, and they shot through before God had a chance to realize His mistake. It wasn't a mistake, of course. God is infallible.

The Nufonians would be touching down in a few hours.

Knowing the Nufonian distaste for scenes, Doll banked on the likelihood that Qwerk would make his move only after the concert was finished. That meant that if they jumped into the saucer right at the end, they'd have a fair chance of making a getaway. Doll had to get the saucer over to the cricket ground, then. She'd explain to the others later.

She glanced at the chronometer. Hoping that the others had come back, she went to Lati's room first and stuck her head in. No one there. A messy array of small sealed bags covered the bed. In the bags were pills and powders, mushrooms and leaves of various descriptions. Doll opened one, dipped a finger into some powder and sniffed. The cocaine launched itself straight into her brain and rocketed around her blue matter. Doll felt her feet lift off the ground. She was spinning like a top. With sudden clarity, she knew exactly what needed to be done. Scooping up all the drugs in her arms, Doll hightailed it to Galgal's engine room. There wasn't a moment to spare.

## "Strap me up, strap me down."

"It's 'tie me up, tie me down' you moron."

"Who cares. I just dig all this bondage and discipline."

"Speaking of."

Captain Qwerk had finally worked out that he could get through God's tollgate by unloading his new sense of humor. Now, followed by his crew of borgs and bots, he was making a final inspection of the saucer before its ejection from Pop, which was docked in lunar orbit close to Mum. The aliens were already harnessed to their seats though, as Qwerk passed by, they clicked open their seat belts, let down their tray tables, and tilted their seats back just to annoy him. Qwerk knew the routine. He passed them in dignified silence and entered the cockpit.

The saucer was a later model than Galgal, larger but sleeker. Ptui! Pop spat out Boyboy like a watermelon seed. *Ziiiiip.*

"Getting hot."

"World's biggest vibro-sauna," chuckled a Zeta Reticulan, reaching under his seat for the inflatable vest which Must Not Be Fully Inflated Until You Are Out of the Spacecraft. That was another favorite trick, pulling the tabs on the vests, screeching the whistles, flashing the lights. But wait, what was this? Groping around under the seat, he'd unexpectedly found a tiny lever. Naturally, he fiddled with it.

"Ow!" cried a Sirian seated across the aisle, clutching his fat head, upon which a dense object had fallen. "Ow!"

While the Sirians fell about in hysterics, an Alpha stretched out a leg and snaffled up the missile with his dexterous toes. "Holy Canopus!" he cried, opening the Hidden Agenda, for that's what it was. Alphas were the speed-readers of the yoon and, just minutes later he'd nearly finished it when Boyboy angled sharply downward and began its plummet to Earth.

"Wheeeeeeeeeeeeeeeeeeeeeeeeeeeeeeeeeeeeeeeeeeeeeeeeeeeeee!" screamed the other aliens as high g-forces plastered them to their seats. "Wheeeeeeeeeeeeee!"

In Washington, within the CONSPIRASEE office, a red light glowed and a buzzer honked for attention. General "Jackal" Mikeson hoicked up his big chin and peered out from between his secretary's legs. "Oh my God," he whistled, seeing what had appeared on his computer screen. "It's the big one. Off that big fat tush of yours, Herman, and call up the troops. Qwerk's in town and we're gonna get his gray ass."

Qwerk steered the saucer straight to Parkes. Several weeks earlier, the government had canceled all funding for scientific institutions. Luella and her crew—convinced they were *that close* to making contact—had been forced to pack up and look for jobs in the woodchipping industry, the only growth sector of the entire economy aside from casinos.

Boyboy passed low over several country towns in Queensland and New South Wales. As Earthlings pointed and stared in fascination and fright, the Sirians, dressed in their spangly jumpsuits, leaned out of the portholes and shouted, "We've brought you Elvis!" Qwerk didn't have a clue as to what they were going on about, but he had too much on his mind to give it much thought.

Parkes wasn't hard to find—a vast webwork of steel and

aluminium rising out of an immense paddock. Its center-piece was a large white dish sixty-four meters in diameter, the place from which the greeting had emanated. When the saucer landed, beside the deserted complex, sheep were baa-ing at the unplugged monitors, and an entire flock of galahs was nesting in the dish. There wasn't a bean in sight.

The babes clearly weren't there either. Qwerk checked his coordinates. He was certain that the message to Pop had been sent from here. Darn. He rifled through the debris at the hastily abandoned scientific outpost for some clue as to where they might have gone. Ah-*hah*.

"We're off to Sydney," he informed the others, fingering an advertisement for *Come to Mothership*. The ad featured a photograph of the Rock 'n' roll Babes from Outer Space. "Let's leave Boyboy here. We can get around easier in Pallas." Pallas was a cigar-shaped craft stored inside Boyboy. Given the right weather conditions, Pallas could pass over Earthling-inhabited zones without being detected until practically the moment of landing.

The babes had insisted on keeping ticket prices for the concert low. The promoters grumbled at first, but when the girls told them that they didn't want any of the profits, that the promoters could keep the lot, they were happy as Larry. Who was still very, very happy.

Different bands attract different audiences. You wouldn't confuse the clean-cut disco bunnies flocking to hear the Pet Shop Boys with the hairy little headbangers who worship Metallica and Twisted Mofo, the beautiful punk girls with their glittery faces moshing for Babes in Toyland with the ponytailed suburban blondes bopping to Le Club Nerd.

But how would you describe, in a phrase, the crowd that was now streaming—pouring, flooding—into the Sydney

Cricket Ground for the Rock 'n' roll Babes from Outer Space? There were hippies in tie-dyed harem pants, North Shore boys in boat shoes, hardcore punks with mohawks, dykes in leather corsets and fishnet stockings, kids on skateboards, New Agers with big curly hair, SF buffs in button-down shirts, pretty gay boys, ravers and ragers of every ilk. It was impossible to generalize even in terms of age. There were oldies who hadn't been to a rock concert since, oh, the Rolling Stones and the Rolling Stones before that, and babies-in-arms who would be told *you were there* when they were old enough to understand it meant something. Many of the punters wore headbands from which bounced two springy antennae, or wore handmade T-shirts with slogans like "Aliens Rock Harder." Some carried stick toys with spinning flying saucers on top.

Luella, who was still looking for work, was there with Aubrey, Aaron, and Jason. Also there were Zach and the rest of the team from Kissed for the Very First Time Records (including Mr. Spinner), all of Newtown, half of Darlinghurst. There were the Mormons, and the drag queen, and Kya, and Groovy Gregory. Ratface had come down from Byron Bay and, yes, Brian the Bouncer and Shareen were there too. Three had come up from Melbourne and Prik Harness and the Angel Pygar from Canberra. The abductees were there, naturally. And Ebola. George, of course, wouldn't have missed it for the end of the world.

Quark dropped the others off at the Opera House. He was surprised that they had all been happy to come to Sydney with him. Normally he'd be making drop offs all over the planet: Moscow so they could play in the subways, Madagascar so they could giggle at the lemurs, the English countryside to do crop circles. But today they all wanted to come to Sydney. Something about having a picnic at Eagle Rock? Who knows? Who cares? It was a beautiful late summer's day, the sky was a cloudless blue, the tiles of the Opera House were glittering in the sun, and the harbor was dotted with pretty white sails. If he could just find those little troublemakers, neutralize them, and retake the saucer, well, hey, hey, it was Saturday and Earth would be Qwerk's oyster.

An oyster's a slippery thing, however. And if Qwerk had just misspent a bit more of his youth, in fact, if he'd misspent any of his youth, he'd have known something was up. Picnic at Eagle Rock indeed.

The truth of the matter was that the aliens had discovered, courtesy of the Hidden Agenda, what the Nufonians really wanted to do on Earth. Make it a better place, sure. If your definition of a better place encompassed the notion of a planet without music, without love, without desire. Without rock 'n' roll. These were the prime factors of Earthly chaos, according to the Nufonians. And they were going to eliminate them, one by one, beginning with their own creations, the very musical, very lovable, very desirable and desirous, Rock 'n' roll Babes from Outer Space. What they did to Michelle Mabelle—that was child's play.

Nufonians knew nothing about Eros, of course.

Doll paced the backstage area, waiting for the others to show. Roadies and crew were rushing back and forth, dragging cables here, hauling them there, testing mikes and switches and lights and lasers. "We have an emergency," she told Baby and Lati when they sauntered in at last. Pulling them away from the hangers-on, promoters, and journalists, all of whom wanted just one quick word before the show, she hurried them into the dressing room and shut the door. "They've caught up to us."

"Who's caught up to us? What are you talking about?" Baby tried to speak the words without guilt, but she wasn't feeling too innocent. She'd deliberately not said a word to the others about Zyggo. Would you change your life just because some big bug blundered up while you were tripping, claimed to be your cousin, and told you to skedaddle? On the other hand, as she told Jake, she was getting ready to pack her bags. Or would be. If she had bags. Who has bags anymore, anyway?

"Daddy Pop. Captain Qwerk himself. He's on his way to recapture us. I don't think it's going to be pretty."

"What makes you think he's here?" Lati asked.

"They've contacted Mum," said Doll. "Now, by my calculations, we've got just enough time to finish the concert and then beat it out of here. I covered the saucer with Enigma Cream—used up our entire supply—and parked it by the side of the stage. The cream will probably start to wear off by the time we start the show, but that's okay. I don't think anyone will try to interfere then."

"Oh, God," whimpered Baby. "I need to see Jake."

*You'll see him. Anyway, weren't you just nattering on about getting a bit sick of the whole Earth gig? You're not being very consistent.*

"A foolish consistency is the hobgoblin of little minds."

*Emerson? You're quoting Ralph Waldo Emerson to me? I must say, I'm rather gobsmacked. I didn't think you read.*

I don't. It's a line from an Angel Pygar song.

*Figures. About Jake. Surely, he's coming to the concert?*

Yes, but God, I need to see him right now.

*You realize I spoil you girls.*

Yes. And we love and worship you for it. We have no other God beside you rarara.

*That's what I like to hear. The second I hear of any funny business with false idols or golden calves or anything like that you're on your own.*

Understood. Thank you. Oh thank you thank you thank you.

Saturna and Skye were dressed and ready to go. They stood in the doorway of the lounge impatiently tapping their feet and looking at imaginary watches as the twins performed their ritualistic preconcert toke-up.

"You know what I think," remarked Skye to Saturna, loud enough for the others to hear. "I think that the boys smoke dope to excess as a way of avoiding the intensity of life, of facing up to their feelings about things."

"That's bullshit," retorted Torquil, trying to think why. "Dope, uh, intensifies the intensity," he hazarded. "Yeah. Of life."

"Yeah," agreed Tristram, exhaling. "You really face up to your feelings. It's like, you see the real face of your feelings." He was onto something here. "The nose and eyes and mouth of your feelings. You can smell them. Real as."

A silence followed. Impatient on the part of Skye and Saturna, philosophical on the part of the twins. "What were we talking about?" asked Torquil, perplexed.

"I'm not sure," said Tristram inhaling, getting paranoid, thinking, why does Saturna always wear *purple*? What does it *mean*? Is it because she doesn't like me?

"Where's Jake?" demanded Skye, drumming her fingers on the banister.

"He, uh."

"He, uh, went upstairs to find a sock," Torquil finished his brother's sentence.

"A sock," noted Skye.

"A sock," repeated Saturna dryly. She and Skye didn't have any trouble with their socks.

"Either of you got a spare sock?" Jake called out from upstairs. "Mine all have egg on them."

"Wow," marveled Torquil. "Did you hear that? *Egg?* That's so cool."

Tristram, on the other hand, didn't like the sound of that *one little bit*. What was egg doing on Jake's socks? Whose egg was it? And why was Skye looking at him like that?

Jake appeared on the landing. Then, abruptly, right before their eyes and, to the accompaniment of a grand flourish of trumpets, he disappeared in a vortex of light.

"Guess he, uh, decided to go on ahead," observed Torquil.

Ping! Jake suddenly found himself backstage.

"I wish you guys wouldn't do that," he said crankily, as Doll stifled a giggle. His Fuct T-shirt had come through inside-out and back-to-front.

Even God had his little jokes.

261

As Jake was putting his shirt back on, Baby pulled him to one side. "We have to talk."

Oh no! Not again! But wasn't everything going well? Like, well enough so that you didn't have to talk about it?

"It looks like we're in a wee nano of trouble. It's a long story, but the short version is that we're going to have to make treks."

"Tracks," Jake said, ever helpful. "Make tracks."

"No, treks. Star treks. They've sent a search party from our home planet. If they catch us they'll force us to go back and who knows what they'll do to us then. Punishmentville for sure. We're going to have to take off right after the concert. If you wanted to come too," she offered casually, "you could. I don't know where we're going, exactly, and I don't know how long we'll be there, but I wouldn't mind, you know, spending some quality continuum space-time with you." As she spoke she hung a plastic ID around his neck. It said "Rock 'n' roll Babes from Outer Space: Access All Areas." "There," she giggled, "it's official."

Jake was over the moon. "Yeah, great," he said. What the fuck was she talking about? Going where? Baby, don't go.

"Babes! Babes!" The cheers for the Babes began halfway through the support band's set. Outside the stadium people were pleading tearfully with the guards to let them in. There were no scalpers—no one who managed to get a ticket would have parted with it under any circumstances. The guards, bewitched by the Babes' presence, let more people in than they should have. Like, maybe twenty or thirty thousand more. By the time the lights dimmed for the Babes, the crowd was hysterical with anticipation. The ambulance tent had already treated dozens of people for whiplash caused by overly boisterous Mexican waving. They'd given away thousands of condoms as the mere proximity of the Babes had brought on a veritable love frenzy.

A strobe projected millions of spinning stars onto a black backdrop. Comets shot through the night and a large hologram of the moon rose above the stage, inciting a great gasp of appreciation from the audience. Next, as lasers crisscrossed the sky, a spotlight came up over the drums to reveal Doll, in a sleeveless black leather minidress, black tights, and knee-high boots, lightly brushing the cymbals. Lati then strode onto the stage in a lime green PVC catsuit, with thigh-high kelly green patent leather boots, and picked up her bass. Her riffs were nearly drowned out by shrieks and screams and the general roar of adulation and astonishment as Baby floated onstage in an antigravity space suit. Wrenching off the helmet and tossing it into the crowd, she shook free her tumbling mass of braids and, still high above the stage, launched into their new hit single "Chaos Is My Best Friend." As she sang, she ripped off the spacesuit, limb by limb, in a space-age striptease, just like Jane Fonda in *Barbarella*, only raunchier. The spacesuit had been filled with helium, and each part she removed floated up into the air above the stadium and then far away. Underneath, she was wearing a minidress made entirely of mirrors, like a disco ball. Her long legs were covered in sparkly black tights, ripped and torn specially for the occasion by Revor, and on her feet were a pair of custom-made silver Blundstones. By the time she'd floated down to the stage and picked up her guitar, the mosh pit was steaming and bubbling like some great witches' cauldron. The magic of the Babes was such that no stage diver ever came crashing to ground, no mosher ever copped a foot in the face, no girl was so much as touched up against her will, and despite the intensity of the mosh, no one suffered even a crushed toe or bruised rib.

Next, they played the ever-popular "Abduction."

> *I wanna be your abductee,*
> *Tied and captured, wild and free,*
> *Oh darlin' you were meant for me.*
> *Prod me with your stethoscope*
> *Stick me with needles—I can cope.*
> *I wanna be your abductee*

The crowd joined in on the chorus with an enthusiastic roar:

> *Tied and captured, wild and free!*

A cheer went up when Revor hunched across the stage to take Doll an extra drumstick, the roadie's roadie in a black T-shirt and sneakers, and with more keys on his belt than even Henry the mixer.

At some point into the fourth song, there was a sudden commotion. All eyes raised to the sky as Pallas descended, rockets blazing. The spaceship blinked and glowed. A strobe light swirled from the nose of the craft and swept the crowd. "HOOWEEE!" screamed the punters. This was better than Voodoo Lounge and Zoo TV and Madonna put together!

A flock of Cherubim appeared next, close on the tail of Pallas, chittering and chattering in their spiraly language like some insane loop on a dance track. Which is exactly what the crowd took it for. More cheers greeted the Cherubim, who flew hither and thither, flapping their wings madly, and shedding feathers over the fans, who enthusiastically scrambled to souvenir them.

The Channel Three news helicopter had arrived on the

scene too, along with a rather distressed paraglider who'd gotten caught in the updraft.

Now the hatch on Pallas popped open and Qwerk appeared in the doorway. The last thing Captain Qwerk ever intended was to become a sideshow at a rock concert. He was trembling so violently that he sounded like someone attacking a giant gong with a hammer, a sound that blended in perfectly with Doll's madcap drumming. Qwerk was rockin' the groove.

Steadying himself, he stepped out now, a Lobot-a-tron semiautomatic pacifier in hand, and immediately shrunk back in horror at the sea of shrieking faces, tossing hair, waving fists, and pogo-ing bodies, more hysteria and erotic energy per square meter than he had imagined could be contained safely in the entire cosmos. And there on stage, the cause of all this insanity and chaos: the Babes themselves.

"Close Encounter You!" screamed the punters, sure that these fabulous FX were the cue for that particular hit. Two teenage girls with pink and yellow mohawks broke through the barricades, ran to Qwerk, gave him a big smacking wet kiss on each cheek and then, flashing the victory sign to the cheering crowd, ran back into the mosh.

It was a Nufonian's worst nightmare. This is what Nufonians like when they come to Earth: Nufonians like a discreet arrival, preferably on some lonely stretch of highway in the middle of the night, when they are least likely to disturb anyone. Meeting Earthlings, they like to keep a certain distance, for Nufonians cherish the notion of, and *this is not a pun*, personal space. They do not like to kiss Earthlings. Even the sex tends to be a bit clinical—recall, if you will, the laboratory-like feel of the sexual experimentation chamber. They always ask politely to be taken to Earthlings' leaders, for they like going through proper channels.

Qwerk, unclinically smooched and improperly channeled, stood frozen as a teardrop on Pluto.

> *I had a dream*
> *about a hill*
> *about a boy*
> *about a girl*
> *you weren't there*
> *in the light . . .*

No sooner did the Babes finish "Close Encounter You" than the punters screamed for "Hangar 99."

At this moment, the Alphas, Sirians, Zetas, and others arrived on the scene in force. Because they had neither tickets nor wings, they hadn't been able to get past the gates, but one of the Sirians remembered something he'd once seen on an old episode of *Twilight Zone* and they passed through a crinkle in time. This put them at the stage ten minutes earlier than when they'd started out. Most of the Sirians were wearing their Elvis jumpsuits, though one had found his ET mask and was wearing that.

A Sirian made the first move. Nimble as, he leapt onto Captain Qwerk's back, wrapped suctiony fingers around his shiny little body and stuck his meter-long tongue straight down Qwerk's ear. Now we know how sensitive Nufonian ears are. Qwerk, paralyzed with pleasure, dropped his Lobot-a-tron. The Sirian briefly extracted his tongue, looked at another Sirian, and mouthed the words "wax-o-rama!" They both laughed so hard at this that Qwerk managed to rouse himself, pick up his weapon, and hold the barrel to the first Sirian's head.

The Babes played on, loud and hard.

"GULP!" cried the Sirian.

The Cherubim chose this moment to descend upon Qwerk. Grabbing onto his knobbly fingers with their pudgy fists, they lifted the small gray high in the air above the stage and gave him a good talking to. They told him that they'd seen him pleasuring his uvula several times on the flight over. They told him that they had found the Hidden Agenda. Then they put him down right on top of the roof of the stage. Qwerk, who, for a cosmonaut, was remarkably afraid of heights and could not even contemplate looking down, was so agitated by now that his limbs began to twitch and jerk and spasm. Nothing life-threatening, but it did make for excellent visuals.

Luella Skye-Walker nudged her husband and pointed to Qwerk. "Haven't seen breakdancing in *ages.*"

"Definitely time for a revival," Aubrey nodded enthusiastically, attempting a shoulder pop, whip, and finger curl. He rubbed his neck. "Maybe not, however, at my age."

"You know, Aubrey, I really wish we'd made contact before the project was wound up," Luella sighed. "Can you imagine how wild it would be if all these aliens were *real?*"

Qwerk's bots and borgs, meanwhile, were taking deep breaths and steeling themselves to venture out into the madness and rescue their leader when Iggy and Revor dashed over and planted themselves at the foot of Pallas's exit ramp. One glance at Iggy, who wasn't even trying to look threatening, and even the notorious borgs of 49 Serpentis retreated. They cowered behind the door, palpitating madly within their pink triangular chests.

And the Babes played on.

> *Warped drive, I'm a-gettin' outta here*
> *Warped drive, I'm switching far for near.*
> *I'd like to be on the same planet as you some day*
> *But even when we're close you're so far away*
> *So thanks for all the Memocide*
> *It's been fun, it's been a ride,*

*Warped drive, warped drive*
*I'm a-gettin' outta here.*

Sirians, being vertically challenged, couldn't see very well at rock concerts. Not quite able to catch what was going on, the Sirian in the ET mask chose this moment to wander onto the stage.

The sight of him spurred the crowd into a veritable frenzy. "Phone home!" they screamed. "Phone home!" Just then he noticed what looked like a SWAT team in full battle dress rush the stage from the other side. In fright, he dived off the stage and landed in the mosh, where he was caught and bodysurfed, passed from hand to hand over the top of the crowd for the rest of the concert.

The Sirian was wrong. It wasn't a SWAT team at all. It was General Jackal Mikeson's TWATS team (Troops for Wasting Aliens To Shit), the enforcement arm of CONSPIRASEE. TWATS were far worse than SWATs. The Alphas and other Sirians and Zeta Reticulans, who hadn't really thought of anything to do yet, now hurled themselves onto the TWATS, hanging upside down off their helmets, sticking suction-cuppy toes onto their faces, trying to tickle them under their flak jackets, and farting up their nostrils. The TWATS weren't the slightest bit flustered by this. This was precisely the sort of situation for which they'd been professionally trained. Suctioning a Sirian off his face, Mikeson signaled for his men to advance on the Babes—who were still madly playing—and then Qwerk.

"Drama-o-rama!" shuddered Tristram from the mosh. In his mind, he leaped up onto the stage and took the TWATS on single-handedly, saving the Babes and earning the total and undivided attention of Lati, who'd never look at another bean again. Except maybe Torquil, when he allowed it. Torquil was thinking the same thing. Here is a picture of slacker heroism: Tristram, looking deeply concerned, re-lights a joint and passes it to Torquil. Then they make their way to the front and tap one of the Sirians on the shoulder.

"Uh, anything we can do?" asked Torquil.

"Cousin!" cried the Sirian, embracing him.

Doll was the first of the Babes to react to all the confu-sion. "Oh, God," she said under her breath as she rolled the drums, "help us. Please. Dear God. If we've ever needed you, we need you now."

CK-CK-CK-CK-CR*RRRAACK!!* A great hole gaped in the speaker stack and a gigantic creature with the face of Phil Collins, the hair of Lenny Kravitz, the body of young Elvis, the dress sense of Dave Graney, the smoldering sexu-ality of The Artist Formerly Known as Prince, the snarl of Johnny Rotten, and the biggest fucken three-necked guitar in the entire yoon burst forth. He was trailing colored streamers and waving a glittering musical staff which He used to lasso the entire division of TWATS.

"KONG FOO SING!" He hollered, commanding them, "Make My day. Dance to the music!" At which point the soldiers turned as one toward the audience, threw their helmets into the air, ripped open their shirts to reveal well-toned chests and, led by Mikeson himself, began gyrating raunchily to the chorus of "In the Sexual Experimentation Chamber (Anything Goes, Everything Cums)."

The fans loved it. They screamed, they laughed, they cheered, they applauded, they pogoed, they moshed, they pashed, they fucked in the aisles. What with the nonstop music, Pallas pulsing on one side, Galgal beaming on the other; what with Qwerk still breakdancing on the roof, the Cherubim cavorting in the air with the lost paraglider and the hovering helicopter; what with the Sirians and Alphas bounding around the stage, ET in the mosh, and now this invasion of dancing soldier boys, not to mention the visita-tion by the ultimate Rock God, blessed be His name, Who was now performing a *filthy* guitar solo of "Stairway to Heaven," this was undoubtedly the best rock 'n' roll stage show in the past, present, and future history of the yoon.

It was so cool, so sick, so full-on, so utterly absorbing and absolutely fabulous that no one even noticed the night sky darkening as an asteroid some twenty-two kilometers in diameter began its approach to Earth.

"Sorry about the rush"—Baby was now standing at the front of the stage and shouting into the microphone—"but as you can see, we're wanted in a few places that we don't particularly want to be wanted in. The life of a rock 'n' roll alien outlaw is a bit like that. We've had a fully mega-mega time on your planet, it's been real *as*, and we love all of you."

What? Jake felt a sudden wave of panic. What was happening? Had she been serious when she said that about leaving? And what did she mean, "love *all* of you." What about *him?* What about *him?*

"You see," she was explaining, "if we don't hightail it out of here sometime around, oh, exactly now, we're dead alien meat. And if you've ever seen dead alien meat, you'll know it's not a pretty sight. So we're off. Don't know where. Don't know when we'll be back. We're just going to get on that big skyway and keep on truckin."

Without *him?* Hey—where had the twins gone? Was *everyone* going to desert him now?

"If you want to come with us," Baby offered, "listen carefully. This is the drill. When I say *rock 'n' roll*, visualize yourself in our flying saucer here, and bang your head three times. All right punters, now—ROCK 'N' ROLL." Hair flew, lacunae opened up in the crowd. Where Larry and the other abductees had been standing, for instance, where George had been, and young Zach, and Skye and Saturna, and Ozone, and Ebola, Groovy Gregory, and even a prominent government leader who'd recently stated that the Babes were his favorite band, better than silverchair even, and Jackal Mikeson's secretary Herman, and Des Blight, and Henry the mixer.

Jake tried to visualize himself in the saucer. He saw the scene of his initial abduction, of himself and Baby playing pool at the Sando, of the first day he and Torquil heard the babes practicing, of the first gig, of touring. He saw himself making love to Baby. Mostly, he saw himself making love to Baby. She was the most amazing girl he'd ever met, they'd had top times, and atomic sex. It was actually true. He *loved* her. With all his heart.

Maybe it really was time to, uh, *commit.* But his skin felt as though it had shrunk a whole size too small for him, his mouth went dry, his palms dampened, and his temples throbbed. He desperately needed a joint and a beer. He needed to think this through.

Baby's antennae had picked Jake out of the crowd. She read his equivocation. A pang rent her heart. "Final call," she said, looking straight at him. *Won't you ride with me?* He looked away. "ROCK 'N' ROLL!" He was still there. He wasn't coming. She knew that now. But she also knew, having read his mind, that he did love her. In his own, strange, Earth boy way. And while part of her wished it could be otherwise, that they could be together forever and ever, she was happy. She was, after all, Baby Baby, wild 'n' free, extraterrestrial extraordinaire, number one rock 'n' roll babe from outer space. There'd be other adventures, other planets, other loves, if not in this solar system then in the next, or the next. Jake would always have a place in her heart, but her heart was a pretty big place.

She could see Doll frantically gesturing at her to hurry up. The borgs and bots in Pallas were now revving up the engine, and God, having done His bit, was tapping His feet and looking at His watch. Qwerk, still on the roof, was the only one to notice the approaching Eros, but his screams were absorbed in the general tumult.

"Thank you very much, Sydney," Baby cried. "Thank you Australia. Thank you Earth. We're the Rock 'n' roll Babes from Outer Space. Catch you next time!" She lifted her guitar into the air and smashed it down on the stage. Lati stomped on her bass and Doll kicked over her drums and tossed the sticks into the mosh, where a thousand hands reached up for them—and lo and behold, the sticks multiplied in the air until there was one for every pair of hands.

As their fans stood and cheered, waving and swaying, Doll revved up Galgal. There wasn't a moment to spare. The saucer rose upward on a solid beam of light, which it then sucked back up into itself with a great big slurp. "Hold on tight," said Doll, throwing the saucer into gear and hanging a u-ee over the stadium with the borg-piloted Pallas in pursuit. Qwerk was still on the roof, gazing with horror upon the fast-plummeting Eros.

Pulling the craft into a sharp right turn, Doll cried, "Okay computer!" and threw all the switches. All the drugs flooded into the engine now. The amphetamines kicked the saucer into a faster and faster velocity. It vibrated and hummed with the speed and cocaine. The acid and mushies were wreaking havoc with the viewing screen, causing little green teddy bears and plates of purple spaghetti to loom up in Doll's sights, but she steeled herself and ran straight through them.

As the saucer passed over the suburb of Wollstonecraft, it

caused a giant sonic boom. Every window in every house shattered with a huge explosion of glass, every knickknack and piece of crockery flew off every shelf.

"Last time I vote for those bastards," exclaimed one distraught resident. "Cunts promised us no aircraft noise if they got into office."

**Eros was really picking up speed** now, and growing hot with freefall. "I'm not afraid to be heavy," he sang. Impact was minutes away. He was so excited just *thinking* about it.

**"What the fuck is this?"** said Baby, looking for some cocktail glasses and discovering, for the first time, the second copy of the Hidden Agenda. "Oh, yuk. Nufonian crap." She opened a window and tossed it out. The volume somersaulted through space at a terrific velocity only to make a direct hit on Pallas, which burst into a thousand pieces of space debris. One of these spun out of control and smacked straight into Eros, which in turn exploded, with an enormous asteroidal shriek of pure bliss, into a million fragments of one hundred percent Pure Love that now showered the Earth.

*YES!* cried all the Earthlings. *Oh yes!*

It was as good for Eros as it was for them.

**In a scene that was repeated,** with suitable variation, in capital cities all over the world, one particularly large fragment of Eros came spinning through the atmosphere to Canberra. The prime minister and Cabinet were having one of their late-night meetings. They met at night because, if too much light were shined on what they were doing, they'd be out of office quicker than you could say "March of the Pigs." BLAM. A piece of space rock crashed straight through the roof of Parliament House and into the meeting room, where it beaned the prime minister. Bouncing off his forehead, it hit each of his men—for they were all men there, even the women—in turn. For a few minutes they slumped unconscious in their seats. Coming to, they looked around with new eyes. The prime minister blinked a few times. "Where were we?" he said, dazed. He glanced down at the agenda before him. The first item of business read "Preventative social justice—imprison poor people *before* they start stealing from the rich."

"That's fucken *ridiculous*," exclaimed the prime minister, tearing off his clothes. He stood up on his chair and shook out his pants. Coins and notes spilled out of the pockets and piled up on the table. "I believe some redistribution of wealth is in order," he declared. "And I think we in this room should set a personal example."

"Hear! Hear!" All the ministers chorused their joy and approval at the prime minister's suggestion. They threw off their clothing and soon the table sagged under the weight of their spare change. It was only some eight billion dollars, but it was a start. And they discovered they could have a lot more fun doing to each other what previously they had only done to the nation.

And so the Rock 'n' roll Babes from Outer Space, with a little help from Eros, managed, quite accidentally, to save the world.

Once Galgal docked into the mothership, the party began in earnest.

George made his way through the revelers and tapped Baby on the shoulder. He looked worried. "Uh, Baby. I didn't realize we'd be taking off in such a rush. I had all the gear in my truck outside the cricket ground. I always thought, you know, we'd need it."

"Doll swooped it up with the Abduct-o-matic as we passed overhead. Sharp chick, that Doll."

"Well," said George, smiling broadly and cracking a tinny—for Doll had had the foresight to abduct the contents of three liquor stores and a Woolies as well—"Cheers."

"Cheers, George," Baby replied, giving him a peck. "Oh, and I'll have that tinny when you're finished. Yours too, Eb."

Doll thought she should take time out to thank God, who was now more popular even than the Beatles.

Thank you, God.


*Pleasure. To paraphrase a Gadflys song, you know that of all My children, darlings, you're the ones I dig the most. Besides, I've always wanted to try out the old deus ex machina thing.*


Leaving the other revelers for a moment, Baby snuck off to her room and picked up the Locate-a-tron. S-P-U-N-K-N-I. No, I won't do it, she told herself. Just let him go. Let it be. She put the device away and returned to the party.

Jake, walking home slowly, studied the tattoo on his wrist. He put on his sunglasses, though it was night, for a few tears had welled in his eyes, and that wasn't very cool, was it?

He pushed open the front door only to find the entire house filled with Sirians and Alphas. They were pulling cones with Torq and Trist. "Cousins!" the Sirians kept exclaiming between giggles. "Cousins!"

Jake walked into the kitchen and opened the fridge door. Nothing but an old tomato and a tin of VB.

He looked at these two things for a very long time before closing the fridge door again.

**Back at the cricket grounds, the** Channel Three helicopter hovered above the roof. The reporter inside was shouting at Qwerk through a megaphone. "Promise us an exclusive," he said, "and you can name your terms."

"Just get me off of here," pleaded Qwerk. "I'll do anything."

**Revor and Iggy sat on their** haunches side by side, snouts to the sky. "Wot sis tory more ningglo ree," said Iggy experimentally, leaning over and nuddling Revor. He was worried about Revor. The little fella hadn't said a word for hours. Revor swung his head round, and forced his odd little mouth into an apologetic smile. He raised a paw to one eye and wiped away the tear which had formed there.

"Oh, Ig," he sniffled. "I will miss them."

"I know." Iggy unhinged his big jaw and opened wide. Revor batted his eyes at the dog. He hooked his front paws around Iggy's teeth and hoisted himself up, over, and in. Turning himself around so that his snout projected just beyond Iggy's lips, he settled down onto the bull terrier's fat moist tongue, the edges of which curled up to cushion him. They sat like that for a long time, Revor's breath coming in long sighs out of Iggy's mouth.

A few weeks later . . .

Jake picked up a piece of greenery from the bowl on the table and studied it under the candlelight. "Wonder why they call it rocket?" he said.

Kya, the yin-yang girl from the Sando, shrugged. "Who cares?" She leaned over the table, rested her chin on her hands, and peered intently at Jake. She was rapt. She hadn't been able to get him to come to her flat for dinner for *yonks*. Now if he'd only snap out of this strange mood he was in. He was still looking at the leaf. "You're very spacey tonight," she ventured.

"Sorry," Jake apologized to the salad. "I'm not very good company lately. I'd better go."

"No, no, no. I didn't mean for you . . . Want me to open another bottle?"

"If you want to."

"Why do you think they call it spacing out?" Kya wondered, scraping her chair back and going to fetch more wine from the fridge. "Think about it. People who don't quite have their 'feet on the ground' are 'space cadets.' We say they're 'off the planet.' But that can be a good thing too. If we want to praise something we say it's 'out of this world.' What do you reckon, Jake, is space as a concept good or bad?"

"Dunno," he mumbled noncommittally, tearing a crust of

bread into little crumbs on his plate. "Space is just a place. The place." He held out his glass and forced a smile. "Sun Ra said that, you know. 'Space is the place.'"

The two of them sat drinking in silence for a few minutes. Kya reached out and put a hand on Jake's arm. She noticed the flying saucer tattoo and traced its outline with a fingertip. More minutes passed without either saying a word. "You really liked that girl, didn't you?" she asked.

"Yeah," Jake shrugged.

"Young Bodies Heal Quickly," she said. "That's how the song goes, anyway."

Jake didn't reply.

"So, you gonna stay the night, Jake?"

Jake sighed. He looked up at Kya with sad eyes. He still thought about Baby all the time. Did she ever think of him, he wondered. Suddenly, his arse itched and emitted a low flat honk. A smile crept over his features. It suddenly occurred to him that Kya was a very cute girl.

"Dunno," he drawled. "What do you reckon?"